The Shattered Visage Lies

The Shattered World Saga Volume 1

Brian Koscienski & Chris Pisano

HELLBENDER
BOOKS

an imprint of Sunbury Press, Inc.
Mechanicsburg, PA USA

HELLBENDER BOOKS

an imprint of Sunbury Press, Inc.
Mechanicsburg, PA USA

For information about special discounts for bulk purchases, please contact Sunbury Press Orders Dept. at (855) 338-8359 or orders@sunburypress.com.

To request one of our authors for speaking engagements or book signings, please contact Sunbury Press Publicity Dept. at publicity@sunburypress.com.

FIRST HELLBENDER BOOKS EDITION: June 2022

Set in Adobe Garamond Pro | Interior design by Crystal Devine | Cover by TGT - dreamstime.com and Lawrence Knorr | Edited by Sarah Peachey.

Publisher's Cataloging-in-Publication Data
Names: Koscienski, Brian, author | Pisano, Chris, author.
Title: The shattered visage lies : the shattered world saga volume 1 / Brian Koscienski & Chris Pisano.
Description: First trade paperback edition. | Mechanicsburg, PA : Hellbender Books, 2022.
Summary: People from across Pennsylvania are waking up with superpowers, but instead of donning spandex and capes to fight crime, they use their new abilities the way real people would.
Identifiers: ISBN 978-1-62006-782-6 (softcover).
Subjects: FICTION / Superheroes | FICTION / Science Fiction / General | FICTION / Fantasy / Urban.

Product of the United States of America
0 1 1 2 3 5 8 13 21 34 55

Continue the Enlightenment!

CHAPTER
1

York, Pennsylvania

Joe clutched his left arm to his chest, broken just above the wrist. He sat on the floor, back against his fake oak entertainment center, resting his left hand on his lap. It throbbed but was hardly noticeable compared to the rippling waves of pain from his right leg, broken at the knee and twisted at an angle. Even that seemed minor, dulled by the fear coursing through his body. The fear of knowing he was soon going to die.

Joe looked at Vincent Carvello, the man who did this. The man who came into his house, the man who worked for Marko. This man, Vincent, even withstood a knife attack. Joe knew he was coming. He owed Marko money and kept skirting the issue, stalling for time. Time ran out, and Joe knew Vincent would come to collect. Joe didn't know that when he tried to jam two steak knives into Vincent's back, they would break, leaving only a slight bruise and a cut shirt.

"Ya know, Joe, there's something different about me," Vincent said, flicking his lighter. He stood in front of Joe like a smiting god, rounded muscles striating with every movement, his black T-shirt doing nothing to hide bulging veins. He had spent most of his time in the local gym, working off the steroids he would inject once a week. His neck was wider than his head, which held a thick nose, broken four times in his life, and cropped black hair. The camouflage pants and black boots made him look like a psychotic army recruitment poster.

"Yeah . . . I . . . uh . . . how . . . how do you mean?" Joe asked, hoping to find words that could get him out of this situation alive. The sweat from his forehead mixed with the blood from his nose and dripped off his chin.

Flip, flick, click. Vincent flipped his Zippo open, flicked the flint roller to spark a flame, then clicked the lid closed. *Flip, flick click.* He focused on the lighter more than Joe, having nothing to fear from the broken man. Why *should*

Vincent be afraid? Two knives were plunged into his back only to break like cheap plastic toys. "Ya know, Joe, I ain't really sure. Couple a days ago, I just woke up like . . . this."

With one last flip and flick, Vincent held the lighter's flame with reverence, like a ceremonial dagger about to cut into a sacrificial lamb. He waved his right hand over the flame, testing it. The swoops became shorter until he finally settled his hand over the lighter, the flame licking his palm. "Like when you jumped me with those steak knives, Joe. You jammed 'em both right into my back, and they just snapped. Not a scratch on me. Didn't even feel much. Kinda tickled."

"Yeah, about that. That was a mistake . . . a misunderstanding. I thought you were someone else," Joe said, trying to muster conviction. He knew he couldn't run, couldn't escape. His only option was to try to get Vincent to leave. "You don't have to—"

"And this right here," Vincent cut him off, ignoring him. "My hand's over the lighter, and nothing. It feels a little warm but no burning. No burning at all."

Joe tried again to show that he was on Vincent's side, to show he was no threat. "Maybe . . . maybe you're made of stone. Or something."

A sinister smile slid across Vincent's face, a smile Joe thought only existed in horror movies. "Yeah, that's it. I'm stone! From now on, call me Stone. My new name is Stone. You got a gun, Joe?"

The word "gun" made Joe's heart clutch. When he heard that word, he knew only one option remained. Beg. "Come on, Vince . . . uh, Stone. Let's just tell Marko—"

"Fahgetabout Marko. Where's your gun, Joe?"

"No . . . uh, no guns here, Stone."

"Damn. I wanted you to shoot me." Still holding his hand over the lighter flame, Stone looked around the sparse living room. There were no wall decorations, just a loveseat about ten feet from the entertainment center and an end table with a lamp; nothing interested Stone until he saw the curtains. "I need to experiment."

A nervous laugh stumbled out of Joe's mouth. "Experiment? What do you . . . wait! No! Don't!"

Again, Stone ignored Joe's pleas as he walked to the curtains. Crying, Joe lunged, grabbing Stone's pant leg with his right hand as Stone held his Zippo under the curtains, laughing as they ignited. "Come on, Joe. Don't you wanna see if I can survive this? See if I can walk outta here without a scratch?"

"Please," Joe cried, spraying blood from his swollen lips. "Don't! Whatever . . . uunnnh . . . whatever Marko wants. I'll do it. I'll pay double. Double!"

Stone yanked his leg from Joe's grip and took a step back to admire his work. The curtains shriveled and smoked as the fire flowed in orange waves, splashing against the ceiling and walls. "I said fahgetabout Marko! Starting right now, I don't work for him no more!"

Joe sobbed. The hungry flames spread to his loveseat and entertainment center, devouring them with cracks and pops. The room was made of fire. But Joe crawled, taking a chance, trying to make it to the door. If he made it out, he could roll, roll out of the flames, roll to freedom. One of the neighbors must have seen the fire by now and dialed 9-1-1. Sure, the police were looking for him, but at least he'd be alive, and then they could deal with this lunatic who thought he was invincible. Prison was better than being burned alive. Fighting through the pain and panic, Joe lifted himself enough to kneel on his left leg and reach for the doorknob. But he missed.

Stone planted his boot in the middle of Joe's back, slamming his chest to the floor. "No more of doin' what Marko says!"

Crying turned to screaming as fire leaped from the door to Joe's arm, burning his sleeve and melting it to his skin. The fire spread up his arm, igniting his shirt in a flash. His skin seared and shriveled, the stench of cooking flesh mixing with the melting fibers of his shirt. He retched between screams, trying to gulp for air. The fire spread across his flailing body, unable to escape from beneath Stone's flaming boot.

"I'm doin' what *I say* from now on!" Stone yelled at Joe. The fire spread from his boot to his pants, then crept up his shirt. "You hear me? I'm Stone! *I'm Stone!*"

The fire consumed him, just another combustible in a house collapsing from lack of support . . .

CHAPTER
2

Camp Hill, Pennsylvania

"Did you see that, Michael? It looked like someone was still in that house," Claire said. Transfixed by the television in the living room, she stood frozen at the kitchen counter, a bagged peanut butter and jelly sandwich in hand. The news program showed a pretty blonde with a microphone in front of firefighters extinguishing the smoldering remains of a charred house. A digital banner in front of the pretty blonde reporter read: "York, York County."

Michael Roseman sat on a stool by the butcher block counter near the kitchen/living room border. Nose buried in the newspaper, he replied, "I'm sure it was nothing, Claire."

Claire returned to packing her daughter's lunch, placing the bagged peanut butter and jelly sandwich into a Powerpuff Girls lunch box. "How would you know? You're not even watching."

Turning a page, Michael glanced over the headlines and examined any article that caught his eye. "I looked up. Saw the house on fire. There couldn't have been anyone inside."

"Well, it *looked* like someone was inside."

"Were they running around screaming?"

"No."

Michael turned to another page and sighed. "Don't you think if you saw someone in a burning house, they'd be running around screaming?"

Claire placed a juice box next to the sandwich. "Maybe it was a fireman, smart guy."

"Well . . . was it a fireman?"

"No. But *you* didn't know that."

Eyes wide, exaggerated, Michael lowered his paper and sat up straight. "I got it! I know what you saw. The house was built on an ancient Indian burial ground, and the fire released all the lost spirits. *That's* what you saw!"

"You're such a dork."

"That's why you married me."

Claire latched the lunch box and turned again toward the television. "Keep telling yourself that. I'll stick with the story that my green card was going to expire, and I was desperate. Sarah! Let's get moving!"

On cue, Sarah ran down the stairs and into the living room. How one seven-year-old girl could sound like a herd of elephants while running down steps had always been a mystery to Michael. But that was one mystery he never cared to solve; he couldn't help but love her enthusiasm. Sarah then skipped from the living room to the kitchen in her blue shirt, matching skirt, and stocking feet, while singing, "Dad-dy's a do-ork. Dad-dy's a do-ork."

In one fluid motion, Michael dropped his newspaper on the butcher block top, picked up his daughter by the waist, spun her upside-down, and held her face inches from his. "Well, it's better than being creepy, you creepy creeping creepster McCreepenstein."

The little girl giggled, loving the sophisticated banter she always shared with her father. "Nuh-uh! You're the creep!"

Wiggling his fingers, Michael tickled Sarah's waist. "Nuh-uh! *You* are!"

Laughing so hard she snorted and could only talk in squeals, Sarah rebutted, "No way! *You* are!"

"You both are creeps!" Claire ended the debate. "And dorks. Here's your lunch, Sarah."

Michael released his daughter, her legs running before he even set her back on the floor. As if discovering the lost tomb of Montezuma, she yelled, "PB&J day! PB&J day!"

Claire handed the lunch box to Sarah, but not before a neck-breaking hug from the little girl. Sarah then clutched her treasure with both hands, tight against her chest, making sure no one could take it, or even *think* about taking it or even think about *thinking about* taking it. She ran from the kitchen at full speed, the only speed she knew, as Claire gave her daily reminder: "Don't forget to put your shoes on before you run to your bus stop."

"'Kay!" she yelled back. "Love you!"

"I love you too, sweetheart," Claire replied.

"Love you more, Creepy!" Michael yelled, mimicking his daughter's enthusiasm. He returned to his paper once he heard the front door slam. Peeking over the top, he saw that Claire busied herself preparing her lunch—a hearty chicken Caesar salad. He also noticed his full, still steaming coffee mug on the countertop in front of him but behind his wife. Holding the paper in front of his face, he thought of ways to connive his lovely wife into fetching his coffee for him. "Five bucks says she forgot her shoes."

Claire laughed. "Suckers bet. And in case you weren't keeping score, you're now both a dork and a creep."

Keeping the newspaper in his entire field of vision, Michael replied, "Now how the hell can I possibly be both a dork and a creep at the same time?"

"See how special you are? Now, if we could only get you to multi-task."

Ah, just the opening he needed. He knew if he kept her talking long enough, she'd provide one. "Speaking of . . . could you get my coffee for me? It's right behind you."

Without even flinching, she knew what to say. "Get it yourself, you bum."

"But it's right there."

"So?"

"So, you're closer. And younger."

The coffee mug in question quaked ever so slightly.

Claire snickered at her husband's pathetic attempts to use flattery to coerce her to do his bidding. "Yeah, nice try."

Turning another page of the paper, Michael couldn't help but snicker himself. *I'm wearing her down; I can feel it.* "Come on. You know you want to."

"Sure. That's why I married you. To get your coffee."

"There you go—now you're catching on."

The mug levitated from the counter and floated toward the butcher block.

Still keeping her back to her husband, as well as the floating mug, Claire laughed. "You're insane."

Michael laughed as well. And that was why he loved Claire. She tolerated his verbal shenanigans, no matter how annoying. "Come on. Please. Please. Please. Please please please pleasepleasepleasepleaseplease . . ."

"The couch must be looking like a mighty comfy place for you to sleep tonight."

The mug hovered over the butcher block island, then set itself down with an audible clack. Michael smiled, thinking Claire fetched it for him; Claire smiled, thinking Michael finally got off his lazy ass for once.

Michael put his paper down enough to take a sip from his mug. "See? Wasn't that easy?"

Claire snapped the top of her salad-filled Tupperware container and placed it in her purse-shaped cooler. She slung it over her shoulder, walked over to Michael, and kissed him on his cheek. "Whatever, dork. I'm off to work. Have a good one."

"Love you too." He slurped from his mug, the victor enjoying his spoils.

Claire shook her head as she walked to the front door. "Now, if we could only get you to pick up your own dry cleaning, we'd be making progress."

Confused, Michael placed his mug on the butcher block top, wondering what she meant by that statement . . .

CHAPTER
3

Harrisburg, Pennsylvania

Marvin Carver sat in the dark on his couch, the only source of light coming from his big-screen TV. He still wore his slacks, shirt, tie, and jacket even though he had returned home from work six hours ago. The way he slouched wrinkled the back of his jacket and shirt, but he didn't care. *Why?* he thought. *Why do I do this to myself?*

Twenty years he had given to his job. Twenty years of working hard and late, never any bonuses or even special recognition. He sacrificed his hair, left with only a gray ring around the back of his head, as well as any opportunity to stay in shape, leaving his body doughy and bloated.

Thelma, thin as a stick and flat as a board with no discernable hips to speak of, entered the living room and watched the light from the television play over her husband, creating sad shadows. In her nightgown and ready for bed, she wondered how much longer Marvin's tantrum would last. "Marvin? Would you like to talk about it yet?"

"Colby," Marvin said, voice cracking from lack of use over the hours. "His name is Colby. I lost out on the promotion to fucking cheese."

Thelma moved behind the couch and ran her fingers across the top of his hairline to relax him. He hated when she did that; it only reminded him of his baldness. "Don't worry, honey. I'm sure you'll get the next one."

"That's what you told me the last time. And the time before. How many 'next ones' will there be for me?"

"Don't talk like that. You've been there for twenty years. Someone will see your strengths and accomplishments. Did you talk to your boss?"

"Yeah. He said I've been there for twenty years and I'm too set in my ways, too entrenched in old philosophies. I can't bring anything new to the table. The cheese-kid just got his MBA. How much can he bring to the table just getting out of college? What does he know about investing? He's never even worked for an investment firm before!"

"It's late, dear. You've had a rough day, and you should get some sleep."

"Fine." He turned the television off and stood. Anything to stop her annoying fingers from sliding across his bald head. "Colby. Fucking cheese."

Marvin skipped his usual bathroom ritual, opting to strip down to his skivvies and slide into bed. He lay on his side, staring at his clock. 12:14. He couldn't help but think that if he fell asleep now, he'd get five hours and forty-six minutes of sleep. He had a compulsive need to do math every chance he got. Numbers came easily to him, almost like they talked to him. That was why he was so good at analyzing company financial numbers for his investment firm. But he couldn't analyze people like Colby could. He couldn't beam on command, disarm, and exude confidence like Colby could.

1:28. If he fell asleep now, he'd get four hours and thirty-two minutes of sleep. His eyes stung with every blink, but keeping them closed seemed impossible. Thelma flung her arm over his and pulled herself closer to spoon. Marvin felt her bony arm dig into his as he watched her hand dangle in front of his chest. A green web of veins lined her paper-thin skin, doing nothing to hide her metacarpals and ligaments. Marvin so wished there were more of her to love, some roundness to get lost in. But her system could tolerate so few foods—no dairy, no peanuts, no pork or beef, few sauces. A pang of resentment shot down his spine as he thought of the time a few years ago when he had a snoring problem, and she sent him to a sleep apnea specialist, yet she balked at every opportunity to see a nutritionist.

2:11. Three hours and forty-nine minutes if he closed his eyes *right now*. Would it matter? No matter how he performed, if he did twice the work or if he simply did the minimal amount expected from him, he'd never leave his cubical. The same cubical for twenty years. He forced his eyes closed and envisioned himself with the business savvy to charm all of the shareholder representatives he met, getting them to give him a tidbit or morsel about upcoming product lines. He envisioned confidence. Until his alarm woke him from his dream.

He hit the snooze button, giving himself respite from the electronic screaming. Thelma slid from the bed to the bathroom to begin her daily routine. The alarm buzzed again; however, when Marvin turned it off, the buzz stayed in his head, bouncing from temple to temple. Digging his palm into his left temple to massage away the pain, he made his way to the bathroom and was treated to his naked wife standing in front of the mirror.

Had it not been for the throbbing in his head and the disappointment in his heart, he might have found the sight of his wife cupping her chest unusual. Instead, he slipped off his underwear and started the shower.

"Do . . . do my breasts look . . . different?" Thelma asked.

"They're fine, dear," Marvin mumbled in reply.

"They . . . they just seem . . . feel . . . bigger?"

"I love you just the way you are," Marvin said with the monotone of a zombie. And like a zombie, he finished his morning routine and drove to work, not realizing that his wife was staring at her naked ass in the mirror when he walked out the door.

In the office, Marvin started to wake up. He did so by standing in front of the conference room door. Any time there was a big promotion, the CEO would meet the promoted candidate in this room to go over forward-thinking strategies and how to implement them into action plans. The rich cherry door, deep in color, made a beautiful barrier, stern yet inviting. Marvin dreamed of meeting the CEO in this room, dreamed of talking to him about action plans. He almost reached out to touch it until a voice came from behind him. "Nice, isn't it?"

Marvin turned to see Colby standing behind him, preening himself. His fingers flicked through his hair, then straightened his tie, then adjusted his cuffs and cufflinks. Sighing, Marvin could only reply, "Yeah."

"Shame we couldn't both make it. Better luck next time." Colby extended his hand.

Marvin had no choice but to shake the hand of the man who stole his promotion and say, "Yeah. Shame. Good luck," while ill thoughts flooded his head. *You make me want to puke. I hope you get sick over this, coming in from college, taking my promotion—that I deserved!*

With one last touch-up to his collar, Colby slid inside the conference room, keeping the door open so Marvin could see what he couldn't have.

Taking a seat at his desk in the same squeaky chair he had for twenty years, Marvin watched. He saw Colby sit, cloaked in an arrogant calm. The middle-aged desk jockey couldn't help but stare and fume, watching this young kid get handed an opportunity like this. Today would be a bad day.

But then he noticed his young nemesis turn a shade of pink.

Colby made the standard move of pulling his collar with his index finger as his forehead started to glisten. He exhaled and shifted in his seat, trying to find a comfort that suddenly eluded him. Using the inside of his jacket sleeve, he dabbed the sweat from his forehead, making the situation no better. Moisture fled his tongue while the hot air from his nostrils burned his upper lip. Then the CEO entered.

"Colby!" the CEO said, extending his hand. "Let me be the first to congratulate you."

Forcing a smile through his aching joints, Colby stood and shook hands. He wanted to say, "Thank you," but instead vomited. His last night's snack and this morning's breakfast ran down his CEO's shirt and slacks, dripping to his shoes. And Marvin saw the whole incident.

A smile grew on Marvin's face as he watched Colby heave a second time. Employees scurried around, some with paper towels for the CEO, some attending to Colby, some content to gossip amongst themselves. Marvin was content to watch Colby lose his promotion . . .

CHAPTER
4

Bellefonte, Pennsylvania

The Schaeffer farm was like any other farm in the area—a hand-built house on excellent cropland with sturdy livestock and residents with a healthy fear of God.

Jeremiah Schaeffer and his family started the day at five every morning, simply sinful to sloth around any later than dawn, except if stricken by illness, of course. He sat at the family table, enjoying the community newsletter while his wife, Dorothy, cooked breakfast. Enough eggs, biscuits, and ham to feed eight. So accustomed to the routine, the children ran from all corners of the three-story farmhouse to the table, seating themselves just as Mother finished setting the food on the table. However, only five children sat at the table.

Jeremiah scowled at Dorothy. Adam's presence was needed for grace. Adam, the first son of the Schaeffers, named so for the first son of the Bible, was cut from the same mold as his father—he enjoyed the blessed bounties from God and never missed a meal. Dorothy could only shrug her shoulders. Jeremiah turned to his other children and asked, "Do any of you know of Adam's whereabouts?"

Mabel, the youngest and at the age where half her teeth were missing, said with a lisp, "His door was closed this morning, Papa. But I did hear stirring in his room."

Still scowling, Jeremiah grunted. He then looked to the ceiling and yelled, "Adam! We have a full day's chores waitin'. And grace to be said."

Nothing.

"Adam!" Jeremiah yelled again, this time with enough force to make everyone at the table jump or flinch. Mabel's cheeks drained to white, fearing she might have gotten her brother in trouble. "Get down here, boy!"

The bed creaked; the whole family could hear it right above their heads. It creaked again, followed by the thump of a body hitting the floor. The parents exchanged looks of concern while the children's looks of confusion bounced from one set of eyes to the next. The sounds of a heavy object being dragged across the floor hovered over their heads. Then a scream.

So filled with horror and fear, the scream froze everyone at the table. Raspy and hollow, it was inhuman and nothing they could comprehend. It wasn't until the noise stopped to inhale did Jeremiah and Dorothy react.

"Jonathan, watch your brothers and sisters," Dorothy said to her next oldest son as she and her husband leaped from the table. The scream filled the house again, this time mixed with spastic sobs.

Long strides propelled Jeremiah to the shotgun over the fireplace hearth. He bounded up the stairs, taking three at a time; Dorothy followed close behind. By the time they reached the second floor, a third scream had come from behind Adam's door.

In tears, Dorothy screamed out as well, "Adam! Adam, we're coming!"

Jeremiah said nothing as he ran, too consumed with anger. Something was attacking his son, his oldest son. With every heartbeat, a memory of Adam would flash through his head. Adam's birth. The first fish Adam caught. The first buck Adam shot. But Jeremiah held no fear, for God carried him, protecting him and his family from the evils of the world. He pumped the shotgun and kicked down the door, ready to wreak God's vengeance on whatever hurt his son. And prayed to God for the opportunity to do so.

Not taking a second to look for Adam, Jeremiah focused on what he could only conceive as an abomination, covered in scales with a thick tail. Disgust coursed through his body as he aimed. Dorothy peeked inside and screamed, a shrill bellow of fear, causing Jeremiah to lose focus as he pulled the trigger. The buckshot missed the monster; it moved with the speed and agility of a snake.

"Adam!" Dorothy cried. Tears streamed down her face while her hands clutched at her chest as if trying to keep her heart from exploding forth. "Where are you?! Where are you?!"

The grotesque creature stopped and held out its scaly hands. "Iiiiiiiissssss meh . . . meh . . . eeeeeee."

"I will send you back to Hell if you hurt my son, demon!" Jeremiah yelled with a fury only found in the Bible itself as he pumped the shotgun again.

Again using inhuman speed, the creature shattered the nearest window and escaped.

Pushing her way into the room past Jeremiah, Dorothy ran to Adam's closet. "Adam?! Adam, it's okay now." She dropped to her hands and knees to look under the bed. "It's okay to come out now. Papa scared the monster away." She couldn't find her son anywhere. Confounded, she joined her husband by the window as he watched the brush and tall grasses by the forest's edge shiver.

"What was that thing? What was it? Where's our son? Where's our boy?" Dorothy sobbed, looking at her husband for answers.

"That was Satan himself. Just as he did in the Book of Genesis, he led Adam astray. And God help me, I'm gonna get him back."

Jeremiah stormed out of the room, leaving Dorothy alone to cry and stare into the forest . . .

CHAPTER
5

Camp Hill, Pennsylvania

Michael held the cantaloupe to his nose and inhaled. Nothing. Then he grabbed it with both hands and shook it next to his ear. Nothing. Resting it in his palm, he held it out in front of him, wondering why people did those tests to determine a good cantaloupe from a bad. A chuckle escaped his mouth when he realized he looked like Hamlet with a melon instead of a skull. If his wife had accompanied him, he would have recited that famous scene, causing her great embarrassment. He envisioned it clearly—she'd tell him to quit being an English professor and then punch him in the arm. He placed the melon in his basket, deciding not to perform an impromptu soliloquy. The grocery store rent-a-cop seemed all too eager to use his pepper spray.

Being a part-time English professor certainly had its advantages. Not only could he reenact Shakespeare using produce as props to embarrass his wife, but his flexible schedule also afforded him the *opportunity* to do so. He loved to be out and about while regular working schlubs toiled away in the office. And, of course, shaping the minds of America's young adults was paramount. Well, at least toward the top of the list of reasons why he loved his job. Maybe not top, but definitely top ten.

Michael finished shopping, paid the clerk, then stepped outside to a warm, sunny day. As he walked down the strip mall's sidewalk, he noticed he was a bit peckish. Out came the cell phone and he dialed his wife's direct line.

"Hello, Claire Roseman speaking."

"Hi. I'm looking for the law offices of Dewy, Screwim, and Howe."

"Har, har. Very funny."

"Well, you didn't marry me for my money."

"No. That's why you married me."

"Ouch. Good one. You wanna do lunch?"

As he talked, Michael walked toward his car on the other side of the strip mall. He stayed on the sidewalk, at a leisurely pace, passing by all kinds of people: kids skipping school, adults who "called in sick" from work, senior citizens, and stay-at-home moms. Such a beautiful day beckoned to all.

"Love to, but can't. I'm working on a deposition that has to be finished soon."

"Workaholic."

"Umm, don't you have papers to grade, slacker?"

"I'm trying to set an example for you."

Michael mingled with a small crowd waiting for the perfect time to venture from the sidewalk to their cars. At that particular spot, the strip mall entrance intersected with the perimeter around the sidewalk, culminating in a three-way stop for vehicles. All pedestrians waited patiently for an SUV entering the mall and a VW bug speeding by the sidewalk. Curt remarks passed among the pedestrians, complaining about the speed both vehicles traveled, unsure if either would stop at the stop signs. The woman in the SUV chatted away on her cell phone while using the rearview mirror to primp her hair. The four teens in the VW smacked each other, playfighting while singing along to the thumping music. Michael couldn't help but notice both drivers seemed oblivious.

"Yeah. I'm sure . . ." Claire started.

"This is crazy! There's no way they're gonna stop in time," Michael said to nobody.

"Stop? Who? What are you—"

Michael stopped listening when he saw a man in his mid-twenties, engrossed with his MP3 player, stroll off the sidewalk right into the path of both cars. The crowd erupted with shouts and warnings, trying to get the young man's attention.

"No! Stop!" Michael shouted along. Out of adrenaline-laced reflex, Michael dropped everything he carried and sprinted from the sidewalk. Not realizing how bad of an idea it was until he got there, he tackled the distracted young man. With both vehicles barreling toward them, Michael only had time to close his eyes and hold out his right hand as if it would provide an adequate shield.

Eyes squeezed shut, Michael felt a warm sensation wash through his body, and the air ripple around him. *This must be what death feels like*, he thought. Then he heard the crash of metal against macadam. By the time he opened his eyes, the crowd of pedestrians went berserk—women shrieking, men rushing off the sidewalk, senior citizens using cell phones to call 9-1-1. The smell of gasoline and antifreeze flowing along the hot pavement filled the air.

Chest burning as he inhaled gulps of air, Michael looked around. The SUV was upside down; the VW lay on its side, the roof crumpled in. The world moved in slow motion, ethereal, as if in a dream. People ran to the vehicles to help the drivers and passengers. Voices echoed and collided, becoming one indistinct warble. Michael turned back to the sidewalk and saw a young man staring at him, no older than his college students. People hustled and bustled all around the young man, crying and hugging each other, pointing and gasping. But the young man just stood there, wearing a hooded sweatshirt with the hood pulled up, hands stuffed in the sweatshirt's front pockets. Unwavering, he stared directly at Michael . . .

CHAPTER
6

Williamsport, Pennsylvania

Widow Emma Montgomery was sixty-four years young. Her husband had been a firefighter and proud of his career path. She shared that pride, even though he ran into his last burning building over two decades ago.

She had never remarried; in fact, she often rejected advances from any suitor who happened to show interest. Being a devout Catholic, she knew the rules of the church allowed her to remarry if she chose to. However, she simply chose not to.

When he was alive, her husband was a healthy man, stronger and sturdier than the young bucks half his age. He attributed that to a strict exercise regimen. Widow Montgomery picked up his good habits and followed her own regimen—step aerobics on Mondays and Thursdays; pilates Tuesdays and Fridays; swimming Saturdays; bringing baked goods to the local fire hall on Wednesdays. And, of course, church on Sundays, as any good Catholic knew.

She considered herself a spry woman. Following the routine of a balanced diet, plenty of positive activity, and a good night's sleep often gave her the feeling of being refreshed and alive every morning. But today . . . today felt different. She hadn't felt this alive, aware, and awake with energy since she was a teen.

Today was Thursday and that meant step aerobics. She completed the class with such vigor that her instructor asked what new vitamins she took. Feeling unsatisfied with the class and needing more exercise, she made a mental note to check her vitamins to determine if she had taken an improper dosage. She decided to jog home to burn off this excess energy.

Emma lived in the suburbs of Williamsport all of her life and never grew tired of it, not once. She smiled as she jogged along the sidewalks of her neighborhood. Clean two-story brick buildings nestled together. Small mom-n-pop shops run by local families for local families. Community was more important than money, where banks closed early while fruits and vegetables were never anything less than fresh. As she jogged through her neighborhood, people waved to Emma, customers and store owners alike. She decided to stop over at the youth center before heading home.

Since the sun shined bright with nary a cloud in the sky, Emma expected to see kids using the outdoor basketball court. She also expected to see riff-raff there but prayed against it as she jogged closer. They came in all shapes, sizes, and colors and dressed in urban apparel: baggy jeans falling off their hips, tank tops or shirts displaying a designer name, bandanas or crooked ball caps atop their heads. *This is Williamsport*, she thought. *Not New York City!* Her heart sank when she saw Jason with them.

Fourteen years old, Jason had no mother, and his father had just lost his job. His father too often hit the bottle between resumes and interviews, so Jason would spend time at the youth center. Emma saw Jason's potential to do great things. But she also saw how he could stray from the righteous path with very little influence from outside forces. However, her Christian duty demanded that she not let that happen.

Jason stood near a bench with two other misbegotten teens, smoking cigarettes. Behind them on the basketball court, a game of two-on-two was underway. Jason just finished embellishing a story to improve his street-cred.

The one teen sucked his teeth and rolled his eyes. "You be trippin'."

"No," Jason replied, "Fo' real!"

Emma jogged over to Jason and said, "You really shouldn't be smoking those, Jason."

Out of reflex, Jason jerked his arm down and hid the cigarette behind his back as if Emma would forget it once out of her sight. Eyes growing wide, his teeth worked over his bottom lip. "I . . . um . . . this is . . . um . . . not what it looks like."

The mysterious burst of energy she'd had today flowed into her confidence as she stepped closer to the three wayward teens. "Just because your father got laid off doesn't mean you should give up on *your* life. If you need to talk, just go inside the center. There are plenty of counselors to talk to. And they care about you, Jason, not like these two losers."

Scowling, both of the other teens stood and puffed out their chests. One of them said, "Yo, Granny! Why you gotta be all up in my grill like dat?"

Undaunted, Emma turned to him and replied, "I don't know who you are, but it's obvious you have some problems with your home life. This youth center is open to everyone. Go talk to a counselor and they will help. If nothing else, I'm sure they could find ways for you to better use your time."

The hooligans laughed as one took a long drag from his cigarette and blew the smoke toward Emma.

The basketball game continued, the players oblivious to the conversation transpiring just off the court. One player tried a half-court shot but missed. The ball hit the side of the rim with a reverberating clang and sailed toward Emma's head, causing the player to yell, "Look out!"

Never pulling her eyes from Jason, Emma stopped the basketball with her left hand and launched it like a missile toward one of the hoodlums. It ricocheted off his cheek with a rubber echo and smashed into the other hoodlum's nose with a crunching squish. Momentum and angle took the ball right back to Emma, who caught it with her right hand. Arcing her arm and flicking her wrist, she sent the ball back to the hoop, sinking it with nothing but net.

Emma's nerves danced under her skin; bolts of electricity skittered from her fingertips to her toes. How did she do that? Her reflexes had never, *never*, been that fast, even in her youth. The speed? The accuracy? Unfathomable! Awe consumed her, slowly giving way to fear. But she couldn't let Jason see any of that. With as much calm as she could muster, she said, "Use the youth center, Jason. Quit smoking and stop hanging around with these losers."

Jason surveyed the damage. The two ruffians writhed on the ground clutching their faces and crying, blood pouring from the one's nose. The four teenagers on the basketball court stood dumbfounded by what they had just witnessed, none noticing the blood on their basketball. Jason looked at the stern face of Widow Montgomery and knew to fear her words or there would be wrath! He sprinted to the youth center, wanting nothing to do with those two writhing teens again.

Emma forced a smile and gave a polite nod to the basketball players. She stepped over the gangster wannabes and continued with her jog. She considered herself a spry woman. Following the routine of a balanced diet, plenty of positive activity, and a good night's sleep often gave her the feeling of being refreshed and alive every morning. But today . . . today definitely felt different . . .

CHAPTER
7

Harrisburg, Pennsylvania

Marvin awoke with a smile. The buzzing alarm sounded like a choir of cherubs. He forwent the snooze button and hopped out of bed. Today was his first day as unit supervisor. He received the promotion by default last week due to his nemesis, Colby, puking on the CEO. But it was a promotion nonetheless, and he whistled his way to the bathroom, where the unusual sight of his wife fastening her bra greeted him.

The only reason she wore one was for a night on the town, not for necessity. Often, people couldn't tell if she wore one or not. Confused, Marvin blurted, "You're wearing a bra?"

She blushed. "I don't believe it, but I actually need one."

Still ecstatic about his promotion, Marvin put his arm around her waist, spun her, and dipped her as if in a ballroom. He noticed her breasts seemed fuller. With a devious smile he pressed his lips to hers and drank deeply from her mouth. She pushed him away and giggled after he playfully snapped her bra strap. "No time to be frisky," she said. "You don't want to be late for your first day as a supervisor."

"Tonight then," Marvin replied as he turned on the shower. "I'd like to take a better look at those. Maybe I can figure out where they came from."

"And what about you?" she said as she ran her finger through the little hair he had. "Your hair seems thicker lately."

Marvin laughed as he got into the shower. "Well, I've been wishing for more hair for the past twenty years; maybe I'm finally getting it. I guess it comes with the promotion? Bonus!"

He smiled the rest of the morning, through rush hour traffic, through orientation, through all the paperwork and meetings he had to attend before he got the keys to his new office. *His* office. It was small, just enough room for his chair and two chairs in front of his L-shaped desk and credenza. A mirror and a framed motivational poster displaying a message about perseverance adorned the wall—the only wall hangings. He closed his eyes and inhaled the aroma of newness. Nothing in it was actually new. The oak desk had its fair share of nicks and scratches, the slate gray wallpaper peeled in a few corners, the mirror and poster glass had dulled from improper cleaning over time. But it was all new to him, and it was *his*, and that was all that mattered.

Taking a seat at his desk, he ran his fingers across the top, feeling every imperfection in the polish. He opened and closed drawers, knowing there would be nothing in them. He stood and walked to the mirror, not recognizing the smiling man he saw. Then something caught his eye. His wife was right—his hair did seem thicker! Moving his face closer, he tilted his head. The ring of hair looked wider, as if his hair finally began to win the territory war against baldness. Just as he moved to prod his hairline with his fingers, his administrative assistant entered.

"Ah-hem," she said, tapping on his door.

Marvin jumped away from the mirror, standing soldier straight, wondering what went through his assistant's mind. "Yes, Trudy."

Standing outside his office, she held out a catalog. "Congratulations, Marvin. It's been a while, but you finally got it. Anyway, flip through the catalog and let me know what you need. Calendars, pens, pencils, that kinda stuff."

"Thank you, Trudy." Marvin sucked in his gut, but he gave up once he realized it still drooped over his belt. Tall and proud, he took the catalog and set it on his desk. "I think I'd like to take a minute and talk to the troops first."

"Very well, sir." She took her seat at her desk, an ersatz sentry station right outside Marvin's office, as he stepped out to address his workers.

"Hi, everyone," he said to get the attention of his staff: Ron, Barb, and, much to his chagrin, Colby. "I just wanted to take a minute to say hi and let everyone know I look forward to the challenges ahead. I've known most of you for a long time, and I couldn't have asked for a better team. If there's anything I can do for you, or if you have any ideas or concerns, feel free to talk to me. I have an open-door policy for anyone. I mean, I'm still the same old Marvin you've known and loved for years; I'm not gonna change just because I'm your supervisor now."

All four of his staff displayed fake smiles and nodded their heads to show they understood. Then Colby stood. "I, for one, am very happy to call you boss. I haven't been with this company long, but one thing I've heard is that you are nothing if not a good leader. I'm sure our time together will be exciting and rewarding and fruitful."

Ron, Barb, and Trudy fought hard to stifle their laughter from Colby's over-the-top routine to undermine Marvin. They also assumed that Marvin believed every word out of Colby's mouth. Trudy dabbed a tear from her eye as Colby approached Marvin, shook his hand, and continued, "I may have been nominated for the same position, but I can see the better man got it. I will give my all to the success of this unit and try my hardest to learn all that I can."

Is this guy for real? Marvin thought, still shaking his hand. *I wish he would just shut up.*

Colby tried to continue but didn't get very far. "I will research every co-pany you gi-- to m- . . . ah-hem . . . gi-- t- me. I wi-- . . . ah-hem . . . I w--- . . . I . . ." He cleared his throat, but that didn't help. He tried again but only made dry, raspy noises. Tapping his hand against the base of his neck, he mouthed the word, "Water."

Trudy ran to the water cooler to fetch him a cup while Barb handed him a lozenge. Confused, Colby returned to his seat while chewing the lozenge and drinking the water.

Marvin put his hand on Colby's shoulder, feigning concern. "Are you okay? Feeling sick again?"

The young man looked up at his boss and tried to talk, but no words came. No words, no whispers, no noises, just a fish on a hot beach gasping for air. He shrugged his shoulders, gave a sheepish smile, and then made the "okay" sign with his fingers.

Stepping back toward his office, Marvin said to his staff, "Well, Colby says he's okay. Let's be troopers, get back to work, and crunch those numbers."

After sitting behind his desk, he giggled but stopped as realization hit him. *I did this,* he thought. *This isn't a coincidence. I've done trend analysis for over twenty years, and I see a trend here—a trend involving me. Colby got sick last week—I made him sick somehow. And today, he lost his voice . . . after I wished he would. Wished? Wishing? My wishes are coming true? That's impossi— I did wish for more hair and it's happening. I can see it! Thelma can see it. And Thelma—I'm always wishing that she was rounder, fuller, and now she needs a bra. This can't be! Can it? Okay, here we go—I wish for a million dollars.*

Nothing. Just the sound of his heart thumping against his eardrums and his heavy breathing.

"I wish for a million dollars," Marvin whispered, blushing at how silly his request sounded once he said it aloud. He chuckled, enamored by the ridiculousness of his words. He repeated, "I wish I had a million dollars." He laughed and started bobbing his head back and forth, almost singing. "I wish I had a million. I wish I had a million. I wish a million dollars would fall from the sky. I wish a million would pour down and shower—" He cut himself off when Trudy entered his office.

"Umm, I wish I had a million, too," she said. "I just wanted to let you know I'll need your supplies request by the end of the day."

"Sure thing," Marvin answered, blushing.

As Trudy left, shutting the door, Marvin felt something deep inside stirring. He caused what happened to Colby, his wife, himself. He *knew* it. It was a trend, and he would figure out how to perpetuate it . . .

CHAPTER
8

State College, Pennsylvania

Right outside Pennsylvania State University's Recreation Center sat the famed statue of their Nittany Lion. The smooth sculpture symbolized everything the college stood for: pride, excellence, power, and conviction. Behind the statue was a small, wooded area containing a few benches for sightseers to rest upon and feed the squirrels. Nora Leung loved to sit here to clear her mind, loved feeding the squirrels and chipmunks. This was her favorite part of campus, the one semi-secluded spot on a campus of over thirty thousand students. There was one problem with this area, though. The Rec Hall hosted the girls' volleyball team.

Practice just ended and the two team captains, Courtney and Lisa, left the building, heading back to their dorms. They strolled across the parking lot to the sparsely wooded area.

Hair matted to her glistening, ruddy face, Lisa beamed, "That was such a great practice! We should totally crush the Buckeyes this weekend."

"Easily," Courtney replied. She jabbed her elbow into Lisa's arm and pointed past the Nittany Lion statue. "Look, there's my creepy roommate, Nora. She's so . . . bleh! I totally hate her."

"Creepy?" Lisa asked. "She looks like any other gothy nerd."

"She loves animals."

"So? I think most animals are cute. And my parents have a dog and two cats."

Courtney's nose crinkled as she sneered, recounting a memory. "No. I mean *loves* them. In a weird way. She has posters of animals. And not like LOLcats. Just big pictures of animals."

"Really?"

"Totally. I tried to be nice to her the first week we moved into the dorm by driving us to the mall, and then she dragged me to the pet store. We looked at the kittens, and she asked to see a couple of them. And she was so totally weird, cuddling them like she was their mother or something, rubbing her face against them and kissing them and stuff."

"Ew."

"I know, right? Now, I just like to totally mess with her. Watch."

Courtney and Lisa approached Nora from behind. Nora knew the girls were nearing the bench, but she didn't turn around. Instead, she continued tossing peanuts to the ground for the scampering squirrels and chipmunks. She knew Courtney would request a favor at Nora's great personal expense, one she obliged to do at least twice a week. But not today.

Standing behind Nora, Courtney folded her hands together, batted her eyelashes, and stood with a twist in her body that exaggerated innocence. She used enough sugar in her voice to cause cavities. "Hey, roomie. Whatchya doin'? Feeding the squirrels again?"

"Umm, yeah." Nora's voice remained monotone and guarded. Leading such a solitary life presented few opportunities for her to speak.

Courtney nudged Lisa again and both girls giggled. "I know you're here at Penn State to be a vet and all, but I thought girls were supposed to stop playing with woodland critters after grade school."

"And I thought the cliquey cool girls were supposed to stop tormenting the nerds after high school. Yet here you are," Nora replied, still tossing peanuts to the ground.

Both Lisa and Courtney rolled their eyes and giggled as Courtney put her finger in her mouth, pantomiming a gag. But Lisa looked past Nora to the squirrels she fed and saw more than she had ever seen before. Ten danced around in skittish movements, as well as a half-dozen chipmunks. It didn't seem normal to her, but neither did she deem the oddity strange enough to interrupt Courtney while she chided her roommate, "Whatever, Nora. Chad's coming over again tonight, so I'm gonna need you to find someplace else to sleep."

"Not this time, Courtney," Nora replied, voice balanced and showing no fear.

Lisa no longer cared about the conversation; her heart beat faster than during volleyball practice. *More* squirrels came in, as well as more chipmunks. She even watched a few rabbits hop close to Nora.

Oblivious to anything other than herself, Courtney put her hands on her hips, her voice turning from sugar to vinegar. "*What* did you say to me?!"

With a confidence her roommate had never heard before, Nora answered, "I said no. I've had to sleep somewhere else three days this week already. No more."

Lisa looked at the low tree branches above them. Squirrels, chipmunks, and even a few raccoons scurried along the branches, running toward them. Lisa felt something wrap around her ankles and looked down. Three black snakes slithered around her feet. Wrapping her hands around Courtney's arm, she tugged.

"I don't care how many times you had to sleep somewhere else! When I say I need the room, then that means you . . . what?! What do you want?!" Courtney could no longer ignore Lisa.

Fear constricted Lisa's voice; she could only point. The trees flowed with fur. The ground undulated and squirmed. Courtney whispered, "Nora?"

Nora stood and turned to face the volleyball players. Courtney and Lisa clutched each other, not recognizing the girl they had been tormenting. The Chinese features that she inherited from her father still existed: circular face, smooth golden skin, straight black hair, rounded cheeks, and thin lips. It was her eyes that were different, her "American eyes," as she called them, given to her by her mother's genes, once wide and emerald green, now inky black with no irises, no sclera. They were black and beady, much like the eyes of all the small animals surrounding the quaking volleyball players. "Things are going to be different now, Courtney. Much, much different. For starters, *you* are going to need to find someplace else to sleep tonight."

Nora turned and walked away just as all the animals attacked. She laughed as Courtney and Lisa screamed . . .

CHAPTER
9

Camp Hill, Pennsylvania

Michael sipped his coffee, holding it with both hands. They still quaked, but not enough to keep him from tasting the rich hazelnut blend. It relaxed him. Being a part-time English professor, he couldn't help but see the irony of drinking a caffeinated beverage to relax, but it calmed him, especially around the police.

The detective's name was Matthew Matthews. Being of average height and stature with a pleasant smile, much unlike the hardened and scowling television cops Michael had expected, made the detective more amenable. That still didn't matter, though. Michael just wanted to answer the questions, get the cop out of his house, and put the whole incident behind him. The media called Michael's actions brave, but he called them stupid, risking his life, the life of his wife's husband and his daughter's father. *Stupid!*

"Thank you for taking the time to talk to me, Mr. Roseman. I'm going to have to ask you some of the same questions you answered with the onsite officers. Since it was such an unusual incident, we just wanted to follow up."

"Okay," Michael said, taking another sip from his mug while Claire made lazy circles on his back with her hand. They sat on stools on one side of their butcher block island, and the detective sat on a stool on the opposite side.

"Good then. All right, in your own words, tell me what happened."

Michael sipped again. "I don't know. This kid was listening to his iPod . . . or whatever they're called . . . and stepped off the sidewalk right as two cars were coming toward him. I jumped out, tackled him to the ground, and closed my eyes. I heard a loud crunch, and when I opened my eyes, the cars were upside down."

"Did you know the young man? The one you tackled?"

"No."

"Then why'd you do it?"

"I . . . I don't know. I just felt I had to do something."

"Okay. Fair enough." The detective paused to flip through the scribblings on his notepad. "Did you happen to see the drivers of either vehicle?"

"Yeah. Yeah, I think the whole crowd got a pretty good look at them. Woman on a cell phone in the SUV, teenagers goofing off in the VW."

"So they seemed distracted?"

"Very. Without a doubt. It was weird, though. They looked like they had no idea they were in a parking lot with stop signs coming up. Didn't slow down at all."

"Weird," the detective repeated as he flipped through more pages. "Now, you said you closed your eyes, so you didn't see how the cars flipped over. Other witnesses said they collided with each other before they got to you. However, the damage done to either vehicle isn't indicative of that. What do you think happened?"

Michael knew the detective was right. He saw both vehicles coming at him. The memory of the looming SUV grill haunted him. Ever since then, if the room became too silent, he could hear the music blaring from the VW zooming toward him. And the strange rush of air that rippled around him after he closed his eyes, he could feel that too. They did *not* hit each other. He sipped his coffee. "They hit each other. They had to, right? I mean, my eyes were closed, but what else could have possibly happened?"

"I don't know, Mr. Roseman. I don't know. One last question—did you see anything suspicious? A person or people acting odd? Or acting contrary to the rest of the crowd? Any events, like flashes or sparks?"

The kid wearing the gray hooded sweatshirt. If Michael closed his eyes long enough, he could see the young man's face, determined and calm, looking at him, not the wrecked cars. The young man was thin with a small frame, shorter than the average man, wearing baggy black jeans. Staring at him. Michael took a longer sip. "Nope. Nothing out of the ordinary. At least, not that I noticed."

Detective Matthews stood, prompting Michael and Claire to stand as well. He flipped his notepad closed and slid his pen into the metal spiral. "Thank you for your time, Mr. Roseman. And your hospitality, Mrs. Roseman. I know you've been through an ordeal, Mr. Roseman, but I hope there comes a time when you realize what you did was very, very brave. Not many people have that kind of heart."

Michael found that statement ironic since he never felt like he possessed "that kind of heart." He never dreamed of risking his life, *this* life he built for himself with his wife and daughter. Michael's eyes fell to the floor, still upset by his actions. There was no way he should still be alive. No way. And he knew it. "Uh, thanks."

The detective nodded as if he understood. "I'll just see myself out. Thank you again."

Claire put her arm around Michael's shoulders as he flopped back down on the stool. After he heard the front door shut, he sighed and took another sip of coffee. The detective was gone, yet Michael felt no better. His heart slammed around in his chest, up his throat, and between his ears. It hadn't stopped since the incident three days ago.

"Michael . . ." Claire started.

"Two people died and the other three are in the hospital," Michael blurted, surprised that the words just fell out of his mouth.

"Michael . . ."

"I could have died, too, Claire. I *should* have. There's *no way* I should have survived."

"Michael," Claire said again, using her hand to lift his chin, forcing his eyes to hers. "You did survive, and you should have. Just because the police don't think the vehicles hit each other doesn't mean they didn't."

"But Sarah . . ."

"Sarah thinks you're a hero. She couldn't be prouder of you if you rescued Santa Claus from a hundred sharks."

Michael smiled. Claire always made him smile. "Speaking of the little creep . . ."

"She's at your folks' place. Probably drawing pictures of you being a super-hero. Tell ya what—I'll go get her and give you a little peace. You okay?"

Michael held his smile and lifted his coffee mug. Jutting out his jaw, he lowered his voice to give an exaggerated bravado found in cartoons. "Yes, ma'am. I will imbibe the healing powers of my magical elixir."

Claire shook her head and grabbed her purse. As she left, she blew a kiss to her husband. "Goof. See you in a bit."

Michael's smile disappeared as soon as he heard the door shut. The coffee in his mug showed the SUV barreling down on him. The VW zooming toward him. The kid in the gray hooded sweatshirt staring at him. The crowd of people rushing around.

The doorbell echoed through the house; Michael jerked, splashing coffee over the edge of his mug onto his hands. He shook his hands as he stood, then wiped them on his shirt as he walked to the door. At first, he thought it might have been Claire, but why would she ring the bell? The detective, maybe? Probably the detective with more questions. What the hell else could he ask? Sure, the incident was odd, but it was hardly . . .

Michael opened the door and was greeted by the young man in the gray sweatshirt, hood up and eyes wild, looking like a sinister monk. Michael's world blurred into tunnel vision, and he couldn't catch his breath.

"What can you do?" the hooded man asked . . .

CHAPTER
10

York, Pennsylvania

Shaken, not stirred. That was how Vincent liked his martinis. Well, he assumed he would like them that way, never having tried one before. Considering himself a beer man, he searched his brother's fridge but found none. Bored and desperate for alcohol, he ransacked the bar area and found bottles upon bottles as well as any mixer he needed. And a drink book. He decided to try a martini while he waited for his brother.

Laughing at the notion of drinking a drink that needed an olive, he took a gulp. Not bad! A second gulp emptied the glass. He poured himself another as he admired his brother's home. The living room alone was larger than Vincent's apartment. Fireplace embedded in the one wall, 60-inch plasma flat-screen between two floor-to-ceiling bookcases on the second wall, the third wall had nothing but glass sliding doors that led to the deck outside and an impressive view, while the fourth housed the bar where he stood. Two large doorways on either side of the bar led to a kitchen rivaling any restaurant. The second martini slid down Vincent's throat with ease. *Yep,* he thought, *this will all be mine soon.*

As if on cue, the front door unlocked. In walked the homeowner, all but wearing a giggling, buxom blonde. They both laughed the lilting laugh of intoxication. But sobriety slapped them in the face when they saw Vincent mixing himself another martini batch.

Vincent's smile beamed like a shark looking at a fattened seal. "Hello, Marko."

"Marko," the girl started, "I thought you said no business tonight . . ."

"Not now," Marko replied, shoving the girl onto one of the plush couches in the center of the living room. "And keep your mouth shut."

The girl crossed her arms and pouted.

Marko turned to Vincent. "Where the hell were you?! What are you doin' here? I've been tryin' to call you ever since I sent you to shake down Joe, and then I see on the news his house burns down, and you don't return my calls. And what's with the shaved head?"

Vincent laughed while rubbing his hand over his smooth head. His hair had burned off during the fire and never grew back. "This? Just a new look I'm tryin'."

"You got no eyebrows, neither. It's kinda weird. Now, where you been for four days?"

"I took a few days to think some things over."

"Think?" Marko laughed. "You don't think. I'm the one who thinks! I do the deals. I make the contacts. I set the pick-ups and drop-offs. You're the muscle. You shake up the people who need shaken up. You don't think."

"After Joe, I decided it's time I started thinking. I went back to my shitty one-bedroom apartment downtown, and I did my thinking. Thinking about this nice place of yours. And I'm thinking you're done."

"Done? What done? What are you talkin' about?"

For dramatic effect, Vincent took his time pouring the martini. He ate the old olive and then dropped in a new one. He raised his glass and made a slow sweeping motion with his arm, presenting Marko's living room to him. "This."

"This? My living room?"

"Ya know, for being the brains, you sure are being stupid. Yeah, the living room! The whole house. Your contacts. Your customers. Your suppliers."

Marko looked at his brother and chuckled. The chuckle snowballed into a laugh that built such momentum only stomach cramps and tears could stop it. He said, wiping his eyes, "That's the dumbest thing I ever heard! You smokin'? Take a snort of my stash? Drunk?"

"Nope. See, Marko, the way I figure, I always thought I was scared of you, scared of what you might do to me if I stopped being your muscle. But that ain't it. I was scared of tryin' to make it on my own. I'm a dumb guy. I know it. I never wanted to try to make my own connections, get my own suppliers and dealers and customers. But now I ain't scared no more."

"You should be if you think I'm just gonna hand this all over to you."

Never once relinquishing his smirk, Vincent tossed back his martini, catching and squishing the olive between his teeth. He wiped his hands on a nearby hand towel and stepped from behind the bar. As Vincent walked closer, Marko saw a glint in his brother's eye, a spark that fortified the truth behind his words. With every step Vincent took, Marko took two steps back.

Vincent dropped the towel on the floor and continued forward. "Well, it looks like I'm just gonna have to take it then."

Marko's face reddened as he backed his way toward one of the bookcases. "This is total bullshit, Vincent! Bullshit! I brought you here from New York. I paid *cash* for that operation to help you sleep. I got you an apartment! I gave you everything you ever needed! Whatever you wanted was yours; all you had to do was ask!"

"Fine," Vincent said. "I want two things. One: I want you to start calling me Stone. Two: everything else. I want it all."

Marko's back hit the bookcase. Without taking his eyes off his brother, he swept all the books off one shelf and then brandished the gun they hid. "Stone, huh? You keep walking and you'll need a tombstone!"

"I knew you'd have a gun. Good. I've been waitin' to see if this works."

A wave of confusion swept over Marko's face, wondering what his brother meant and what drugs he took to make him act like this. However, his anger returned, not caring what his brother was on, just mad that he had the gall to act this way. He thought of pistol-whipping him once he got close enough, but Vincent's sudden conviction mixed with his already enormous size scared Marko. He gave his brother a job, made him important, and *this* was how he thanked him? Betrayal! This was betrayal, plain and simple. Marko pulled the trigger.

The bullet struck Stone's right shoulder, angled upward, and sunk into the ceiling. Gripping his shoulder, he yelled, "Ooooow, fuck! That really hurt!" He moved his hand and looked through the hole in his shirt. No blood. No wound. No bruise. He laughed and kept walking.

Marko squeezed the trigger four more times, all four striking Stone, making him yell and curse each time. Close enough now, Stone snatched the gun from his brother's hand and smacked him across the head with it. Blood ran down his face, and Marko fell to the floor. Stone tossed the gun aside and wrapped his hands around his brother's throat. And squeezed.

Marko grabbed Stone's wrists, hoping to pry them free but to no avail. He looked into his brother's eyes, and his voice squeaked out, "Vinny, please . . ."

"Vinny?" Stone repeated. "You haven't called me that since we was kids. And I told you—I'm Stone now!"

Marko kicked, twitched, then fell limp like the towel Stone discarded moments ago.

Stone turned to survey his new house and saw the blonde on his new couch. She sat almost in a fetal position, holding a pillow in front of her as if it could possibly help. He strode over and stood in front of her.

"Are . . . are you gonna kill me, Mr. Stone?"

Mister Stone! He liked that. "Everything's mine now. Why should I keep you?"

She stopped shaking enough to move the pillow aside and slide to the floor. On her knees, she undid his pants and answered his question . . .

CHAPTER
11

Williamsport, Pennsylvania

Widow Emma Montgomery needed to confess. Her devotion and guilty heart forced her to confess as soon as possible whenever she sinned. Thanks to that same devotion and guilty heart, confession happened about as often as a leap year. But yesterday, she sinned.

On purpose, she smote two teenagers. They deserved smiting, but it was not her place to do so, not her place to pass judgment. Her Almighty Lord and Savior had a monopoly on that duty. And she did it with such vigor; she slept not a wink last night, fraught with guilt. She needed to confess now, which led her to the local tavern.

The priest of her church, Father Maclusky, was young and forward-thinking, liberal enough to encourage the congregation to call him Father Frank. And liberal enough to enjoy the occasional libation at the local tavern. He argued that the Bible had no rule against it and assured anyone who asked that he never drank in excess. Emma never felt comfortable with the fact that he had a desire to get a drink first thing Friday morning. However, he had never done anything to bring shame to his name or the church. So, in she went.

If any comfort could be found, it was with the fact that she, the Father, and the bartender were the only people in the establishment. Sidling up next to Father Maclusky, she took a seat at the bar.

"Emma Montgomery? What an interesting surprise this morning," Father Maclusky said, taking a sip of beer from his mug. Emma's eyes followed the mug from the bar top, to his lips, back to the bar top again.

"Father Maclusky—"

"Father Frank," he interrupted, implying he wouldn't listen unless she played by his rules.

"Father . . . Frank . . ." Emma forced from her mouth, pained to veer so greatly from tradition. "I need to confess."

Father Maclusky laughed. "Emma, we're not at church. I'm not even wearing my collar."

One of her new reflexes dictated that she look him over; she didn't know why, but she couldn't stop herself. Picking weak points along his knees, elbows, shoulders, neck, and nose, she saw he wore khaki cotton pants and a white casual shirt with three buttons, the top one undone. "I still need to confess."

He sipped his beer again; her eyes again followed. "What exactly could you have done that is so bad you can't wait until tomorrow when I'll be at church listening to confessions?"

She told him. Everything from feeling different, the strange new energy coursing through her every waking second, to her newfound courage in standing up to ruffians, to how she handled them with devastating alacrity. Father Frank listened speechless, too stunned to even drink. Upon the completion of her story, he found it surreal to even blink. This thin woman took down two healthy men, one quarter her age, in a way that would make a ninja jealous. Father Frank laughed. "Emma, I'm sorry. I don't mean to laugh. Do you realize how incredible this story sounds? How can I possibly—"

Emma noticed the house darts resting on the bar nearby. While Father Frank disparaged her, she scooped up all three and flipped her wrist. Fifty feet to the back wall, all three darts struck the bull's-eye. Father Frank choked on his words.

Dumbfounded, he forgot his beer and scampered to the dartboard, not blinking once. As if discovering a new species, Father Frank examined the darts from all angles, his face an inch away. All three darts shared the same hole. So entranced, he never heard the three muffler-deficient Harleys approach, nor did he hear their raucous owners enter the tavern. Curious about the slack-jawed skinny man looking at the darts in a dartboard, they ambled right to him.

"They're called darts," the one biker said, his voice rough and raspy, as if he gargled with broken glass every morning. "If you'd like, I can school you. It'll cost you, though."

Father Frank pulled the darts from the board and turned to the men. Each had beards exploding from their faces as well as waists rounder than their barrel chests. A bandana on the head of one, a cowboy hat on another, a backward ball cap on the third.

Heart strumming up and down his ribs, Father Frank wanted to run. But he could not pass up this opportunity. Bible passage after Bible passage ran through his head, telling him his ill-conceived thoughts had no place being there. But, damn! This temptation was far too great. He pointed to Emma and said, "No. But she'll be happy to school you. It'll cost you, though."

"No!" Emma yelled but was drowned out by the eruption of laughter of the three bikers.

Walking to her with a hastened pace, Father Frank handed the darts to her and folded his hands over hers, offering comfort and permission. "Emma, don't you see? What you did yesterday was out of love to protect Jason. A shepherd has every right to protect his flock. You have done nothing wrong . . ."

The electricity ran through her body again, and that scared her. She turned to Father Frank for help but instead found he wanted to pull her deeper into the pit. She tried to protest. "But gambling . . ."

". . . does not break any of the Ten Commandments," Father Frank interrupted. His hungry eyes devoured her as he escorted her to the dartboard, closer to the three bikers. "Don't you see? You have a *gift*, one *given* to you by *God*. And you are being called upon again to teach a lesson. I promise you, Emma, any money won will go to the church. I promise."

Realizing this skinny man was serious about his challenge, the biker with the bandana produced his own darts from a small plastic case. "You're serious? I wanted to play a few rounds today anyway. May as well take your money as a warm-up."

Giving Emma no chance to rebut, Father Frank laid down the terms. "Let's play 301. Ten dollars a point."

The biker chuckled and shook his head in disbelief. "You're on, but you better pay up once I—"

The electricity within Emma consumed her. She could fight it no longer and let go, truly feeling as if God were the pilot and she, as copilot, was left to observe. Faster than two blinks, she launched all three of her darts with her left hand, all three once again finding the exact center of the dartboard. Before they even hit, she used her right hand to snatch the three the biker held and threw those, which joined the others at the bulls-eye. Spinning into a crouch, she swiped a small knife tucked in the side of the biker's boot and flicked it at the dartboard. The knife sank deep into the colorful cork, the largest section under the number "1."

Father Frank beamed as if touched by a ray of sunshine from Heaven itself. "Six times fifty, plus one. That's 3,010 dollars, please."

The biker with the bandana grabbed the Father by his shirt, his hair-covered fist as big as the priest's head. "Only three tosses per turn, buddy."

Before another word could be spoken, Emma chopped at the pivot point of the biker's elbow, forcing him to release Father Frank. Using her other hand to grip his elbow, she lifted upward, forcing the biker to punch his own face. Adjusting her hold on his arm, she jumped and flipped, landing behind the behemoth. Using his own weight against him, she pulled his arm back and kicked the back of his knee, sending him flailing into a table. He groaned in pain, the table nothing more than tinder around him.

His friends had been in bar fights before, considering it their hobby. But never with a senior citizen who moved faster than they could think. A broken chair and two well-placed chair legs to their throats later, they writhed on the ground, gasping for air.

"I think it's time we go," Father Frank said and grabbed Emma by the arm to hurry her from the tavern, fleeing from the shouts of the bartender.

Once they reached the outside, Emma yanked her arm from the priest. "Let go of me!"

"Emma, please—"

"No! I trusted you! I came to you for help, and you tried to exploit me! You tried to use me, tell me my gift is a blessing, only to use me! To make you rich!"

Widow Emma Montgomery stormed away, ignoring Father Maclusky's pleas. For the first time in her life, even after her husband died in the line of duty, she felt alone . . .

CHAPTER
12

Harrisburg, Pennsylvania

"Your numbers are crap!"

Marvin stared at the report that his boss, Mr. Salinger, had just slammed on his desk. He looked up at his angry boss, whose red face made his thick gray hair look like plumes of smoke from an erupting volcano. His shirt buttons strained to contain his girth; his short tie rested at an angle on his prodigious belly while parts of his neck rolled over the collar.

"I've been a supervisor for only two weeks," Marvin rebutted, feeling his ire swell.

"Doesn't matter. It's still your unit, your numbers." Salinger's breath reeked of cigarettes and stale coffee.

Marvin knew where this was going but played along anyway, just wanting to hear the words. "I made a return of seventy-four basis points for the month. Johnson's unit made eighty-seven and Savinski's made ninety-five. I'm not lagging behind by that much."

"I can't believe I even have to say this—annualize them! God, I still can't believe the old man upstairs chose you over Colby!"

There it was, what Marvin had waited for. Colby. The fucking cheese. Salinger hired Colby specifically for this job, but when he had that moment of physical indiscretion on the CEO's pants, the CEO saw Marvin and promoted him on the spot. And Salinger had been riding Marvin ever since, pointing out every flaw and misstep, usually with other people around.

"Fine!" Marvin snapped. "Anything else?"

Mr. Salinger placed his hands on Marvin's desk and leaned in. Marvin held his breath to avoid inhaling the fumes coming from his boss's mouth. His heart beat fast and furious. Then Marvin realized—that wasn't his heart. He glanced down and saw that his finger touched Mr. Salinger's.

"I assure you, Marvin," Mr. Salinger growled. "You're on very thin ice."

Marvin sat wide-eyed, no longer able to feel the heartbeat once Mr. Salinger stood and turned to the door. Mr. Salinger's parting words were, "And everyone knows you're getting hair plugs!"

Looking into his mirror, Marvin ran his fingers along his hairline. So much had grown over the past two weeks that people noticed. Hair plugs? Fine. Let them think that. He had more pressing issues.

Once alone, Marvin opened a drawer and pulled out an unmarked file containing handwritten, loose papers listing every odd occurrence over the past two weeks. Colby's vomiting and loss of voice. His wife's changing body and his own. There were lists of experiments and results, all failed. From wishing to cursing to repeating his routines. He thought he found a pattern with touching, but those experiments yielded nothing except an awkward moment with Trudy when he left his hands on her shoulders too long. However, Mr. Salinger made him realize the one flaw with that experiment—he touched her clothing. Excited, he picked up a pencil and scrawled at the bottom of one sheet: "Skin-to-skin." One more experiment. And he knew just the test subject.

Marvin grabbed three folders, each with a potential company in which to invest, and exited his office, shutting his door hard enough to command his staff's attention. They looked at him through pitying eyes, trying not to laugh, yet feeling embarrassed for him at the same time. They had heard what Mr. Salinger said. And they agreed with it.

Colby walked over with his Cheshire smile and put his hand on Marvin's shoulder. False sympathy oozed from his words. "I guess we can't win 'em all, huh, boss?"

This was who they wanted, his staff and his boss. This twenty-four-year-old know-it-all. They liked him more than Marvin and—worse—respected him more. Trudy, Ron, and Barb would follow him anywhere, while Mr. Salinger would help him reach new heights. Not Marvin, though. Not yet.

His employees gave him substandard research about potential companies to invest in, merely summarizing the companies' prospectuses, giving Marvin very little to analyze. Colby did the research. However, he would tell Marvin a potential company was not worth investing in and then give the research to Savinski. Colby picked the companies, Savinski invested in them, getting his ninety-five basis points. No more!

Marvin placed his hand on top of Colby's and smiled. This was it! He could feel Colby's skin tingle, hear it sing to him. Marvin said nothing, but one thought, one silent command, ran through his head—*piss yourself.*

And Colby did.

Marvin looked down and jumped back, letting out a very loud, "Whoa!"

Colby stood in stunned silence; his coworkers stared with mouths agape.

"Well, I'm glad to see someone's excited," Marvin said, trying to sound as stern as possible. Then he slapped one of the files against Colby's chest. The young man, still shocked, took it. Marvin then took the other two files and tossed one onto Barb's desk, the other onto Ron's desk. "Here are a few companies I want researched. And I mean researched. No more of this cookie-cutter bullshit that you've been giving me. I don't want anything recited from the shareholder service hotlines. I want you calling these companies' officers, employees, customers, and vendors. I want you projecting inventory, marketing, and identifying sales and trends. I want you to understand the regions they're in, the countries they have buildings in, the workers' mentality. I want you to predict the goddamn weather and how it will affect the companies that you're researching. I'm an analyst. Give me something to analyze!"

Marvin looked at his employees, their faces red with shame, eyes wide with shock. He looked at Colby, then down to his crotch, then over to Trudy. "Trudy, be a dear and help Captain Pissy Pants clean up. Maybe even set up an appointment for him to see a urologist." With that, he left for the day.

Marvin wore a smile from ear to ear the entire ride home. His speech was perfect. The looks on their faces were priceless. And the knowledge that he did it, he caused Colby's accident, tickled him inside his chest. The possibilities this presented!

He burst through the door of his house with an energy he had never felt before.

"You're home early," his wife greeted him with a smile.

Without saying a word, he strode to her and removed her top. He saw that she spilled over the confines of her A cup. Out of mercy for her bra, he unclipped it and released the prisoners. He undid her jeans, now a size two from a size zero to accommodate the hips she had gained in the past two weeks. He stripped himself and then held his wife close, chest to chest, legs to legs. He heard her heartbeat, felt the blood through her veins, tasted the air she breathed, smelled every pheromone she released. Her body sang to him . . .

CHAPTER
13

State College, Pennsylvania

Nora smiled, satisfied with her work. Her roommate, Courtney, sat in the hospital bed, bandaged and bruised, looking miserable. Her normally full hair looked limp, patches noticeably missing, her scalp scabbing over where locks had been torn out by the root. Her pretty, pretty face was scratched and cut, some chunks bitten off that would leave scars. *Yes,* Nora smiled, *very satisfied.*

She watched—spied—on Courtney, sitting in her hospital bed, surrounded by her father, her father's lawyer, and a representative from the college.

"How could you allow this to happen?" Courtney's father snapped at the representative. The lawyer placed a hand on her dad's shoulder, trying to calm him.

"Sir, I assure you that we had our entire campus maintenance crew *scour* the campus looking for the animals that attacked your daughter. It's unbelievable, but we can't find a single animal," the representative said.

Nora laughed.

"What's unbelievable is the lack of control you have over the animal population! How can it be so out of control that a rogue group of animals found a need to attack my daughter?"

"Sir, I assure you—"

"Assure me? Assure me? How can you assure me of anything? How—"

"Jim, please," the lawyer said, halting the assault. "Let's handle this the proper way. It's for the best."

"Fine," Courtney's father snapped. He looked at the representative and said, "Get out. Just get out of here, now."

The college representative did as instructed. As he left the room, Matthew Matthews knocked on the door and poked his head inside. "Excuse me? I know this is a bad time, but I'm Detective Matthews. I was wondering if I could ask some questions about the . . . incident?"

Courtney's father shook his hand and introduced himself. "I'm Jim and this is my daughter, Courtney. This is my lawyer, and I'd like him present."

"Not a problem," the detective said.

Hmm, Nora thought. *Didn't think the police would get involved.* She continued to watch, preparing for a distraction.

"I know you've been through quite an ordeal, Courtney, but can you tell me what happened?" Matthews asked.

"Yeah! I got attacked by a bunch of animals!" Her voice was shrill and angry. Nora loved it.

"Animals," the detective repeated, writing on his notepad. "What kinds of animals?"

"Squirrels and chipmunks and snakes . . . God, I hate snakes . . . and . . . and rabbits."

"Rabbits? Attacked you? Alongside . . . snakes?"

"Yes! That's what I said!"

Nora knew what the next question would be. She watched and listened to the whole conversation through the eyes and ears of a chipmunk perched on a ledge outside the hospital room window. She used the woodland creature as a mobile camera, sure to cause little suspicion if detected. Concerned about what she heard through the creature's ears, she commanded the chipmunk to gnaw at the corner of the window's screen.

"Very well," the detective said. "Did anything suspicious happen? Anyone acting unusual or contrary to how a normal person would act?"

Eyes filled with venom, Courtney focused on the detective. She knew Nora had something to do with this. That freak! She waited for the right moment to tell someone about her roommate. Somehow, she did this. How her eyes became creepy and black. Just as Courtney's lips curled, as her voice started to form the words, she saw something out of the corner of her eye.

The chipmunk burst through the screen, jumped onto the floor, and scurried toward the bed.

Courtney screamed with such horror the lawyer covered his ears, and her dad froze, never before hearing such a noise in his life. Courtney squirmed, legs kicking and arms flailing, as if pushing against an invisible wall. And she screamed again. She fell from her bed, ripping the IV line from her arm and getting tangled in her sheets. Convulsing on the floor, Courtney punched and kicked her father as he tried to help her from her feet and keep her from hurting herself. "What?" he asked. "What is it? What's wrong?"

"Animal!" she screamed, blindly pointing toward the window. "Animal!"

No sooner did Nora command the chipmunk into the room, she ordered it back to the window. It perched itself on the sill so Nora could watch the events in the room through its eyes. She so loved the sound of Courtney screaming. Just as the men in the room looked where Courtney pointed, Nora ordered the chipmunk back through the screen to escape. She relinquished control and had to blink a few times, acclimating her eyes to her current surroundings.

Nora sat naked against a tree, deep in the forest of Mt. Nittany. She laughed again, replaying the sights and sounds she had heard in the hospital room, remembering the college representative's confusion about the complete lack of animals on the campus since the incident. She laughed because they were all with her.

Field mice and chipmunks scurried across her body, many up her neck and onto her head, nestling within her hair. Their tiny claws tickled her skin as they scampered. Squirrels roved across her body; however, their claws were too sharp for her chest. They were content to run along her legs, stretched out along the dirt floor of the forest. Black snakes joined in the celebration, slithering across all parts of her body from fingertip to toe. She had to remind them not to eat the mice while with her. The rabbits snuggled close, their fur keeping her warm. She stroked a raccoon that found a comfortable spot on her lap. Even though she was naked, very little of her skin was exposed.

As a little girl, she would pile all her stuffed animals on her bed, sleeping on top of them, cuddling among them. Now fate gifted her a new reality, here with her friends she had loved her entire life. Sure, Courtney would eventually give the police her name, but how could they find her? They couldn't. No one could.

She smiled and leaned back, resting her head against the tree, careful not to hurt any roaming critter. She closed her eyes and let her mind wander, listening, feeling. Connecting with all the animals in the area, she shared herself with them, listened to them. She felt the flocks of birds flying overhead. A mountain lion wandered the peak of the mountain over a mile away. A black bear was in the valley on the other side. Two mountains over she felt pain . . . heartbreak? The pain was so deep she clutched her stomach. Tears fell from her eyes. But she couldn't tell what kind of animal it was, couldn't see through its eyes or smell what it smelled or hear the sounds around it; she just felt its pain.

Most of the animals leaped from her body as she stood. However, the snakes hugged her tightly, and the mice stayed within her hair. The raccoon perched itself on her shoulder as she walked; walked toward the miserable creature in pain . . .

CHAPTER
14

Camp Hill, Pennsylvania

"Who are you?" Michael yelled.

Annoyed that Michael didn't answer his question, the young man in the gray hooded sweatshirt said, "Derrick. What can you do?"

"Do?" Michael asked, getting annoyed as well. "I can call the cops if you don't get the hell outta here, that's what I can do!"

"No, you can't."

"Yes, I can."

"No. You. Can't."

Michael closed his eyes and pinched the bridge of his nose. He didn't know what to do. Standing in front of him was the one person who seemed to know what happened during the car incident. And he was completely incoherent. Michael wanted to talk to him about that day, but now, he wasn't sure how this loon could help. "Let's try this again. What do you want?"

"I want to know what you can do."

"Okay, I'm done." Michael backed into the living room. He left the door open to keep an eye on this guy. He wasn't really afraid of him since he was half a foot shorter than Michael and seemed malnourished. But Michael certainly didn't feel comfortable around him. "As soon as I find my phone, I'm calling the cops."

After the words left his mouth, Michael wanted to slap himself. Why tell him that? Just give him an invitation to cut the phone wires and go psycho! He hated when people did that in the movies, and now he did it himself. However, he couldn't find a phone.

It was on the butcher block island where he left it. He knew it! Keeping one eye on Derrick, Michael looked on the kitchen counter where one of the chargers sat. Empty. Then he looked in the living room, on the coffee table and end tables. Nothing. "I have four freaking phones but can't find one when I have a psycho kid outside my house?"

Derrick entered the front door and walked toward Michael. "You can't find your phones because I won't let you see them. That's what I can do."

"You steal phones? That's what you can . . . *hey!* Get the hell outta my house!"

Derrick continued to walk into the living room. "And I'm not psycho. I can do things, and I got this . . . this . . . vibe about you, and I know you can do something because I've seen it, but I just want to know what it is you can do."

Heart racing, Michael backed toward the kitchen counter where he kept the knives, cursing himself for letting this kid know he was going to call the police. Where the hell were the knives? Claire always accused Michael of never paying attention, but he knew where the knives were. They were right here! In a wooden block! Ten steak knives and almost as many specialty knives. Right here!

"See?" Derrick continued. "This is what I'm trying to tell you. I'm hiding the knives from you. That's what I can do."

"Stop!" Michael yelled, holding his hand up to Derrick. He felt cornered, and then his eyes started to tear, a burning sensation erupting behind them. The warmth spread down his neck and through his back, traveling the entire length of his extended arm, rushing through his body. Derrick flew back, as did the couch and coffee table behind him.

Michael stared at his hand. *Where did that come from?*

"You can push things!" Derrick shouted, excited.

With adrenaline still coursing through his body, Michael snapped his hand in front of himself again, feeling the same warmth flow through his body, a torrent of invisible energy bursting from his fingertips. The young man flew through the air as if Michael had punched him square in the chest. Derrick toppled over the back of the couch and hit the floor with a thud. "Ow."

"Impossible," Michael whispered, staring at his hand as if it were the smoking gun at a murder scene.

"You can stop hitting me now," Derrick said, limping around the couch and rubbing his arm. "Your phones and knives are back."

Barely hearing his guest, Michael glanced up to see his cell phone on the butcher block island. As if getting slapped in the face, the clarity of the moment returned, and he spun to look at the charger, now cradling the landline phone. He spun again to see the knife block, exactly where and how he remembered it. "What. The. Hell. Is. Going. On."

"I don't know," Derrick answered.

Michael spun to look at his guest. Derrick jumped back and crouched, holding his hands in front of him while yelling, "I really don't know! Please don't hit me again!"

Sweat formed across Michael's brow as a chill ran through his body, sapping all color from his skin as realization washed through him. "Is . . . is that what happened? At the mall?"

"Yeah, pretty much. The cars were coming at you, and you put up your hand. You pushed them away. It really looked like they hit each other and missed you, but I was watching. Watching you."

How did this happen? What was this? Michael couldn't fathom what he saw, let alone what he just did. He did this? He couldn't believe it. He looked up at Derrick and noticed his hood was off. The thin young man had brown hair that he gelled to the center, creating a fake mohawk. "You look familiar . . ."

"I had you for English last semester, Professor Roseman," Derrick said, confused that Michael hadn't recognized him this whole time.

"You did? Okay, yeah. Now I remember. You were real quiet. Didn't participate much."

"Well . . . the class kinda sucked."

"Excuse me?"

"You're not very inspiring."

"Candor. Noun. Frankness or openness of expression."

Derrick blushed and lowered his eyes. His hands found refuge in the front pocket of his sweatshirt. "Sorry."

Michael chuckled. "Don't be. You're only telling the truth."

He couldn't help but look back at his hands. "How . . . did you know I could do something?"

"I don't know. It was like I got this weird vibe thing going on. I saw you in my sleep, in dreams and stuff. I saw your house. And the feeling got more and more . . . intense! Like, the closer I got to you. I mean, that's why I was, like, freaking out when I got here. My head was on fire from the inside," Derrick explained. He became more animated as the story went on, his hands motioning with every word.

"Well . . . what do you feel now?"

Derrick looked up to the right, then to the left. Surprised, he looked back at Michael. "Ya know . . . nothing. No headaches. No burning. I feel fine."

Michael heard a hum come from the basement. "Shit! The garage door! My wife's home! Get out!"

"What? Why?"

"I can't tell her about this yet."

"Why not?"

Michael rushed over to Derrick and pushed him toward the door. Derrick resisted but moved along. "I just can't. Not yet. Not until I . . . we . . . figure out what's going on."

"When are we . . .?"

"Tomorrow. At the mall food court. Noon," Michael said with one final push, sending Derrick across the threshold. Before the young man could respond, Michael shut the door . . .

CHAPTER
15

Bellefonte, Pennsylvania

Adam Schaeffer looked at his hands. His heart sank, as it did every time he looked at his hands. The fresh blood started to dry, turning from slick red to cracked brown. He plunged both hands into the shallow stream, running his hands over the rocks to scrub away the blood. As he scrubbed, he practiced his speaking. "My. Name. Isss. Adam. Ssss . . . ssss . . . ssssaeffer. My. Name. Isss Adam Ssssaeffer."

His lips were thicker, more cumbersome. It took some time to get used to them extending from the front of his face all the way back to the sides of his face. His tongue was thinner and longer, much longer—long enough to snatch a dragonfly from the air over a foot away—and it still couldn't perform all the tricks it once did to allow proper speech. But he practiced. He knew his father was looking for him, hunting him. If his father found him, Adam knew he wouldn't have much time to explain.

Water rolled unfettered across his scales as he pulled his hands from the stream. The blood was gone; his hands returned to green. He dunked his head into the stream to rinse the blood from his mouth. The thought of inhaling, drowning himself to end it all, crossed his mind. But that act would condemn him to Hell with no chance of penance. He lifted his head from the stream, and tiny waterfalls flowed from his face. He saw his wavy reflection.

God made man in His divine image. At least that was what Adam learned from church. But he knew that God did not look like this. What did He look like? Did this mean Adam was not to be with God or part of His divine plan? Impossible. Adam's heart was filled with God's word; he knew it. Knew it! Or maybe Adam was no longer part of man—humanity. Did God suddenly deem him no longer worthy?

"I. Am. A. Hu-man. Be-ing. I. Am. A. Hu-man. Be-ing," Adam said to his reflection.

He doubted his own words when he looked at the rabbit skins. Minutes ago, he stumbled upon a nest of rabbits. He smelled them in their burrow. Using his new claws . . . no, hands . . . they were still his *hands* . . . he found them within three scoops. They tried to run, but Adam now possessed a speed he had never fathomed. Two adults and six babies. He swallowed the babies whole and broke the necks of the adults. His fingers tore through their soft bellies as his teeth scraped the meat, guts, and bone away from the skin, their pelts unappetizing. He stared at the rabbit skins. Could a human being really do this?

Job, he thought, recalling the Bible story. *The trials of Job*. But that didn't stop him from sitting on the forest floor and crying, if it could still be called crying. He pulled his legs to his chest, wrapping his arms around them for a false sense of comfort. Then, he felt it.

Adam lifted his head and looked through the forest. He . . . heard? . . . felt? . . . something. Where? He stood and turned in circles. Where was it? *What* was it? He ran, his senses tingling. He smelled . . . what did he smell? It overwhelmed him, and he felt that he was getting closer. He came upon a thick patch of blackberry bushes. It was on the other side. As heady as the sensation was, he decided to err on the side of caution and peek through the brush, slowly moving through the thorny bushes. There! He saw it! It was . . . a girl?

Nora Leung looked right at the blackberry bush, right at him. Still covered in squirming snakes and skittish small animals, she smiled at the bush. "I know you're there."

She saw movement as the branches wiggled. She knew he wanted to run. "It's okay," she said, her voice alive and energetic. "I'm not going to hurt you."

Adam crawled out from the bushes, almost slithering on all fours. Free from the jagged brush, he slowly stood, still ready to flee.

Nora's eyes widened and her jaw went slack. The animals leaped and slithered from her body, leaving her naked before him. Her lips quivered as a tear slid down her cheek. She whispered, "You're beautiful."

Adam stood, embarrassed and ashamed. Over seven feet tall, he stood like a reptile molded onto a man's frame. Even though his head resembled a lizard's, his eyes held the soul of a confused young man. Out of nerves, his forked snake tongue flicked across his muzzle. His toned body was covered in tight emerald scales. An impressive tail sprouted from the base of his back, ten feet long and always moving.

Nora stepped toward him and he stepped away. She reached out her hand and reiterated, "I'm not going to hurt you."

Adam drew his hands close to his chest, uncomfortable. "You. Are. Nay-ked."

"Yes. And so are you."

Adam had never seen a naked woman before. His tongue flipped out of the right side of his mouth, across his nostrils, then again from the left side. His stare coated her body. Her small brown nipples stood out against her golden skin, as did her triangular patch of black hair. Nora smiled when she noticed that his eyes canvassed her body. Continuing to walk closer, she said, "What's your name?"

"My. Name. Isss. Adam. What. Isss. Your. Name?"

"Eve."

Adam's eyes shot up to meet hers, her inky black eyes. "Really?"

"No," she said smiling, standing within a foot of him now. "It was a joke to make you relax. My name is Nora."

He smiled too, exposing two rows of teeth, pointed like an alligator's. He felt relaxed around her despite his recent torrent of emotions.

Nora reached out and placed her hands on his chest. She made small circles, then slid them up to his shoulders and down his arms. His skin appeared slick and slimy but was as smooth as the snakes Nora kept as companions. She slid her arms around his waist and rested the side of her head against his sternum.

Confused, he gently placed his hands on her naked back, cautious of his claws. Maybe it was a sign from God?

"There's more like you, Adam," Nora said, still hugging him.

More like me? he thought. It *was* a sign . . . .

CHAPTER
16

Philadelphia, Pennsylvania

LaKeisha LaRue was beautiful once. Back in high school. Her dark chocolate skin was smooth and seductive; her big, brown eyes expressive, able to capture any man's gaze. And her tits were to die for. She loved how they caused men to walk into walls. Then she got pregnant at fourteen and again at sixteen. Now, she was the oldest twenty-two-year-old she knew.

She stared in the mirror of her tiny bathroom. Wrinkles. She had wrinkles by her eyes already. Sucking her teeth, she mumbled, "Shoot, girl." Wrinkles. How did that happen? They used to be wide open and alive; now, they were half-shut and dead with apathy. Back then, she was built like a statue. Now, she was built in layers. Her first chin layered onto the beginnings of a second chin. Her tits rested on her belly, which layered over her skirt. Her ass went from J-Lo to Jell-O overnight. But she really didn't care—she still got sex when she wanted it. She just had to lower her standards.

She didn't plan on getting any today, so she threw a thick band over her head and slid it up to the top of her forehead, pushing her kinky hair straight up. It looked like an explosion, but at least it was out of her eyes. She squirmed into a tube top that exposed her belly, boobs, and the stretchmarks of both. And a thin skirt for comfort. She found a chip on the fingernail of her left index finger and rubbed it, again sucking her teeth. She sighed in disgust when she failed to remove it. The system provided a place for her to live and food for her and her kids with little left over for her nails.

Exiting the small bathroom, she walked into the small living room of her small two-bedroom apartment. Her children slouched on the floor, slack-jawed, staring at the television. She knew she could find ways to abuse the system like some of her friends, but damn, that took a lot of work, and LaKeisha just couldn't be bothered. She also knew she could free up some money by taking a one-bedroom rat-hole down the block, but this was the nicest building of rent controls. Her kids got their own room, and the drugs weren't as rampant. Even though getting pregnant ruined her life—at least that was what her mom said, who was only seventeen years older—but she was satisfied. Well, at least she wasn't hateful like some of her friends. And she loved her kids. She smiled as they watched television, remembering how excited they were to get their own rooms when they moved in here. Her mind drifted to similar smiles during birthdays and Christmases.

As if someone lit their pants on fire, both children jumped up and looked at LaKeisha. Eyes wide, they both ran to her with open arms. They hugged her as hard as their little arms would allow. "I love you, Mommy," the oldest one said, burying his face in her leg. Her younger child followed suit.

A little surprised by their sudden burst of affection, she bent down and enjoyed the moment of four loving arms hugging her neck. She smiled. This was nice. Then she heard the rattle of keys outside her door.

"Oh, shit," she whispered, standing. She peered through the peephole in her door and saw her next-door neighbor, Darnel, trying to unlock his door.

Shooing her children back to the television, she explained, "Okay, babies. Back to TV. Mommy's gonna go say hi to our nice neighbor, Darnel."

Dazed and confused, the children did as instructed. Once they devoted their full attention to the box, she slipped into the hallway, shutting the door behind her.

"Hey, Darnel," she said, adding a playful drawl to the E's.

He glanced over his shoulder. "Oh, hey, Keisha."

LaKeisha smiled and then wondered why she bothered. Darnel was gorgeous. Almost a foot taller and five years older, she knew she never had a chance with him. His T-shirt did nothing to hide his muscles, rounded from a two-year stint in prison, and his jeans shaped everything below his waist just right. His smooth skin, just as dark as hers, caused her to lick her lips, dying for a piece. But she knew that she could never get any, for he only got with white women. Then he turned around again, this time with fire in his eyes.

Darnel looked at her as his tongue slid across his bottom lip. His eyes moved up and down her body, and a blaze flowed within her. LaKeisha knew the look he gave her but didn't think it possible. Until he unbuckled his belt.

LaKeisha's eyes almost shot out of her head as his pants fell to the floor, his penis hanging to his knees. Within seconds it stood firm, ready to do its job. A

torrent of warmth and wetness flooded her. She had heard stories about how big
he was but didn't believe—couldn't believe.

"Come here," he ordered. She felt the heat of his breath from across the
hallway.

Shocked and excited, she stepped over, looking up and down the hallway to
make sure there were no observers. Once within his reach, he grabbed her and
threw her against the wall. The decorative crown molding that ran along the
wall dug into her back, but she didn't care. It was going to happen! She waited
all her life for this!

LaKeisha tried to kiss his lips, but he didn't make them accessible as he
bent down and grabbed the bottom of her skirt with both hands. He ripped it
in half; her legs turned to jelly. He tore off her thong as well, dropping it to her
skirt on the ground, casualties of lust. She tried to kiss his lips again as he stood
but to no avail.

Darnel placed his forehead and both forearms on the wall above LaKeisha's
head, not seeming to notice she was even there. Instinct guided his erection,
sliding into her with one thrust, filling her and spreading her like never before.
She was thankful that she was so excited—if not, that move of his would have
hurt more. He had a few inches to spare but tried to shove them inside anyway;
his monomaniacal drive became more apparent with every thrust.

A warm wave flowed from her belly, up her spine, and to the base of her
neck with every push. Darnel tried harder and faster to force his entire self into
her. The warm wave turned into exciting lightning strikes, then bolts of searing
pain. She felt as if her guts were getting beaten with a lead pipe as her feet left
the floor with every slam from Darnel. Not wanting to ruin the moment, she
reached up and wrapped her arms around his neck while throwing her left foot
onto the small ledge of the crown molding. She pulled herself up and wrapped
her right leg around the small of Darnel's back.

Too out of shape to be trying something so athletic, LaKeisha's arms and
back started to burn, and she had trouble drawing a steady breath. But the pain
was worth it. She had Darnel and he was fucking the hell out of her!

Just as she closed her eyes, determined to ignore all the pain and focus on
what was going on between her legs, he finished. With one last painful thrust,
she felt him release. Again, she didn't care because it was *Darnel.* Thoughts
flooded her mind. What did this mean to him? Would they see each other
again? Fuck again? She couldn't wait to tell her friends or the girls at the salon.
She got Darnel, and he only liked white women. She tried to think of something to say to her lover but noticed he wasn't done yet.

Darnel remained inside of her. He slowly started to slide back and forth again. The sliding turned into a rhythmic pumping. At first, this excited LaKeisha, but then she realized her slickness had turned to stickiness. He was no longer gliding but now forcing.

"Dar . . . Darnel. Wait . . ." she huffed, out of breath.

Pulling away from the wall, he moved his arms to her back to support her and looked into her eyes. She didn't recognize him. She only saw a dog in heat. And like a dog in heat, he latched onto her neck with his teeth. Thrusting faster and panting harder, he squeezed her tighter and tighter. His grip became unbearable, lust consuming him to the point of making her an inconsequential participant. She couldn't breathe. She wanted to scream but didn't, afraid her children would answer her call for help and see her like this. Panic consumed her; fear tore the lust out of her heart. She was afraid. Then Darnel stopped.

As if doused in a bucket of ice water, Darnel's erection withered, and he pulled his face away from her neck to look at her. His pupils were pinpoints; fear strangled him. Terrified, he dropped her. Pain shot up her back as she landed on her ass. So afraid, Darnel could only speak in shaky grunts as he tried to run but tripped over the pants around his ankles. Trying to scream, he kicked and flailed his pants off. Wearing only a sweaty T-shirt, Darnel ran.

Gasping for breath, LaKeisha leaned against the wall. Her whole body hurt. Her back and crotch throbbed to the rhythm of her heart slamming against her chest. Her legs quaked every time she moved them. Sitting in a puddle of sex mess, she cried . . .

CHAPTER
17

York, Pennsylvania

Stone paced his new living room. Something didn't feel right today. When he woke up this morning, he simply . . . couldn't feel. But he could still taste, so he mixed himself a martini—he had grown quite fond of them over the past week—and decided to get back to business.

After killing his brother and claiming the house and business and everything else he owned, Stone went looking for information. Lucky for him, the blonde bimbo, who seemingly came with the house because she never left, not only knew where to find the wall-safe but knew the combination. More information could be found on Marko's computer. It took a couple days to get to it, but again, with the bimbo's help, Stone was in business.

When Stone first made phone calls to let people know that he had taken over for Marko, he was treated to laughing at the other end of the line, followed by a hang-up. Marko had made it look so easy, and Stone started to regret killing him. Then the bimbo reminded him that the only advertising in *this* business was word-of-mouth.

A garage downtown doubled as a chop shop, and Stone knew the guys who worked there. The guys knew how to party, and they were also on Marko's payroll. One night, Stone interrupted their poker game to give them the news. They laughed. Frustrated from being laughed at, Stone busted up the place. Of course, the chop-shop guys took offense and pulled their guns, a futile act. Two broken necks, several cracked ribs, and a few busted kneecaps later, the word was out. Stone was the new Boss—and you *didn't* fuck with him!

The suppliers didn't care either way. As long as the cash made it to their pockets, they didn't care if it came from a scrawny Italian guy named Marko or his psycho brother who thought he was made out of stone. The distributors were the ones Stone had to get under control. The inventory flowed, and he had to keep things moving. One slip-up and the cops would be all over him. Or worse—he'd lose money.

The bimbo handled the numbers. Not well, but better than Stone. He let her take care of the books, but he watched over her shoulder, pretending to make sure she was doing everything right. She talked a lot, which annoyed him, but he got better at ignoring her. And the sex was phenomenal.

She was outside in the pool, and he watched her as he mixed up a martini batch. The morning chill spread into the cloudy afternoon. That didn't stop her from slipping into a bikini and jumping into the pool. Beginning some ritual, she then got out and ran to the hot tub. A few minutes in there sufficed, and off she went to dive into the pool again.

"Crazy bitch," Stone mumbled to himself, pouring his martini. The glass shattered as he reached for his drink. Confused, he rubbed his fingers together, then his hands, but felt nothing. He squeezed his hands together, hard enough for veins to pop out of his forearms, resulting in only the slightest sensation of pressure.

He started to panic. The thought of not being able to *feel* anything freaked him out. Opening one of the drawers, he found the corkscrew. He grabbed it, unable to feel the wooden top in his palm or the metal between his fingers as he gripped it, and placed the palm of his other hand on the bar top, unable to feel that either. He stabbed his hand with the corkscrew. Nothing. He did it again. And again. Harder and faster, over and over again, until the bent metal finally snapped from the wooden handle, garnering only the most minimal pinprick of sensation.

"What the hell are you doing?" the bimbo asked, standing in front of the glass doors, done with her afternoon swim. Wet locks of hair streaked across her face and over her shoulders in seductive patterns. The jewelry in her navel glistened. Her nipples fought hard to escape from the flimsy yellow material of her bikini top.

"I can't feel anything."

"Yeah, we get it. You're Stone. You're big and mean. Raaaaahhhrr," she said with bored sarcasm. She mimicked Frankenstein's monster, her silicone jiggling.

Stone loved her tits. He didn't care how fake they were; they were huge and fun. There had been times over the past week he had forgotten what her face looked like but not *those* tits. His pants bulged as he watched her. "Get naked."

Sighing, she replied, "Now?"

"Now!"

They both made their way to the nearest couch. With a tug at two strings, she fulfilled his request and sat on the couch, leaning back to accommodate. Stone stripped as well and strode over with a sense of urgency, hard as his name implied. Without so much as a kiss or a peck or even a friendly touch, he grabbed her hips and shoved himself in. She pushed against his shoulders as her face contorted to a grimace. "Oooooow! Foreplay, asshole!"

"I can't feel anything," he said to nobody as he pulled out and plunged in again.

"Well, I can, and it doesn't feel good, you dick! Now slow down and give me a minute to catch up!"

"I can't feel anything," he repeated, his voice quaking with fear, sounding like a lost child. His thrusting became furious.

She squirmed, fighting against his grip. "Yeah, you said that, and it's not getting any better for me! Let me go!"

He did, only to grab her again, this time by her throat. Panic consumed him, his eyes wide with terror. Fear grew with every thrust, as did his grip. "I can't feel anything!"

The bimbo's hands wrapped around his wrists, fighting so hard her fingernails split and broke. Unable to scream, her mouth stayed open. Her eyes held as much fear as his. Frustrated by the lack of any sensation, unable to feel her from the inside, the skin of her neck, or the heat from her twitching body, Stone pulled her by the neck, then shoved her head back into the couch. He continued to pull and push her head as he pumped with his hips, well after she had died. An hour later, he finally came . . .

CHAPTER
18

Harrisburg, Pennsylvania

One week. One week was how long it took Marvin's magic touch to make Colby's tooth fall out. He took the right incisor, making the young man look lopsided whenever he smiled. Marvin noted that in his notebook. Little notes and expounding rhetoric jumbled together on page after page of documented experiments. Most of them involved Colby.

In his notes, Marvin recorded the sensation he felt when he touched people's skin, usually Colby's. Finding the right words to describe the sensations eluded him. Communicating? Not exactly. Singing? Closer. Spying? Better, but not perfectly accurate. Marvin enjoyed the sensations, feeling the inner workings of anyone he wished. But it was the *manipulation* that thrilled him. Especially Colby.

Colby served as a petri dish for three experiments, counting the most recent that came to fruition—the loss of his tooth. Notes described how Marvin had to prolong a handshake to find the right nerves. Once he found them, it only took a casual brush of the fingers during a paper exchange to kill them. Marvin had ordered the nerves to cease functioning. One week later, Colby visited the dentist for an extraction.

The other experiments involved weight gain and hair loss. One week garnered results, but only Marvin noticed the visual effects because he knew what to look for. However, whenever Marvin touched Colby, he felt the extra fat cells and noticed fewer functioning hair follicles.

Of course, Marvin experimented on others. The random outbreaks of acne drove Trudy mad. A rash on his inner thigh provided Ron with more than one embarrassing situation. Nosebleeds sent Barb to the doctor just a few days ago. He even experimented on himself. For the first time in years, his hair claimed more territory than his baldness. Other "follicle-ly challenged" men hounded him for his secret. He always responded with a smile and said, "A magician never tells." And for the last seven days, he ate ten candy bars during lunch and topped off his dinner every night with an entire quart of ice cream. His efforts resulted in the loss of an inch from his waist. It still flopped over his belt, but his experiment yielded promising results. But the work he prided the most was his wife.

Marvin smiled, thinking of how her breasts exploded from not needing a bra to a C cup. He planned on stopping them around a double D. A thought struck him as he flipped through his notes regarding his wife; before it fled, he wrote: "Give her more back muscle to properly support her tits."

She needed size-4 pants now. Marvin reviewed a stray scribbling in one corner of his notebook to stop at a size 6. Just the other day, he noticed her ribs were gone, smoothed over by her "mysterious" weight gain. God, he hated seeing her ribs; it made him feel like he lived with a zombie.

He placed the notebook back in his desk drawer and locked it. He had to tell her soon. Even though she loved shopping for a new wardrobe and the attention her new figure garnered, she worried. A diet that disallowed most of the food in the grocery store could never yield such results. And she fretted over Marvin as well. How did his hair grow back? How did a man who ate a quart of ice cream for dessert every night lose an inch from his waist? He smiled again—after all these years, she still noticed him.

"Hi, Colby," Marvin heard Trudy's voice outside his office. He saw the young man stride past his door. Feeling like a secret agent, Marvin moved from his desk toward the door, careful not to make a sound, and watched Colby interact with Trudy.

"Hi, Trudy," Colby replied, his voice still resounding with confidence.

Trudy touched Colby's arm, an extension of her concern. "Hey, I just heard about your tooth. I'm so sorry. What'd the dentist say?"

"It's crazy. He has *no idea* what happened. The nerves to that tooth just died. No reason. Just died."

Trudy covered her mouth with a hand and shook her head, partly to cover the dime-sized pimple sprouting from the left corner of her mouth. "That's such a shame. Does he think it'll happen again?"

"They're gonna do some more tests, but God-willing, everything should be fine."

God has nothing to do with it, Marvin thought as he slipped out of his office after Colby left Trudy's desk.

It was Wednesday. And Wednesdays were when Colby met with Savinski to tell him which companies Marvin looked at investing in. Marvin tried giving him companies that were dogs, but Colby would just talk to Barb and Ron, compiling the true list that way. Did Barb and Ron know about Colby's secret meetings with Savinski? Didn't matter. It was going to end today—Marvin was sure of it as he strode toward his competitor's office. Having more hair made him feel empowered.

On a mission, Marvin walked past Savinski's administrative assistant. She paid him no heed, so he backtracked, slipped into Savinski's office, and shut the door.

"What are you doing, Marvin?" Savinski asked from behind his desk.

Marvin used to admire Savinski. The man had been alive ten years longer than Marvin and been in the investment game twelve years longer. But he looked phenomenal. Trim but athletic, his body made any suit look dapper. His smile could get more than any bribe or blackmail, and his styled silver hair only added to his panache. But ever since Marvin got his promotion and became Savinski's equal, on paper at least, Savinski became an embittered man who undermined Marvin and swayed his employees against him. That was going to stop now.

"It stops now," Marvin blurted out, feeling like the smallest kid in the schoolyard standing up to the bully.

Savinksi smiled that damn smile. "Marvin, why don't you have a seat."

Marvin sat in a chair in front of Savinski's desk but continued, "I know you've got Colby in your back pocket, stealing my companies from me."

"Then fire him. Problem solved."

Marvin felt his body sweat. His palms burned while his forehead chilled. He furrowed his brows, remembering this was how he *used to* react. Not anymore! He *willed* himself to stop sweating. He *commanded* himself to be brave. "No. You leave my employees alone."

Savinski laughed. "Marvin, you're too funny. You're acting like you actually *deserve* the promotion that gave you this job. You didn't earn this. Just give Colby to me and be done with it."

Waves of anger crashed against Marvin's heart. He clenched his fists. He cowered to this type of condescending attitude for twenty years, not just from Savinski, but from *everyone! Twenty years!* "No more. Leave my employees alone."

Savinski remained stolid. "Marvin, come on. Colby hates you. All your employees do. Give it up, and I'll put in a good word for you with Salinger. He'll ease up on you, and you can coast through to retirement."

Marvin leaned forward; his brows dug so low that his face hurt. He felt his lips snarl when he talked. "You talentless hack. You can't tell the difference between an assets page and the hooker's ass you supply to all your contacts."

Savinski laughed. Then he leaned forward himself, placing his folded hands on his desk. "That has got to be the worst insult ever. Now get out of my office. And take your hair plugs with you."

"Didn't care about the insult. Just wanted you to get closer," Marvin mumbled as he grabbed Savinski's right hand with his left.

Confused, the older man tried to pull back but couldn't escape Marvin's vice-like grip. His body sang to Marvin, giving up every secret it had. Marvin saw the gray in his lungs from too many cigarettes but not enough for his needs. No signs of cancer. A mild infection in his bladder wasn't enough either. But Savinski enjoyed red meat and potato chips. Marvin swam through Savinski's rivers of blood, looking for the right atoll.

There was one right at the top of his spine—the gateway to his brain.

The artery constriction hindered the blood flow already, coated with a layer of cholesterol plaque. The right nerve spasm at the right time around that artery closed it off, catching a bevy of platelets. When the spasm ended, it was too late. A clot formed. Savinski stroked. And Marvin felt the whole thing.

At first, Savinski had no clue. His brows furrowed as he prepared to unleash a verbal tirade since Marvin refused to relinquish his hand. Physical violence might have crossed his mind; Marvin agitated him *that* much! But then the lack of blood flow to his brain, panic rippling through every nerve. Desperation pumped through his body with the beat of his heart, the blood forbidden to move beyond the impasse. The temperature of Savinski's body rose as sweat streamed from every pore. Finally, his bulging eyes locked onto Marvin's, horror mixed with realization. He knew Marvin did this. He knew.

Once Marvin felt everything cease, he let go of Savinski's hand. The empty husk of an old man collapsed on his desk.

With impeccable timing, Colby opened the door and froze. Emboldened by his meeting with Savinski, Marvin got within an inch of Colby and whispered, "Your 'other' boss just had a stroke. You're stuck with me now." Marvin exited the office bumping Colby's shoulder with his own.

"Call 9-1-1," Marvin said to Savinski's admin assistant as he strode past, his voice as calm as if he had asked for coffee.

Halfway to his office, a harrowing thought struck Marvin. Tormenting Colby tickled him like a child on Christmas morning. Molding himself like a sculptor with clay felt great. And having a hot wife surpassed all those feelings. But at that moment, he realized one thing—he was thinking too small . . .

CHAPTER
19

Camp Hill, Pennsylvania

12:30. *Half an hour late*, Michael thought, looking at his watch. He looked around the bustling food court. It was small, only ten restaurants, but serviceable. Plenty of lunchtime options. He opted for a big cup of boardwalk-style French fries.

Most of the patrons consisted of other mall employees. Women of all ages wore sleek slacks and blouses or fun spring dresses, labeled from whichever clothing store employed them. Pimply-faced and shaggy-haired young men from electronics stores or game stores or music stores sat with women attractive enough to be considered out of their league. *I could never get a woman like that at his age*, Michael thought, watching a blonde flaunt her cleavage while talking to a young man wearing droopy pants and a wrinkled shirt two sizes too big.

Senior citizens populated quite a few tables, enjoying their retirement. Michael watched one couple, white-haired with bodies surrendering to the fight against gravity, still very much in love. He wondered about "their story" and studied their mannerisms, thinking they'd make great characters for a book. A few yuppies walked in front of his field of vision, streamlined in dark suits and red ties. On days like this, he could empathize with them—he had to be back to work after lunch. Of course, the reality of the situation was that he had a class to teach from 2:30 to 3:30, and then he could call it a day.

Michael shoved two fries into his mouth and looked at his watch again. 12:45. He shook his head and rolled his eyes. He came here to meet a kid who said he found Michael by . . . vibing? . . . and then mentally hid his knives and phones from him. Ridiculous. They scheduled this meeting to talk about Michael's strange ability to . . . push? . . . things. More ridiculousness! Although, it did explain how Michael survived two oncoming vehicles barreling toward him.

And it was impossible to deny he threw Derrick through the air just by thinking about it. Or did he? Derrick could have jumped? Thrown himself? Derrick had been a student of Michael's and freely admitted that the class sucked. Maybe he needed a practical joke as restitution?

Looking around to make sure no one ruined his feeling of anonymity, Michael dumped the rest of the French fries from the 32-ounce cup onto his tray and set the cup on the table. He rested his palms on the table behind the cup and drew in a slow breath, remembering the warm feeling in the back of his head. He felt it! Slow and steady, he released the warmth, letting it flow through his arms. *Slide the cup across the table, slide it slowly across the table*, he thought. The warmth exploded from his fingertips.

The cup popped into the air, spinning end over end. It landed in the center of the empty table in front of him and bounced. Momentum exhausted, the cup landed at the base of the next table, at the feet of two college-aged girls.

Shit!

Not everyone saw what happened but enough to blush Michael's cheeks as he stood. He did what he always did in awkward situations—he smiled and let his mouth take over.

"Sorry. Circus clown learning a new trick," he said to the patrons of one table. "Cup was getting mouthy with me. Had to teach it a lesson," he said to others. "Sorry. I bet my invisible friend that I could make you look," he said to the two girls as he picked the cup from the floor. Their silent sneers spoke volumes. He returned to his seat, not wanting to see if they had pepper spray in their trendy purses.

Hoping to make a clean escape, Michael didn't even sit back down. He lifted his tray and dropped the cup on it, ready to sacrifice his uneaten fries. Then, he saw Derrick.

Still wearing his gray sweatshirt, hood up, Derrick flung open the glass doors. He located Michael and hurried toward him, taking long strides. His eyes were wide again. "Professor!" he yelled, oblivious to how much attention he attracted. "Professor! I'm vibing again!"

Michael smiled the smile of a man surrendering to humility. He simply sat back down and waited for crazy, hyper, vibing Derrick to join him. In the meantime, the patrons who witnessed the flying cup incident looked at Michael and smiled as well. A few even looked around for a hidden camera. He glanced over to the two college-aged girls he disturbed earlier. They made no effort to hide their disgust and eye rolls. Michael swore he saw one girl mouth to the other, "Perverted, creepy, old guy."

"Professor," Derrick huffed, out of breath and taking a seat in front of Michael. "I'm vibing again."

"Really, Derrick?" Michael said with patient sarcasm.

"Yeah. Started last night. An old woman. I keep seeing this old woman. Not old like you, but *old* old. *Real* old."

Not sure what to make of the whole situation, Michael said the only thing that came to mind, "Derrick, I'm thirty-seven."

"Really? Yeah, she's older than that. Like thin-with-gray-hair old. Up north."

Michael felt his pulse race just watching the animated young man, hands flailing, eyes flittering as he talked. When he didn't talk, his feet bounced, both legs in perfect rhythm while at least one finger tapped the table. Pressing his fingertips to his temple to circumvent the impending headache, Michael asked, "Are you on Ritalin?"

"No. We gotta find her to make this stop—that's how it stopped with you—when I found you. The vibe's not as strong as it was with you, which makes me think she's a little farther away than you were when I first felt your vibe, so I'm thinking about an hour to an hour and a half north of here, which isn't too bad, especially if we leave now . . ."

"Derrick . . . we're not going anywhere right now."

"What? Why?"

"For starters, I have to get back to work soon. Second, I came here to talk to you about what's going on with us. Third, it's difficult to be around you when you're all spastic like this."

Derrick leaned forward and blinked rapidly as if trying to scrub away the images he saw. "Professor, I can't help it. She's all I see. When I shut my eyes, there she is. I gotta go find her to stop the vibing. I'll head up now and call you when I find her and figure out what she can do."

Michael's mind flooded with images of an old woman having a heart attack after being accosted by crazy, hyper, vibing Derrick. Michael couldn't allow that. He picked up his empty fry cup and placed it on the table in front of Derrick. "Here, look at this."

"I don't under—"

"Derrick, please," Michael's voice shifted from sarcasm to compassion, pretending that Derrick just needed help comprehending Shakespeare. "Focus on the cup. Don't look at me, or the food court, or anyone in the food court. Just the cup."

Michael paused to let the young man slouch forward and stare at the cup. "Just keep looking at the cup and try to calm down. When you blink, you see the woman. Yes, it's freaky, but just try to accept it. And take deep breaths."

Michael's drive-through meditation tactic worked. Well, as best it could. Derrick's fingers still strummed the table, but his legs stopped bouncing. "Okay, Derrick. Do you think you can do this—relax for a couple days?"

"Yeah," Derrick replied, sounding surprised by the answer. "Yeah, I think I can."

"Okay. Good. You do this: You go home and stay relaxed. Meet me at my house, day after tomorrow, 8 a.m., and I promise we'll find this woman together. Deal?"

Still staring at the cup, Derrick agreed. "Deal."

"Okay, Derrick, I gotta go back to work. You all right?"

Breathing easy and steady, Derrick answered, "Yeah. I'm good. But you wanted to talk about what's going on with us?"

"It can wait. We'll have plenty of time in the car ride up north."

"Okay." With that, Derrick stood and walked out of the food court and into the parking lot, taking the empty 32-ounce French-fry cup with him.

Michael could only watch with his mouth hanging open. No one who witnessed his entrance even noticed he left. Did that even happen? Michael thought maybe he dreamed it all, or maybe he vibed Derrick, seeing him every time he closed his eyes. And what about his "pushing?" It was real—he knew it. But it couldn't be. Impossible.

Just as Michael stood and turned, he watched the two college-aged girls stand and walk away. However, he overheard the one say to the other, "Can you believe that creepy, old guy tried to hit on us by throwing a cup at us? Ugh!"

Embarrassment ate a hole through Michael's gut. No dream could produce such a painful feeling. No more denial. It was real. He had some strange ability to push things with his mind. Now what?

CHAPTER
20

Near State College, Pennsylvania

The sun barely made it through the thick tree canopy, creating more shadows than not. Dust and dirt floated through the shafts of light, magically scintillating. Jeremiah Schaeffer didn't believe in magic. He believed in his Almighty God, Lord and Savior. He also believed that the devil existed—he had to believe that if he believed in God. He knew of the sins the devil brought to man. He knew of evil; he smelled it, wafting thick and rotten through the morning air. He knew it well because he had been tracking it for ten days now.

Hunting rifle in hand, Jeremiah moved through the forest as if on angel's wings. The crunch of dead leaves and small twigs underfoot made sounds no more noisy or suspicious than that made by any other creature that lived in the forest. Oak and poplar and locust trees populated the forest, just like the part of the mountain near his home, where he had hunted all his life. He even passed the occasional birch, cutting off a piece here and there to chew. Even though he had never been on this part of the mountain before, he moved through it as if he belonged. God had granted him access since he was on a mission to find and exorcise evil. A mission to save his son.

Jeremiah's teeth ground together just thinking about the incident. The devil assumed the form of a serpent once again and infiltrated Jeremiah's house, stealing his first-born son. Every time he blinked, he saw the undulating abomination in his son's bedroom. It escaped with his son. He didn't actually see his son, but he knew the evil demon had kidnapped him. There was no other logical explanation.

Tracking it was easy. Jeremiah had a hunting rifle in his hands the day after he took his first steps. This land was his playground as a child and his livelihood as a farmer. These mountains were *his*! Jeremiah reckoned that the serpent towered around seven feet tall, with a tail longer than its body. Jeremiah's size-13 hunting boot fit inside the beast's footprint without touching the edges. The footprints, the trail its dragging tail left, the broken branches and twigs, all made for easy tracking.

Jeremiah slept only when his body collapsed and ate when his vision blurred. He had a light sleeping bag and opted to eat whatever berries he could find, saving the beef jerky he packed for an emergency. He dropped a bit of weight but didn't worry. God was on his side.

For ten days, Jeremiah hunted the monster. For the first eight days, it moved south along the stream, fast, the speed of a slithering snake fast. But something had slowed it down for the last two. Jeremiah caught up to it.

He could smell it.

A small hill rose before him, and on the other side was the beast. Hearing the unholy noises the monster made, Jeremiah dropped his backpack and sleeping bag, keeping only his rifle and as many shells as he could fit into his pockets. He crept up the hill, remaining as quiet as a grazing deer. The air moved toward him, so his scent blew away from the creature. He reached the top and peered at the bottom of the other side. He made the sign of the cross and prayed.

The monster, scales as green as bile, danced and celebrated, covered in black snakes. Two dozen slithered all over its body, around its chest, down its legs, over its head—the salacious movements made Jeremiah feel like he had snakes of his own squirming in his stomach. Disgusting, blaspheming *filth*! Hissing and howling, calling forth the powers of Hell!

Adam squirmed and twisted. Nora sat next to a tree fifty feet away, commanding the snakes to play with him. Their smooth scales slid across his smooth scales. They tickled! He gyrated and fidgeted his feet as one snake or another slid a silly way across a sensitive scale. Laughing, he twisted and turned. Until he saw his father pointing a gun at him.

With the reflexes of a lizard, Adam leaped out of the way. The bullet missed, followed quickly by the exploding crack of Jeremiah's gun. Despite his bulk, Adam hopped from behind one tree to another with grace and ease, toward his father. He knew this moment would come, and he practiced for it. "Pa-pa! It'sss me! A-dam!"

"Satan!" Jeremiah screamed back and raised his rifle. "What have you done with my son?!"

With another pull of the trigger, tree bark exploded where Adam once was. He avoided the gunshot and scaled the trunk of a nearby tree. He jumped to another tree, but he stayed closer to the ground, trying to get closer to his father.

Finally, he jumped down, landing within ten feet. He stood with pleading eyes and outstretched arms. "Pa-pa. It'sss. Me. Your. Ssson. I. Am. Adam. Sssaeffer."

Jeremiah heard the words. Tears rolled down his cheeks. At least he knew what happened to his son. He raised his rifle and aimed right at Adam's head.

Before he could pull the trigger, a squirrel fell from an overhead tree branch, landing on Jeremiah's arm. Then another. A dozen squirrels attacked him from above while black snakes wrapped around his legs from below.

"Don't worry, Adam," Nora said, walking from behind Jeremiah. "I have a wolf coming from about a mile away. He'll be here soon."

Jeremiah turned and saw a naked girl with eyes as black as the pits of Hades. Anger and relief swirled within his belly. Maybe there was magic in this world? Black, evil magic from sullied temptresses. "Witch!" he yelled and trained his weapon on her, ignoring the pain from two dozen biting creatures. Once she died, this would all stop, and Adam's soul would be released!

"No!" Adam screamed. He lunged forward. Panic made him clumsy. Reflexes forced his father to move. There was a spine-chilling squish. Then the thump of a two-hundred-pound man hitting the forest floor.

Adam looked at his left hand, slicked crimson with bloodied chunks of fat and flesh sliding down his fingers. Strips of flannel stuck to the tips of his claws. He knew what happened before he even looked down at his father, clutching his waist. With every waning heartbeat, he twitched and lurched forward a bit. His intestines continued to slide out, piling in front of him.

Pain stung Adam's eyes, running from his head to his chest, squeezing tighter and tighter. "Pa-pa. I'm. Ssssorr-ee. I. Jumped. You. Moved. I . . ."

Jeremiah's eyes held hatred. Only hatred. "Monster," he muttered with his last breath. His body convulsed one last time.

Adam wheezed, gulping for air. He shook, unable to cope. Thoughts of his widowed mother flooded his mind. His brothers and sisters, too. He saw them crying. Tending the farm by themselves. Empty.

"Adam," Nora said as she walked past. "We need to go."

Adam wanted to stay. He wanted to bury his father or take his body back to the farm, at least get it away from the scavengers. He wanted to kneel and pray, beg for his father's safe entry into Heaven, as well as his own forgiveness. Instead, he took one last look and turned to follow Nora . . .

CHAPTER
21

Pittsburgh, Pennsylvania

The Blue Line Star Health Insurance Company building glimmered like a beacon of hope, the sun reflecting off the five floors of black glass. During cloudy days, the building glowered like a foreboding tower of doom with impenetrable windows. Blue Line Star's mission statement focused more on the "beacon of hope" for the community. Other buildings near it were taller, a few shorter but wider. However, this one was the most noticeable, with its spectacular angles producing a star-like design. On the inside, the atrium in the center of the building stretched to the glass ceiling, allowing heaven itself to cascade the lobby with light. Three thousand employees found some sense of awe as soon as they entered the building, ready to begin their workday. The atrium provided a reflective respite for any employee needing a break. Except for the I/T department. Like many other companies, the I/T department was located in the basement.

This bothered most of the techs. But not Kevin Keller. He led a solitary life anyway, leaving his house only to go to work, get the latest video game, or see the occasional movie. Being in a windowless environment never bothered him. Plus, he got to see more of the building than just about anyone when he fetched a broken computer and then returned with a fixed one. That was what he did. Fixed them.

"Dude! Done already?"

Kevin turned to see Bob, his coworker and friend. Tall and lanky, Bob smiled and moved with the confidence and effortless flow of a spider. His sky-blue polo shirt and khaki pants didn't fit him, or more accurately, he didn't fit into them. Kevin had the opposite problem—his sky-blue polo shirt and khaki pants hugged his waist past the point of comfort.

Tightening the last screw of the computer's cover, Kevin smiled, blushed, and replied. "Yeah."

"Damn. You've been *en fuego* lately!" Bob said, sidling up to Kevin's work area. Bob ran his hand up his face, scooping his bangs out of his eyes so he could get a better look. His hair was long and straight, like an overgrown bowl cut. Kevin kept his hair short and tight, setting his trimmer to "1" every Monday. Not knowing anything about style, he felt more comfortable doing that. A small patch of a beard grew from the bottom of Bob's lip to the tip of his chin. Still not knowing anything about style, nor having the ability to grow facial hair in any uniform fashion, Kevin used an electric razor every morning.

"I still can't believe how fast you fixed it," Bob continued. "All right, let's go interface with the plebians."

They loaded the computer onto a small work cart, and off they went to deliver it. This was Kevin's favorite part. Not the delivering but watching Bob. Despite the fact that no one would ever consider him an attractive guy, Bob was good with women. Sometimes smooth and mellow, sometimes animated and off the wall, he always made them laugh. In a good way. From originating point to destination point, Bob would have to stop and spend some time flirting with a woman. Kevin was content to watch, never speaking himself. If the conversation ever shifted his way, he'd simply blush, smile, and nod. Today they stopped five times before they made it to their destination.

"So, where's this going?" Bob asked, snatching the fix-it form taped to the computer.

"Umm," Kevin replied, unable to even say the name. Nervousness constricted his throat.

"No way. No. Freaking. Way!"

Blushing, but not smiling, Kevin whispered, "Shh. Dude, keep your voice down."

Bob bounced all around Kevin like an out-of-control pogo stick. "Have you figured out what you're gonna say yet?"

"Umm," Kevin replied, still pushing the cart housing the lone computer.

"Dude, you can't lead off with that. Come on. This is your one big chance. You've been waiting for this for, like, ever. Seriously, dude, you can't pass this up." To emphasize his point, Bob held up the fix-it form an inch from Kevin's eyes in case he forgot the love of his life: Debra Verone.

The rest of the trip to her desk, Kevin had to withstand the Bob barrage: "Dude, come on. Dude, seriously. Dude, you need to. Dude, seriously. Dude, duuuuuude."

Once at her cubicle, Kevin felt a slight sense of relief that she wasn't there. Then his heart seized when she poked her head out from the neighboring cubicle while on a cell phone. "Yeah, I know. Oh wait, the computer guys are here with my new computer."

She moved the phone away from her mouth and looked at Kevin. "Go ahead, guys. Just let me know when you're done," she said. A stylish elastic headband held back thick locks of cinnamon hair. Perfect white teeth gleamed from her perfect smile, trapping Kevin like a deer in headlights while her bright emerald eyes turned him into roadkill.

"Okay," Bob said, saving Kevin from a heart attack. Once she moved back into the neighboring cubicle, Bob smacked Kevin's arm. As they did their job, they communicated with hand gestures while eavesdropping on her phone call.

"I know he was attractive," she said, her voice deep but smooth, holding a sophistication beyond her years. "But he was too immature. I'm finally ready for a nice guy. A stable guy."

Bob pointed to Kevin, then pointed to the neighboring cubicle where she conversed, then shrugged his shoulders, wondering what the problem was. Kevin blushed and shook his head while plugging the CPU into the wall.

Debra's alluring voice continued. "I'll be thirty-two next month. It's time for me to settle down and find a guy who wants to do the same thing."

Bob rolled his eyes and threw his hands to heaven, wondering how the thirty-three-year-old Kevin could sit back and do nothing. Kevin blushed and shrugged his shoulders while he hooked up the monitor.

Debra laughed so smoothly that it caressed Kevin and gave him goosebumps. "Yeah, I know. Nice, stable guy looking to settle—what a fairy tale, huh? I think the computer guys might be done. I'm gonna go. Bye."

Bob rested his face in the palm of his hand, the only way to keep himself from blurting out, "Kevin loves you!" to her.

Kevin turned the computer on. Debra entered her cubicle, greeted by her log-in screen. She looked over at Kevin and smiled. "Looks great, guys. I can't thank you enough."

Gesturing toward her keyboard as if presenting it to her for the first time, Kevin managed a, "Heh?"

If the situation weren't so sad, Bob would have laughed. Instead, he shouldered the attention. Breaking into his best fast-talking, used-car salesman shyster voice, he said, "We rotated the tires, changed the oil, bled the transmission, flushed the radiator, greased it, lubed it, washed it, and winterized it. You should be good to go for another three thousand miles."

Debra shook her head and laughed. "Well, that's good to hear. What was wrong with it?"

"The mouse was bad."

Shock and confusion swept across Debra's face. "The mouse? Really?"

"No. Not even close. Why would you think it was the mouse? Who told you it was the mouse? See, that's why you should always let us professionals handle it."

Debra laughed again, melting Kevin's feet to the floor. "I will certainly keep you guys in mind the next time my 'mouse' wrecks my machine."

With that, Bob pushed the cart with one hand while pulling Kevin away with the other. As soon as they escaped far enough out of earshot, Bob began the admonishing. "Dude, that was the poorest display of manship I've ever seen. Dude, come on. What's going on in that shaved head of yours? You've loved her ever since you got hired here, which has been like forever, by the way, and you *always* take the fix-it call from anyone in her department, just so you can see her. You finally get a legit chance to interface and you choke?"

"I don't know," Kevin mumbled. "I guess I just interface with computers better than people."

"See? You just gotta take what you love about computers and find it in people."

Bob looked at Kevin, his hands in his pockets and shoulders dropped in a miserable slouch as he trudged along. Bob then looked over his shoulder to see if anyone could possibly hear what he was about to say. "I was the same way."

Kevin looked up, one eyebrow raised in disbelief. "Really?"

"Yeah. So I got a hooker."

"What?" Kevin screeched, then tittered like a schoolboy.

Bob jerked around to see if anyone heard. "Dude! That's what I'm talking about. That's what you gotta get over."

"No way, man. No way."

"Dude, I'm serious. I was shy, even more than you. But I got a hooker and she helped me out. I was able to . . . you know . . . practice. And I'm not just talking about the fucking . . . although, that was nice too . . . but I got over my fear of women. Hookers helped me be the man I am today."

"Are you serious?"

"Totally. Dude, you have a problem. Like a *real* problem. Support groups are amateurs helping amateurs. A therapist costs two to three hundred dollars *an hour*. A hooker is two hundred for the whole night, and you get some great hands-on experience. Get it? Hands . . . on . . . never mind. But I'm serious about the hooker."

Kevin gave Bob a blank stare.

Bob put his hand on his friend's shoulder. "Dude. You need to experiment. Interface with a real person like you do with a computer."

Experiment. Interface. Kevin liked the sound of that . . .

CHAPTER
22

Harrisburg, Pennsylvania

Marvin sat on the corner of his bed, wringing his hands together. *New hair, new confidence*, he thought to himself. This was it. He was going to tell his wife.

Thelma fought with her bra in the bathroom, a B cup she couldn't quite clasp. She tried to get the front clasps to meet, crushing her breasts together. There! Finally. Her chest spilled out over the top, and she shook her head. How did they get so big in a few weeks? Looking in the mirror, she shook her head. "That's it. I'm calling a doctor today."

Marvin stood and walked to her. His jaw muscles flexed and unflexed, clenching and unclenching his teeth. His eyes held concern, a secret. "Don't call."

Pointing at her chest, she turned to look at him. "I have to, Marvin. Look at these. I mean, I love them, but it's not natural. How can your sudden hair growth not concern you?"

"Because I'm responsible."

Thelma squinted, a smile forming, ready to turn into a laugh as if she thought it was a joke. However, Marvin's sullen eyes told her this was no joke. "What? What are you talking about?"

Marvin sighed. More serious than when he proposed to her, he continued, "It's me, dear. I'm doing this. Your boobs. Your hips. My hair, my waist. I'm doing this."

Thelma still wanted to laugh but wondered if she should call the local hospital to cart him away in a straightjacket. "Marvin. You're scaring me. You don't really believe that, do you?"

Marvin reached for her hand and placed it in his, as gentle as if he handled a butterfly. "I'll show you. Now, try to talk."

Still concerned about her husband's sanity, she wanted to let him know that help was a phone call away. But when she tried to talk, no words came out, just a high-pitched squeak. Confused, she placed her free hand at the base of her neck, cleared her throat, and tried again. Nothing.

"I've just made your larynx swell," Marvin explained. "Here, now I've taken away your laryngitis."

Thelma frowned and moved her lips. Nothing happened until, ". . . being ridiculous." She winced, shocked to hear her voice.

With his free hand, Marvin pulled a few tissues from a nearby box. He handed them to his wife and spun her so she could see herself in the mirror. He placed his hands on her shoulders and said, "Okay. Don't freak out over this one because I could never hurt you, but I just popped a few capillaries in your nasal passage. We should see a couple drops of blood soon."

Before she could tell him that he sounded more insane than before, a scarlet drop rolled from her nostril. Her eyes widened as she watched it touch the top of her lip. Her mind raced, causing her to blink rapidly as she touched the tissue to her face. "Marvin. I . . . I . . . I . . . That doesn't prove . . . I mean . . ."

Still proving his point, he grabbed her hand and gave it a loving squeeze. "In about five seconds, you're going to have to piss very badly."

Five seconds was all he needed to turn and leave the bathroom to give her privacy. She wanted to refute his claim but couldn't. The urge struck her like a punch, and she dropped her ass to the toilet seat.

After he heard the flush, Marvin looked back at the bathroom. His wife exited, wide-eyed. "Marvin. What's going on?"

Sitting on the edge of the bed, Marvin watched as Thelma made her way in front of him. "I don't know, honey."

"How? How did this happen?"

"I don't know. I have *no* idea."

"How long?"

"About three weeks ago. The day Colby puked. I did that. But I didn't know it at the time."

Thelma's eyes darted back and forth, looking for reason and sanity. But *this* was sanity. This *did* happen. "How do you do it?"

"I . . . don't know. It's like people's bodies talk to me when I touch them. Small stuff like your nosebleed and laryngitis I can do right away. Bigger things like your hips and boobs and my hair take longer."

She looked at her husband, her eyes reddening with latent tears. "And . . . and it doesn't bother you that you don't know how this happened?"

"It took me a couple weeks just to figure out I was doing it. I wanted to make sure it was *me* doing it. And I want to enjoy this first. I deserve this—*we* deserve this. I want to give us what we could never have before." He punctuated his sentence by putting his hand on her belly.

Confused, Thelma searched her husband's face for some clue to his riddle. He gave a sheepish grin and raised his eyebrows. She caught the hint. A smile ran from ear to ear; her bloodshot eyes released the tears they held. She put her hands to her mouth. "You mean?"

"Yes. I can fix it."

"A baby?"

"Yes."

"But we're both forty-five. How?"

Marvin slid her a sly grin. "Honey, I'm aging us in reverse. Next month, you'll have D cups and I'll have a full head of hair. The month after, you'll have the skin of a model and I'll be chiseled. I can read your body; it talks to me. Everything will be fine."

Thelma smiled. Her whole body smiled, it glowed. Every trepidation she had about her husband's shocking news went to the wayside. Placing her hands on his face, Thelma knew she had never loved her husband more than that moment when she believed she could conceive.

They saw a specialist over a decade ago, wondering why there was no pregnancy after years of trying. The doctor used the phrase "inhospitable environment." No alternative, no procedure, was affordable, and that ended that. If Marvin could do what he said he could do, give her the one thing to complete her life, it would be worth the wait.

Thelma gave Marvin her most devious smile, then looked at her chest and said, "So, you made these?"

Marvin smiled as well. "Yep."

Leaning forward, she unclasped her bra. Her breasts burst from their confines, smacking Marvin in the face. He and his wife fell onto the bed. She laughed and said, "You do good work."

Marvin decided that he'd be late for work today. He needed to make an environment hospitable. Having not gotten dressed yet, Thelma was naked and ready to go, helping Marvin squirm free from his clothes. Her body was everywhere on his. Singing to him. Her joy permeated every cell, strummed every nerve like a harp.

Thelma set the tempo, allowing Marvin to concentrate on fixing her. But something was wrong. Marvin felt her womb, her uterus, her fallopian tubes.

He understood them, their functions, how they worked. But he couldn't change them.

He breathed through his nose, trying to delay the inevitable while his wife writhed away. Concentrate! Why wasn't he able to command these areas? Because he didn't have them? Nonsense. He felt them; they sang to him like every other part of her body. Or maybe it was the *knowledge* of them. Reading about skydiving and actually jumping from a plane were vastly different concepts. Just because he knew *how* they worked didn't mean he could work them.

Trudy had kids! So did Barb! Three of them, in fact. He touched them enough over the past week to know their bodies inside and out—literally! For this journey with his wife, he needed a roadmap. Common sense could get him from Third Street if he stood on Second Street without a map. However, with no map, the difficulty skyrocketed if he had to get from Second Street, Harrisburg, to Third Street, Wichita.

Still feeling his wife grind his erection, still feeling her heartbeat and sweat and hot breath, still feeling her every cell, he called upon his memory of Trudy and Barb. Walking through their bodies as easily as walking through a house with many rooms, he felt how they had been pregnant, how they sustained life from within. A roadmap!

Marvin couldn't keep from releasing much longer. Even he had limits. And Thelma kept grinding faster and harder. He knew how to fix her now. The salinity balance shifted to peak, the acidity levels adjusted to optimal. The trail of glucose from her entrance to her egg couldn't get more inviting. Her environment became very hospitable.

Marvin released, injecting his sperm as deeply as he could. The half-cells began their trek, every one of them containing a Y chromosome . . .

CHAPTER
23

Camp Hill, Pennsylvania

Michael started his day like any other: he showered, dressed, ate a few pieces of toast, opened up the paper, and tried to connive Claire into getting his coffee for him while she packed lunch for herself and their daughter. But today, he just went through the actions so as not to raise suspicion. While flipping through the paper, not a single word caught his eye, too busy wrestling with his inner dialogue about morals:

I should tell her.

I can't tell her. And what would I tell her? "Honey, I can push things with my mind."

Why can't I tell her?

Because she's a lawyer—she'll overanalyze the situation and barrage me with questions I can't answer.

But I should tell her because she is *a lawyer and possibly the smartest person I know.*

So, why can't I tell her? Does that intimidate me? That she's smarter than me? And more successful? And the breadwinner with a real job while I go off and play pretend-intellectual with other fake intellectuals?

Oh, hell no! That's great! I got a sugar mama! What man wouldn't want a sugar mama?!

Sugar mama! Boo-ya!

Michael continued to dole himself mental high-fives until his daughter ran into the kitchen, exchanged raucous morning greetings with her parents, collected her lunch box, and ran to her bus stop sans shoes again.

"I'm surprised the school hasn't contacted Child Protective Services on us yet for continually sending her to school with no shoes," Claire said, putting the finishing touches on her chicken Caesar salad.

"I'm just happy she puts on clothes before she runs to the bus," Michael replied.

He glanced at the clock and prayed that Derrick continued his habit of tardiness. 7:45. *Keep smiling*, he thought. *She's a lawyer. She can smell fear. Why am I afraid? It's not like I'm doing anything wrong. If I'm not doing anything wrong, why does it* feel *wrong?*

"Bye. Love you," Claire said as she aimed for the front door. "And I have my book club tonight."

"Love you more," Michael replied, starting to sweat. He almost escorted her to the door, which would have broken the routine. She would have known something was amiss! A near-fatal flaw!

The newspaper dropped as soon as the door closed. Michael sprinted from the butcher block island to the front door window in two heartbeats. Strong, thudding heartbeats rattled his ribs. Sweat formed along his hairline as he watched her drive away, suspicious of nothing.

Then he paced. And paced. And paced. He walked to the door to look out the window for Derrick. Then he walked to the living room to look out that window, hoping to distract himself. Then to the kitchen to look at the microwave clock. Then to the front door. Living room. Kitchen. Front window. Back window. Microwave.

Stop! I'm doing nothing wrong. Just hiding a freaky new mental ability and a crazy new acquaintance. Seriously, what would I tell her? I have no idea what's even going on? I'm acting insane.

The knock on the door interrupted Michael's thoughts. He answered and saw Derrick standing there, still wearing the gray sweatshirt with the hood up, still staring at the empty 32-ounce French-fry cup. *I guess insanity is a relative concept*, Michael thought.

"You didn't stare at the cup the whole time you were driving, did you?" Michael asked, looking over Derrick's shoulder at the gray Cavalier sedan, rust along the edges, duct-taped side mirror, rear door missing a door handle. He didn't need to look too hard to see that a coat hanger kept the muffler from falling off.

"No," Derrick replied, turning toward his car.

"Umm," Michael stopped him and nudged his head toward a black Explorer. "How about I drive."

"Why?"

"So . . . you can concentrate on your vibing. Just tell me which way to go."

Derrick shrugged his shoulders in indifference. He and his cup joined Michael in the Explorer.

The trip started well, much better than Michael could have imagined. Other than the occasional outbursts from Derrick giving last-second navigation changes, they shared pleasant conversation. Michael learned that Derrick was twenty-three; lived with his grandparents in Gettysburg; had four tattoos but zero piercings because they were too painful; played no sports in high school but had an aptitude for numbers and would have gone to school for architecture if the industry hadn't become so corporate and soulless, so instead opted to become an artist, mainly acrylics, but really any medium that struck his muse; worked at both a local McDonald's as well as apprenticed for a tattoo artist; his biggest crush was on a nature-nut named Nora that he met at a church camp when he was twelve; even though he was good with his hands when it came to sculpting clay, he sucked at metal shop in high school; he hated cauliflower because he saw faces in it, usually of old teachers; and he had a dog named Tucker that had irritable bowel syndrome.

Derrick learned that Michael had a wife and daughter.

During a rare occasion when Derrick took a breath, Michael asked, "So, when you vibe, you . . . what? See the person you're vibing?"

"Yeah, but it's . . ." Derrick paused and looked at his cup. "It's more than just seeing. It's like really feeling it, too. My heart speeds up the closer I get to them. And my mind's just racing, racing, racing with the person. First you, then this old woman."

"So after we find her, are you gonna vibe someone else?"

"I have no idea. I don't know."

"How'd you hide things from me? The phones and the knives when we first met?"

"It's like I could just see what you were thinking. *Left! Left here! Now! Here!* I saw you were looking for your phones and your knives, so I made you think they were gone."

After a tire-screeching left turn, Michael rolled his eyes and continued. "Did you make me hallucinate? Did you mess with my brain?"

"I don't know."

"How could you not know? Am I gonna get brain cancer from this? Or . . . or . . . or get it fried like those old stoners who hang around the organic food stores?"

"Dude, I don't know. I just . . . just do it. It just happens. I've made, like, a group of people all see the same thing at the same time before. Does that help?"

"Oh, God. I'm gonna be brain-fried. Wear tie-dye. And I hate Birkenstocks."

"Right at the stop sign! *Right at the stop sign!*"

Frowning, Michael stopped, then made a right. "You know, you're like Bill the Cat."

"Umm, what?"

"Bill the Cat? Bloom County? Opus? It was a comic strip that ran in the newspapers that would irreverently poke fun at certain societal issues, and . . ." Judging from the blank look on Derrick's face, Michael realized it would have been easier to explain the influence of *Beowulf* on modern western literature to his seven-year-old daughter. "Never mind."

Derrick turned his attention back to his cup, his fingers drumming the sides. His feet bounced both of his legs. "We're getting closer."

"Good. We've been driving for about an hour and a half. I want to leave by noon."

"Okay. Why?"

"What do you mean 'why?' I want to get home by two since my daughter gets done with school around three."

Derrick pulled his attention from his cup and stared at Michael. His eyes probed Michael's face.

"What?" Michael snapped.

"You haven't told your wife yet, have you?" Derrick asked, his gaze flat and cunning.

"Did you read my mind? Is that something you can do? Vibe and make hallucinations and give brain cancer and read minds?"

"I can't read minds. You look all guilty and stuff. So why haven't you told her?"

Michael gritted his teeth, and his hands strangled the steering wheel. "Because I don't want to get her involved. Because I'm hoping between me, you, and this old woman we're looking for, we can figure out what happened and then go tell a doctor or someone, get it reversed, and have life go back to normal."

"You . . . don't like being able to push things?"

"Not with my mind! No, I don't! I don't know how I'm able to do it or why I'm able to do it. Hell, that's probably giving me brain cancer, too! Between 'pushing' things and you making me hallucinate, my brain'll squirt out of my ears in a year or two! So, no, I don't like to *push* things. I don't like that you can *vibe*. I don't like that there are people in this world who *can* push things mentally or vibe or make people hallucinate! I don't like that we're on our way to find someone *else* who can push or vibe, or maybe even *worse*! It fucking freaks me out!"

Derrick's stare remained blank until Michael finished his tantrum, then twisted his lips into a wry smirk and said, "Diatribe. Noun. A bitter, abusive denunciation."

"Don't make me pull this car over!" Michael shouted, his face reddening.

Derrick's eyes widened as if they tried to escape from his head. All color disappeared from his face as sweat percolated along his brow. He shouted back. "Pull the car over!"

"What?"

"Stop! We're here! *We're here!*"

Michael slammed the brakes, the antilock system kicking in to prevent fishtailing. Both occupants lurched forward, then smacked the seatbacks once the Explorer finished its stop.

Both men calmed themselves with shaky but cleansing breaths, leaving their mouths dry. Michael turned to Derrick and said snidely, "I bet you were a joy on family vacation road trips, weren't you?"

"She's in there. *There*," Derrick said, pointing to the house they parked in front of.

Both men exited the Explorer, Derrick bringing his cup with him. Michael noticed Derrick's eyes were glazed, darting up and down, left and right, unable to focus on anything. *Yeah*, Michael thought, *this'll be fun*, as they walked to the front door, passing a mailbox labeled Montgomery.

CHAPTER
24

Williamsport, Pennsylvania

Widow Emma Montgomery sat at her kitchen table, looking into the dining room and staring at its far wall. On one was a small painting of Jesus, benevolently holding his hands in front of Him, palms pointing upward. A ray of light from above cascaded onto Him. On a small, round table just below the painting was a picture of her late husband—a headshot, one of the few with him smiling. In front of the picture on the table was a lit tealight in a small cup-shaped glass votive. Emma asked each picture for help, for guidance. She had been doing this every day, from sun-up to sundown, for days.

She prayed to Jesus while keeping a lit candle burning for her husband. What should she do? Why was this happening? She asked, or more recently begged, for understanding, even just a shred of clarity, maybe a sign of some sort to give her direction. These new abilities frightened her, and she needed to know why God gave them to her. She felt lost, so very lost, especially after turning to Father Maclusky only to find he wanted to profit from her new abilities. He was why she missed church for the first time in two decades. He was why she missed her aerobics classes and why she didn't make her weekly trip to the fire hall with baked goods.

Sighing, she realized there would be no such epiphany today. She took a sip of warm tea and looked at the flashing red light of her answering machine. Twenty messages. She heard them all, listening when each caller left them. A lot of them from Father Maclusky as he begged for her forgiveness. A few social calls from her friends. One from the guys at the fire hall, hoping everything was okay since she didn't visit this past Wednesday. Resigning herself to erase the messages and make a few phone calls, she stood. Then her doorbell rang.

Without thinking, "Who is it?" slipped from her lips.

"Ms. Montgomery?" a man asked.

"We know you're in there," a second man said, his voice younger.

Taken aback by such an unusual comment, she rushed to the peephole of her front door. The two men seemed rather unassuming; one was in his mid-thirties in a plain T-shirt and jeans, and the other was in his early twenties, wearing a gray sweatshirt with his hood pulled up. He held an empty 32-ounce cup. The older man seemed rather disgusted with the younger man.

"Ms. Montgomery?" Michael asked again. "You don't know us, but we were wondering if we could ask . . ."

"What can you do?" Derrick blurted, interrupting his partner.

Michael turned to Derrick, and his whispering did nothing to hide his frustration. "Will you quit saying that? That's a horrible way to start."

A look of self-disappointment washed over Derrick's face. "Why?"

"It's creepy. It's like a really bad pick-up line. The worst ever."

"It's not that bad. It's to the point."

Michael's brows knitted as he stared at Derrick until the young man's eyes met his. "Have you ever gotten laid?"

Derrick's eyes fell to his feet. "Yes. Lots of times."

"Not since I've met you, that's for sure."

Emma gasped when she heard the vulgarity of the older man. How dare he challenge the young man's virtue, especially a young man who looked to him for guidance.

She watched as the older man cleared his throat and returned to statue-straight perfect posture, ready to recite complicated lines from a choreographed theater production. "Ms. Montgomery, I apologize for the interruption. My associate and I were wondering if we could sit down and talk to you a bit. I don't know how to accurately put this, but we believe that . . ."

"We were wondering if you had any new special abilities," Derrick interrupted again.

"Will you stop *doing* that," Michael whisper-shouted at Derrick.

Special abilities? Emma stepped back and placed a hand over her mouth. How did they know? What did they have to do with this? But how did *they* know about *her*? From her front door, she looked into her dining room at her pictures. From this angle, she swore the arms of Jesus extended toward her, casting the rays of Heaven in her direction. Her late husband's smile twinkled with a gleam, and he appeared to be winking at her. A sign? Was *this* her sign? Her help that she had been begging for?

Emma peeked through her peephole again. The older man still admonished the younger one. "If you keep freaking people out like this, someone will call the cops. Now, will you just please let me do all the talking."

Not understanding why the older man displayed such brash hostility toward the younger one, she felt the need to come to his rescue. Feeling this was the perfect opportunity, she opened the door and looked at the stunned men. "I'm Emma Montgomery. And to whom am I speaking?"

Michael smiled, loving the sophistication in her voice. If only he could get his students to speak as well as she. Hell, if he could get his students to speak other than when called upon, he'd do backflips. He knew he would get along with this woman. "Hello, Ms. Montgomery. I'm Professor Michael Roseman. And this is Derrick."

Dishing out a cold shoulder for Michael, Emma turned to Derrick with a smile and extended her hand. "Derrick . . . Roseman?"

Derrick cupped her hand in his and leaned over, kissing the back of it. "I'm very pleased to meet you. But, no, it's Derrick Sharper. No relation to Michael."

Emma's smile ran out of space to spread as she placed her free hand at the base of her neck and gave an "oh my, aren't you a sweet dear" look at Derrick. She then shot Michael a "see what happens when you speak for others" glare, but he missed it. His full attention was on Derrick, wondering how such a spaz could dole out charm like that.

"Could I interest you gentlemen in some tea?" Emma asked Derrick.

"That'd be lovely," Michael replied.

Emma didn't move until she heard from Derrick. "Yes, ma'am."

"Wonderful! Now, if you'll please follow me." She turned and went right to her kitchen.

Frustrated beyond words, Michael grabbed Derrick by the arm and whispered, "What the *hell* was that about?"

"I live with my grandparents, remember? I know what old people like."

Okay, Michael thought, entering the house and shutting the door behind him. *But that still doesn't explain why she doesn't like me! What's not to like? I'm well educated and more than willing to flaunt it. A sophisticated older woman like her ought to love that.*

Derrick and Michael took Emma's offered seats at the dining room table before she went to the kitchen to prepare the tea.

Even though Michael would never admit it, especially under the accusatory condemnation of his wife, he sometimes had a short attention span when it came to certain activities—"sitting" and "not reading" being two of them. Eyes wandering around the house, he noticed it was cozy: the front door opened into a small living room, a half-wall divided the kitchen from the living room while it could only be accessed by traveling through the dining room first. A set of stairs that shared the same carpeting as the living room led to a second floor. His eyes swept across the sparse walls, stopping on the painting of Jesus. Wincing, he thought it might look better on the wall of a trailer.

"Do you believe in Jesus, Professor Roseman?" Emma asked as she poured a tea for him.

"Sort of," he replied.

She laughed a charming old lady laugh, one that undermined Michael's last statement while captivating his heart. "How does one 'sort of' believe in Jesus?"

"Well, there's no denying the influence of Jesus, in a historical and world-wide sense. However, I'm not sure I'm into all the miracles and whatnot. I mean, between the time he was born and now, there have been billions of people passing one message—"

Emma interrupted him by asking Derrick the same question, pouring his tea. "Do you believe in Jesus?"

"Yes, ma'am. I attend church with my grandparents."

Emma sat across from him, reaching to put her hand on top of his. "That is positively delightful!"

Oh, sure, Michael thought to himself. *Now is when you're lucid. With me, I get rambling, hyper, creepy guy vibing every five fucking seconds. But throw an old lady in front of you, and you turn into Casa-fucking-nova!*

"Is that your husband?" Derrick asked, nodding his head toward the picture on the small round table.

Emma sighed with a beaming smile. "Late husband, I'm afraid."

"We'd love to hear about him."

Wait, Michael thought. *Did he just say "we?" Oh, dear God, no . . .*

Finally pouring herself some tea, Emma replied, "I'd love to tell you all about him."

Much to Michael's chagrin, she did . . .

CHAPTER
25

Philadelphia, Pennsylvania

The club's music thumped to a synthetic tribal beat. Patterns had been fed into oscillators, coupled with preprogrammed electronic drums to create unique beats, usually two or three per second. Airy keyboards wrapped the sounds with ponderous, catchy melodies, but the omnipresent beat kept people moving, grinding. Men and women consumed beer and mixed drinks, enhancing their virility through elixir. They displayed and exchanged primal ideals. Body heat created the humid atmosphere in the small club where, off to one side, by the bar, sat LaKeisha LaRue and her best friend, Camilla.

"I'm hot!" Camilla complained, holding her drink in one hand, pinky out, while fanning herself with her other hand.

"We just got here," LaKeisha replied.

"I don't care." Camilla took a sip from her drink, then looked at LaKeisha with pursed lips and dark eyes full of attitude. "It still *hot!*"

Camilla watched the dance floor, looking for anyone she knew. LaKeisha watched the way Camilla's usually golden skin absorbed the flashing lights. Green, then blue, then red, changing her from a Mexican to just another person at a club. She glanced at her own arms, completely exposed by her pink tank-top, and they changed to the same colors. In a dance club, everyone was the same color, the color of the dance floor. Green, then blue, then red.

LaKeisha wore a thick denim skirt one size too small, hoping the material would help push in her waist while camouflaging her hip width. Her legs were still nice, free from the ravages of time for now, and glistening from body lotion. Her outfit must have worked because she and Camilla drank for free as soon as they sat down.

Two men approached LaKeisha and Camilla. Young, handsome, and muscular, the three qualifications Camilla looked for in a man. LaKeisha's standards were similar; however, these men just weren't doing it for her—neither of them was Darnel.

It had been five days since she walked down the trail of indiscretion with Darnel. It took three days for her crotch and insides to stop throbbing. Another day for the muscles in her arms, back, and legs to heal. Her tailbone still hurt, though. Sitting still came with discomfort. But Darnel was all worth it.

Sipping her drink through her tiny straw, LaKeisha turned to watch the dance floor, her mind replaying her intimate moment with Darnel. She didn't care that both potential suitors turned their attention to Camilla. She just watched the dance floor. The shifting, colored lights changed to a strobe light that shifted from night to day in half-second intervals. Her vision blurred, the people turning into one moving mass, while her mind's eye focused on Darnel, her man. He touched her rough. So? She had rough before. He didn't kiss her. So? He just didn't like kissing, and the biting was kind of hot; it just surprised her. Now that she knew he was a machine who didn't roll over and snore in her ear when finished, she could be more prepared for next time. And the size of him—dear God, the size! LaKeisha giggled as a warm tingle flowed in between her legs.

Smiling, she set her drink on the bar top and turned back to watch the dance floor. Her eyes immediately focused on a pair of naked breasts flopping to the beat of the music. The girl's flimsy blouse was hiked up to her neck. A pair of man's hands slid around from behind, clamping themselves to her chest. LaKeisha then saw the girl's miniskirt cinched up as her dance partner took her from behind. Putting one hand over her mouth to stifle a laugh, LaKeisha said, "Oh. Oh no, they ain't!"

LaKeisha stared for a few more seconds to confirm what she watched. Still snickering, she turned to her friend and said, "Camilla. You won't believe what I'm see—" She was interrupted by the sight of her friend.

Sandwiched between two thrusting men, all LaKeisha could see of Camilla were her hands on the one man's shoulders and the tangle of feet where her skirt and thong were.

Surprised but still giggling, LaKeisha said, "Girl, you so nasty!" She turned to see if anyone else noticed, only to find more couples and threesomes, in all stages of nakedness, having sex. Men with women. Men with men. Women with women. Clothes were strewn along the floor and tables, torn off or pulled off, all removed in haste. Grinding and gauging done to the thumping beat of the music. It seemed to get faster as LaKeisha felt the beat of her heart surface to her chest and shoulders. Then the pulsing made its way lower.

Through the white-hot flashes of the strobe light, LaKeisha watched bodies writhe in ecstasy, all in some form of nudity—partial or complete. Sweat glistened on everyone, making them seem like carnal gods demanding worship. *What kind of club is this?* she thought, the tingling between her legs becoming undeniable. She started to wonder about Camilla's tastes, this club being her suggestion, one LaKeisha had never been to before. Then she wondered why she wasted time thinking about things other than all the men presenting their beautiful bodies!

Still sitting on her barstool, she hiked up her skirt a bit, just enough to remove any potential discomfort from her hands going to where they needed to be. Her left hand held her thong to the side while a couple fingers from her right hand slid through her slick. She leaned back against the bar and smiled while her finger pressed languid circles into her clit. She watched the men move and thrust and pump and shove, fantasizing that one of them would take the time to do to her what she did to herself. She fantasized about Darnel, hoping he would do just that the next time they got together. She did love the moving and thrusting and pumping and shoving—after all, that was what made a man a man—but, damn, just once, she wished for some soft and slow stroking with a finger or a tongue.

As her finger moved faster and the warmth turned into electricity, she looked around the club, wanting to focus on the right guy. There! There was the one to watch while she took herself to the promised land! Tall and dark-skinned, sweat glued his flimsy shirt to his body, accentuating every ridge of his muscles. With his pants dropped to his ankles, his bare ass worked furiously, ravaging a fake-titted white girl from behind. Watching them, LaKeisha couldn't help but speed up as well. The music thumped twice as fast as her heart, and he pumped twice as fast as the music, the white girl just a meaningless piece of meat in his strong arms. He started to adjust his stance and turned, LaKeisha getting more excited to see his face.

It was Darnel.

LaKeisha's finger stopped and she immediately went dry.

How could he do this to her? What they shared in the hallway was kind of like this, but it was still special. To her! They didn't even talk about it. She wanted to give him some time to gather his thoughts, sift through his feelings. It only seemed fair since she knew damn well what she felt and thought. But did he call her? No! Instead, he slipped his dick into some white hooch the first chance he got! At a club! In public! In front of people LaKeisha might know! Especially after she told all her friends what they shared. And now he was back to white women!

LaKeisha's blood boiled, not sure where to direct her ire—to Darnel or the whore he was fucking. She wanted to break it up and give him a piece of her mind. Then she wanted to grab that slut by her hair and punch her square in the face. However, she would never have a chance—Darnel beat her to it.

Surprised, LaKeisha sat and watched Darnel and the white girl just stop cold. In a blinding rage, the girl spun around and raked her nails across his face. Ignoring the cuts, Darnel reeled back and punched her, his fist as big as her head. Nose crushed, she flopped to the floor; the pooling blood sparkled from the strobe light. Darnel kicked her repeatedly in the stomach.

LaKeisha noticed the same scene repeated throughout the club. Men who shared an embrace now exchanged blows. Women who rubbed against each other's legs now clawed at each other's eyes. And the men who had their way with women now pulverized them.

Before LaKeisha could react, a hand grabbed her shoulder and pulled her around on her barstool. A topless Camilla stood in front of her. The two men who had sandwiched Camilla now wrestled on the floor, exchanging blows. Camilla reeled back, her full breasts jiggling, and punched LaKeisha just below her right eye.

Stars exploded from out of nowhere, dazzling LaKeisha's field of vision as she fell backward off her stool. Arms and legs as useless as noodles, she flopped to the floor. The cement felt cold against the side of her head as the music and strobe lights faded away into unconsciousness . . .

CHAPTER
26

Near State College, Pennsylvania

Adam woke to a raccoon scurrying across his head. He laid on the forest floor, curled up in a nest of leaves, a squirming ball of snakes over his feet. The occasional chipmunk or squirrel skittered over his shoulder or along his thigh. Behind him was Nora, the warm press of her chest against his back.

He luxuriated in her skin against his scales, drinking in every second, memorizing the feel. Her hand slid up and down his arm, her fingers and palm exploring his scaled flesh. His thoughts turned to white noise every time her hot breath caressed his back.

"Are you awake?" she whispered.

"Yesss," he replied.

"Still thinking about your father?"

"Yesss."

It had been three days. He couldn't shake the dread, the terrible hole he had created for his family. Family meant supporting each other, being there for one another. He ran from home because he scared his parents. He understood their fear. Wanting to let everyone's emotions cool down, Adam sought respite in the forest, hoping to make sense of what happened. Then he would go back to his family, to their comfort and understanding. Instead, he transferred his curse to them, tearing his own father's guts from him, tearing his father away from his family.

Nora's hand slid up his arm to his shoulder, then down to his chest. She gave a slight pull, signaling him to roll over. He did. The leaves rustled and crunched as he moved to his back. She rested her head on his arm and nuzzled. Her moist exhales sent waves of electricity through his arm. Continuing to glide across his chest, her hand made small circles as she moved it lower. Her left leg slithered over his left leg as the black snakes slithered over his right leg, her thigh warm against his.

"You need to let go. You need to forgive yourself. He would have killed you, killed me. You saved me," she said. He felt her lips dance along his bicep; the sensation blurred his vision.

Adam's heart raced. He couldn't move. He couldn't sweat. He couldn't blush. Her warmth against his body was intoxicating. Her hand created a path of happiness; her fingers left a trail of joy as it swept across his waist. Shame chased ecstasy through Adam, knowing her acts were impure and seductive, yet he let her do them anyway. Her hand massaged where his privates once were, now just a barren expanse of more scales. And he let her. Maybe this was why God punished him? Because He knew Adam would fail another test from Eve's temptations in Eden. But why dole out punishment before any crime had been committed? This wasn't right. She had touched him like this every day since they met, and he still wasn't comfortable with her nakedness. He wanted it but had to stop it.

"I. Can't," Adam said, sitting up, cautious not to upset her or any of the other animals.

She misunderstood his intent, sitting up as well and snuggling close to him, her right hand stroking his back. "I understand. Losing a parent is difficult."

Not having any experience with women to fall back on, Adam changed the subject as best he could, hoping not to offend her, "How. Closss. Are. Othersss. Like. Me?"

Nora rested her head against Adam's arm. Her cheek, soft. So soft. She sighed and said, "I felt another like you before we went to sleep last night. About ten miles south of here. I'll see if I can find . . . her . . . again . . .?"

Adam felt her skin go cold. She jumped to her feet, her body tense. Adam wondered if he did or said something wrong. Turning to look at Adam, her eyes widened. Even though they were solid black, Adam could see the fear in them. A lone tear rolled down her cheek. Her lips quivered as she spoke. "Adam . . . something's wrong. We have to find her. Now."

Adam sprang to his feet and started running with Nora, but he shot past her like a bullet, still unaccustomed to the speed and power of his new body.

"Adam!" she called out, twenty yards behind him. He ran back to scoop her up. Cradling her five-foot frame in one arm, he took off again.

Curled up, she nestled her face into the base of his neck while he ran as fast as he could. The panic in Nora's voice spurred him on as she barked out a direction change over the sounds of cracking branches and rustling leaves. He didn't know how fast he ran, but any time a whipping branch made contact, it stung. One clipped Nora's leg and would surely leave a welt. Adam didn't slow down; he couldn't. He used his other hand to block the branches as they whistled by. It opened him up to more abuse, but he didn't care; he needed to find the other creature like him and keep Nora safe during the journey.

Adam kept this pace for half an hour. Nora weighed less than a hundred pounds, and at first, his arm barely registered her weight. Halfway there, her weight hurt, sending fire through his arm, chest, and back. Subtle shifts staved off cramps but did little to relieve the burning. Churning legs fared no better. He became adept at using his tail for balance, so he demanded pure power from his legs. They burned from the inside just as hot as his arm. But he had to keep moving, had to find another like him, had to see who else God punished.

"Stop!" Nora yelled, her hands over her face for protection.

Adam stopped and glanced around, looking for something, anything. Nothing. He swore to himself, feeling the full wrath of his muscles now. His whole body throbbed, pounded, to the beat of his heart, even down to the tip of his tail. Tongue out and panting to cool himself, his breath was so hot it steamed and rippled the air around him. Voice pained and raspy, he asked, "Where?"

"I don't know. This was the area I last felt her presence. But that was last night." Nora breathed in gulps as if she ran the ten miles.

"What. Do. You. Feel. Now?"

The hollowness in her voice chilled Adam much more than what she said. "Nothing."

They searched in silence, often wandering from each other. What were they looking for? The anticipation strangled Adam; the need to find another like him burned deep in his belly. Then he noticed the air tasted musty. His tongue still draped from his mouth. It never occurred to him before that reptiles sensed smell through their tongues. Cooled down enough to regain control of his tongue, he started flicking it in and out, collecting samples, then analyzing what he collected in his mouth. He smell-tasted the green leaves from the trees. Then Nora's salty skin. Then he smelled . . . raw meat . . . ?

Nora screamed.

Faster than a lightning strike, Adam found Nora and the source of the raw meat scent. Instinct dictated he protect Nora, hugging her while she buried her face in his sternum. While he comforted her, he examined what caused her outburst. A dead bird.

The only thing left was the torso, entrails hanging out. But that was enough for Adam to see that this creature was another like him, no longer human. Dull brown feathers covered the entire body. Wings sprouted from the shoulders and sides, but human hands appeared at the tips. The eyes were wide and round with a foot-long beak. It was a girl. It didn't look like a woman; it just smelled female to Adam. Dead. Torn in half and covered in bugs, her legs nowhere to be found.

"Bastards," Nora whispered, finding the bravery needed to look at the grim scene.

"What?" Adam replied.

"Look." Nora walked closer, using her disgust and anger to give her the strength she needed. She pointed to the creature's right shoulder. A bullet hole, still fresh. "Some fucking small-minded asshole did this! Or the group of them since stupidity seems to flourish in numbers. Instead of embracing something new, something so beautiful, they killed it!"

Adam didn't feel convinced. He couldn't deny the bullet hole, but that didn't explain half of its . . . her . . . body being missing. The skin near the separation, as well as her remaining entrails, had been chewed on. "What. About. Her. Legsss?"

Frowning, Nora's nose crinkled and her lips snarled as if her entire face tried to shield her eyes. She saw the chew marks as well. "There is a cougar on this mountain. And a bear that passes through. I've even felt a stray dog here and there. Scavenging isn't the noblest of ways to survive, but it must be done."

Adam stared at the mangled bird-person's body. This could have been him. His father wanted to shoot him—shot at him—with every intent to kill. His father thought Adam was Satan incarnate. Adam realized that this forest was his true home now.

Nora wrapped her hands around Adam's left hand. "We should go. There's another one like you close by. Only a few more miles south of here."

Adam pulled his hand free and walked a few paces from the carcass. "Not. Yet."

Disgruntled that he asserted himself against her, Nora replied, "Adam. We don't have time for this. If a group of rednecks with guns did this to . . . her . . . then there's a good chance they're still around."

"That. Can. Wait. Sssee'sss. Ssstill. Hu-man." Adam dropped to his knees and clawed away huge chunks of earth, digging a grave . . .

CHAPTER
27

Harrisburg, Pennsylvania

Looking in his office's mirror, Marvin straightened his tie—a solid red that shimmered like a polished ruby when the light hit it right. It formed a tight and crisp triangle between the buttoned collar before exploding into the form of power. Perfect. Marvin always liked red.

Smiling, he ran his fingers through his hair. *His hair!* The sides and back borders of hair had closed the gap, converging on the small patch of baldness atop his head. He saw a few stray hairs in the area, planted like flags marking sites for future conquest.

He put on his suit jacket, finding it tighter in the shoulders, looser at the waist. He patted his belly: still too large but no longer flopping over his belt. Shifting his shoulders in his jacket, he enjoyed the discomfort of the tight material, this being the first time he ever felt the sensation. Never before had he experienced such muscle growth. He didn't need a roadmap to make muscle, just a little time on the internet to get the gist. However, there were two hard-core muscle-heads in the company, so Marvin shook their hands and made roadmaps anyway.

Tomorrow he would get new suits. With his recent promotion, he could afford it. And this promotion certainly wouldn't be the last. He needed to dress better since he looked better. And since he was an expecting father.

Thelma had been pregnant for a week, and all went well. Triplets. All boys. All gestating to perfection. Marvin never gave much thought to a family. Ever since he and Thelma discovered they couldn't conceive, he'd pushed the thought right out of his mind. But now that she was pregnant and he had the ability to make sure the boys grew to perfect human specimens, the concept kind of tickled him. There were thirteen pregnant women in the company, and he used them all to make roadmaps.

"Okay," he whispered to himself. "Time to start stage one."

He turned to leave but stumbled over his gym bag on the floor next to his desk. He chuckled and pushed it under the desk with his foot. That was stage two.

Stage one involved meeting with Salinger, his boss, regarding the recent vacancy in the department due to Savinski's fatal stroke. Marvin had an idea of how the meeting would go, but he at least wanted to give Salinger the opportunity to do the right thing.

"Good afternoon," Marvin said to Salinger's administrative assistant. "How are you?"

"Last meeting of the day," she replied with a smile.

"I'll keep it brief. I promise," Marvin replied with a wink. He turned and entered Salinger's office, closing the door behind him.

The older man behind the desk pulled off his reading glasses and tossed them aside. His collar seemed too tight for his flabby neck as his jowls drooped, making him look like a basset hound in a tie. "Let's get this over with, Marvin. What do you want?"

Refusing to sit, Marvin wore a smirk of confidence, the same smirk he wore when he last spoke with Savinski. "I want Savinski's people."

"Don't be stupid, Marvin. Your people don't even like you, so why would I give you his?"

"Well, it would save you from having to hire a new manager, as well as—"

"Colby's getting his people."

"Excuse me?"

"I'm promoting Colby. He's getting Savinski's unit."

Marvin certainly didn't see this coming. He knew very well Salinger wouldn't just give him Savinski's people. But to have the audacity to promote Colby? Reprehensible! His smile drew tighter as he took a stand. "No."

Salinger's face reddened, creating a harshness against his gray hair. He shot Marvin a look so icy it threatened to freeze him where he stood. "What do you mean, 'no'?"

Trying to make his new body and new hair seem intimidating, Marvin crossed his arms over his chest. "You're not taking Colby from me."

Taking offense to Marvin's newfound posturing, Salinger decided to do some of his own and stood. "Let's not forget one thing, Marvin. I'm your boss. You don't tell me what to do with personnel."

Marvin uncrossed his arms and then folded his hands behind his back, displaying his lack of fear. He even took a step forward. "Just because you're my boss doesn't make you competent. You're not taking Colby from me."

Incensed, Salinger stepped forward himself. Standing eye to eye with Marvin, he growled, "Just because you lost a couple pounds and are getting new hair doesn't make you any younger. I have a few years on you, but I swear to God, man, you don't dare get physical with me."

"Really?" As casually as dusting away a piece of lint, Marvin reached for Salinger's wrist.

"Is this some kind of joke?" Salinger asked, looking at Marvin's hand gripping his wrist.

"You tell me," Marvin mumbled, his anger exploding from a broken pressure cooker.

Salinger started to curl his fingers into a fist, ready to take any means necessary to end this nonsense, but he felt suddenly flush. Sweat streamed from his forehead, his chest, his back, his armpits. It burned to blink. Breathing became labored. He felt his heartbeat ripple through his whole body.

"Your pulse is up to 180 beats per minute," Marvin said, glaring at Salinger through icy eyes. "Let's ramp you up to 220."

Vertigo tugged at Salinger, forcing him to sit on his desk and use his other hand for stability. He didn't need to test his pulse to know Marvin was right. He felt his heart rev behind his ribs, like a dragster gunning its engine. Pain shot through his whole body with every breath, and his exhales lasted twice as long as his inhales. Now 240 beats per minute. He felt heat, only heat and sweat, cascading from every pore of his body. Up to 280 beats per minute. Blood screamed through his arteries and veins; he *felt* the fast flow. Ticking up to 300 beats per minute. His eyes bulged and his throat closed. His carotid artery ruptured.

Salinger's corpse slumped to his desk. His skin paled, becoming clammy as half his blood flooded his chest cavity before his heart stopped. Marvin yanked Salinger's arm, forcing his body to fall to the floor, making his heart attack look more natural.

Triumphant and tall, Marvin lorded over Salinger. Every memory of every night he had to work late, every special project dumped on him, every idea he had that went ignored because of this fat, gray-haired bastard swirled in Marvin's head. Never an iota of respect. Never even a pat on the back of acknowledgment. But this man would die—*did die*—for Colby. *Colby!*

"Colby's my bitch and I'm not done fucking him yet," Marvin growled at Salinger.

Using a mirror in Salinger's office, Marvin took a minute to primp, making sure he looked just as good leaving as he did when entering. Satisfied, he stepped over Salinger and exited the office, quickly closing the door behind him.

Salinger's admin assistant looked up and smiled. "Wow. That *was* a quick meeting."

"I always keep my promises," Marvin said, flashing a smile in return. "As an added bonus, Salinger told me to tell you to call it a day."

"Really?"

"Cross my heart."

"You don't have to tell me twice." She shut down her computer and grabbed her purse, none the wiser until tomorrow morning. Back in his office, Marvin locked his door and retrieved his duffle bag. Unzipping it, he pulled out a change of clothes: jeans and an old T-shirt. After a quick change, he locked up his office and left for the day. Time to start stage two.

Satisfaction oozed from his every pore, from his office to the respite home of a local rehab facility, where he met his wife. So grateful for the gifts Marvin received and the conception he gave her, she suggested they give thanks by helping those less fortunate. At first, he resisted the idea, but when she suggested spending an hour or two at the rehab, Marvin supported the idea and lauded her as a saint.

Introductions were made to recovering crack and cocaine addicts, marijuana and acid burnouts, crystal meth and ecstasy zealots. But Marvin only saw roadmaps . . .

CHAPTER
28

Pittsburgh, Pennsylvania

Stella was a hooker. She understood this. For a while, she tried to disguise it with words like "call girl" or "professional companion." Even now that she worked for an "escort" service, she knew she was a hooker. She even knew how it happened.

Growing up in a small coal-mining town only afforded a girl so many options in life. Even as the prettiest girl in town, partying always seemed the best life choice. That eventually led to nights of blow jobs and hand jobs by the dumpsters behind the local convenience store. But she did well enough in school to get accepted to Pittsburgh University, hoping an education would change her life.

The only thing that changed was that instead of giving blow jobs and hand jobs to motorheads and stoners, she gave them to frat boys. Many at the same time, usually in front of a camera. She took enough psychology classes to know she had low self-esteem and the attention from men fulfilled her. It only took five minutes of a bad taste in her mouth or ten minutes of stroking some skin to get the attention she so craved.

Of course, being drunk more often than not led to poor grades; now, her only area of expertise was blow jobs and hand jobs. Sex changed from hobby to career. She screwed up and she was self-aware enough to know she screwed up. She knew a lot of things about herself. What she didn't know was that she wouldn't see the end of the day.

Stella looked at the piece of paper she used to write down the information the escort service gave her. Sheridan. Room 505. One guy. No cameras, nothing kinky. Should be an easy job. She found the room and knocked on the door.

"It's open," a voice called from inside.

Stella opened the door and stepped back. A slight bit of anger washed through her as she peered into the pitch-black room. "Oh, no, no, no. Too dark. I'm not coming in."

"Wait! I'm sorry. I'm sorry. Hold on. Wait." Anxiety quaked the man's voice. It was nasally and wheezy. A nervous fat kid looking to pop his cherry.

Stella stayed in the hallway with her arms crossed, watching the darkness. She saw a bit of movement, then the butane flash of a lighter to light a candle. After lighting four more candles, he illuminated enough of the room for her satisfaction.

Entering the room and shutting the door, she looked at her John. She was right about him being nervous and fat, but he seemed older than she had guessed. Clean-shaven with tightly cropped hair, probably done himself, he stood frozen, looking at her with dopey deer eyes.

"Sorry about the dark. I was trying to set a mood," he said. The remorse in his meek voice plucked her heartstrings.

She smiled and softened her voice as if talking to a scared puppy. "It's okay. I didn't mean to freak out about the dark. A girl can't be too careful, you know."

He smiled as well, fighting to keep his eyes from shifting to the floor. His fingers fidgeted with each other.

Stella glanced around the room, looking for hints about what to expect. In the center of the room were two beds. At the foot of the beds were the two nightstands pushed together. The nightstands held two plates, two forks, two wine glasses, a bottle of champagne, a tray of lasagna, and one of the candles. The trash can held the empty box that the lasagna came in with easy-to-follow microwave instructions. The little girl deep inside of her melted from the sweetness of his innocence.

"So . . . what's your name?" she asked.

He debated. When he placed the order with the agency, he used the internet, a fake name, and a fraudulent credit card number. He hadn't thought if he should use his real name or not. If he decided not to, his first choices were either "Anakin" or "Neo," but he didn't want to sound as geeky as he truly was. He wanted to be the opposite of that, which was the whole point of getting a hooker. Thinking she would find it too creepy if he took the time necessary to come up with a good fake name, he went with his real one. "Kevin. Kevin Keller."

That wasn't the name the agency gave her, but she figured he just made up a name to feel less embarrassed about needing a hooker. Especially since this looked like it might be his first time. As far as fake names went, at least he used one that sounded real as opposed to using some machismo-filled character from a science-fiction movie. She never saw any of the movies, but she had been with enough awkward recluses to hear all the names. She continued to smile and use soothing tones. "So, Kevin, I see you made dinner. Most of the men I meet don't make dinner."

"Oh," he said, almost apologizing. "I didn't know."

Stella placed her purse on the floor and sat on the chair meant for her. "That's okay. It's very sweet of you."

A mousy smile crept across his thick lips as he sat in the chair at the other end of the makeshift table. Even though shadows played across his face, Stella knew she made him blush. A sad thought crossed her mind—what if that was the first time a woman ever called him sweet? She continued, more from her heart now, "So, Kevin. What's the occasion?"

Kevin winced a bit from the question, not fully understanding the concept of small talk. Most of his conversations took place at work, all logical and to the point. Banter was unnecessary. His naturally squinty eyes squinted even more as he tried to process the question. "Uh, I just wanted to practice."

Pretty sure that Kevin wasn't going to, Stella took the initiative and served the lasagna. "Practice? Practicing for anything special?"

Displaying another squinty frown, Kevin didn't like how this was going. Superlative questions. He simply wasn't wired to handle them properly. "Practice interfacing. With women."

Stella giggled at his word choice while pouring some champagne. She guessed with certainty that he was a virgin. That tickled her because he'd be quick, gentle, and it'd actually mean something to him. "Interface. The first thing you need to do, sweetie, is stop using the term, 'interface.'"

No interfacing? Ridiculous. Then what was the point? Kevin did not like where this evening was headed. "I don't understand."

Stella thought now would be a great time to reach out and place her hand on top of his. Surprised that he didn't flinch, she caressed the back of his hand with her fingers. Finding his watch unusual, she traced it with her fingers. It seemed very thick and heavy. "To communicate with a woman, well, we like conversation. We like to talk and share our thoughts and feelings."

Conversation? *More* directionless talking? Senseless chattering? Emotions? This was all going wrong. Kevin couldn't interface with women. Kevin couldn't interface with people. He could only interface with computers. But he wanted, so desperately wanted, to interface with Debra Verone. Time for an upgrade!

Under Stella's fingers, Kevin's watch hummed and shifted. She felt small pieces slide and shift. Just as she tried to jerk away, dozens of wires pounced from the watch and sank into her skin.

Stella's body seized, every muscle flexed from the crash of pain, a shocking burn exploding from her wrist. It hurt too much to even scream; the contorted muscles in her neck squeezed her throat, only allowing a guttural growl to escape. She tried to pull away, but her arm wouldn't move, couldn't escape the grasp. With jolts of fire raging through her body, she swiveled her hips and kicked her legs. Driven by anger and frustration from the nonstop burn, she pounded the table with her other hand. The table's contents fell to the floor, the candle's flame extinguished.

The wires entered her skin and snaked their way up her arm, pushing by nerves, scraping along bone, and burrowing through muscle. Stella tried to scream again after a ragged, choking inhale but could only produce another raspy growl with an occasional squeak, spraying snot, sweat, and spittle from her lips. She still tried to pull her arm away to no avail. She tried to kick Kevin with her legs but instead smashed her toes into the table or stomped the floor from burning convulsions. She used her free hand to rake the skin around the wires, praying for some form of release. Then more wires pierced her other hand.

Stella produced silent sobs, thrashing about in her chair. Her arms burned and itched, and she couldn't free them. Fighting against the rigid muscles of her neck and back, she forced herself to open her eyes and look. Copper filaments slithered in and out of her skin as if she were nothing more than a rag doll sewn by the hands of a sick seamstress. Through streaming tears and burning, *dear God, the burning*, she followed them to their source—Kevin's bizarre watch.

As if any other workday, Kevin opened the drawer to the nightstand to retrieve some tools he had put in there. Hard drive. Processors. Converter chips. Logic cards. More wire. Sensors. Pliers. X-acto knife. Soldering iron. Duct tape. Ready to start his project, he looked at Stella. She still twisted and flopped, trying to free herself from the wires. She was so beautiful but still so flawed. He would fix that. Time for an upgrade . . .

CHAPTER
29

Williamsport, Pennsylvania

Widow Emma Montgomery sniffed and dabbed away a stray tear escaping her eye like the dainty old woman she seemed to be. She'd just finished telling Michael and Derrick about her brave husband's last sprint into a burning building.

Derrick held her other hand and looked at her through solemn eyes. He said in hushed tones, as if talking in church, "Amazing. Really, really amazing."

Emma gave a bright smile, proud of the man who graced her life with such devotion. "Thank you."

Michael looked at his watch. Noon. "Those were some very touching stories, Mrs. Montgomery. Unfortunately, Derrick and I have to leave within the hour. I was hoping we could talk about your . . . new abilities? Maybe we can find a connection . . ."

"Oh, I'm sure you two can stay a bit longer," Emma interrupted. She noticed empty teacups and stood to get more from the kitchen.

"Really, we can't," Michael replied.

"Yeah," Derrick confirmed. "He still hasn't told his wife about his new abilities and has to get home before she does."

"Thanks, Narc."

"Hey, I'm not keeping secrets from *my* wife."

"You're not married! You wouldn't understand."

Emma opened the silverware drawer to get a spoon for the tea. "Well, I used to be married, and I certainly don't understand."

Michael's cheeks flushed, warming from Emma's interrogation spotlights. "I don't want to burden her with my problems. I'm sure your late husband would have done the same thing."

Before he punctuated his last sentence, knives, forks, and spoons whistled toward Michael's head. But nothing hit him. By the time he realized he should duck, he no longer needed to. He snapped forward and turned around to see two-dozen utensils piercing the wall, outlining his head. Little old woman or not, a flurry of expletives formed at the back of his throat. But thanks to Derrick, they never made it out.

"Whoa!" the young man yelped. "Totally Blue Raja!"

So confounded by Derrick's statement, Michael let his angry eyes do the talking and turned to face him.

"Blue Raja," Derrick repeated. "From *Mystery Men*? The movie? With . . . Ben . . . Stiller? Never mind."

Shaking, a little from fear and a lot from anger, Michael turned back to Emma. Again, he didn't need to speak to convey his feelings.

"My husband shared everything with me," Emma said. "He would have most certainly shared something like this. As I would with him. I spent the past week wishing he were here so I could lean on him, turn to him for guidance. I spent the past week wondering what to do with this gift."

"Gift?" Michael asked. "How could you—either of you—consider what we're going through a gift?"

"And exactly what are you going through, Professor Roseman?" Emma asked.

Michael turned to Derrick and looked at the 32-ounce empty cup in his hand. Finally catching on to non-verbal cues, Derrick set the cup on the table and moved away. Michael needed little concentration to feel the warmth, the flow, the release. The push popped the cup in the air, much like it did at the mall. "I can 'push' things."

"And this has you so upset you feel the need to hide it from your wife?"

"Yes! How could it not? I can *move* things with my *mind*! It's not natural. I didn't do well in any of my science classes, but I did well enough to know I shouldn't be able to do that. Despite the fact that you are obviously fit and healthy, a senior citizen shouldn't be able to throw utensils with the precision of a laser beam. And no one, especially a kid barely out of college, should be able to make people hallucinate!"

Michael's eyes bored into Emma's. She saw that he spoke his true feelings from his heart, probably for the first time today. She didn't care for his haughty attitude or the way he talked down to Derrick, but she could see he had a difficult time with what was happening. How could she blame him? She just spent the last week as a recluse, shutting out the people who cared for her and questioning everything, from her faith to her sanity. Feeling he needed a bit of a break, she turned to Derrick. "You can make people hallucinate?"

"I'm . . . not really sure. I don't know if I can make people *see* things or if I make them *think* they see things," Derrick said, retrieving his empty cup.

"Oh. That sounds very interesting. Can you make me see something?"

"Uh, I'm pretty sure you don't want me to do that right now."

"And why is that?"

Michael huffed, a cross between a cough and a laugh. "Because he'll give you brain cancer."

Not liking the glibness in his voice, Emma chose not to respond to Michael. She dealt with misbegotten young men at the youth center, always encouraging them to reach for their full potential. She offered Derrick the same looks and tones. "Ignore his rubbish. I'd like to see your talents."

Derrick's eyebrows rounded upward as sad eyes apologized to Emma. She readied more words of encouragement but found she didn't need them. Her husband stood right next to her.

Her hands jumped to her mouth. Emotion tore through her like a tornado. A single thread of rationality telling her this was an illusion weaved its way through a tapestry of temptation to lose herself in what she saw. Her voice abandoned her as tears streamed down her face.

Michael couldn't see the illusion, but judging from Emma's reaction, he had a fair assumption of what she saw. He leaned across the table and placed his hand on Derrick's arm. "Okay, Derrick. I think that's enough."

As soon as her husband disappeared, she found herself calm again. Surprised at her quick composure, she reached for more tissues to wipe away the tears. "Oh my. That *is* something."

Derrick's eyes welled up as well. "I'm sorry. I'm so sorry. I . . . I don't know how I do it. I don't know if you saw him because he was what *you* were thinking of or because I was thinking of him. It . . . it just happens."

"Don't be sorry, Derrick. I should be thanking you. That was a truly remarkable moment. God definitely blessed you with quite a gift."

There it was again. The word that screeched through Michael like fingernails down a chalkboard. "Gift." Emma just implied that Derrick should make *more* people hallucinate *more* often. This kid probably needed his name to be sewn into his underwear, and she *encouraged* him to mess with people's minds? Or was it the other word that freaked him out? "God." This had to stop.

"Emma, he just said he had no idea how he does that. He can make people *see* things without knowing how, without knowing if there are any side effects. That's not just irresponsible—it's dangerous."

"Professor Roseman, I feel fine. And I'm assuming he made you see some things as well. Are you experiencing any side effects?"

"Not at the moment, but I don't know what *could* be happening. And we don't know what else he can do."

Emma's encouraging smile returned, and she looked back at Derrick as he wiped his eyes. "Do you know if you can do anything else?"

"I vibe."

"Vibe?"

"Yeah. It's how I found Michael and how we found you."

"Yeah," Michael snorted. "And he can't explain that either."

Emma shifted her smile, patronizing, to Michael. "Professor Roseman, life can't always be explained. That's where faith comes in. Religion isn't some kind of sideshow magic trick at a carnival like you seem to think it is. It's trust. It's a sweeping answer to unanswerable questions. Derrick doesn't need to explain 'vibing' to me. And as far as I can tell, you can't explain how you 'push' things, can you?"

"No, I can't. But that's why I'm here. That's why I wanted to meet you, to see if there are any connections among the three of us, to see if there's a pattern, to *explain* things. I don't want religion; I want answers!"

Awkward silence followed; all eyes averted from each other. Derrick's leg started to bounce and his fingers drum-rolled on the table. "Um. So, now what do we do?"

Michael sucked his teeth, shook his head, and rolled his eyes—the frustration trifecta.

Scowling at Michael, Emma addressed Derrick. "I think that's a very good question. God gave us these gifts. He wants us to use them."

Derrick's leg halted, his fingers stopped drumming, and his eyes widened as the seed Emma planted sprouted into a clinging vine. "She's right. We have to use them."

Being a professor, Michael knew very well how a young man's mind worked, knew where this conversation's journey would end even before it began. "No. Derrick, stop."

Derrick's eye darted back and forth, as if speed-reading a script only he could see. "It makes sense. We can do *more* than everyone else. We have these abilities, these . . ."

"Please don't say it. Please don't say it," Michael repeated, closing his eyes.

". . . powers!" Derrick continued. "Don't you see? We can use them. Use them to help people. We can be . . ."

"God, I will *so* believe in You if You make him stop talking."

". . . heroes! We *have* to do this. There's nothing else we could do with them. We . . ."

The idea of Derrick suggesting that they run around in capes, tights, and masks was the last straw. It didn't just break the camel's back; it shattered it, crushed the camel to a bloody pulp, kicked it in the ribs, and then spat on it. Childhood comic books and cartoons flowed through Michael's head—his, Derrick's, and Emma's faces replacing the heroes of the stories. Derrick as his sidekick. No, there were more years between him and Emma than there were between Derrick and him. Would that make Michael *her* sidekick? Didn't matter. This was stupid. Beyond stupid. He went to a hospital for help only to find the doctors locked away while the lunatics ran the asylum. He was done.

Michael slammed his palm on the top of the table, hoping it was enough to get Derrick to shut up. It was. "Derrick, we're leaving."

Michael stood with a calm he hadn't felt in weeks while both Derrick and Emma expressed their dissatisfaction. He ignored them and walked to the front door. Once he reached it, he turned. "Mrs. Montgomery. Thank you for your hospitality. You have a lovely home. However, I hope to never see you or your home again. Derrick, let's go."

"I'm not leaving," Derrick replied, frowning.

"You can't make him do anything," Emma jumped in.

"Derrick, your car is parked by my house. And I live in a nice neighborhood. If my wife, who is a lawyer, by the way, comes home and sees it, she will undoubtedly have it towed away. Either I take you to your car or you stay here. Either way, I have zero intention of ever seeing you again after today."

Pouting worse than Michael's seven-year-old daughter, Derrick jumped up from his chair and stomped out the front door. "Emma, I'll be back in a few hours."

Without so much as a look back, Michael got in his Explorer and Derrick followed, slamming the door once he was in. Silence accompanied them all the way back, and Michael smiled the whole ride home . . .

CHAPTER
30

Carlisle, Pennsylvania

Haley Mitchell was ten years old. Last night she dreamed about being an adult and owning a horse farm. Endless acres of rolling fields speckled with patches of forest stretched from one horizon to the other. Chromatic butterflies filled the air, as did the soft scent of chocolate. She would tend to each horse personally, feeding them sugar cubes and combing their manes. She would ride each one, taking them for a brief run to stretch their muscles. She liked the way the wind made her long blonde hair flow. And each horse wore a headset attached to the cell phones strapped to their flanks.

Haley awoke with a smile from that dream. She loved horses. Then she got sad. Usually, when she dreamed about being an adult and owning a horse farm, she had fought with her parents the night before. She sighed, watching the clear mask that covered her nose and mouth fog up. The cool, moist air that pumped through the mask took the fog away.

Sitting up in her bed, shifting aside pink sheets, she removed the mask and set it on her nightstand, next to the sleep apnea machine that produced the cool, moist air. At first, she hated it when she got it a year ago, but now she didn't mind it too much, sometimes forgetting she even wore it. She clicked the machine off and set out to start her day.

Her Disney Princesses clock displayed 10:23. She found it odd. Even though it was a Saturday, her parents never let her sleep so late. They must really be mad at her about last night!

Haley shifted to the edge of her bed and her feet dangled over, toes flirting with the floor. She found her slippers, large and fluffy and brown, displaying a smiling horse's face: Bullseye from *Toy Story 2*. She slipped them on and treaded with trepidation out of her room, wondering how mad her parents were at her.

No noise from downstairs. This late in the morning, she expected to hear something: Mom in the kitchen, Dad watching TV, the two of them talking. Nothing. Not even their lawnmower going.

Tiptoeing down the stairs, she wanted to call out, but fear held her back. How mad were they? Pausing mid-step, she recalled yesterday's argument. During school, her friends teased her about not having a cell phone. She had an mp3 player just like theirs but no cell phone. Deflecting her anger toward her parents, she came home and demanded a cell phone. Probably not the best strategy. She fought with them on and off throughout the evening, including yelling and screaming until an earlier-than-usual bedtime, concluding with an "I hate you!" and a door slam. She remembered flopping on the bed and crying, frustrated that her parents wouldn't get her a cell phone and mad at her friends for creating this situation. She remembered her entire body tingling, feeling warm before she fell asleep.

She had never used such harsh words with them before, and now, on the stairs, her gut twisted from the notion. She needed to apologize and explain, no matter how mad at her they were. Dad always said that talking solves everything. Time to see if he followed his own advice.

She padded from the stairs to the living room. The television was on, but she could barely hear it. It was turned down to the nighttime level her dad would watch it at so it wouldn't disturb her sleep. But no Dad. No Mom. No one. Standing behind the couch, she noticed something unusual about it. Something on it. Dust? A small pile of dust, no bigger than her fist, was on the top of the couch back. Confused, she walked around the couch to see a larger pile of dust on the floor and the biggest pile on the couch itself. Haley immediately thought of her dad getting in trouble with her mom because he smoked and now made a mess on the couch with the ashes. However, it seemed like quite a bit of ash to her, too much from any one ashtray.

Still looking at the dust piles, she backed out of the living room until she made it to the hall that led to the kitchen. Once there, it took only a few steps to enter the spacious kitchen with numerous light-inviting windows. She found another pile of dust.

Anxiety touched her heart as tears touched her eyes. What was going on? She skulked over to the pile and stared at it—a foot in diameter and coning to a peak. Why would her mother sweep the mess on the floor into a pile but not throw it out?

"Mom?" she said. She looked around the kitchen and through the windows, but the mysterious dust pile on the floor always pulled her back. "Mommy?"

Did they really leave her alone in the house? They talked about it before but decided to wait until she was twelve. Where were they?

"Dad? Daddy?" Haley called out as she moved through the dining room and into the enclosed porch. She didn't know what to do. She thought about going outside but became suddenly afraid, not wanting to get into more trouble. But where were they? Pressing her face to one of the screened windows, she looked to her neighbors' houses. No sign of her parents. From one house to the other, she stared ferociously, her eyes and head hurting from concentrating so hard. Still no sign of her parents. She looked slowly, panning from left to right. Until the face of a large bearded man popped up in front of her.

Shrieking as if watching Disneyland burn to the ground, she threw herself away from the window, her rear slamming to the floor. Every safety lesson she had been taught disappeared from her memory. Running, safe room, 9-1-1 never crossed her mind. She just sat and shrieked.

The man jumped back. He pointed to his hat with a "UGI" label and the nametag on his shirt that read, "PAUL" and said, "Whoa! Sorry! I'm Paul, Paul from UGI . . . the gas company. I'm just here to read your meter, little girl."

Haley didn't hear a word. She saw stranger danger, and her parents were nowhere to be found. She saw a guilty man, an axe murderer, a psycho killer, a vampire cyborg ghost pirate, who must have done something horrible to her parents. Him! This scary guy! And her entire body felt warm from the inside.

The scary man stopped moving and stood very still. Then he started shaking. His eyes widened and he looked at his hands. Quaking more, his skin started to shrivel and his clothes became baggier and baggier. He went from prune to raisin to balled-up paper. Then, in a puff, to dust. A pile as large as the one in Haley's kitchen.

Haley stopped screaming. She couldn't blink. Couldn't breathe. Her chest hurt. Her jaw throbbed. She knew what happened to her parents . . .

CHAPTER
31

Near State College, Pennsylvania

Adam and Nora meandered through the forest. The day was beautiful, the weather perfect. Nora wanted to enjoy the stroll. Adam wanted to find the next creature that looked like him. He wanted to find someone who understood what he went through: the pain, the isolation, the fear. He wanted to hurry but instead walked slowly with Nora, following her lead.

Nora stopped. She felt *him*, nearby, the other creature, no, human—like Adam. She couldn't see through his eyes or hear through his ears, but she sensed him. She sensed it was a him. And she sensed . . . he . . . was . . . very . . .

"Adam?" she said, turning to her half-man, half-lizard companion. "Are you hungry?"

Adam wanted to argue, wanted to tell her to hurry and find this other creature, that he grew more impatient with every passing minute. This was no time to think about food! However, he said, "Yesss."

"Why don't we break for a quick lunch?"

"Okay," Adam sighed, not agreeing with her suggestion. But he did it anyway.

Adam trudged over a small roll on the mountainside, leading to a shallow gully. There he would find a rabbit and two squirrels, all old and past their prime. Nora made sure of it. Being a good-hearted young man, Adam always hunted far from Nora, trying not to offend her by eating the very animals she loved and communicated with. But Nora's love for nature came with an understanding—nature cannibalized itself. Some animals ate other animals. She accepted that. However, she leveled the playing field as best she could, trying to bring about a certain fairness. She warned a family of young foxes to flee from the gully and changed the direction of a pregnant doe. However, the aged rabbit and two old squirrels had all led full lives, mating often and filling their bellies even more. They would be the ones to sate Adam's appetite today.

Once Adam disappeared from her sight, Nora began her own journey. She followed the roundness of the mountainside in the opposite direction, sloping into a miniature valley. She left her entourage of critters behind, commanding them to mill around and enjoy an acorn or two. She reminded the snakes not to eat the mice and chipmunks and then found a nearby blackberry bush for them to share. Her feet shuffled through the carpet of ferns and fallen leaves as she made her way to the valley, made her way to . . . him. The other.

As she made her way through the valley, she couldn't help but breathe harder, almost panting through her mouth. With every step, her nipples tingled, suddenly rock hard and hurting. She cupped her hands over her breasts to massage them, alleviating some of the pain. The tingling between her legs started to distract her, taking shorter steps, her thighs brushing together, worsening her primal itch.

With every step, she sensed she was getting closer to him. Felt it with—through—her whole sweating body. She smelled him. And he smelled like no man ever before. His presence sent her hormones into a frenzy. Adam excited her but never like this! And he didn't have the means to satisfy her even if he could ignite these fires within her.

She stopped by a thick grouping of young oak trees, their canopies not more than twelve feet off the ground. He was in the trees. Eyes watering, she looked at the leaves, trying to find him. She could only hear her pounding heart and felt it everywhere between her hands and feet. Sweat ran down her neck, matting her hair to her back, while her lust ran down her legs. She couldn't find him. A torrent of frustration swirled within her, and she panted, "Come out."

There was a moment of silence, too long and agonizing for Nora. Then a rustle of leaves. By the time she saw the movement, he had jumped from the branches, landing in front of her.

Towering a foot and a half over her, Nora almost collapsed from catharsis. He was beautiful, more so than she could imagine, more so than any fantasy she ever had alone under her covers with only her fingers and battery-operated lovers. Her head came to his sternum as she took a step forward and buried her fingers in the soft orange fur of his chest. Her hands flowed over the rock-hard ripples of his muscular chest, leading up to fur-covered shoulders, then down to solid arms bigger than her thighs. The fur tapered away by his elbow, exposing forearms of white skin. However, thick tufts encircled his wrists, each housing hands bigger than her head and a thin, razor-sharp claw from each finger. Her eyes continued down his body, following his tapered waist to a nappy patch of orange fur that concealed his privates. Powerful hips led to tree-trunk thighs. Again, the fur tapered away, all but disappearing by his knees, white shins led to orange furry paws. She soaked in the vision of this creature from bottom to top, stopping at his eyes—human eyes—in the giant face of a cat.

"What's . . . your name?" she huffed.

"Samson," he replied. His voice was deep but as raspy as sandpaper brushing a brick.

Taking one more step closer, Nora wrapped one arm around his waist while pressing her cheek into his chest fur. Her other hand rubbed up and down his thigh and over his hip, from front to back. "Nora."

What the fuck is wrong with this chick? Samson thought. Never in his fifty-five years of life did he ever imagine waking up one day as a giant cat and being forced to live in the exile of the mountain forests only to find a hot Asian chick horny for giant cats. Before he woke up as a giant cat three weeks ago, he could never have gotten a woman this hot. Of course, he spent thirty-eight of those fifty-five years in the cab of a big rig, hauling everything everywhere to make enough money for booze, cigarettes, alcohol, truck-stop whores, and beer. That quickly led to a gut twice as big as his chest, hair slicker and thinner than the dental floss he never used, and the abandonment of most of his yellowed teeth. Truck-stop whores were all he could ever get. And many of them had fewer teeth than he and showered even less. None of them were as hot as this giant-cat-loving Asian chick grinding against him. Then he wondered why he thought so much about this instead of just taking her. *What the fuck is wrong with me?*

Nora turned around and started to rub against his leg while her hand ran over his crotch. His erection slid out from a pocket of fur. She dropped to her knees, pressing her face and chest to the forest floor. Presenting herself as any animal in heat would, she growled two instructions, "No claws. No teeth."

"Cool," he replied, knowing he didn't have the savvy to say anything better. Not like this situation could get any better! He knelt behind her and gently grabbed her hips and thighs, careful of his claws. The last thing he wanted to do was break any of her rules and have this dream end. He raised her hips with ease and slid in. Nora moaned. Samson knew very little about women but watched enough porn to know *that* was a *good* moan. Still cautious of his claws, he developed a steady rhythm. She gasped, groaned, and panted, her fingers extending and contracting, grabbing at dirt and dead leaves.

Samson expressed his joy with a feral howl, deep and hollow like any other cat singing to its lover. *Don't ruin this, don't ruin this,* he thought to himself, his thrusts getting faster while still focusing on his claws. But something caught his eye, and he looked up. On the ridge a hundred yards away stood . . . one freaking huge lizard! And it looked *pissed!*

Adam ate a rabbit and two squirrels for lunch. They were old and offered little chase. He then looked for Nora, hoping to get back on schedule with the finding of the nearby creature. Passing through the large gathering of critters he called travel companions, he wondered where Nora had wandered and why she left the animals behind. Then he heard a feral moan, a restless cat singing a summertime song of lust. He followed it over the slope of the mountain. He froze, looking into the small valley below. Nora had found the other creature.

Even though Adam came from a strict household with an excessive fear of God, he still went to public school. He knew exactly what he saw. And it disgusted him. Shame stirred his frothy anger in the scalding cauldron of betrayal. Primal rules mixed with teenage logic. Adam saw an adversary with something he thought belonged to him. He attacked.

Samson swore the lizard ran on two legs, but it attacked with a slithering speed he thought only possible by a snake. In a very compromising position, Samson couldn't defend himself against Adam's flying tackle.

The two once-human creatures tumbled together with snarling growls and haunting howls, claws and teeth articulating their fury. One fought to preserve a shattered love that never existed; the other for survival against a foe with unknown motivations. Deflecting critical attacks to minor bites and cuts, each participant surprised the other by being swifter and more agile than expected. Finally, Adam's rage gave him the advantage, sinking his teeth into Samson's arm, forcing the cat-creature to spit a chilling hiss. Adam brought his claws to the cat-man's throat for impending victory. Until . . .

"Adam! Stop!" Nora screamed.

Not comprehending, Adam relinquished his grip and jumped away from the cat-creature. "What. Isss. Going. On?"

Still on the ground, Samson instinctively licked his arm. He smelled Adam's youth. "What the fuck is wrong with you, kid?"

Nora stood between the men. "I didn't want you two to meet like this. I'm sorry, Adam. This is Samson, the other like you we were tracking. He and I had . . . have . . . a connection."

Adam stared at Nora; her eyes begged him to leave her alone with Samson for them to finish. If he could, Adam would have blushed from both anger and embarrassment, feeling like a victim of a cruel high-school prank. Nora reached for him and he stepped away. With fevered red cheeks, she asked, "Adam. Please. Just . . . just five minutes. And then we can all meet properly."

"Better make it ten, junior," Samson said while standing. "You kinda ruined my mojo."

With no acknowledgment, Adam turned and walked away, back over the ridge with the other animals. He found a large rock and sat, hoping to sort through his violent emotions and racing thoughts. Which were of a teenager? Which were of an animal?

The three dozen snakes converged on him, faithful friends. A few of the other animals skittered around him. The raccoon, Nora's favorite, passed too close. Adam ate it in one bite . . .

CHAPTER
32

Harrisburg, Pennsylvania

"How do you like our new doctor?" Marvin asked, admiring the fit of his suit. He had it for only three weeks but sent it in for much needed alterations.

Thelma sighed as she joined him in the admiration, her hands picking a piece of lint here, shooing a wrinkle there. "He's nice. He's just different after having the same doctor for almost twenty years."

"You'll adjust. It had to be done, though. After going from a no cup to a D cup and a size zero to a size six, while maintaining such a thin waist like you did, I'm sure it would have raised suspicions."

"You're right. I know you're right. I'll get used to him. But you know my waist won't be thin for much longer." Thelma stepped back and patted her belly.

Smiling, Marvin placed his hand on her belly as well and leaned in to steal a kiss from her soft lips. "But thanks to my magic touch, it'll only last half as long. Right now, the boys are two months along, even though they've only been in there a month. And then your body will spring right back to the way it looks now, thin waist and all."

Thelma kissed him back. "This is all so amazing, Marvin. Absolutely amazing."

"And it's only going to get better, my dear." With a wink and a smile, Marvin went to work. For the entire drive, he ran his hands through his hair, sifting the thick strands through his fingers. A full head of hair! It looked better than it did when he was a teenager. Then again, it started an early retreat once he hit eighteen. By the time he graduated college, he could fit his whole hand in the bald spot. As his hair disappeared, so did his confidence. Then he met a skinny girl with wacky food allergies. And she didn't care about his thinning hair. They married and he found work at Gunn & Dunn Investments, LLC. She stood by his side as he toiled away in a cubicle and more hair fell away in a shower drain. It seemed only fair that she stood by his side while his hair returned and he ascended the corporate ladder.

Marvin's administrative assistant, Trudy, greeted him with an enthusiastic, "Good morning, sir." The shaky smile and panicked look in her eyes made Marvin think of her as a fearful puppy hoping her master never leaves her again. She held out a handful of missed calls papers. "Here are your messages, sir."

"Thank you, dear," he said, smiling. As he took the papers from her, his fingers glanced across her hands, rewarding her. A calm washed over her body. Her eyes went from wide and frenzied to hazy and half-shut as she slouched back into her chair. For the next five minutes, she'd be able to do little else. She slurred a whisper, "Mr. Pavel's in your office."

Marvin feigned surprise just in case she was lucid enough to notice he was still there. "Really? Okay. Thank you, Trudy."

She replied with a dopey smile.

Mr. Pavel was the company's vice president and in charge of Marvin's division. He was a nice enough man but certainly dropped the hammer of Thor when he had to. But for the past couple of weeks, he had been having some issues.

"Good morning, Mr. Pavel," Marvin said to the man sitting in his chair. Pavel had been a linebacker in college and that could still be seen in the sixty-two-year-old man. Today, he looked rather pale.

"Carver," Pavel replied, mustering a pained smile as he stood.

The men shook hands. However, Pavel released quickly as he shifted from ghost white to seasick green. He pulled his decorative silk handkerchief from his breast pocket and held it to his mouth. Looking for support while he fought nausea, he sat on Marvin's desk.

"Are you okay, Mr. Pavel?" Marvin asked.

After a minute of embarrassing silence, Pavel's color shifted back to haggard white. "No. And that's why I'm here to see you."

"Excuse me?"

"Damnedest thing. Over the past couple weeks, I've been having bouts of severe nausea. But only at work, only here. Home, I'm fine. Doctor checked me out and said there's nothing wrong with me physically. Said it must be psychosomatic. Stress getting to me. What happened to Salinger and Savinski must be freaking me out. I talked with my wife, and we decided it's time for me to retire."

Marvin just played along. "Retire?"

"Yes. And I'm recommending you to the old man to take my spot."

Playing his cards perfectly, Marvin knew with Pavel's recommendation to the CEO, he'd be a vice president within a week. "Me? But I haven't been in Salinger's job all that long."

Pavel stood and nodded toward the door. Marvin exited his office and then walked down the cubicle-lined aisles with Pavel. After his promotion to Salinger's old position, Marvin decided to take a more hands-on management approach. Before his promotion, there were two managers, him and Johnson. However, when it came time to interview for Salinger's old job, Johnson kept missing his appointment, mysteriously falling asleep in his office. Marvin won the job, and Johnson subjected himself to a battery of tests for narcolepsy. Since all the test results were negative, Marvin fired Johnson and now had twelve employees answer directly to him.

Pavel strolled along, peeking into everyone's cubicles. Every single one of Marvin's employees worked with a burning in their blood. Unblinking eyes darted from work papers to financial statements to spreadsheets to risk management models to news articles back to work papers. Every employee researched a company, from Fortune-500 mega-conglomerates to small mom-n-pop shops looking for a venture capitalist's seed money.

As Pavel and Marvin walked past Barb's cubicle, she turned around. With clammy skin and hands shaking like a junkie needing a fix, she looked past Pavel to Marvin only. "Mr. Carver! I have exciting news. Look at these numbers I've come up with. That small chain of restaurants who wanted a loan? Profitable. Beyond profitable. We shouldn't loan them the money. We should make a push to buy them outright."

Marvin glanced over the numbers on her computer's monitor as well as the reports scattered across her desk. She was right. And Marvin got very excited as images of commissions and incentives and bonuses for him danced through his head. "Excellent work, Barb. I'll contact them tomorrow and get the ball rolling."

As he leaned forward to look at more reports, he put his hand on her shoulder under the guise of needing balance. However, he just wanted to give her a reward. His finger slid across her neck. Gates opened and the dopamine flowed through her brain. Barb slouched in her chair with a loose smile, staring into space. Even if she remembered to thank him, she couldn't—every nerve in her body took a lunch break. She'd be catatonic for five minutes and rather wistful for another fifteen. Marvin would come back later and release some more, but he'd mix in some adrenaline to keep her excitement at high levels.

Pavel and Marvin continued walking, heading back to Marvin's office.

"Amazing," Pavel said, shaking his head. "From what I hear, none of your employees even like you. You obviously know how to motivate. You're bringing money into the company. That's why I'm recommending you for a promotion. To fill the hole I'm leaving."

After a quick handshake, Pavel went to meet with the CEO while Marvin eased into his leather chair and basked in his own glory. Two more steps to go. Only the executive vice president, who doubled as COO, and the old man himself, the president/CEO.

Colby knocked on the door and invited himself into Marvin's office. The young man looked haggard. His hair was extra spiky in a desperate attempt to cover the newly formed widow's peak. Due to an ever-expanding waist, his clothes no longer fit properly; his shirt fluffed out along the beltline, his pants too tight there while baggy everywhere else. A trail of acne flowed from his forehead to his chin. His natural attractiveness hadn't disappeared, but he was now far from perfect.

Without saying a word, Colby dropped an envelope onto Marvin's desk. He tried to leave, but Marvin's question stopped him. "What's this?"

For the first time since Marvin met him, Colby sounded nervous. "My letter of resignation."

Marvin laughed. There was no way he'd let his favorite squeak toy leave. "Colby. You're twenty-four. You're a kid. You haven't even been here two months. Don't you think the next place will call here looking for a reference? How's it going to look that you couldn't even last two months on your first job out of college?"

"But you're making me an admin assistant. I have a master's degree, Marvin. I'm more than that."

Marvin laughed again. "More than that? Are you serious? You puked on the CE-fucking-O! You pissed yourself! And look at you—you're losing hair and gaining weight. You're missing two teeth, and the grapevine tells me you might lose a third."

"I . . . I . . ." Colby stammered, eyes welling with tears.

Marvin sighed for drama, internally relishing every ounce of Colby's pain. Would Colby be kind if roles were reversed? If not for this miracle of Marvin's, Colby would be a manager and Marvin would be a cubicle hermit. What would Colby have done? What would that fucking cheese do? "Look. Pavel just told me he's retiring and I'm going to take his spot. Yes, you're still going to be an admin assistant. But you'll be an AA to a VP. Come on, son, you know you bit off more than you can chew here. I'm just trying to help you out."

Marvin decided to buy himself a bottle of Dom on the way home tonight to celebrate his great acting performance. Colby apologized and sniveled, *finally* showing his true colors. Marvin dismissed him but was *far* from through with him . . .

CHAPTER
33

Harrisburg, Pennsylvania

Naked, Stone paced the room. He curled and uncurled his fingers, making and unmaking fists. He didn't know what to do. He wasn't smart enough to comprehend what was happening, so how could he possibly formulate a plan for what he should do next?

Stopping in the middle of the tiny bedroom, he squeezed both his fists as tight as possible. His arms shook and veins bulged. He felt nothing. So frustrated, he punched himself in the face, square in the mouth. Then again, this time in the nose. Nothing. He didn't feel his fist hit his nose and didn't feel his nose against his knuckles. He started pacing again.

Following a bloodied trail, he took three steps, turned then followed the blood streaks back for three steps. The saturated carpet could absorb no more, and crimson pools formed around his feet with every step. More blood dripped from his waist and down his thighs to the carpet. He didn't care. It wasn't his carpet or his blood. It all belonged to the dead hooker on the bed.

After strangling his brother's bimbo a month ago, he quickly learned that was the only way he could get off anymore. He limited himself to twice a week and used only hookers. Women threw themselves at him any time he stepped out of his Ferrari. But he couldn't use them because they might have families or friends who would notice them missing. He felt he was at least smart enough to realize that. No one cared about a couple of dead hookers every week. Especially since he didn't keep using the ones from the same town.

Thanks to his late brother, Stone now had business dealings in all the surrounding cities, as far as Philly, Baltimore, and DC. Since he had trust issues, he micromanaged using hands-on deals and problem-solving. Every town had whores, whether street trash or ones who called themselves fancy names like "escort." Every town had whores.

He had business in Harrisburg, close enough to York for him to drive. A couple of distributors tried to double-dip by taking the percentage Stone offered to move junk, then charged addicts more than they told Stone they were charging and kept the profits. Nothing more than street hustlers, but Stone was running a business. He couldn't allow his other distributors to get the same bright idea. So he drove up to Harrisburg to take care of business.

With a garage full of cars, he had one for each occasion. For handling stupid punks, he always took the '69 Camaro. Always. He had inherited his brother's business only two months ago, but he made enough personal trips that, in certain neighborhoods, a '69 Camaro meant a couple people were going to get their heads knocked together.

The distributors were a few ghetto teens who only stayed in school to push the junk. They heard the rumors about Stone being bulletproof but figured he just wore a vest and decided they'd be ready for him. He didn't wear Kevlar on his head, now, did he? That'd be where they'd aim. Their plan was perfect, and they readied themselves when they heard the '69 Camaro pull up, growling like a lion prowling the jungle.

The street urchins invited Stone into a section-eight living room, showing smiles and feigning compliance. Then sprung the trap. Laughing and howling, they emptied clips as they danced around the drug lord from York. Their celebration was short-lived, though.

Stone felt nothing as bullets ricocheted off his ears, eyes, and cheeks. Rounds bouncing in every direction, they struck all four walls and the floor as well as the ceiling. Stone made short work of the wannabes, breaking noses and ribs before breaking their necks. He forgot to keep one alive, too disturbed by the circumstances. He felt nothing, and that freaked him out.

Over the past two months, he had become increasingly numb. It scared him, but as long as he could get off, he never thought too much about it. He still felt bullets, finding himself in situations where he was shot once or twice a week. Well, he used to feel bullets. These three punks *unloaded* three full clips. And he didn't feel a single thing; no pinch, sting, or even tickle. Nothing.

He sped away in his Camaro, confident that citizens who heard the shootings would tell the cops a mysterious figure jumped into any car other than a Camaro, and went looking for a hooker. He felt nervous, hoping he could still feel enough to get off. The steering wheel creaked from the pressure of his hands squeezing it. They should have been sweating, but they weren't. Glancing in his rearview mirror, he noticed not a drop on his forehead. No sweat after a fight? No sweat from being so scared? How was that possible? He found a streetwalker at a convenience store a few blocks away.

She was tall but skinny from being a junkie. Her tits sagged and her size zero skirt almost fell from her hips. She was twenty, looked forty, and was missing a tooth. Stone took her because her face still held a vague memory of prettiness, and he needed to know if he could still get off.

They headed back to her place in an abandoned building that once held four apartments. Two were used for the homeless and the junkies, while the other two were "owned" by the hooker's pimp. Within a second of locking the door, he tore off her clothes.

He pushed and thrust and pumped and poked. Nothing. He had at her like a starving dog would a bone. Nothing. He tried the move that always worked before; grabbing her by the neck and squeezing, using it as leverage to push and pull harder. Nothing. She slapped and punched and kicked, trying to get him to relinquish his grip. He did. She tried to scream, but as soon as she opened her mouth, he filled it. He pushed and thrust and pumped and poked. Nothing.

Her arms flailed in a panic. Her legs tangled in the bedsheets, looking for any leverage; any she could find was negated by Stone's firm grasp on the back of her head. She could feel nothing else except the burning constriction from mouth to stomach as she heaved. Having eaten nothing in two days, nothing came out. She desperately gulped for air on every thrust; her nose had swollen shut from him bashing her face into his impossibly hard pelvis. She could no longer control her retching and gagging, and the noises coming from her mutated into inhuman sounds, a malfunctioning alarm clock signaling the end. A stinging from her teeth pushed past the panic and fire in her throat. The stinging soon exploded into lightning bolts of pain, her teeth tearing free from her gums as her face continued to get smashed against his body. Blood and teeth erupted from her mouth with twisted coughs and vomit. Each push forced her jaw open more until one thrust snapped it from her skull, putting an end to her torture. Stone kept thrusting even after her body stopped twitching. Nothing.

Now he paced the room, her blood oozing from his waist to his feet, as his feet squished it from the carpet.

What the fuck happened to me? He cried. Tears and snot streamed down his face. He couldn't feel the wetness or flow. Out of habit he wiped his nose across his forearm and couldn't feel that either. A panicked moan warbled from his throat, sounding like a wounded animal, a scared child unable to fully comprehend the extent of a bad situation. *What's goin' on? How'd this happen? How do I stop?*

From sheer frustration, he punched himself in the face again. Nothing.

He liked the feeling no pain part. Always had from day one. But the feeling nothing part? Not being able to feel his dick? Not good! Not good at all! He needed to fix this. And now! But how? How? How? How? He punched his own face again.

The blood-saturated path led to a window, and Stone went to it hoping to get some fresh air or get an idea or find a sign. He discovered all three. A tiny square sign, so small it had been ignored by vandals, stood across the street. A blue sign with a white H and an arrow . . .

CHAPTER
34

Camp Hill, Pennsylvania

Saturday morning meant one thing to Michael—quality family downtime. After a fifty-hour workweek, Claire needed the relaxation. Although her recent weeks had been more like sixty hours, even seventy during one week, with a trip to the office last Saturday, she was home today. After putting in a grueling week in which he spent seven hours teaching class, three hours in his on-campus office, and two hours grading papers, Michael also needed a break.

Claire sat in her "comfy chair"—a plush pink armchair that matched the rose color in the swirling patterns on both the couch and loveseat—while reading a book for the book club she would be attending tonight. She sat ninety degrees, askew, her legs dangling over one arm of the chair while her back rested against the other arm. Michael stretched out on the loveseat across from her. Newspaper in hand, he read the morning away. Although, he sneaked a loving peek at his wife now and again. He loved her and loved to look at her. Saturdays transformed her from a high-octane, power-suit-wearing barracuda with lipstick into a girl who liked to curl up on her comfy chair and read a book. Suits made Michael uncomfortable and edgy. He never trusted anyone in a suit. But once his wife cracked a book, he felt safe and secure. There was nothing more down-to-earth than reading a book.

With a strategic turn of the newspaper page, Michael went back to wife-watching. He loved the way she read, moving her lips the whole time. Usually, her eyes moved faster than her lips could possibly keep up, so her lips just opened and closed with the occasional pucker. However, her lips didn't move today. And neither did her eyes. She just stared at a page, mouth shut. He then noticed that over half the book remained unexplored. Quite a bit of reading before the meeting tonight! An impossible amount, actually. As Michael thought about it, she joined this book appreciation club over a month ago and had been reading the same book. Could that be true? The same book?

Something had to be troubling her. It was obvious she was just staring into space, exploring the recesses of her own mind. Something at work? A case she was working on? Something that confounded her lawyering skills? *Which lawsuit was she talking about last night?* Michael wondered. He scolded himself for being so selfish and inconsiderate for not listening when she talked. He had a sugar mama! Why risk losing that by not giving a modicum of attention when she talked?

Michael lowered the paper, giving it an extra rustle for dramatic effect. "Good book?"

"Hmm?" Claire asked, looking at Michael through half-glazed eyes. It was the same look their daughter gave whenever she watched too much television without moving, breathing, or blinking. Now Michael knew where she inherited that look.

"I just asked if it was a good book?"

"Oh." Claire smiled a sleepy smile and shifted in her comfy chair. "Yes, very good. Intriguing."

"Got a good bit left before the meeting."

Claire tilted her book to look at the number of remaining pages. A slight twitch in her face hinted that this surprised her. Her disarming smile returned. "I'll skim through some parts. One of the advantages of being a lawyer—we read nothing. Just skim through contracts looking for keywords to use against our opponents."

Michael wanted to press the issue. But how did he express that he wanted her to talk about what bothered her without stating he didn't listen to a single thing she said last night or come across as accusatory? He breathed a sigh of relief when the doorbell rang.

No sooner had their visitor taken their finger off the button when the ceiling above Michael and Claire came alive. Their daughter, Sarah, had been demonstrating her desire to show off her adult skills. She took advantage of any chance to answer the phone, use the microwave, insert the straw into her juice box, or answer the door. She squealed as she jumped from her bed, resulting in an earth-shaking thud. Little legs hammered the floor as she sprinted to the stairs. All but falling down the stairs to get to the front door, she screamed, "I got it!"

Both Michael and Claire laughed, loving Sarah's enthusiasm. Michael pulled himself off the couch and dropped the newspaper. "Don't forget to ask for them to identify themselves first."

"Who is it?" she yelled at the door with enough strength to knock down the walls of Jericho.

After a short pause, Michael and Sarah heard an older woman's voice, smooth and confident. "Hello, sweetie. My name is Emma, and I'm looking for Professor Roseman."

Michael frowned and opened the door. The tone of his voice cut the temperature in half. "What do you want?"

"We need to talk." Emma displayed a cordial smile, glancing down at Sarah's curious eyes.

Michael reached down and turned his daughter 180 degrees by her shoulders. His stomach cramped as he forced himself to talk in a softer tone. "Thank you for getting the door, dear. But this is for Daddy, so go back to playing. Okay?"

Sarah huffed and trudged away. "Fine."

Michael's scowl returned as he stepped outside and shut the door. "What the hell do you want, Emma? I thought I made it perfectly clear that I never wanted to see you again."

Her smile shifted to a look of placating concern. "It's been about two weeks, Professor Roseman. I was just wondering if you had thought any more about . . ."

"There's *nothing* to think about. I haven't thought about it since we met, and I'm hoping never to have to think about it again. I want nothing to do with this, Emma. So why don't you just get back in your . . ." Michael looked up to see what kind of car she drove. A Lincoln, which didn't surprise him in the slightest. But in it, he saw a familiar sight—a young man in a gray sweatshirt, hood up, hugging himself as he rocked back and forth. "Oh, great! You brought Derrick with you?"

"He needs your help." Emma's eyes held the delicate mix of fear and desperation. She worried about Derrick, but she was also scared of him. Michael saw it in the way she looked at him. It wasn't often that Emma looked like a sixty-four-year-old woman, but this was one of those times. "He started vibing five days ago."

"Have him focus on that cup I gave him." Michael tried to sound dispassionate.

"Derrick was so hurt after you left that day. He got in his car and came right back to my house. He took the cup you gave him, crumbled it up, and threw it out."

Just like Emma had done to Michael's heart. He looked up to the sky and released a slow, pained sigh of exasperation.

As if she knew what he wanted to say next, Emma continued, "We tried other objects for him to focus on. Even other cups. He said he wanted to try to control it, ignore it, like you would. Today it was too much, so I drove and he gave me directions. We ended up in front of the Gunn & Dunn building."

"In Harrisburg? So why didn't you go in?"

"He was too upset. He kept saying that he's stupid and couldn't talk to people, and he'd embarrass me."

"Why would he . . . think . . . that . . . ?"

Emma's glare told Michael what he already knew. It was his fault. And she wanted him to fix it.

"Fine! What do you want me to do? Talk to him?"

"I want you to come with us."

"Emma . . ."

She reached out and grabbed his hand. "Please, Michael. You don't realize how much he looks up to you. You calmed him down and helped him with this 'vibing' thing he does. He can't ignore his gifts—his abilities—like you can."

Michael looked into Emma's car and watched the young man rock back and forth. He was lost and confused. Emma's words bounced through his head—Derrick couldn't ignore this. He couldn't even control it. "Wait here."

Michael slipped back into his house, wondering what to tell Claire. He hastened his step, opting for a more blitzkrieg communication style. As soon as he stepped from the foyer to the living room, he turned and went into the kitchen.

"Who was at the door?" Claire asked from her comfy chair. "Sarah said it was an old woman. She told me, 'Not old like you and Daddy old, but old like Grandma.'"

Michael rifled through a cabinet near the sink containing Tupperware and other plastics. He spoke loudly, barely louder than the ruckus he made. "Couple of students doing poorly in my class. I'm gonna go to campus with them and help them out for a few hours."

"An old woman? And it doesn't bother you that they came to our house?"

Even over the noise of plastic bouncing around the confines of the wooden cabinet, he sensed the angst in her voice. He had to move fast if he expected to make it out of the house without more questions. Found it! A 30-ounce plastic sports thermos. It was dark blue with white letters: "Harrisburg Area Community College." It was capped with a white lid and thick plastic straw. He snatched it, shut the cabinet door, and walked out of the kitchen toward the foyer. "You're never too old to go to college. I told them it was unorthodox to come here, but I'm giving a test Monday, and they really need help. Shows initiative."

As he trod through the foyer, he heard his wife ask, "And the sports thermos?"

Opening the front door, he shouted over his shoulder, "In case I get thirsty! I gotta get going! I'll be back before your reading group! I love you!"

He shut the door before he heard a reply.

Derrick sat in the front passenger seat. Still rocking, he looked up and saw Michael walk past the back door. Trying to hide his actions, Derrick turned to wipe away the tears and snot from crying for two hours. But Michael saw.

Michael slid into the backseat right behind Derrick and shut the door. Emma sat in the driver's seat and started the car. Derrick still rocked back and forth.

Michael handed the plastic thermos to Derrick. "Here you go."

"What's this?" Derrick asked so fast Michael barely understood the words.

"Something for you to focus on. We're gonna do it just like we did with Emma. You give the directions, and when we get there, I'll do the talking."

Derrick held it with both hands. His rocking slowed and soon subsided.

Satisfied with the result, Michael buckled his seatbelt and said, "All right. Let's do this." He couldn't help but think about how he'd lied to Claire. He hated doing it, but as long as Emma and Derrick were involved, he'd have to do a lot more of it . . .

CHAPTER
35

Harrisburg, Pennsylvania

None of the office buildings in downtown Harrisburg stood out from one another. All sharing the same general shape, they only differed in color and height. Even then, they all still looked the same to Michael. Although Michael worked in Harrisburg, his campus was tucked away in one corner of the city that bordered the river. He rarely came downtown. It always gave him an overwhelming sense of dread.

Emma parked in a nearby garage, then she and Michael followed Derrick, his brisk pace leading them to a cold gray building. Derrick was more lucid thanks to the sports bottle Michael had given him, but he was still frantic, walking with jerky, uncoordinated steps and muttering to himself. Just about every pedestrian he passed on the sidewalk thought he had recently escaped from a mental ward. Not giving an argument to the contrary, Derrick stormed through the lobby, entered the nearest elevator, and pressed all the buttons.

Derrick had visions of the man that caused him to vibe. Images of a middle-aged, overweight, balding man flashed through his head like a broken movie projector, only showing every tenth frame. He saw the man working in an office environment, or cubicle farm, as Michael repeatedly referred to it. He also saw the man's name displayed on the wall of a cubicle: Marvin Carver.

The elevator stopped at every floor just long enough for Derrick to poke his head out and get a sense of whether they had found the right floor. Doors closed. Next floor.

Michael scowled while staring at the floor indicator. His fingers drummed against the railing. His foot tapped. Emma could take no more of his impertinence and whispered, "This shouldn't take much longer."

Being the only three in the elevator, Michael found no problem being candid. "Did you see all the suits running around? Especially on a Saturday! And every floor we've stopped on was nothing more than cubicle farms stretching from horizon to horizon. Mindless drones, typing their lives away, hoping they get a chance to be the next suit."

"Suits?" Emma asked.

"Businessmen. Corporate shills. Soulless monsters. Twenty-first-century boogeymen. The 'greed-is-good' problem with America today."

"Now, why on earth do you think that?"

"Venal. Adjective. Open to bribery. Capable of betrayal for a price. Marked by corrupt dealings. Corruptible."

"You are a piece of work, Professor Roseman. Anyone without a solid sense of spirituality is capable of corruption."

"When was the last time a beatnik ruined thousands of lives by stealing billions of dollars while receiving million-dollar paychecks?"

"When was the last time a 'suit' set fire to an abortion clinic? Killed hardworking scientists trying to find cures for diseases just to set animals free? Sank boats to save whales? Bombed communities for jihad?"

Michael could have argued until he was blue in the face, having done so on many occasions, much to his wife's chagrin. But what was the point? Emma was entrenched in her ignorance. He'd never be able to show her the light, let alone get her to change her mind. However, she did get Michael to question his spirituality. Why did he do this? Why didn't he turn the old lady away when she rang his doorbell? Why did he feel the need to continue lying to his wife? And why the hell haven't they found the right floor yet? Do they *have* to stop at every freaking floor in this rancid building filled with suits and ties and filth and disgust and . . .

"Here!" Derrick shouted. "This is the floor!"

"Good," Michael said, barging past Derrick to exit the elevator. "Just let me do the talking."

Shaking off his frustration, Michael approached the receptionist with a smile that showed her he sympathized with her because she had to toil her life away answering phones. "Good afternoon. I was wondering if we could meet with Marvin Carver?"

The receptionist offered a smile in return, showing that he could get off his high horse anytime and stop looking down his nose at her. "Do you have an appointment?"

"No."

"The nature of your business, sir?"

Michael had no idea what this Marvin Carver fellow did here. But he knew Gunn & Dunn was an investment firm. He took a stab in the dark. "I'm looking for an investment advisor."

"Well, I'm sure I can have another representative talk to you . . ."

"No. Mr. Carver only, please. A friend recommended him to us."

Suspicion oozed from the receptionist as her eyes slid from Michael to Emma to Derrick, whose wide-eyed trembling made him look like a chihuahua. Glaring at Michael through I-don't-get-paid-enough-to-put-up-with-your-bullshit eyes, she picked up the phone and dialed. "Mr. Carver? There are a few people here who would like to talk to you about investment advice and possibly set up a new account . . . No, I don't believe they're from that corporation . . . Not that one either, sir. I believe they are seeking advice about a personal account . . . Yes, I suggested that, sir, but they asked for you specifically . . . Okay, thank you."

Marvin hung up the phone and wondered who could possibly be here to set up a new personal account. And asked for him by name? As a newly-appointed vice president, he had nothing to do with that. Questions stewed in his mind as he made his way to reception. Once he arrived, more questions stewed.

"Hello? I'm Marvin Carver," he greeted the oddly matched strangers.

Michael's face froze in a look of confusion. He turned to Derrick for an explanation. The young viber described Marvin as overweight, balding, and old. The Marvin Carver who greeted them was trim, young, and had a show-quality head of hair. Even Emma couldn't stop herself from shooting Derrick a similar look.

"Now what?" Michael whispered to Derrick through a forced smile he displayed for Marvin and the receptionist.

"It's him," Derrick whispered back.

"Are you sure?"

"Yeah. I stopped vibing."

Marvin stopped short, confused why this small group of people asked for him by name, then whispered among themselves when he arrived. Putting his hands in his pockets, he asked, "How . . . can I help you?"

"We're looking for an investment advisor, and . . . well . . . here we are," Michael said through a fake smile.

"I'm the vice president of research, so doling out advice is not my particular forte. If you'd like, I could give you the name of an account manager who—"

"You were recommended to us. Is there someplace we could go to talk?"

"Recommended? By whom?"

Sweat beaded along Michael's hairline. Memories of discussions with his school's theater professor about the importance of improv turned into a harsh I-told-you-so since he never gave the acting skill much credit. "Umm, we can discuss that later. In your office, maybe? A conference room?"

Marvin's diplomatic smile waned. He had found humor in the way this guy was dressed—loafers, relaxed khakis, a loose cotton shirt with a floral pattern that was one lily away from being considered "Hawaiian," and a hairstyle that would have been "hip" three years ago. It amused Marvin. But that no longer sufficed, and his smile became forced. Marvin pulled his hands from his pockets and started to turn. "Look, I'm very busy and—"

Sensing Marvin's impending retreat, Michael stepped forward with an outstretched hand. He knew no suit could resist a handshake. They could never pass up an opportunity to press their flesh against a potential victim. Michael tried to wrangle the devil and used his soul as bait. "I'm sorry. We didn't start on the right foot. I'm Michael."

Hoping this gesture would hasten the strangers' departure, Marvin stepped forward as well and grabbed Michael's hand. Marvin saw fireworks. A refreshing coolness washed through him, like taking a cold shower on a sweltering day. A constant strum rippled through Michael, from his head, to his arms, and out through his fingers. Michael's body sang to Marvin, but a song far more complex than any he had heard before.

"Are . . . you okay," Michael asked, forcing a release from an uncomfortably long handshake. "You seemed to space out there for a minute."

Marvin snapped back to reality, and his diplomatic smile returned. "Oh? Sorry about that. Just thinking about my schedule. It so happens I can squeeze you in now."

With an outstretched hand, Marvin approached Derrick like a hungry vampire. "And you are?"

"Derrick," the young man replied, grasping Marvin's hand.

Michael was the fireworks display, while Derrick was the grand finale. The neurons in the young man's brain fired and popped at speeds greater than Marvin had ever imagined possible. And the leaps made from one synapse to another seemed acrobatic. The fastest way to make it from here to Australia would be through Earth as opposed to around it; however, that couldn't happen with the limited resources available. But Derrick's brain made it happen. With impossible leaps and unlikely connections, it was, simply put, wired differently.

Derrick also pulled his hand from Marvin after a too-long handshake. He shot a confused glance at Michael, who could only shrug his shoulders while Marvin moved on to Emma. Giving the older woman little choice, he clasped her hand and shook, so excited he forgot to ask for her name. Electricity flowed from her body to his. Her entire body felt like one giant reflex waiting to burst free, a billion coiled springs set for release at any moment. It didn't just sing to Marvin; it was the whole damn orchestra!

As demurely as possible, Emma freed herself from Marvin's clutches. "Emma Montgomery. Very pleased to meet you."

"The pleasure is all mine," Marvin replied, unconsciously licking his lips. Before him stood three incredible roadmaps . . .

CHAPTER
36

Philadelphia, Pennsylvania

LaKeisha stared at herself in the mirror, watching how her skin reacted when she pressed her fingers to her right cheek and released. Still a bit puffy. The swelling had disappeared from the side of her nose to the top of her lip. Almost gone from her cheek, right where Camilla punched her. The doctor said she was lucky her "friend" didn't break any bones in her face. At the time, the swelling and pain had been so bad that she thought the doctor was wrong. After all, he was a doctor who saw patients on welfare. But now, it looked as if he might have been right—no broken bones and "the system" had worked.

She had been in the welfare system her entire life, and it had never done her wrong. It paid for her to be born, and it paid for her babies to be born. A few years ago, she had a severe sleep disorder, and the system even paid for her to have a specialist fix it. Some of her friends and family tried to abuse it, but she always thought they did more work trying to stay home from work. LaKeisha just took what they gave her and liked it. The only thing the system couldn't give her was an explanation for why her best friend punched her and why her boyfriend's dick was in another woman.

"Bitch," she whispered as she thought about Camilla and how she hadn't called yet with a reason or apology for punching her at the dance club. Sadness mixed with frustration as she thought about Darnel. He hadn't called since the dance club either. Hell, he *still* hadn't called her since their hallway boom-boom a couple weeks ago! Disgusted, she sucked her teeth and left the bathroom.

Alone in her apartment, she strolled to the couch. She gave the kids to her mom for a couple days. She couldn't deal with them and the throbbing cheek at the same time. It was a crazy cycle—they would fight, then she'd get mad and they would fight more, then she'd get madder and they'd fight even harder. Too much drama. She *had* to send them away. Get some peace, quiet, and much-deserved time to herself. However, no sooner had she sat down when there was a knock on the door.

It was almost noon; good television time started soon! She sucked her teeth in disgust and shouted, "Who is it?"

"My name is Detective Matthews."

"Already talked to the cops!"

"We have some follow-up questions, ma'am."

Realizing she'd lose less television time if she'd just talk to him rather than trying to shoo him away, she stood and stomped her way to the door. She peeked through the peephole to see him holding his badge out for her. He asked, "May I come in?"

She opened the door, displaying her contempt, and kept her back to him, flicking her hand in the air as she walked to her kitchenette. "Shut it behind you."

"I know this is an inconvenience for you, Miss LaRue. I just want to thank you in advance for your time."

"Whatever," she mumbled. LaKeisha opened the fridge and buried her head inside. She found the orange juice immediately but extended her search for dramatic effect.

"I just have a few questions about that night in the club."

Still not looking at him, she shut the fridge and put the orange juice on the small counter. She flung open a cabinet door and pushed her mismatched glasses around as loudly as possible without breaking them until she found one she liked. "Details was in the next day's papers."

"Actually, outsider details only. No one involved had any comments. All of them said they really didn't remember what happened. Do you remember?"

Attitude flowed from her mouth like the juice she poured into the glass. "Told you cops before. Everybody doin' the bump-n-grind, then went all gansta on each other."

"Can we start from the beginning?"

"Look . . ." she started, but when she turned and got a good view of the detective, she rethought her attitude. He wasn't like any cop she'd seen before. He dressed stylish, like something out of *GQ*. Not only that, he *looked* like a model from *GQ*. He draped his coat over the back of the chair he was about to sit in. A dark blue tie matched his dark blue shirt that struggled to hide the fact that he was built like an athlete, like Darnel. And tall like Darnel. Detective Matthews sat and LaKeisha gave him a good once over. His thick black hair, slicked with styling gel, couldn't have been more perfect with his smooth olive skin, pronounced nose, and set jawline. "Detective *Matthews*? You look Italian."

Matthews felt a wave of heat hit him, surprising since he just removed his jacket. He watched LaKeisha as she walked toward him. Braless, she wore a gray shirt two sizes too small that had the word "bebe" in faux glitter. From shifting and stretching, the middle of the shirt tucked itself under her breasts, clinging to their fullness. Her nipples poked between the loops of the first "B" and second "E" while her tits rippled with every step. She wore tight gray sweat shorts. Matthews could see enough of her jiggling ass to notice the material flowed in and out of her cellulite ridges. Her stretchmark-covered waist remained exposed and drooped a bit over the top of her sweat shorts, bouncing as she walked.

The detective smiled at her comment. "I get that a lot. So, you entered the club. By yourself?"

"Nah. With my girl Camilla." LaKeisha's eyes coated Matthews better than the peeling paint on her walls.

Matthews shifted in his seat while flipping through his notepad. "Talked to her. She was very upset about what she did. She said she didn't even know why she did it."

LaKeisha looked down and scowled. She cracked the knuckles of one hand with her thumb. Damn Camilla. Damn that no good Darnel, too!

A chill ran down Matthew's spine as he felt his brows furrow. He looked around for an air vent. Strange how he went from hot and happy to cold and angry.

Pushing both Camilla and Darnel from her mind, making room for only the fine-looking man in front of her, LaKeisha looked back to Matthews. "It's nuthin'. Maybe she lost her groove with the two guys she was gettin' nasty with?"

The heat and happiness returned to Matthews. Not even realizing it came from within, he looked around for air vents again. "About that. Was there any warning that it was going to become a full-blown orgy?"

"Nah. Just happened."

"And it didn't surprise you?"

"Yeah. It was crazy. But I jus' thought it was one of them type of clubs, ya know?"

Matthews' mouth went dry, and he found it difficult to swallow. The tips of his fingers and toes burned. An erection formed and he had no idea why. By the time he realized that his judgment had slipped away, he had no sense to stop it. "So . . . what did *you* do?"

LaKeisha's heartbeat quickened. Just thinking about what she did, how she had touched herself like that in public, made her cheeks warm. Blood pumped through her whole body, but she only felt throbbing between her legs, remembering the hard-bodied men getting busy with the beat of the music and the heat of the night. She looked at the detective through heavy eyes and said, "I jerked off."

Detective Matthews awoke to the sound of sirens. He opened his eyes to see the cracked ceiling of a dark room, lit only by the outside streetlights. A pillow was under his head, and a flimsy sheet covered his naked body.

What the fuck happened?!

His training prepared him for situations like this. Not *specifically* this, but unexpected situations. No panicking. Deep breaths. He didn't seem to be in danger, so he took the time to understand his environment. He was in a bed and heard snoring. He saw an explosion of kinky hair on the pillow next to him and the body of a naked black woman attached to it. LaKeisha. He was in her bed.

What the hell happened?

His dick let him know immediately with a dull, steady ache as he rolled on his side. A full bladder kicked his gut to the beat of his heart. He felt the salty coating of dried sweat over his body as he sat up. The taste in his mouth and the smell of his breath confirmed it. He certainly didn't need to be a detective to figure out what happened.

How did this happen?

Matthews weighed the pros and cons of trying to use her bathroom to piss and wash his face before he left but decided against it. She snored away now, but he didn't want to risk blowing his chance of sneaking out. He found his pants and put them on. He grabbed the rest of his clothes and shoes and walked out her bedroom door. The clock on her wall read 12:45. Over twelve hours since he arrived. No wonder his dick hurt!

How did this happen?

Matthews put his shoes on in the living room and shirt on in the hallway. He received a few stares along the way, people wandering the halls here and there, either leaving or heading to one of the apartments with thumping music. Shaking his head as if it helped shake away the cobwebs covering his memories, he fought hard to recall the past twelve hours. At her table, asking her questions. He thought her clothes showed too much of her body, needing some time at the local gym. Then . . . then he *wanted* her. Something primal made him jump her. He remembered grabbing at her, trying to tear her clothes off while tearing his own clothes off. On the kitchenette floor. His tongue in her mouth, her ass in his hands. On the couch. Her thighs squeezing his waist. On the living room floor. Their hands grabbing at each other. In the bathroom. Her thighs against his face. In her bed. He still couldn't recall any moment, just random pictures from a perverted photo album.

How did it happen? Matthews chuckled. He knew it was her. That was why he visited her in the first place. Despite his desire to take an hour-long shower with a wire brush, it made perfect sense. As did the orgy at the club and then the sudden riot.

Matthews pulled out his cell phone as he exited the building. "It's Matthews. Yeah, LaRue. I think we can really use this one. Move her to number two on the list . . ."

CHAPTER
37

Harrisburg, Pennsylvania

Marvin watched as his guests looked around his office like tourists in a new city. Only two offices in the building were bigger: the executive vice president's and the president's. Marvin would occupy them soon enough and had started his day formulating plans on how to do that. However, these guests provided an interesting distraction that might even expedite the ladder-climbing process.

Emma and Derrick gawked open-mouthed, never dreaming an office could look so luxurious and elegant. Every wall hid doors and shelves that could be opened or moved by remote or Marvin's computer. Half a dozen television screens, all tuned to news and business channels, could play hide-and-seek with one infrared pulse. Even the keyboard and monitor appeared from secret compartments of his cherry wood desk. "The wonder of tomorrow mixed with the wisdom of yesterday," he called it. Michael sneered, not trying to hide his contempt for such ballyhooed excess as demanded by the corporate world.

Not waiting for them to get entirely acclimated, Marvin sat in his throne-like leather high-backed chair and asked, "So, why are we all here?"

Both Derrick and Emma turned to Michael. Apparently, having a doctorate in the English language meant others thought he could speak it well. "Umm . . . well . . . this will sound very strange . . . especially if we're wrong . . . but we think you may have special abilities."

"Special abilities?" Marvin repeated, arching his eyebrows in an effort to make this pompous jerk feel less comfortable.

Michael hated Marvin already. Marvin's condescending stare in this cold museum of decadence made Michael nervous. "Heh. Yeah. We . . . each of us . . . just one day woke up with a new extraordinary ability. And Derrick here has an ability he calls 'vibing,' where he can find other people with these abilities. He found me. And Emma. And his 'vibe' says that you, too, have some sort of . . . special . . . ability . . ."

Nonplussed and impassive, Marvin sat in his chair, hands folded together more for theatrics, staring at Michael with eyes of smoldering coal. Michael fought every urge to fidget or show any other sign of the intimidation he felt. Marvin was just another man in a suit, another rat looking for the most cheese. He wasn't the gym teacher who embarrassed Michael in grade school or the jocks who teased him in middle school or his father who belittled his liking of classic literature in high school. *Don't be nervous.* Marvin was just another man. *Don't blush.* Marvin was just another man. *Don't sweat.*

Marvin's stony face finally cracked when he asked, "So, what exactly is your extraordinary ability?"

"I push things."

"Push? Things?"

"With my mind."

"You mean telekinesis?"

"Limited telekinesis. I can only push."

Marvin fought with his twitching lips, the gatekeepers to the belly laugh locked deep within, begging for freedom. He looked at Michael the way Michael looked at his seven-year-old daughter whenever she went into exasperating nonsense trying to explain how everyday items work, like the television remote or telephone or microwave. The man in the suit slid his desk organizer, a collection of cherrywood cups holding silver-plated pens and pencils, to the edge of his desk. "Okay. Push this."

Michael choked down his hatred for suits, for being in a building full of them, for having one sitting in his smug throne talking down to him. He forced himself to relax, deep breath in through his nose, slow exhale over his lips. Then he saw a small wastebasket, cherrywood as well, the last vestige to the mundane in this office, on the floor next to Marvin's desk.

Warmth built at the base of his neck. He released it. Like snapping a whip, the sensation rolled down his arms and shot from his fingertips, his hands pointing at the pen-pencil holder and base of the trash can. Both jumped in the air; both threw their contents. Paper floated in the air around Marvin, who remained as immobile and indifferent as a plastic figure in a snow globe scene that had been shaken.

Before Marvin could even think of words to express his exasperation and condemn the actions of this guest, disrespectful enough to scatter trash about his hospitality, Emma showed her special ability. She plucked the six writing instruments out of the air, five with her left hand, one with her right. However, she wielded the one in her right hand like a miniature sword, stabbing at the floating papers. Not a one touched the ground. Blocking the flight of the trash can with her knee, it slid to her foot and rested open end up. With a graceful swipe against the side of the wooden trash bin, she scraped the papers from the pen. With a flick of the wrist and a twist of her ankle, she returned three pencils to one cup, three pens to another, and the trash bin to the side of Marvin's desk.

Marvin regarded Emma with a bright smile. "Now, *that* was quite impressive."

"Yep," Michael interjected. "She's now the perfect killing machine."

Emma stabbed Michael with an icy glare, wondering how a man with his social stature could be so insensitive.

Michael rolled his eyes, wondering what the hell he said now to offend her.

Marvin observed their relationships. Derrick and Emma gave him a form of leadership, and he had no idea how to use it. Power was sometimes wasted on those who didn't want it; it was certainly wasted on Michael. Holding his smile steady, he turned to Derrick. "And what is it you can do again?"

"I vibe. That's how I found you. And Michael and Emma. I can also make you hallucinate, but I'm not sure how it works. I don't even know if it's what I'm thinking or what you're thinking or what I think you're thinking."

Marvin chuckled and placed his hands in front of his body, signaling surrender. Not wanting to take the chance of Derrick exposing any secrets, he said, "Whoa! No need for that. After what I've just seen, I certainly believe you."

Derrick blushed as his eyes found his feet, as they so often did when he became nervous. "So . . . um . . . what . . . can you do?"

Marvin's eyes swept over the other three people in his office. They all wore their hearts on their sleeves. His eyes stopped on Michael. He could feel, see, hear, and smell Michael's disdain. He could taste it, bitter medicine Michael forced down Marvin's throat. If not for Michael, he might have told them the truth. But it behooved Marvin to be as guarded as possible, for now. "I'm afraid it's nothing quite so spectacular as you may have hoped. Certainly not as imposing as what you have demonstrated. I have a mild case of the Midas touch when it comes to people."

"You can turn them into gold?" Derrick asked, not realizing how stupid his question sounded until actually spoken.

"I think he means he can fix people," Michael answered. "Heal them. Control them."

Marvin laughed. "Hardly the case, Michael. I can relieve sinus pressure. Dull a headache. Stop the sniffles. As sad as it is to say, I'm merely an efficient and cheap form of cold medicine."

Derrick's disappointment was evident. "We were hoping you'd join us."

Marvin cocked his head as if Derrick spoke a foreign language. "Join you?"

"Since we have these . . . gifts . . . we thought we could, ya know, use them. To help people."

The gates crumbled and Marvin's belly laugh was unleashed. "I do admire your enthusiasm, son, but starting a little do-gooder club certainly isn't for me."

Michael frowned. It was one thing for Michael to belittle Derrick, but it was completely unacceptable for Marvin to attempt such a feat. Typical suit— invites regular people into his world just to belittle and gloat. Michael had half a mind to tell this societal monster to go to hell. However, it was the other half that overruled, intimidated to the point of silence.

Amazed again by Michael's lack of character, Emma realized she would have to be the one to say something to the classless Marvin Carver. Michael sure had no problems belittling old ladies and young men who were unsure of their place in this world, but he showed a surprising lack of backbone when it came to the "suits" he hated so much. "Now, Mr. Carver, was that necessary?"

Marvin wiped a tear from his eye as he finally stopped laughing. "No, no. You're absolutely correct, Emma. Derrick, I apologize for my indiscretion. I must admit I'm a little overwhelmed by all of this."

"That's okay," Derrick said, head hanging low.

Marvin checked his Rolex, making sure everyone saw this action. With a press of a button on his phone, he summoned his administrative assistant. "I must again apologize—I have an upcoming meeting I cannot cancel."

Upon finishing his sentence, the door opened. In walked a frumpy-looking kid, about Derrick's age. His hair was neatly styled, but his clothes didn't fit his partially doughy body too well. And a couple teeth were missing. *He could be a good-looking kid if he'd hit the gym*, Michael thought.

"This is Colby," Marvin continued, standing. "He's my admin assistant. He'll show you out and collect your contact information from you. I do appreciate you coming. Although I don't believe I'm what you're looking for, I will certainly stay in contact."

Pleasant farewells were exchanged and the door shut.

Marvin sat in his chair and closed his eyes. He reviewed each of their road-maps, one at a time, never examining too much at once, as if savoring a rare and forbidden delicacy. He reviewed the synaptic connections of Derrick's brain. He peeled away layer after layer of Emma's nerve bundles, examining the way they interacted. He learned how Michael's brainwaves mixed with his body's natural electrical pulses to create his unique "pushing" abilities. Then he felt something else, a tickle in his mind, an afterthought he almost discarded. Finding this piece of information useless, he passed over it as he reviewed Derrick's roadmap. He ignored it again in Emma. But Michael had it, too. As did Marvin.

Rarely Marvin wondered how he received his incredible abilities; any time such thoughts crept into his mind, he pushed them out with the sprouting of new hair follicles or loss of old fat cells. He knew enough about addiction to know that a true alcoholic didn't care where his booze came from, as long as he had it in his hands. But this new information irritated Marvin, stuck in his mind like a mote in his eye. He found something he could no longer ignore. It went beyond coincidence.

He discovered a unifying factor that connected all four of them . . .

CHAPTER
38

Near State College, Pennsylvania

This is it, Adam thought. Perched high in a treetop, he watched Nora and Samson stroll through the forest, dozens of forest creatures in tow. *This is my life now.*

Adam lost all sense of time since he awoke as this abomination, this circus sideshow lizard-snake-boy freak, and ran from the farm. Two months? Two months since he killed his father? Two months since his personal apocalypse?

With the inherited grace of a lizard, Adam scurried down the tree a bit and leaped to another tree, then another, staying a little ahead of Nora and Samson. He watched them. The world had ended and only Adam knew it. An emptiness gnawed at his insides as he realized Nora and Samson were the new, twisted Adam and Eve.

Adam should be thankful for Samson's arrival. The lizard-snake-boy felt little comfort around the naked Asian girl from the first moment he met her. She was weird, or so he first thought. But with the discovery of Samson, Adam learned at least once a day how deep her sickness truly went. How else could he describe her? Her willingness to be . . . taken . . . by a mutated cat-creature? A knot twisted in Adam's gut as he thought about all the times that she had touched his scaled skin in promiscuous ways, her hands sliding around his face, chest, and between his legs. Would he have had relations with her if he still had a method? Would he care about finding other half-animal creatures like himself if he could be with Nora in the same capacity as Samson? The knot in his stomach untied itself, replaced by chills squirming up and down his spine as he wondered about his pain—disgust for the unnatural acts committed by Nora and Samson every day or jealousy?

He crouched, perched in the treetop, a declaration of his defiance, alone if not for the snakes to keep him company. They hung from him like drooping clothing, squirming strands of drapery. Most flowed along his body, up then down, down then up, as a form of companionship. At first, Adam thought Nora forced them to like him, but now he could feel the inherent kinship between himself and the snakes.

He watched as Nora and Samson made their way closer to the tree where he and his slithering brethren were perched. Instinctively, the snakes tightened their grip on the lizard-snake-boy. He bounded from one tree to another, again putting some distance between himself and his companions shuffling along the forest floor, stopping at a tree infested with box-elder bugs. After he ate her favorite raccoon, Nora had been mad at him, so he deemed it wise to stay away from her for a while. Box-elder bugs made great snacks for him and his legless companions.

Watching the snakes snap up the bugs with red bodies and black wings, looking like fireflies without the affable glow, Adam realized that they were his only friends, his family now. He wondered how his human family fared. If his mom could forgive him. She believed in the word of the Lord more than any person he knew, but the act of accepting his serpent form and slaying his father seemed unforgivable. And his siblings? Would they understand? What did they know about the loss of their father and oldest brother? What were they telling their friends at school? Yes, life had ended for Adam two months ago, and it was indeed an apocalypse only he knew about. The world didn't end with nuclear fire or rampant disease or any of the four horsemen. It ended with mysterious green scales, an Asian girl with ink-black eyes, and an ill-mannered cat-creature on a futile trek to . . . where?

Adam peeled back a piece of bark to reveal a squirming patch of grubs. He flicked his tongue and caught two dozen squirming bugs. With another flick, he snatched another dozen box-elders from a patch of the tree a sunbeam warmed. His brethren joined in the feast.

As box-elders flowed across the tree and grubs poured from the trunk, Adam noticed a nearby branch as thick as his arm was dead. Exerting little effort, he snapped it off, sending it crashing to the forest floor after smashing against other branches on the way down. But his suspicions were correct—the hollowed, dried branch contained more food. A nest of earwigs oozed from the new hole, as if the tree itself bled. A chill ran down Adam's spine. The earwigs aimed right for him.

Out of instinct, he backed away, although he couldn't fathom why since his skin was thick enough to dispel any bites or stings. The same instinct dictated the snakes regroup close to him. He found the earwigs' actions odd—prey, even having a bug's brain, never ran toward a predator.

Adam then noticed the box-elders and grubs, both sets of insects swarming toward him and the snakes. The grubs crawled across his clawed hands while the box-elders flew around his face, throwing themselves into his eyes and nostrils. Eyes closed, his tongue whipped in and out of his mouth as he tried to get his bearings, but he caught a thick coating of bugs with every flick. He felt the earwigs cover his feet and move up his legs, hundreds of pincers trying to pierce his skin. More than a few were successful.

Tail flailing and arms swinging spastically, he danced around on the thick branch. But being blinded, with panic taking over, made his situation less enviable. His foot slipped. He couldn't adjust his awkward body. He blindly reached for the branch, for anything, as he fell.

Snapping a few branches on the way down, he landed with an impact that made Nora's teeth rattle. She and Samson ran to the squirming lizard-snake-boy. Quick to his feet, he cleared his eyes with one hand while slapping random places on his body with his other.

"What the hell's wrong with you, boy?" Samson asked, his cat face doing little to hide contempt and confusion.

Nora smacked Samson's arm with the back of her hand, then ran over to Adam. "What's wrong, Adam. What's going on?"

"Bugsss," Adam replied. He stopped slapping himself, but his heart still raced as he examined his arms and legs.

Laughter exploded from Samson. "Bugs? Big, bad snake boy is afraid of bugs? I thought you ate them for snacks?"

A deep rumble from Adam's throat accompanied a deeper glare from his eyes. His thick lips curled up to reveal saliva-slicked teeth running the length of his snout. Then he felt Nora's soothing hands on his scales and her fingertips gliding over his arm. For the first time since meeting the cat-person, Nora came to Adam's defense. "Shut up, Samson. He does have quite a few bites. More than what would be natural."

Nora then crouched to examine Adam's legs. Squashed earwigs and grubs and box-elders coated his shins and calves. Using a handful of dead leaves, Nora wiped them off his legs to reveal more bite marks. "Adam, what happened?"

"Sssswarmed . . . at me. Sssomething'sss . . . not right."

"No. Not at all." Nora stood back up and slowly scanned the forest. She used the eyes and ears of nearby animals. Her heart raced as she jumped from mind to mind, from robin to deer to squirrel to snake. One patch of forest remained out of her reach, a patch of forest all the animals avoided. "Something is very wrong. This way. It's not far."

The naked Asian girl grabbed Adam's hand and started walking toward the anomaly. The stings of Adam's bite wounds subsided as a comforting warmth returned to his heart. He was back in her good graces. Not as he had hoped, but enough.

"Wait a minute!" Samson yelled. "You just said 'something is very wrong,' and now we're walking *toward* the something that is very wrong?"

Adam looked back at Samson, and his lizard-snake face did little to hide his contempt and confusion, and said, "Pusssy."

It was Samson's turn to growl and bare his teeth, but neither Adam nor Nora took notice as they continued forward. Samson had little choice but to follow . . .

CHAPTER
39

Harrisburg, Pennsylvania

Marvin stared at the empty 16-ounce Starbucks cup on his desk. It wasn't working. He even removed the cardboard sleeve, and still nothing. He stared harder, frowning to the point of a headache. Why the hell didn't it work?

For over a week, Marvin followed the roadmaps. Or tried to, at least. He saw how Michael's brain worked, how it produced the "push." But Marvin couldn't duplicate it. He shifted his brain cells, moved them to be more efficient, rewired them to produce the staggering brain waves needed, and tapped into the parts evolution forgot about to create the necessary electrical pulse. He made that part of his brain just like Michael's, following every twist and turn the map had to offer. Nothing.

Frustration grew. Marvin even held his hands out, mimicking what Michael did during his initial demonstration. He stared. He concentrated. He frowned and gnashed his teeth. Holding his breath, he squeezed every bit of energy he had into this task; every vein and artery pulsed louder and harder with each beat of his heart. He heard his blood swish through his ears as warmth built at the base of his neck. Releasing the warmth, it flowed down his arm and through his fingertips. The cup shimmied, but only because he had huffed a harsh breath of frustration at it.

Trying to accomplish at least one goal, travel down at least one road to the final destination using these new roadmaps, he grabbed his silver-sheathed pens and pencils, three of each. Replicating the same electricity he felt in Emma, his fingers and toes tingled. Synapses fired faster. Nerve endings cracked like whips. The world moved slower. A photographer couldn't capture images crisper or clearer. Marvin juggled all six objects with ease. Each object had perfect spin with every throw and felt balanced with every catch. Knowing the capabilities of the old woman, he tried to replicate her actions. A small water stain blemished his pristine ceiling near where he sat, and he knew Emma could drive all six writing instruments through it. He wanted to do the same. However, as soon as he took his eyes off the flowing circle of silver, he lost control. Bobbling the pens and pencils, they bounced off his desk and floor, leaving only one in each hand. He looked at the stain but couldn't target it. He threw the remaining two out of anger rather than controlled precision, hitting the ceiling nowhere near the stain.

Seething, Marvin ran his hands through his thick head of hair, a new nervous habit he never wanted to remedy. Pretty sure he didn't want to make himself hallucinate, and not sure what the hell "vibing" even meant, Marvin explored Derrick's roadmap no further than a cursory glance. But even with that, he felt the same thing—a roadblock.

He didn't want to admit it, but now he saw little reason in avoiding such admission. Something was blocking him, something kept him from performing the same actions he had witnessed a week ago. Something blocking . . . or something lacking? Was he missing a piece of the puzzle? Did they have something he didn't? That was ludicrous since he had a special ability himself. Maybe he had something? Maybe it was something they all had?

Marvin sat back in his chair, the weight of his body tilting it back. Time for some meditation. He closed his eyes and inhaled slowly. He focused on his breathing, then his heartbeat. He visualized a tour through his bloodstream, visiting muscles and organs along the way. His body sang to him and he listened. Like a quality-checker on an assembly line, he compared his internal workings to the other roadmaps he had on file. He imagined holding his heart in one hand while holding Colby's in his right, his lungs in his left hand, and Barb's in his right. One at a time, he looked at his organs against all the others he had stored in his memory. Nothing. Then again, he had no idea what he was looking for, and the human body had billions of hiding places. He needed help.

Turning to his computer, he pulled up the address book in his Outlook and found the one name he wanted. Michael Roseman. He tapped a button on his phone, and the dial-tone hummed through the speaker, filling his office. Soon after came the beeps from dialing, three rings, and a disoriented, "Hello?"

"Michael?" Marvin asked, smiling a fake smile to sound convincing. "This is Marvin. How are you today?"

"Who?"

"Marvin Carver. We met a little more than a week ago when you, Derrick, and . . ."

"Okay, okay, okay. I remember . . . am I on speakerphone?"

"I just wanted to talk to you about—"

"Why am I on speakerphone?"

"I don't think that's important. I wanted to talk—"

"Is there anyone else there with you?"

When he first met Michael, Marvin knew the professor disliked the corporate world. But he had no idea the level of paranoia he would be dealing with. Gaining a new appreciation for the customer service reps who had to deal with the general public every day, Marvin massaged his temples. "No, Michael. There's no one here with me."

"Then why am I on speakerphone?"

Was this guy for real? Marvin rolled his eyes and stifled a laugh, wondering how this lunatic made it through day-to-day life. He picked up the headset. "Here we go. This better?"

"Much. Thank you. So, to what do I owe the pleasure?"

"I've given some thought about our abilities. Our common bond that makes us unique—"

"Hold on." Growing weary of getting repeatedly cut off, Marvin heard rustling noises, guessing Michael had put down a newspaper of some sort. He heard Michael's muffled footsteps and then finally a door shutting. "Okay. I've moved to a different room. We can talk now."

Marvin rolled his eyes. "Good to know."

"Now, what is it again you want to talk about?"

"Our abilities, Michael. What do you know about them?"

"Nothing."

"Have you done any research?"

"No. Derrick and Emma are more interested in this than I am. I'd rather not do what I do and just move on with life. You should call one of them."

"A religious nut and a flake? No, thank you."

"Hey! Derrick's a good kid. A bit . . . off . . . but a good kid nonetheless."

Gritting his teeth, Marvin apologized. "Sorry. What I meant was you and I are family men closer in age. In fact, let's do dinner with our wives."

"What?"

"This Friday."

"I can't . . . we can't . . ."

"This Saturday, then."

"Umm?"

"Next Friday."

"Okay." Marvin could hear the frustration in Michael's voice. The professor undoubtedly agreed just to get him to stop firing days at him. It didn't matter why he accepted, just as long as he did. Marvin needed to touch Michael again, needed to review the roadmap again.

"Wonderful. I'll have Colby call you later this week with directions to my house."

"Uhh . . ."

Click.

What an ordeal! Marvin thinned his blood, dilated his sinuses, and numbed a few nerve endings to get rid of his headache. Once refreshed, he stood and walked out of his office to look at his employees, all hunched at their desks scouring pages of numbers because of their addictions to being in the office. *Time to make a few more million*, Marvin thought . . .

CHAPTER
40

Near State College, Pennsylvania

As the sun set, pre-twilight rays cast eerie shadows about the forest. Trees loomed as stray vines reached their tangled fingers to snatch the souls of unsuspecting victims. A slight breeze pushed through the treetops, causing an itchy rustle through the leaves and making the tall trunks creak and groan. The foreboding forest prepared itself for a sinister night, and Adam could smell it in the air.

The young man certainly enjoyed being back in Nora's good graces, but at what cost? He remained by her side as they skulked into a small patch of forest through which no animal dared to venture. Every animal Nora commanded refused to cross the invisible border; even the birds flew out of their way to avoid it.

As soon as the trio crossed the line, a sense of dread reached inside of Adam and squeezed his heart. His stomach clenched and his breath became labored. They should flee; Adam knew it. Even Samson felt it. The cat-creature's fur bristled thick and full as his eyes darted from tree to bush to rock, searching for the unknown danger he felt with his very soul. But Nora pressed on, and so did Adam and Samson.

As quietly as the leaves and twigs on the ground allowed, the three interlopers crept forward. A breeze whispered through the trees, carrying the scent of decay and rot. Samson and Adam exchanged a look as they smelled it, their new animal instincts telling them to run away. Samson's wet nostrils flared and then contracted with each breath. Adam's tongue involuntarily flicked in and out of his mouth, looking for more pleasant tastes in the air.

The threesome slinked from behind one tree to the next. The silence unnerved them—no animal noises, not even a stray bird chirp. All they heard was their own heartbeats with such ferocity they each swore it was someone else's. Then a break in the trees revealed their goal—a ramshackle cabin.

Once it came into view, the girl and her two monsters stopped and shared looks of concern; would the girl's monsters be more frightening than what scared the forest's animals away from this unassuming cabin? They pressed on despite instinct and common sense telling them to turn and forget all about it. Turn and continue living in blissful ignorance. Turn and continue their quest to find other man-creatures. All three knew it was too late when they heard a familiar tune glide through the air. A twangy banjo carried forth an ominous warning.

Deh—de—deng—deng deng-dengggg.

Of the three, only Samson had seen *Deliverance*. His ass cheeks clenched while his fingers spread, readying his claws. Bursts of fear exploded in his heart with every step, every inch closer to the cabin. The warning came again, the second part of the duel in the form of whistling.

Twe—t—twee-twee twee-tweeeeee.

The girl and her creature-men moved on. She hoped they would be strong enough to protect her. Adam shared the same hope, while Samson hoped he would be fast enough to escape whatever danger lurked around this cabin. Still, they crept closer. Closer to the cabin. Closer to the whistling. Closer to what had been spooking the animals of the region. Close enough to hear the creaking of a rocking chair on a squeaky wooden porch. Close enough to almost jump out of their skin when they heard an old man's voice break the silence. "Y'uns can stop creepin' aroun' back there."

The trio stopped, once again looking at each other, hoping anyone had an answer or even a plan. Then the old man spoke again. "Yeah, y'uns three. Come on 'round front."

The three did as instructed but still clung to caution even though desperation gnawed at the pits of their stomachs. As they walked around the side of the cabin to the front, they saw exactly what they thought they'd see—an old man in a rocking chair with banjo in hand. His long, stringy hair and beard were supposed to be gray with various shades of white, but instead, they both looked yellow, unwashed for a very long time. Without a shirt on, his emaciated torso didn't look human, his hair-covered chest didn't move with his hairy belly when he breathed, accentuating what looked like deep scars from his sternum along the bottom of his rib cage.

As Nora walked into his view, the old man set his banjo on the porch and shifted in his seat, making room in his loose pants for his newly formed erection. "Daaaaaaamn! Y'er a sweet thing up close! I thought my eyes were goin' wacky on me, seein' a Chink walkin' 'round the forest nekkid."

Nora noticed that his scars weren't scars, but folds of skin, bugs crawling in and out from under the folds. Ants and earwigs and termites crawled out from his ribs and down his legs while flies and wasps and box-elders flew out from the same flaps of skin. "See, I been watching y'uns three for some time now. An' I been hopin' you'd come visit."

"Visit?" Nora asked, her eyes trying to follow all the bugs clamoring from under the old man's skin. "You wanted us to come here? Why?"

The old man squinted at her as his dry tongue scraped across his peeling lips. "Shit, girl, you can't be dumb. I want you. I figure if a girl like you is willin' to take it from a freaky cat-thing, then you'd be up for just 'bout anytin'."

The lechery in his voice rippled through Nora's mind. She tried to reach out for help, her mind searching for animals to protect her, but she couldn't concentrate. Every time she found a bear or feral dog or mountain lion, she'd see the flow of insects pour out from the old man's skin and lose her connection with the animal. Her skin crawled, and her fingers went cold as her stomach went sour. She began to panic.

Both Adam and Samson moved in front of her, standing between her and potential harm. However, Samson continued advancing. Snarling, he bared his teeth and gums. "Fuck off!"

"I'm afraid I can't do that, boy," the old man replied, standing from his rocking chair. He didn't look imposing until his ribs split away from his body along the seams that produced the insects. Still connected to the top of his sternum, his flesh-covered ribs hinged outward like the opening carapace of a beetle. Three-foot-long insect wings unfurled and thrummed, lifting his whole body in the air. There he hovered, only his spine wrapped in skin connected his shoulders to his hips. His protruding belly quickly deflated, the skin flopped over his belt buckle, and it released the remainder of the bugs he housed.

Disgusted but unimpressed with the sign of aggression, Samson attacked. With the roar of a wildcat, he bounded forward, his claws begging to slice into the creepy old man. So focused, he didn't see the cabin shake.

The wood creaked and the roof shifted, as if the small house stretched after waking up from a nap. It hummed and buzzed. As if popping a boil, a column of living black burst from the window closest to Samson.

Millions of insects slammed into Samson, stopping him mid-leap. A chitinous tidal wave swept Samson backward. Insects bit and burrowed through his fur as they swarmed for his eyes, ears, and mouth. With a howling hiss, Samson spat in pain as he pounced to his feet and bounded away, leaving Adam and Nora alone.

"Nora . . . run!" Adam yelled to the naked girl, who would stand no chance if the swarm turned its attention toward her. She did as instructed, sprinting the opposite way Samson ran. Adam had to buy her some more time and could only think of one thing to do, even though he knew the outcome.

As fast as his serpentine muscles allowed, he rushed toward the old man, now cackling in amusement. Befalling a similar fate as his companion, Adam was knocked out of the air by the swarm. The force of impact squished hundreds of bugs against his skin, and his body left an indent in the ground. His tongue whipped around, not an inch of it without a buzzing insect glued to it. He snapped to his feet, his hands swiping against his face, hopelessly trying to create a pocket of air for a quick breath. No luck. Eyes closed, he leaped straight up. Just enough distance separated him from the swarm to take a quick peek, finding a sturdy tree nearby.

Adam jumped to the tree, clinging to it. He paused to open his eyes again and was punished. The swarm slammed into him again, crushing him against the bark. He pushed and jumped, blindly waving his arms, hoping to catch a nearby tree. Success! This time he took no pause before he jumped again, barely cracking his eyelids to find the next tree. Then the next. And again. He fled further and higher with every leap.

Panic finally subsided when he noticed the swarm no longer pursued. Tongue flopping free, he panted as he looked around the forest, forty feet from the ground. He lost sight of the cabin. And he prayed he gave Nora enough time to escape . . .

CHAPTER
41

Harrisburg, Pennsylvania

Michael navigated his Ford Explorer through the ornate metal arch with the words "Madison Manor" scrawled across the top, faux-iron ivy vines twisting their way over the whole structure. Michael had no doubt that the developer named the "manor" after his daughter. He followed the GPS directions that guided him through streets named after the rest of the developer's family, from Tanner Drive to Pamela Road, finally stopping on Timothy Drive. Claire sat in the passenger seat, as quiet as a leopard poised to pounce, and took in the scenery.

So new, none of the homes even had lawns yet; minimal sprigs of grass poked through the crisscrossing straws of hay, blanketing plots of dirt. Those who owned the bulky houses concerned themselves more with hurrying the contractors to finish with the most square footage rather than landscaping. Soon enough, they would continue to compete with each other by bringing in the trendiest and most expensive landscape design firms possible.

Both Michael and Claire thought the houses in this neighborhood lacked soul. What the houses lacked in angles and flare, they certainly made up for in windows and decorative brick, the newest trend in homes. Boxes with roofs, each house boasted a unique pattern of windows and an ostentatious collection of brick. Some facings contained individually handcrafted stones, while other houses used bricks imported from South American countries. The affluence of prosperity washed Michael away.

"So," Claire started, still looking out the passenger side window. She turned her head just enough to look at Michael and show him a wry smirk. "Any other secrets you've been keeping?"

Her smirk worried him; he wasn't sure if she was joking around or enjoying herself by making his guts twist and turn. Her smirk looked awfully knowing, ready to trap him in his web of secrets. Michael chuckled, trying to play it cool, huffing a puff of air out his nose. "What do you mean?"

"Investment manager? That's *so* against your character." Her smirk stayed, and her lips parted slowly as she spoke, showing her teeth, a shark smiling at a fattened seal.

"Just trying to take more interest in our finances. Wanted to explore other avenues and learn about different types of resources available." Michael willed himself not to sweat, not to show any sign of fear.

"You do realize investment managers invest in *corporations*, don't you? The very foundation of everything you stand against?" Michael loved Claire with all his heart. He courted her for a few years and then took a vow to love her and only her. However, during moments like this, she looked like a piranha with lipstick.

"What? It's not like any human being can escape the influence and products of corporations. This will give me a better understanding of which companies do what and which are worse than others."

"Still sounds a little suspicious to me."

"One of my students recommended this guy. I gave him a call, and he invited us over for dinner. What's suspicious about that?" Michael punched himself on the inside, knowing never, ever to ask his lawyer wife a question in an argument, even if he wasn't entirely sure if they were arguing.

"Well, now that you ask—how about the fact that Professor 'Just-Give-Me-Tenure' is listening to and communicating with his students. I mean, you sure have been spending a lot of time with them. Very secretively, too, I might add."

Red flags, red lights, and sirens went off in his mind. He saw an opportunity to shift the argument, still uncertain if that was what they were doing, even though he knew he shouldn't. "No more time than you spend at your book appreciation club." He saw her smile fade, but too much momentum had built up to keep himself from stopping. "Are there any secrets you're keeping from me?"

An average husband would have realized he struck a nerve. A corporation-hating husband of a lawyer wouldn't be able to see that due to his thanking God, the stars, and nature that she didn't rip his throat out with her teeth. Michael held his breath, waiting for her response, and breathed an internal sigh of relief as she opened the door. "Let's go meet our potential investment manager."

Michael followed Claire to the front door of the behemoth that sat at 5 Timothy Drive. He knew he shouldn't do this, especially after narrowly escaping a pseudo-argument with his vicious wife, but he couldn't keep his eyes

off her ass. Her jeans shaped it perfectly, accentuating the curve of her hips
and allowing the world to see that three hours on the StairMaster every week
benefited its user. He wanted to just reach out and grab it right now, or pinch
it at the very least, and . . .

"Hey, Warren Buffet," Claire interrupted as she pressed the doorbell button. "Think you can take your eyes off my ass long enough to fetch our paperwork that you forgot?"

Michael looked at his empty hands, then back at the SUV. He jogged over
to the vehicle and retrieved the manila folder of bank and broker statements.
By the time he made it back to the door, it had been answered and Claire
welcomed in. Feeling every bit the daft dolt, Michael rang the doorbell. The
door opened before Michael pulled his finger from the button. Then all color
fled from his face.

It had been seventeen years ago, a time when Michael's boyhood was giving
way to his manhood. Every memory of every day of a summer internship seventeen years ago came crashing through his mind, a tsunami against a mountain.
Her. She stood before him now as she did seventeen years ago. Surprisingly,
she looked just as young now as she did then; her skin actually seemed fresher
and healthier. And her body now! Seventeen years ago, she was rail thin, but
today! Michael could tell that she was pregnant, but she still had hips and tits a
Victoria's Secret model would kill for.

Michael looked into her eyes and saw the same woman he had met seventeen years ago. "Thelma?"

Thelma took a step back to get a better look at the man who seemed to
know her. She looked him up and down, but it was his eyes that gave him away,
his eyes that broke down the door that barricaded the one room in her mind she
hadn't visited for seventeen years. She whispered, "Michael?"

Upon realization, a sappy smile slid across his face. "Yes. Thelma, it's
been . . ."

"Oh, my God," she whispered, her voice quaking in fear. Her supple skin
turned pale and clammy. Her bottom lip quivered as she backed away, her eyes
welling with tears. "Oh, God, no."

"Whoa, Thelma, it's okay," Michael whispered, catching on that this was a
secret she hoped never to reveal to her husband. "I won't say anything. Promise."

Her retreating stopped. Wiping away her tears, she smiled. "Oh, I'm so
sorry, Michael. I didn't mean to react that way. I feel so silly."

"Don't be. It's okay. We all have our secrets."

Color returned to her cheeks, and her smile hid any evidence that the two of them had met before. "Yes, I know. Marvin's told me all about your little secret."

Taken aback by her comment, Michael used his smile to hide his true feelings. "I won't tell if you won't."

"Deal."

Michael hid behind his smile most of the evening. From the pleasant introductions to hors d'oeuvres of pinwheels and bacon-wrapped scallops to a fine pre-cocktail. Michael found these situations rather comforting. He always found hiding behind pompous veneers much more appealing than expressing any form of feelings to strangers while wasting conversation hunting for theirs. He loved college functions and charity events, and this situation was no different, just with fewer participants.

Pretentiousness was a subtle dance, not one for amateurs. One mistake in footwork could prove fatal, or worse—embarrassing. Michael found an able partner in Marvin. Much to the professor's surprise, the suit kept up his end of the conversation on topics of literature and history but not enough to challenge Michael's expertise. However, Marvin displayed a vast knowledge of science and world politics, but Michael kept an admirable pace due to participating in similar conversations at similar soirées. The two men put on quite the show for their wives, exchanging pats on the back and fake laughs. Feeling comfortable enough to leave the women alone, they slipped into a different room.

Grilling Michael past the point of discomfort, Marvin asked if he, Emma, or Derrick had discussed the possible origins of their abilities. Again, Michael had to stress that he didn't want the ability to "push," nor did he want to talk about it. He was perfectly content leading a "push"-free life with his wife and daughter. If he couldn't get rid of his ability, he'd do his best to ignore it. However, Marvin kept digging for information until dinner.

Michael made it through the meal without killing Marvin. Although the suit discussed investment strategies with Michael and Claire, he took every opportunity to jibe against the professor with comments about trust and security. After the meal, they retired to the den for a sherry.

Claire sat next to Michael on a plush loveseat, crossed her legs, and sipped her drink. "Please forgive me for prying, Thelma, but how many months are you along? You are by far the most radiant soon-to-be mother I have ever seen."

Placing both hands on her protruding belly, Thelma smiled. "If you're going to compliment me every time you ask a question, then, by all means, pry away! We're at five months now with triplets."

A look of genuine shock struck Claire. "Triplets! My God, woman, I had a miserable enough time with one child when I was at five months."

"I remember," Michael slipped in. "You were sweating nonstop."

"I was performing the greatest miracle a human being could perform, and the only memory you have is of me perspiring? No wonder nature entrusted women with the task," Claire replied with an exaggerated eye roll that elicited laughter from all four people. "Seriously, Thelma, you look marvelous."

Patting her belly again, Thelma said. "You're far too kind."

"Any other children?" Michael asked, admiring the nutty aftertaste of his cordial. After his question, he raised the glass to his lips for more.

"None. These will be our first," Marvin answered, his voice carrying the pride of an expecting father.

"Wonderful," Claire said. "And how long have you two been married?"

"Twenty years," Marvin and Thelma said, both of their voices ringing with joy.

Michael gasped as the sherry touched his lips, his violent inhale pulling the alcohol too fast, splashing the back of his throat. He coughed, his whole body convulsing as his lungs fought to expel the violating liquid.

Embarrassed, Claire reached over and patted his back. She tried to make light of the situation. "Not used to drinking such a fine wine, dear?"

In between gulps of air, Michael squeezed out, "We gotta go."

"But—" Claire started.

"No. We really gotta go," Michael worked in between coughs.

After Claire took care of the goodbyes since Michael didn't have the physical capacity to do so, she took him by the arm and escorted him back to their Explorer. Not so coincidentally, Michael's coughing fit ended.

"What was *that* about?" Claire asked as they shut the car doors.

"Remember that internship I had seventeen years ago? The one—"

"The one where an older woman showed you some affection and you became a slutty whore for a summer? Yeah?"

"Thelma was that woman."

Claire laughed. "So? That was seventeen years ago? What's the big deal?"

"And how long were they married?"

"Twenty . . . *oh*. So, that makes you a *dirty* slutty whore."

"Yeah, thanks."

"Okay, so what's the worst that can happen?"

What indeed? Michael thought, fighting off an ominous chill while glancing one last time at Marvin's ostentatious house before driving away . . .

CHAPTER
42

Near State College, Pennsylvania

Adam leaped from one oak tree to another, then froze. Thanks to his reptilian physiology, clinging to the rough bark took little effort. He didn't move, watching and listening as the forest settled from his minor disruption. He inhaled through his nostrils—old habits die hard. Creating a new habit, he flicked his tongue, tasting the entire world in a second. Nothing. He sprung to another tree, repeating the process.

It had been an hour since his encounter with the old cottage dweller and his bevy of bugs. An hour since he last saw Nora. His search was slow and methodical, but he couldn't risk being discovered.

Images of the fight—if he could even call it that—kept flashing through his mind between leaps. Did he give Nora enough time to escape? He wished he had been better prepared. But how *could* he have been? Wanting to flog himself for not trusting his animal instincts, he wondered if that would have been enough? Samson felt it too, though, yet did nothing either. He proved to be nothing more than a coward, running off when faced with the slightest hint of danger. Slightest hint? Samson did get blindsided by a swarm of millions of drones. And Adam also ran from the same "slightest hint" of danger. Was he as big a coward as Samson? No, no, he must not think like that—at least *he* tried to protect Nora, tried to help her flee.

A chill ran down Adam's spine as he thought about Nora's safety. He felt her. He didn't know how, but he felt her inside him. His heart, his mind. He couldn't read her thoughts or see where she was, but he felt her. So, she must, at the very least, still be alive. But was she okay? Hurt? It would have been difficult to outrun any number of insects, even with her unique ability to get animals to do her bidding. Even if she had sent dozens of forest creatures to their doom to protect her, which she would *never* do, the odds of a naked young woman surviving a swarm that vicious, unscathed, seemed insurmountable. But Adam knew she was alive, and he kept looking.

Continuing with caution, he pounced from tree to tree. Not only did he not know where to go, but he had also forgotten where *not* to go. Blind during his harrowing escape, Adam lost all sense of direction. He had no idea where the cabin was and wouldn't know unless he stumbled upon it again. He couldn't trust his instincts at the moment, the animal feelings of impending danger, because his adrenaline *still* coursed through his body, keeping him at an elevated level of paranoia. *Everything* seemed dangerous now, everywhere, at every moment. But he kept moving.

All was quiet and Adam jumped again. He developed a rhythm: jump, wait, flick tongue, repeat. Even though he remained vigilant, the pattern soothed him. Jump, wait, flick tongue, repeat. Jump, wait, flick . . . what?

His right hand tickled. He looked to see it covered in ants, caterpillars, and earwigs. A squirming glove made from waves of insects, rising then falling in on themselves as they crawled up his arm. Shaking his arm, he launched himself, skittering from tree to tree. As if in a convulsion, he used his other arm to smack and slap the insects away until his right arm turned bug-free. Whatever calm he had found in the past few minutes died, splattered with the insects on his scaly arm. A nervous volcano erupted deep within, spewing adrenaline throughout his body.

Continuing to move, Adam took less time between leaps. That insect conglomeration was not natural. That old man might be nearby, and if not, he certainly knew Adam's location. *Keep moving*, Adam thought. *Just keep moving*.

Just when Adam felt in control again, another trap sprung. Flying insects of all shapes and sizes congealed on his face. Hacking and spitting, he blindly shot from tree to tree, his arms and tail flailing while in the air. Once free of the winged demons, he moved again, faster, giving even less regard to his stealth. He was ambushed again.

Stinging and biting bugs attacked his feet. A few times he lost his footing, the itching and pain too much to bear. Too panicked to cling to the trees with his reptilian pads, he relied on his claws, both hands and feet, as he tore through the forest. Shredded bark flew with each jump; branches snapped and leaves fell with each hurried pounce. *Just keep jumping. Keep running. Keep moving south. Straight south . . . no!*

South. The first mini-swarm attacked and forced him southeast. The second forced him to move southwest. The third came from the north, pushing him straight south. He was being corralled. To the old bug-man? Then Adam saw it.

Adam didn't know if reptiles saw in color or not, but he could. And his eyes were set close enough to the front of his head to still see in three dimensions.

About forty feet away on the ground, slowly creeping among the trees, Adam saw fluorescent orange. A hunter. *What is he hunting? Me? Impossible! How would he even know about me?* Still hugging the tree, Adam's mind rolled and swirled, a torrent of ideas, thoughts, and emotions mixed together, but no conclusion. Until the ants came.

A line of ants crawled up his left hand, using his index finger as a bridge. Then a second train of ants chugged their way along his pinky. He wiggled his fingers, trying to knock them off, but only a few fell away. They kept coming. Adam's eyes shifted from the ants to the hunter, who lurked just below Adam's tree. He flicked his tongue, snatching as many ants as he could, dozens at a time, but still not enough. The squirming black slowly covered Adam's emerald skin.

Concentrate. Just ignore them until the hunter leaves. No sooner did that thought pass through his mind when heard a familiar buzz coming from behind him. He turned just as dozens of hornets swarmed his face. They clogged his mouth and nostrils, stinging and biting whatever they touched. It was too much for Adam.

He fell from the tree but scrabbled for cover as soon as he hit the ground. A blast of handheld thunder cracked the air, and bark exploded from a nearby tree. Streaking through the forest, Adam shifted from ground to trees, staying low. The hunter fired again, his shot nowhere near the lizard-snake-boy.

After missing the second time, the hunter pursued while grabbing his walkie-talkie. "Cal! Cal! It's heading toward you! Big lizard thing!"

Adam ran, ran and clawed as fast as his body allowed. Ran right into the ambush. One pause, one short pause to look over his shoulder was all it took for Cal, a barrel-chested man with a barrel-sized gut wearing camouflage and a ponytail under a camouflaged hat, to let loose an arrow from his compound bow. A scant second after a whistle, an arrow tore through Adam's left leg.

Adam froze. He looked at his leg like it was alien. He saw what happened, but his brain failed to comprehend it. The pain and blood flowed simultaneously. Before he could decide that the wound was his single most painful experience, he heard the thunder of a Winchester again. The bullet hit the back of his right shoulder and went straight through the front. The force of the impact knocked him to the ground. Pain from his shoulder and his leg rippled and collided at his stomach. Fire roared within, burning everything inside of him. The inferno burned his guts like they were made of thatch, his heart nothing more than tinder. His eyes squirted tears, trying to extinguish the flames, but the fire roared on, turning his mind to ash. He shut his eyes to stop the fire, but it took his sight, his consciousness, leaving only blackness . . .

CHAPTER
43

Pittsburgh, Pennsylvania

Kevin's right hand rested on the mouse while his left shoveled chips into his mouth. His eyes darted from one open window to the next on his computer's monitor. He had four windows open, dividing his screen into four equal parts. Three screens displayed different internet sites, each opened long enough to peruse the data he sought. The fourth window was a spreadsheet where he took notes and made charts and tables from his findings. Websites opened and closed, bouncing from medical sites giving the in-depth workings of human anatomy to sites listing schematics for defibrillators to online shopping to libraries to collegiate databases to cybernetics. Whatever he gleaned to be important went in the spreadsheet. Words and numbers appeared as fast as he could think, while three mouse arrows darted from link option to picture to scroll bar. All without moving his hand.

"Quittin' time, Keemosabee," Bob said, entering Kevin's work area.

Faster than a blink, Kevin's monitor flicked to cyan; the windows disappeared, leaving no trace of ever being open. No one saw the wire that retracted from the mouse into the oversized watch on Kevin's right wrist. He stood, wiping potato chip crumbs off his shirt, leaving tiny spots of discoloration from the grease. "Cool."

Bob smiled and shook his head at his friend's cluelessness. They departed for the trek to their cars, often interrupted by Bob's need to flirt with any woman that crossed their path. Kevin reacted with his usual smile and silence while Bob prattled on to an array of giggles and laughs.

Being Friday, the women with whom Bob flirted inquired about him and his friend's weekend plans. Kevin would answer with a shrug and a smile. At the same time, Bob either exaggerated about going on top-secret CIA missions or answered with an ambiguous, "I'm keeping my options open," which garnered him invites to two happy hours and a Saturday cookout. Kevin was also invited to all the functions, but more as an afterthought of politeness, because everyone knew he'd never attend even if they truly wanted him there. It was a typical Friday after work until a familiar voice stopped Kevin and Bob in the parking lot.

"Oh, hey, guys."

The men turned to see Debra approach them. Bob's mind raced, flipping through scenario after scenario as if the list of possible outcomes was held in a Rolodex. He wanted something flirtatious but not over the top since he wanted to include Kevin in the conversation. His friend loved Debra, and he wanted to give him every opportunity to talk to her yet feel comfortable around her. Bob examined his words carefully, looking at the possibilities each phrase would lead to. However, the one scenario he was not prepared for was Kevin actually opening his mouth and saying, "Hi, Debra."

Bob froze. He looked up for the plague of locusts, to see if the sky turned to the color of blood. Kevin's response was one of Biblical proportions, and Bob wanted to make sure he wouldn't be caught in the middle of it. No raining frogs. No flaming hailstones. He turned his attention back to his friend and the woman he had been pining over for years.

"Hi, Kevin," she replied, surprised that Kevin talked to her. "What's new?"

"You leave earlier," Kevin noted, his words more fell from his mouth than actually spoken.

Bob cringed. Even though his pride welled, because obviously he taught his ward well, so did his concern, wondering how Debra would react to his comment. Would she think it endearing that he knew that? Or creepy, like he was stalking her?

Debra tilted her head and smiled, her eyes gleaming, impressed that he cared enough to notice. "I usually do. Had to finish up an important report. Stayed a bit later."

Bob thought of a hundred ways to respond, each a suggestive way to continue the conversation, a few even implying the conversation should continue over drinks. Over a hundred responses and Kevin chose, "Oh."

Much to Bob's surprise, that was enough. Despite the lack of encouragement, Debra asked, "So . . . what are your plans for the weekend?"

"Got a date," Kevin answered.

Bob's face went numb, and his knees turned to jelly. His brain felt like a hive of angry bees. Did his friend—the same friend who could barely talk to a woman in any form of social situation—just tell the love of his life he had *a date*?! Oh, this was too much!

Blushing, Debra was taken aback, half from shame thinking Kevin didn't, or couldn't, date and half from . . . jealousy? Debra knew for years about Kevin's crush on her but never thought much of it. She knew she was an attractive woman and also knew she also couldn't control who thought she was. Kevin had always been a bit awkward and quiet, but nothing intimidating or threatening. In fact, he had always treated her with respect. Too many men she considered "her type" would hold entire conversations with her chest or make blatant advances to the bedroom. It wasn't until her last breakup a few weeks ago that she realized she wished she could find a man more like Kevin. Two days ago, she decided to get to know Kevin better, maybe break him out of his shell a bit. Make a little project out of him. She would never have expected him to have a date!

"Oh," she replied and smiled. "Very . . . very good for you. I hope you have a lovely time."

Kevin's cheeks reddened as well. "Thanks."

"Well, you have a good weekend." Debra lightly touched Kevin's shoulder and then continued to her car. So shaken by what happened and embarrassed by her preconceived notions, she forgot all about Bob.

Watching her until she was far from earshot, Bob let loose, "Oh . . . my . . . God! Dude, that was great! You're an animal!"

"What?" Kevin asked, wondering why his friend showed such exuberance over a minimal verbal exchange.

"Dude? First of all, you actually talked to her! That was fucking awesome! Second, didn't you see? She was totally jealous!"

"Jealous?"

"Totally! Monday . . . you listening? . . . on Monday, try to run into her. I'm serious. Run into her and she'll be compelled to ask you how your date went. Guaranteed. When she does, just tell her you took the girl to dinner, bought her flowers, talked about feelings and shit, but there was no spark."

"Lie?"

"Lie your ass off! And make sure you let Debra know that you're not gonna see this chick again. Wait . . . is this girl a . . . practice . . . girl?"

Bob's question confused Kevin. Why should it matter if his date was a prostitute or not? A woman was a woman, and a machine was a machine, plain and simple. In fact, a woman and a machine were very similar, just different operating systems. A woman's was far more complex, but Kevin felt he would figure it out soon enough. "Prostitute? Yeah."

"Very nice, very nice. No wonder you're so relaxed, getting laid on a regular basis and all. But I think it's time you graduated from that. And the newspapers said the police found another murdered hooker the other night. You don't want to be a part of that anymore. Too dangerous. But I don't think you're ready for Miss Debra, your princess in the tower, yet. Next two weeks are busy for me, but after that, we'll go out, me and you."

Kevin didn't feel comfortable with that at all. He had a lot to learn about women, too many experiments to perform, too much data to pour through before he tried to meet some for free.

Bob saw the reservation in his friend's face. "Much to learn, still have you, my Padawan learner. That's why I'm here. I'm your animal spirit sent to guide you. Don't worry, just let me do all the talking. That way, I'm the one getting slapped and pepper-sprayed. You just jump in when you feel comfortable. Cool?"

Kevin couldn't help but chuckle at the *Star Wars* reference. "Cool."

"Rock on!" Bob made the heavy metal devil sign with both hands before bounding off to his car. Kevin smiled and shook his head. But it quickly faded as he made his way to his own car.

Women were complicated. This thought preoccupied him the entire drive home. Bob said to make Debra jealous. Why? Women need to feel jealous to solidify their emotional being? Or was it to realize their true emotions in the first place?

As soon as Kevin returned home, he cooked dinner. Baked ziti. It was simple enough to make, tasted rather good, and sounded mature for a single man to make. He still needed some practice, though. He scooped out healthy-sized servings on two plates and took them to his basement.

The table was in the center of the room; just enough light from the upstairs touched it to help guide Kevin. Once he set the plates down, he lit the two candles, which added some more light, enough for him to see his date.

Her name was Candy. Her real name was Mary; Candy was her working name. Since Kevin didn't understand the need for two names, he acknowledged her only as Candy, the first name she used with him. She told him her real name two days ago as she begged for her freedom, pleaded with him to let her go, and screamed in pain as he weaved wires in and out of her skin and muscle. Two days in this dark basement, naked and sitting on a wooden box with a hole in it, enduring his insane mockeries of dates with all the follow-up questions when

Kevin was with her, waiting in handcuffs with duct tape over her mouth when he left her alone.

Candy was tired. She never thought she could be this exhausted. When he removed the tape and cuffs, she couldn't even muster up the strength to massage her wrists. Three years ago, she dropped out of school and ran away from home. She found a flophouse and wanted to save enough money for a plane ticket to Hollywood. Then she caught a whiff of cocaine and had been sniffing it ever since, by any means necessary. And that led her to take a ride with a shy, fat guy back to his house. Here. This basement. Hundreds of different colored wires erupted from her skin like Kevin had shredded a rainbow and sewn it into her. They no longer hurt—they itched. Each and every one of them. But when she scratched them, fire blazed up her spine and seared her eyes to the point of vomiting. Scratch or hurt? Irritation or pain?

Candy looked ahead, trying not to look down at the baked ziti in front of her. The meal didn't repulse her—it was the wires. The more she looked at them, the more they itched. And the dozen sticking out of each nipple unnerved her, as did the two-dozen flowing from her vagina.

All the wires led to a server under the table, and the server fed output to two monitors located on either side of Kevin's chair. Getting comfortable in the chair, he looked at each monitor to see if they worked properly. "The date is commencing."

Candy knew to eat and compliment. "Delicious."

The processor attached to her right temple hummed, as did the hard drive attached to the left side of her head. They itched as well, a thin tenacious itch that shot between her ears. She shifted her jaw from side to side, alleviating some of the itch.

Kevin watched the monitors, studying her response. She lied. She lied a lot, mostly every answer she had given to every question he had asked. Candy was certainly an irrational specimen. Maybe being a hooker made her overly irrational? Whatever the case, Kevin grew impatient. He had one final experiment. "I have a new girlfriend."

Candy looked across the table, her eyes wide with hope. Silent tears rolled down her cheeks. Her quivering lips twitched into a smile. If he found another girl, even if she wasn't *truly* his girlfriend, he'd be done with her and release her. Candy hated hoping that another person would have to endure this torture. All she knew was she couldn't do it anymore. The itching. The burning. The hours and hours of useless crying. The fear. If there were another woman to replace her, it'd all be over! "Really? That's . . . that's wonderful."

Kevin studied the monitors. She told the truth. His statement made her happy. He couldn't imagine that was a response from jealousy. He realized Bob was right; he needed different experiences in different environments to study women. He needed new experiments. This experiment was a failure . . . .

CHAPTER
44

Harrisburg, Pennsylvania

Fear. Stone still *felt* fear. The tightness in his chest, his spine turning to ice. Fire in his lungs. He hadn't been scared many times in his life. The first time he went to prison, he had been afraid. A big tough guy on the streets, roughing up average people and stealing their money, he learned fear when he was finally caught and thrown into the zoo. He kept to himself and hit the weights hard. He used his fear to push himself forward, to exercise when he didn't want to, to do push-ups instead of sleep. He eventually turned it into anger, fighting his way to the top of the food chain, taking a broken nose in exchange for giving broken fingers and shins. When he eventually got out, his brother took him in, utilized his talents. Stone had left the fear in prison, forgetting it ever existed. Until now.

Stone was hot. He couldn't *feel* the heat, but he knew he was hot. Hard and fast, he was panting like a dog in an oven. His tongue even flopped from his mouth. But no sweat. Why wasn't he sweating? He turned on the air conditioning in his car but had no idea if it helped. He couldn't feel the air move. In fact, he couldn't feel the steering wheel or the seat upon which he sat or the momentum when he hit the gas pedal or brakes. But he felt fear. He felt his stomach churn and even tasted the acid mist from his nervous belches. Did he really feel it, though? He wasn't sure if he felt it or just thought he felt it because he was so damn scared of what was happening to him. And what the fuck was happening to him?!

His mind raced faster than his car down the alleyways, running stop signs and hitting potholes. When did this happen? He blinked fast as his eyes darted back and forth, unstoppable signs of trying to access recessed memories. A couple months ago. What the fuck happened a couple months ago? Did he eat something? Get bit by some strange animal or bug? Get sick with some crazy virus? Drink some fucked up water? His old apartment! The one he lived in before he inherited the mansion from his deceased brother. It had mold all over the place. Roaches and rats, too. And it was in York, for God's sake! What a shithole that town was! Dirty industries either polluting the air or catching on fire or exploding! Stone deduced that he got infected with something, and this—*this*—was his body's fucked up way of dealing with it. It didn't matter because the hospital was near, and the doctors would figure it out and fix him.

Stone parked his car a block away and ran. He was a new crime lord, and he was sure his name would be known. But not his face. Every time he had to shake down one of his street lackeys for fucking up the works, they'd play dumb. Well, now it was his turn to give it a try.

He sprinted around to the front of the hospital, the twilight skies doing little to hide him. Anyone who saw the topless, shoeless man running to the hospital did nothing more than a double-take and moved on with their lives. Once to the front of the building, he walked through the doors, past the stares and the gasps of the people close enough to see that dried blood painted him from sternum to toes. He aimed for the check-in and prepared himself to play dumb. He knew nothing. He knew nothing.

Halfway to his goal, a nurse in blue scrubs saw him and approached. "Sir, what happened?"

"I don't know."

"Is this your blood?"

"I . . . I don't think so?"

The nurse escorted him through a set of doors to the ER. "Are you feeling any dizziness or nausea? Are you okay to walk?"

"No. Uh, yeah. No, I'm fine. I can walk."

The nurse led him to one of the rooms and donned a pair of latex gloves. "Drop your pants and lie down on the bed. Let's make sure you're not the one bleeding here, Mister . . ."

Stone obliged. "I . . . don't know."

The nurse shot him a look as she approached with hydrogen peroxide and a small cloth. "You . . . don't know your name?"

"No."

"Do you know what happened or whose blood this is?"

"No."

"Uh-huh," the nurse replied, the skepticism in her voice evident. After half a dozen swipes, the crimson cloth was saturated. She tossed the cloth in a biohazard container and got a new one to continue. However, she went much slower, her eyes examining his body, looking for any punctures or lacerations. "Well, at least you told the truth about one thing—this blood's not yours. And you have no wounds. So, how 'bout you cut the crap and tell me why you're here?"

"I need to see a doctor."

"Street fight? Knife fight? One of those stupid underground fight club things?"

Playing dumb didn't work, and he wasn't a bright guy, so why did he think he could pull it off with a nurse? Stupid! His fear returned. His eyes widened in panic. "Look, I really need to see a doctor."

"Yeah? Looking for a little fix? A little morphine?"

"What? No. I . . . dammit! Fucking listen to me! Gimme a doctor now!" Stone's heart sped up again. Or at least he thought it did. Did it? Why wouldn't this nurse just do as he asked? He wanted a doctor to see him, to fix him. And now this nurse was being a smartass, and it really freaked him out.

"Okay, calm down. Just calm down," the nurse said, backing away from Stone and toward the door.

Stone knew that look in her eye. He lunged as she opened the door. The nurse ran from the room, only to be yanked back in by her ponytail. Rage mixed into Stone's fear and panic concoction as he slammed the nurse's face against the wall. He couldn't feel the force he used but assumed it was substantial since he pulped her nose and crushed her skull.

By the time her lifeless body hit the floor, an orderly and a security guard had tackled Stone. Two more orderlies stormed into the room, followed by another guard. A flurry of fists and feet slammed against Stone, and he didn't feel a thing. For the first time since prison, Stone fought with men bigger than him. But their bulk was nothing. Noses were crushed and fingers snapped like meat-wrapped sticks. A headbutt finished one guy completely. Stone even bit one of them. And he felt nothing, not even shots to his crotch.

When he finished, he left the room, greeted by screaming people and flashing lights. In a building full of doctors, how was it not possible to find one? Then again, Stone realized, he was in a building full of hostages. He was going to be seen by a fucking doctor . . .

CHAPTER
45

Harrisburg, Pennsylvania

"Trite. Adjective. Lacking power to evoke interest through overuse or repetition. Hackneyed," Michael said to no one as he tossed one of his student's essays onto his desk. The deplorable essay matched the serious lack of talent and intelligence as every other essay on his desk. His students possessed the writing skills of eight-year-olds! His daughter could have done a better job! This was why Michael exerted little effort to teach—there was little effort put forth from his students to learn.

Frustrated, Michael ran his hand through his hair and checked the time. Almost eight o'clock. His heart sunk when he realized he had been in his on-campus office for almost two hours. He always retreated here after an argument with Claire.

He didn't even know how it happened. Right after dinner he made a smartass comment about her book appreciation club. He thought it was great that she expressed interest in the arts, especially since it took her mind off her lawyering, but he found it odd that she never wanted to discuss the literature with him. An English professor! His smartass comment was nothing out of the ordinary. He felt that if he didn't make one, then she'd worry. However, after he said it, she flipped out. She accused him of accusing her of keeping secrets, that he was checking up on her, snooping, not trusting her. Under fire, Michael did what he always did—he ran away.

Looking at the stack of essays in his inbox, he decided he could tolerate only two more. He dreaded looking at them, but if he knew what was coming next, he'd have happily chosen to read the whole stack. Picking up the first one, he never even had a chance to read the title when he heard a knock on his door. And then it flung open.

In rushed Derrick with his manic panic eyes. Although they were opened cartoonishly wide, they weren't darting around. "Professor! You gotta come! We gotta go!"

Not able to help himself, the words shot out of Michael like a reflex. "Is Timmy stuck in a well again, boy? Is Timmy stuck in a well?"

Emma walked in behind Derrick and put one hand on his shoulder. "Derrick, remember—try to calm yourself and your words will come easier."

Derrick closed his eyes and took a deep breath. "There's a problem at the hospital. Some guy is going nuts. He already killed a doctor and a nurse and few orderlies. I think he's got powers like us."

Sighing, Michael pinched the bridge of his nose, hoping to stave off the impending headache. "How did you two find me?"

"We called your house and your wife told us where you were," Emma answered. "And it sounded like she was crying. If you two are fighting and you'd like to talk about it—"

Michael snapped his head up and glared at the gray-haired woman. "You called *my house?*"

"We said we were your students," Derrick said, confused by Michael's ire.

"I told you two . . . I even used small, simple words . . . stay the hell away from me and my family!"

"But . . . people are in trouble," Derrick whined.

"News flash, pal—people are always in trouble. That's why there are policemen and firemen and EMTs. *They* handle the trouble."

"Not *this* kind of trouble!" Derrick snapped back. "If this guy has some kind of powers and is not ignoring them like you are, then *we* are the only ones capable of stopping him."

"Emma . . ." Michael pleaded, looking to the only other adult in the room.

Emma crossed her arms and struck a pose of defiance. "Michael, I am the wife of a firefighter. I know what is right and what is wrong. I know it takes sacrifice to do the right thing, while all you have to do to be wrong is sit on your lazy ass in your office while other people—*good* people—rush in to—"

"Okay, okay, I understand your point of view!" Michael interrupted by leaning forward in his chair while waving his arms in front of him. "So, why don't you two run along now."

"Michael, please," Emma started. "There is a *reason* God brought us together like this. Even though you may try to ignore your abilities, you still have them. We need your help with this."

"No. Now get out."

"Is this the kind of man you are? Is this the kind of father you want to be for your daughter? To show her that men are cowards? To . . . why am I wasting my breath on a husband who keeps important secrets from his wife."

Michael stopped listening after he heard the word "daughter." Emma was right. He was being a coward. A lazy coward, spiteful to a young man, possibly the only person other than his daughter who looked up to him. And he did have . . . an ability. A unique and strong ability that he could use to protect himself if things got out of hand. Plus, he sometimes liked to say he was a writer, and writers need experience. "Okay."

Derrick smiled from ear to ear. Emma even smiled as well. They both quickly faded once Michael continued, "There are some rules, though."

Emma and Derrick just stared, daring not to think about the possibilities that would come from this man's mouth. However, surprising them, Michael's demands made sense. "First and foremost, if this guy, or whoever, does not have abilities like us, then we will *not* get involved. We will become nosy bystanders and let the *police* do their jobs. Understand?"

Emma and Derrick nodded.

"Second. We avoid the media. No interviews. No cameras if at all possible. I want no one to know I'm involved, and that means no one knows either of you are involved. Got it?"

Once again, Emma and Derrick nodded.

"Now, Derrick, I know you're probably going to wet yourself over this, but we need masks of some sort. I don't know if—" Before Michael could finish, he noticed a backpack slung over Derrick's shoulder. He removed it and placed it on Michael's desk. Michael's heart fell into the empty well of his stomach as Derrick unzipped it.

"No!" Michael yelled. "No, no, no, no, no!"

"Derrick! You didn't!" Emma even scolded.

Blushing, Derrick stammered, "I . . . uh . . . went to a sporting goods store and . . . another . . . store . . ."

Michael reached into the bag and pulled out a black Under Armour top and a black leather mask. The mask had openings for the eyes, nose, and mouth, and a silver zipper adorned the mouth opening. "Derrick. This 'other store' didn't happen to be a fetish shop, would it?"

"Um . . ."

"Oh, God!" Michael shouted, his face contorting to twists of disgust. He dropped the mask and wiped his hand on his shirt.

"That one is yours."

"You can't be serious. You absolutely cannot be serious! I'm not wearing that."

"We don't have time! We really gotta go!"

Michael once again turned to Emma for help, and once again, he felt greatly disappointed. She had already put on her mask, which was nothing more than a neoprene sleeve that covered her whole head except her face. Due to the tightness of the material, it pulled at her face, diminishing many of her wrinkles. Stunned, Michael could only stare, getting a glimpse of how attractive she had been decades ago. Wondering why he stared, Emma walked to a small mirror on the wall and peeked. She giggled like a little girl. "Oh my! I haven't seen this face in years."

Ignoring how ludicrous the situation had become, Michael shoved his mask and Under Armour sports shirt back into Derrick's backpack and tried to restore seriousness. "Derrick's right. Let's get moving and we'll fix ourselves up in the car."

Keeping her mask on, Emma left the office. Derrick grabbed his backpack and followed. Michael turned off his light and locked the door. He jogged to catch up to Derrick and grabbed him by the arm. "Derrick," he whispered. "This isn't some kind of game, okay? I know you're very excited about this, but I want to remind you there's no reset switch."

Indignant, Derrick yanked his arm away. "Just because I want to do the right thing doesn't mean I don't understand the dangers involved. And just because I'm younger than you and kinda spaz out here and there doesn't mean I'm a child. Now, let's go."

Michael felt ashamed for thinking so lowly of Derrick. But he still couldn't shake the belief that Derrick was too gung-ho, jump in with both feet, damn the consequences about this escapade. Yes, Derrick was an adult, but a reckless one. And Emma seemed to side with him quite often. Did she do so to spite Michael? Or did she actually share Derrick's shortsightedness? Michael was clearly the only one who had foresight and the ability to use it. He had a foreboding feeling in his gut that this couldn't end well . . .

CHAPTER
46

Harrisburg, Pennsylvania

When Michael was ten, his father forced him to join a football team. Young Michael had no desire to play any sport, let alone one where the difference between success and failure depended on his strength and ability to hit other people. He hated practices and hated the games even more. He didn't even know the rules of the game. The rare times when Coach allowed him off the bench to play defense, he would pray to God that the ball carrier never came his way. God let him down repeatedly, sending the ball carrier in Michael's direction quite often. And every time, he'd do the same thing—plant his feet and close his eyes. And every time, one of two things would happen: either he'd miss the ball carrier completely and be embarrassed, or he'd be leveled by the ball carrier and be embarrassed. The play would be over, but the anxiety never waned.

Hours before he even had to suit up, all during practice or game time, and after they ended, long into the evening, his heart would hammer sharp nails into his chest. His hands would shake. The urge to cry was present the whole time while he talked himself out of running away. He suppressed those memories a long time ago, never caring to feel so scared and confused again. Tonight, they all came rushing back.

Michael breathed through his mouth; his breaths were short and quick but strong enough to rattle the zipper pull dangling by the corner of his mouth. He wore the leather mask he said he would never wear. He wore the spandex sports shirt made by Under Armour. However, he stuck with his khaki slacks, refusing to wear the leather pants Derrick picked out. Why the young man thought they would be comfortable was beyond Michael. Derrick was obviously going for aesthetics rather than function. That fact couldn't be more evident than Derrick lacking the wherewithal to choose a ski mask instead of this uncomfortable fetish wear covering Michael's face! And Derrick's "disguise" wasn't much better.

The young man wore his standard jeans and a gray hooded sweatshirt, hood pulled up. His "disguise" came in the form of massive ski goggles with chartreuse frames and square lenses. Michael once again had no idea what look Derrick went for. However, Emma's outfit made more sense.

Other than the neoprene head covering, now complete with a pair of swim goggles, black spandex covered the rest of her body. Michael was both impressed that a sixty-four-year-old woman had such an athletic figure and depressed that he was almost thirty years her junior and far from being as fit. Maybe Michael should have fought his fears as a child and tried harder in sports? He certainly would be more conditioned for this. Conditioned physically, certainly not mentally. Nothing could have mentally prepared him for running from building to bushes to building to alleyways to get close to a hospital surrounded by police.

The hospital sat at the edge of the city, between Front Street and Second Street. Front Street traversed parallel to the Susquehanna River, offering bridge access every few miles. Local and state police closed off two blocks of Front Street and Second Street. The authorities relegated the media to Second Street, trying to corral the chaos while keeping Front Street available for service vehicles. Convoys of ambulances kept a steady stream of moving evacuees to other local hospitals. Fire trucks stood ready, hoses connected to fire hydrants, ever vigilant. Street police and mounted officers with bullhorns pushed the crowds back, moving them along the side streets connecting Second to Third.

The east side of the building held the main entrance, visible from neither Front Street nor Second Street. However, a driveway from both streets converged to a small paved area for patient pick-up and drop-off in front of the main entrance. Police vehicles clogged the paved area, creating a hypnotic red and blue strobe. The officers stood ready, communicating to other teams and their superiors via walkie-talkies.

This is insane! Michael thought. *Insane-insane-insane-insane-insane! Why did Claire have to flip out over me being stupid? Why couldn't she have simply laughed it off like she does every other time I'm stupid? But tonight? No! She has to start an argument and force me to go to my office, making me an easy target for the May through December Bonnie and Clyde! This is so fucking insane!*

Michael, Derrick, and Emma crouched and ran closer to the hospital, staying as far away from the media circus as possible. Any time a rogue bystander came close, or more police enforcements ran near, Derrick would make himself,

Michael, and Emma invisible. He simply plucked the images of three people dressed like fetish party attendees from their minds as they made their way past.

"It makes me nervous when you do that," Michael whispered as the three of them settled behind a row of bushes, less than a hundred feet from the main entrance clogged with armed policemen.

"Why?" Derrick asked, peeking around the bushes, counting the officers.

"It doesn't unnerve you to have someone walk right past you and look right at you, yet not see you? Are you sure that will even work with getting into the hospital? If you miss even one officer, he'll see us and shoot."

"Okay, okay," Derrick snipped. "Let me try something."

The young man closed his eyes and focused. A warmth spread from the top of his skull to the back of his eyes. He saw past his closed eyelids, saw each of the officers standing in front of the hospital, saw into their minds. And found the one unifying factor he hoped for.

All the police turned to the main doors as they flung open, Stone standing there panting. Taking advantage of the officers' shock, he sprinted across the small paved lot and into the small structure leading to a nearby parking garage. Snapping out of their surprise, the officers drew their weapons and pursued, barking into their walkie-talkies. Not wanting to let the perp escape, none stayed behind. Emma and Michael had no idea why they hurriedly abandoned their posts.

"Derrick, what did you do?" Michael asked, watching Derrick stand.

"Made them see the guy run from the hospital."

Michael and Emma stood as well, cautiously following Derrick's lead toward the front doors. "You sent them on an illusionary goose chase?"

"Yeah. You just told me that making us invisible freaks you out, so I had to do something."

Michael wanted to argue but found his booming heartbeat too distracting. "Do you at least know what the guy looks like?"

"Huh? Yeah. Big guy. Football player big. Huge muscles. Bald. His nose looks like it's been broken a few times."

Derrick's description didn't ease Michael's anxiety. Tunnel vision wrapped around everything Michael saw as he ran behind Derrick and Emma to the hospital's front doors.

The trio paused and looked at each other, hoping to find even a modicum of inspiration behind someone else's eyes. Fear. Apprehension. Panic. Concern. Doubt. Michael's vision quivered with every thump of his heart. The smell of leather consumed him with every desperate inhale. He couldn't stop his hands from trembling. "Are we really going to do this?"

Emma's eyes were wide, apprehensive but ready. "Michael, we have to."

"Right. But if that guy is a regular person, nothing like us, we get the hell out of there."

Not exactly the inspiration of Churchill or Eisenhower, but it would have to suffice as Michael grabbed the door handle and pulled . . .

CHAPTER
47

Carlisle, Pennsylvania

Matthew Matthews drove through the neighborhood, as serene and picturesque as a postcard. If Norman Rockwell were still alive, he'd finish his career here. Matthews expected to see bluebirds and rainbows while the squirrels paused from their scampering to sing Disney songs. He hated the suburbs.

He lived in Harrisburg, which wasn't too far away and certainly not the largest city, but it was still a city, surrounded by buildings and restaurants. Everything was within walking distance, and he never had to stay in his apartment other than to sleep. Matthews was sure that was why he hated the suburbs; they represented standing still, stagnation.

Even though his job brought him to places like this, Matthews loved it. Constant travel, as of late. He just returned from Philadelphia last week. He had a great time there: ate at great restaurants, caught some theater, hit a museum. He even got laid. It was by an out-of-shape welfare mother of two, but still. Afterward, he snuck out of her place and moved on with his life. Cities allowed that. Suburbs didn't. There'd have been phone calls, pressure to see her again, awkward moments if they ever ran into each other again. Matthews lacked a certain fortitude to lead such a lifestyle. He pondered for a moment as he realized he would have to see LaKeisha again. However, the circumstances would be different when that time came.

Those same circumstances might lead him back to this neighborhood. But he had to be sure first. Finding the right address, Matthews pulled over to the curb and parked. As soon as he got out of his car, the suburban noises assaulted him. Two lawnmowers whirred off in the distance, possibly a third, Matthews suspected. They buzzed like hornets between his ears. The only thing he noticed more than the mowers were the barking dogs. Four of them with four different barks and four different rhythms. A large dog shot off a booming woof, took a few seconds to reload, then shot again. The *rat-a-tat-tat* of a smaller yippy dog never paused. A couple medium dogs barked in uneven variables, like two boxers too drunk to stand, arguing who was a better fighter. But all four dogs tried their damnedest to leave their mark on Matthews' brain by repeating their message over and over and over. Matthews leaned back into his car to get some aspirin from his glove box and thanked God that his apartment building disallowed pets.

Armed with his notepad and pen, Matthews followed the driveway to the small path of gray brick to the porch decorated in the light tans and powder blues of country style. His headache doubled with every step; the machine gun yippy dog got louder as Matthews approached the house. That damn dog was inside! *This girl better be worth it*, he thought.

A ring of the doorbell yielded a sad-looking woman in her early forties. When she opened the door, the dog's barking worsened, almost echoed. With every bark, Matthews' brain punched the inside of his eardrums. The woman was unfazed. How could that dog not bother her?

"Mrs. Muller?" Matthews asked.

"Yes?" Her voice was as sullen as her droopy face.

"My name is Detective Matthews, and I'm here about the deaths of Mr. and Mrs. Mitchell. Is—"

"Such a shame, isn't it? My sister was so young. Thank God whatever happened to her and her husband didn't happen to their daughter."

"Yes, I'm very sorry to hear what happened to—"

"Did you ever figure out what happened yet? Any leads as to what caused it? My husband searched the internet looking for clues as to what could have happened. He looked at gas leaks and radon leaks and all forms of radiation. He'll be home soon if you'd like to talk to him and look at what he found?"

No wonder this woman couldn't hear the *yip-yip-yipping* of her dog; she couldn't even hear the other half of the conversation she held. Though, Matthews had a hard time hearing her talk because of that *yip-yip-yipping*.

Part of the job, he told himself. *All part of the job*. "Ma'am? We don't have any 'leads' yet. And I'm actually here to talk to Haley. We really haven't had a chance to interview her and get her side of the story."

Mrs. Muller paused, processing the concept of the detective wanting to talk to Haley about the mysterious demise of her parents. While she thought, the dog's barking stopped. Apparently, Mrs. Muller did such a good job of ignoring the dog that she didn't notice when it stopped barking. Matthews recited silent prayers to every god and deity he could think of for such a miracle.

"Haley?" Mrs. Muller said. "Yes, yes. Certainly you can talk to her. Please, come in."

Matthews stepped into the typical suburban house, so fake in its desire for homeliness that it completely lacked any soul. The hardwood floor of the foyer led to the living room carpet, a muted gray that could go with any color of furniture, which happened to be plum in this case. Reprints of modern art adorned the white walls that had stencils of purple grapes on flowing green vines. As typical with these newer houses, one room opened up into another. The seeming lack of walls made Matthews rather uncomfortable. The living room led to a dining room, which led to the kitchen.

"She's out in the sunroom," Mrs. Muller said, pointing to a set of sliding glass doors giving the dining room a "stunning" view of the backyard. She veered toward the kitchen and continued, "I'll just whip up some iced tea. The blend I've been using lately has always been my sister's favorite . . ."

Matthews took his turn in the ignore-the-conversation game and cautiously opened the sliding glass door. The annoying yips of the dog had been coming from the sunroom. Haley was in the sunroom. What happened to her parents was no longer a mystery to Matthews.

He entered the sunroom slowly, as if through a minefield, wearing a big, bright smile. The house's lack of personality extended to the sunroom as well. Thin brown carpet spread through the whole room while tasteful jungle print pillows and cushions rested on wicker furniture. Mini tiki torches made their homes on small wicker tables. Within a couple steps to the wicker couch, Matthews heard the whispering.

"I'm sorry, Rascal. I'm sorry, Rascal. I'm sorry, Rascal," Haley whispered over and over as she sat on the floor, hugging her knees, talking to the pile of dust in front of her. Matthews knew very well that Rascal had been desiccated.

"Hi, Haley," Matthews said, his voice soft and soothing. He still smiled.

The young girl jerked and spun where she sat, quickly wiping the back of her hand over her eyes to erase the tears. Matthews kept smiling and using hushed tones to comfort her. "It's okay. My name is Detective Matthews. I just came over to say hello."

Looking worried, she glanced from him, to the remains of Rascal, back to him again.

"It's okay, Haley. I know what happened."

She sniffled. "You do?"

"Yep. I also know it was an accident," Matthews' voice remained soothing yet reassuring. He walked around the wicker couch to Haley and the pile of dust. Crouching, he continued, "And if you ask me, Rascal deserved it."

"He kept barking and barking," her little voice quivered. "I told him over and over to stop, but he . . . he wouldn't listen."

"Yep. I know." Matthews flipped open his notebook to the last page. He used the cardboard back of the notebook to scoop up the ashes. "There's nothing to worry about."

"But . . . but my aunt will be mad at me."

Matthews stood and made his way to the screen door that led to the backyard, balancing the ash pile on the cardboard. Concluding his precarious journey, he opened the door and dropped the ash, letting a stiff breeze do the rest. "Your aunt never needs to know about this."

"Promise?"

"Promise. It's our little secret."

A smile appeared on Haley's face. But disappeared just as fast once her aunt entered the sunroom carrying a tray holding three glasses of iced tea. The little girl couldn't look away from Matthews, her eyes wide from fear.

Mrs. Muller tilted her head and furrowed her brows, wondering why Matthews stood by the door. He saw the confusion on her face and answered her question before she could ask it. "Rascal needed outside, so I let him."

Haley's face relaxed and even allowed a faint smile.

Mrs. Muller's face went from sullen to downright anxiety stricken. "Without a leash?"

"I'm sorry. I didn't know this neighborhood required them," Matthews replied.

Haley's aunt placed the tray on a small coffee table and hurried to the windows. With a heavy sigh, she asked, "It's not just that. He's prone to running away. Did you see where he went?"

Matthews stepped away from the door over to the coffee table. He picked up two glasses and handed one to Haley. With her aunt still staring out the window, he gave the little girl a knowing wink. "The wind took him that way."

"Oh, that dog. I knew we named him right. He is such a rascal. One time—"

Matthews took a sip from his glass and placed it back on the tray. "Thank you for your hospitality, Mrs. Muller, but I really must be going now."

The woman paused mid-story, taken aback by Matthews. "What about Haley?"

"She and I had a nice talk, and I found out everything I needed to know. I'll see myself out. Bye, Haley."

"Bye!" Haley beamed, her smile as bright as the sun, happy that Matthews helped her out of a bad situation.

Matthews made his way back through the house and out the front door. As soon as he got back to his car, he dialed his cell phone. "Hey, it's Matthews. Just met Haley Mitchell. Move her to the top of the list . . ."

CHAPTER
48

Gallitzin, Pennsylvania

Pain. Burning, searing, throbbing pain. Bright starbursts woke Adam, exploding behind his closed eyelids. Each white pop of electricity brought a ripple of agony from his shoulder to his chest and head. He didn't want to open his eyes.

When he lived at home, when he was *human*, there had never been a day he didn't greet with anticipation and vigor. No matter how unpleasant a school day awaited him, even with the flu, his eyes snapped open as soon as he awoke, ready to begin the day. Chores amid cold winters didn't diminish his zeal. Nothing could. Until now.

He knew his situation was dire, but not to what extent. That could wait. He hoped if he kept his eyes shut long enough, he'd slip out of this horrific nightmare into a carefree dream and finally wake up in his bed at home. But he knew that wouldn't happen. It hadn't happened for the past two months, so why should now be any different? Just more, constant pain. He swore that every nerve in his body led from his right shoulder to his right eye, sparking livewires conducting frazzled electricity. But he still couldn't bring himself to open his eyes, couldn't bear the thought of what he might see.

He inhaled slowly, expanding his chest with his lungs, filling them with as much air as they allowed. Sore spots around his ribs made themselves known, but nothing felt broken or damaged like his right shoulder. Then he felt his body sway a bit. Confused, he curled his toes and felt nothing beneath them. He then shifted his left shoulder, his right still tormenting him, and realized his hands were above his head. As he turned his wrists and flexed his fingers, unsure if his right hand responded since it was numb, he felt the cold metal of shackles and chains tight against his reptilian skin. He was hanging above the ground by his wrists.

Dread swept through Adam. He argued with himself about opening his eyes, weighed the pros and cons, and finally honored his father's teachings about "being a man" and facing the world with eyes wide open. So, he did and saw . . . the inside of a barn.

There was nothing unusual about the barn; small, with only two animal stalls on each side and the typical hayloft along the perimeter. The smell of animals—their dirty fur, their feed, their waste—still lingered in the air. Due to Adam's acute sense of smell, he could tell there hadn't been animals in this barn for a few weeks now. Except for the giant rabbit currently hanging next to him.

"About time you woke up," the rabbit mumbled.

That rabbit wasn't truly a rabbit, more of a misfit hybrid like Adam and the cowardly Samson. His torso—Adam assumed it was a "he" by his voice—was fairly human-shaped, thin and wiry with a regular person's arms, chest, and waist. Short and stumpy, his fingers resembled the toes of a rabbit, and his thumbs jutted out from the base of his wrists. They seemed awkward but functional. The tops of his legs and haunches were thick with muscle and tapered to his feet. One was missing, a stump where it should be, fur caked and matted brown from blood, mostly dried, but with some spots still oozing. The other was long and wide, just like a rabbit's.

Adam tried to speak, but his dry throat refused to work properly. "W . . . wh . . . where . . . ?"

"Where are we?" the rabbit person moaned. "Hell. That's where."

"Hah . . . How . . . ?"

"How long have I been here? How did I turn into such a freak? How long are we stuck here? I have no idea!"

Finally showing signs of life, the rabbit person lifted his head. His nose and cheeks no longer looked human. But his crooked teeth and angry human eyes looked alien against the tan fur. His floppy ears twitched but remained drooped over his shoulders and against his back. The unkempt fur covering his body was a few shades darker, nappy, and formed curls clumped from dirt.

Adam flicked his tongue across his lips and along his cheeks, even out of his mouth, hoping to pull any form of moisture from the air. "Neh . . . name . . . ?"

"My name? You ready? Robert. Yeah, Robert fucking Rabbit. Ha ha, fucking funny! Not bad enough, these rednecks chain me up and cut my fucking foot off, but they have to come up with as many fucking name jokes as their tiny little inbred brains can handle."

"Ah . . . Adam."

"Well, Adam, don't tell them your name. Don't fucking tell them anything! They already have it in their fucking KKK heads that we're all Satan spawn and it's their God-given duty to round us up. They caught me a few days ago. They had another, a girl named Carla, but she escaped."

"Bird . . . girl?"

"Yeah! You seen her?"

"She'sss . . . dead . . . shot."

Robert looked at the closed barn doors and lurched forward, chains rattling. "You fuckers! You ignorant, backward, toothless, sheep-fucking fuckers! We're not the devil! We're not evil! I'm only fourteen, you inbreds!"

Adam watched as Robert twisted and pulled, struggling against the chains. His ire subsided after a minute, too tired to continue his tantrum. The fur on his cheeks darkened as it absorbed his tears. "It's not fair. It's not fair."

Adam and Robert spent the next half hour in silence. Robert was too tired for anything other than wallowing in self-pity. Adam's throbbing shoulder demanded all of his attention, and his mouth seemed to refuse all forms of moisture. He knew nothing he said would make the situation any more tolerable. But after half an hour, Adam thought of something to say.

"Robert?"

"What?"

Before Adam could continue, the barn doors shook, followed by the sounds of unlatching padlocks and clanking chains. They flung open once all the locks were undone. In walked three men, two carried shotguns. The one without firearms led the way, walking straight for his prisoners. He wore a light blue denim shirt, top buttons undone to expose a white T-shirt, dark blue jeans, and hiking boots. He stopped about five feet from the creatures in chains and introduced himself. "I'm Mayor Myers and I'm the only one keeping you two alive. The big guy's Sheriff Winston, and the smaller guy is Albert Buckley, the owner of this barn and the land it stands on."

Robert couldn't stop himself from saying, "Better known as Inbred, Red Neck, and Sheep Fucker."

"Yeah, keep talkin', Bugs Bunny, and I'll cut off your other foot," Albert said. He started to approach Robert, but Winston stepped in his way. Winston was a hulking man wearing flannel, jeans, cowboy boots, and a Stetson. Even his beer gut seemed to be made of muscle. Although he worked the fields every day for the past thirty years, Albert just didn't have the size to challenge the sheriff.

"You best be keepin' your mouth shut, boy. Whole town wants to lynch you and lizard boy here."

"Then let them! Just get it over with!"

"Now, settle down. I don't want no killing. We're just as confused as you are. We heard there's a cat-creature like y'uns running around these mountains, so once we bring him and Carla in here, then we're gonna call the FBI and let them handle you. So . . ."

"Carla's dead! You fucking killed her!"

"We didn't kill her, boy. We just wanted to keep her locked in here for her own safety. She—"

"I . . . sssaw . . . her . . . dead . . . body . . ." Adam forced out with labored breaths. "Shot."

The mayor furrowed his brows and turned to Adam. "Now don't you be a bigger problem than Robert Rabbit here . . ."

Mayor Myers paused, waiting for Adam to confess his name. Adam gave nothing more than icy silence.

". . . very well, lizard-boy. But listen good. We shot her once to get her here. She escaped and hurt a few people in the process. If she's dead, we didn't do it, and it's best you keep that to yourself unless you want an angry mob razing this barn with yinz in it."

Adam responded with a glare, pushing the pain of his shoulder out through his eyes and into the mayor. The mayor answered with a glare of his own. He turned to leave, and the armed men followed. "Come on, guys. Let's get that cat-creature, and get these freaks outta here."

As the three men left, both Adam and Robert heard Albert say, "Still think we should kill 'em."

With a thud, the men shut the barn door and chained it back up. With every rattle of the chains, Robert's head sunk deeper and lower against his chest. With a deflating sigh, he asked, "Adam?"

"Yesss?"

"What was it you were going to tell me before those bastards came in?"

"Help . . . isss . . . on . . . the way."

Adam closed his eyes and felt Nora nearby. And she was getting closer . . .

CHAPTER
49

Harrisburg, Pennsylvania

Empty. The hospital was empty. Michael didn't know what he expected but certainly not empty. When he first heard the news of some madman running around, "shredding the hospital," according to Derrick, Michael imagined dead and bloodied bodies everywhere. Silly images of thriller movies came to mind: lights flickering, holes in the walls, wires dangling. None of that. The reception area was unscathed and well-lit. No one around, not a soul. Yet Michael felt the compunction to crouch and tiptoe as he walked. And he couldn't bring himself to talk above a whisper. "Now what?"

"This way," Derrick said, rushing toward the nearest stairwell.

After Derrick, Michael, and Emma made their way through the stairwell doors and attacked the first flight, Michael asked, "Where are we going?"

"Ninth floor to maternity. Heard on the police scanner that he was holding the maternity ward hostage."

Emma gasped. "What kind of monster holds babies hostage."

"We're about to find out."

"Ninth floor?" Michael asked, taking pause. He couldn't help but look at Emma as he continued, "Should . . . all of us . . . be taking the stairs?"

Emma knew an ageist remark when she heard one. Realizing her words would have little impact, she let her feet do the talking. Starting with a light jog, her feet padded against the staircase one step at a time. She took the next flight faster and the one after that even faster. Michael and Derrick listened to the soft scuffs of her feet get faster and farther away until they finally stopped on the ninth floor.

Derrick shook his head and continued up the stairs. "For someone who teaches, you sure have a hard time learning."

Michael followed, contorting his face and flapping his lips mockingly, the same way he knew his daughter did behind his back after a scolding. He had to stop doing that by the sixth floor to focus on breathing. By the ninth floor, he needed to rest and placed his hands on his knees. The sports shirt did a great job of diffusing the sweat, but the mask was unbearable. However, Michael endured, knowing that hospital cameras would capture his image once they entered the ninth floor.

While gasping for air at the top of the landing, Michael's thoughts drifted to his daughter and wife. Why wasn't he at home with them? He was no hero and he knew it. If he had any inner strength, he would have been able to say no to Emma and Derrick. He should be at home with his wife, who was undoubtedly glued to the television, watching live feeds.

"Let's go," Derrick whispered as he opened the stairwell door. Michael took a painful inhale and followed Emma through the door.

The police had set up shop on the ninth floor, and Michael had no idea why he was surprised. Was it a fear of being this close to the police? Or did they hammer home the reality of the situation? Whatever heat was generated by climbing nine flights of stairs suddenly vanished. Michael's bones froze solid, chilling him to his soul. Yet the trio pressed on.

Not speaking and letting Derrick take point so he could make them invisible if any stray eyes glanced in their direction, the three moved along the hallways and ducked into empty rooms when necessary. Finally, they found a room that hid them without obstructing their view of the nursery.

In the center of the large hall, the small nursery had four walls of thick plexiglass, allowing for friends and families of new mothers to ooh and aww over the blessed gifts, no matter where they stood around the room. Today, the only people outside the room were state troopers pointing guns at it. Five newborns were inside, all awake and crying, wondering why their first day of life had been filled with nonstop screaming and noise. Also in the room were four terrified nurses and two very shaken doctors. In the center, the cause of all the madness, stood Stone, shaken, terrified, and wide-eyed.

"What's wrong with me?" Stone screamed, eyes wide with panic. "What the hell is wrong with me?"

"I— I— I don't know. I don't understand what's happening," one of the doctors stammered.

"Try again!"

"We've already broken six needles trying to—"

"Then try a different fucking needle! You're the one who said you needed a blood sample! Just try again!"

"O-o-okay. Okay." One of the nurses handed the doctor another needle.

For the seventh time, the needle shattered against Stone's skin. And for the seventh time, Stone flipped out. He grabbed the doctor's shirt with both hands and screamed, "Why is it doing that? What is going on with me? Why can't I feel anything? Why?"

The officers with their rifles trained on the large man shifted and squirmed. They all wanted to take the shot and end this madness. Each one knew if this escalated any more, they might have to, risking the lives of the doctors and nurses and babies in the process.

Emma had seen enough. "We have to stop him."

"Oh, yeah?" Michael replied. "Let me guess, God's your copilot and He gave you an idea."

Even though the swim goggles distorted her eyes, Michael could clearly see her glare. "Actually, yes. We need to lure him out of there. Derrick, make me invisible to everyone except the psycho. I'll go in and lure him out."

"Wouldn't it be better if you were invisible to him too?"

"No. If he can't see me, he might flip out more and hurt the babies. This way, I can get him away from them."

"But once he leaves that room, the cops will start shooting. If they can't see you, you might get hit."

"If they can see me, that would bring about too many questions, and it might distract them. Once I get him out of the room, Michael, help get the doctors and nurses and babies out of here."

Michael peeked back out. There were only five babies. The nurses should be able to carry them all with ease. He still didn't like the idea, but, "Fine. Let's do this."

Derrick knelt to get more comfortable. "Okay, Emma. You're good to go."

"Are you sure? I can still see her."

"Yes, I'm sure! Now go."

And Emma went. Doing cartwheels from the room to the entrance of the postpartum area, she moved with a speed and grace that beguiled Stone. He froze, capable of doing nothing more than stare as she stood in the doorway. A dozen armed policemen, four terrified nurses, and two scared doctors all wondered why Stone had stopped screaming and what the hell he was looking at.

Seeing the needles shatter against his skin and hearing how bullets had no effect, Emma knew not to engage him hand-to-hand. Instead, she picked up a container of talcum powder and ran up to the large man. Before Stone had time to even blink, Emma squeezed the container. Three rough jets of powder filled his eyes.

"Argh!" Stone screamed, dropping the doctor and rubbing his eyes. He blinked enough away to focus on the mysterious woman in the black neoprene. "Bitch!"

Stone grabbed at her but missed. He lunged for her again as she jumped backward. One more leap backward was all it took to get him into the middle of the room.

Confused, the police watched the large man swing and grab at the air around him. He took a step forward and swiped the nothingness in front of him. He lunged a few more steps. Once he made it out of the nursery, all the men in the hallway jumped on their radios to update their commanding officers. Then they all received their orders: wait for him to be far enough away, then open fire. All the men watched through their rifle sights. Bullets from standard-issue handguns had bounced off his chest and back, as they would if he wore Kevlar. None of these officers were there to see that. He was now shirtless, and they had high-velocity rifles. Anyone's round could take him down. Or so they thought.

The first trigger pull led to a dozen more trigger pulls. The doctors and nurses tried to cover their ears while protecting the babies as a mysterious man wearing a leather fetish mask aided their escape. The explosions of rifle fire rippled through the air, and the tremendous noise dropped Michael to his knees to cover his ears. Once the noise stopped, Michael looked up to see the large man standing unscathed, panting like a rabid dog. The large man looked at the police like they were raw meat. And he attacked.

"No!" Michael screamed, not knowing what else to do as he watched Stone kill two officers by slamming their heads together. The other ten men jumped on their radios and drew their handguns. Bullets and blood and screams sprayed the room. By the time Michael ran back to Derrick, the mayhem was over, and one lone figure dominated the room. And one old woman sat on the floor, leaning against a wall, clutching her bleeding leg.

Derrick stared and shivered. It all happened so fast. He focused so much on keeping Emma safe, he didn't protect the officers. He couldn't stop the mad-man. And Emma *still* got shot! He was going to die, and he knew it. This was all too real! That indestructible man would kill Emma and then come over and kill Derrick. Strangle him or rend him limb from limb or . . . The sting of a slap pulled Derrick from his swirling thoughts. He looked up to see Michael crouching down in front of him. "Turn her invisible. Now!"

Still shaking, Derrick focused enough to make Emma disappear from Stone's mind. Confused, Stone looked around. Up and down. Throughout the room. And then, behind him, he saw two men crouched in the doorway of the stairwell.

Michael grabbed Derrick's arm and said, "Go help Emma. Take her mask and your goggles and her goggles and whatever you call a uniform and get rid of it!"

"But . . ."

"All the cameras are destroyed. The psycho must have taken care of them. And keep me visible. He has to see me. Got it?"

Just as Derrick started nodding his head, Michael saw the large man notice him.

Adrenaline fueled, Michael shot across the room and down a hallway. Growling with blind rage, Stone followed. The large man frothing at the mouth was clearly in better shape than the English professor in a fetish mask. He gained ground with every step. Michael sprinted, as best as his body would allow him, to another stairwell and stopped. Fighting through the burning in his legs and lungs, ignoring his throbbing heartbeat punching his whole body, Michael focused on the warmth building at the base of his neck. He nurtured it, commanded it. And once Stone was close enough, Michael released it. The air rippled between the men. Stone's feet left the ground as he slammed into a wall. Anger exceeding anything human, Stone jumped to his feet and continued pursuit. Michael continued to flee.

Running down the stairs as fast as he could, Michael could only think, *Don't trip. Don't trip. Don't trip. Don't trip. Don't trip.* When he heard the door slam open and Stone's growls echo through the stairwell, Michael pushed himself to move faster. Just as he reached the first floor, Stone was only half a flight behind. Michael swore he felt Stone's breath on his neck. Using fear as a motivator, Michael leaped through the door and spun, pushing the warmth from the base of his neck through his fingers, knocking Stone off his feet once more.

Michael landed on his hip and thigh in the lobby. He jumped to his feet and . . . dear God, his leg wanted to fall off! *Move! Keep moving*, he yelled at himself. Two policemen in body armor holding rifles watched in shock as Michael scrabbled to his feet.

"Hey!" one of them yelled as Michael sprinted toward the exit.

"Run!" Michael yelled back.

When Michael reached the exit, he heard the door burst off its hinges and Stone scream. The sound of the officers' guns didn't even phase him anymore. He just kept running until he left the building.

Making it through the exit doors, he sidestepped and threw himself against the building. Back and arms straight, he couldn't believe he was trying a tactic he had once seen on a cartoon. But standing before him were a dozen more police officers, staring at him in stunned silence. Not knowing what else to do, he placed his index finger in front of his lips as the universal sign for "Shh." Before the police could react to such a ludicrous gesture, Stone burst through the doors and ran into the middle of the small parking area.

It worked! Michael was behind Stone now. But more importantly, Stone stood between Michael and the Susquehanna River.

The warmth grew at the base of Michael's skull. He never gave much credence to visualization, but he imagined tearing down gates and breaking down large doors to expose a fire, an out-of-control inferno. The warmth grew to a level Michael had never allowed before. Sweat flowed over his whole body. His hands shook. It actually hurt to keep it back. Just as Stone turned, Michael unleashed.

As if being punched in the chin by a tornado, Stone was ripped from the ground and thrown into the air. In a low-level arc, Stone flew toward the river. And with a plunk, he disappeared into the water.

Still stunned, the police simply watched as a smaller man in a leather mask somehow pushed a psychotic behemoth half a block into the middle of a river. They turned their attention back to Michael. His stomach still in knots, Michael had plenty of warmth left. He extended his hands and used it, knocking all the police off their feet long enough for him to run.

He sprinted between trees, across streets, and from building to building. He took his mask off and found a place to rest, between a building and a few trees. He plopped on the ground and panted as his lungs begged for air even though every breath set them on fire. The cold brick he leaned against did nothing to stop the sweating. Images flipped through his mind like snapshots in a macabre photo album. Pictures of the needle breaking against Stone's skin. Stone killing a dozen armed cops. Emma's bleeding leg. Stone flying in the air. Guns. Blood. Everything that personified primal fear. Michael wanted to puke, but his stomach simply cramped too much to allow that to happen. And he wanted to cry. Not because of what happened, but because of how exciting it had been . . .

CHAPTER
50

Harrisburg, Pennsylvania

"No. No. No!" Marvin shouted into the phone before he slammed the receiver down. If he didn't have the ability to stop headaches before they happened, he'd have one now. That was the third time Derrick had called asking for Marvin's help in dealing with the lunatic at the hospital. Why would Derrick think Marvin, an up-and-coming vice president of a prestigious investment firm, would be willing to help? The ignorance of youth, Marvin guessed.

And speaking of ignorant youths . . . Marvin paged his assistant. And Colby came running.

"Yes, Mr. Carver?" Colby asked as he walked into Marvin's office. The young man looked a dozen years older than his actual age. He kept his hair spiky in a faux-mess sort of way, refusing to change his style even though his hairline retreated from his forehead at an alarming rate. The three missing teeth didn't help either. And neither did the weight he had gained over the past few months. His chin was barely distinguishable from his neck, and his waist rivaled his chest in girth. But he still had youthful eyes, and Marvin knew that beneath the piggish exterior was a cool *GQ* model dying to be free.

"Have you found that doctor I asked you about?"

"Yes, Mr. Carver. Dr. Zillin is with the Central Pennsylvania Sleep Institute."

"Still?" Marvin mumbled to himself.

"Are . . . you having sleep problems, sir?"

Sir? Marvin liked the sound of that. It took three months, but he finally broke Colby. Not only did he step on the man who once stepped on him, but he held him down and crushed him beneath his shoe. But it still wasn't enough.

Over half of the employees in the company answered to Marvin, and they all worked fifty to seventy hours a week. They had to. Not because Marvin told them to, but because of the addiction he gave each and every one of them. Deep within them was a chemical desire to find the right answers, produce the best numbers, and keep Marvin happy. But Colby was different, a separate experiment in Marvin's lab. He had no addiction like the others, just the astonishing physical changes he had endured over the past few months. Colby saw some form of change every day in his mirror, as did his coworkers. However, no one pointed out his physical degradation except for his boss. Marvin molded Colby's body like a petulant child with a glob of clay, but the true manipulation was psychological. Marvin's words hurt worse than thinning hair, an expanding waist, or missing teeth. And Colby always put in eighty hours a week. Minimum.

"No, Colby. No sleep problems." Marvin would have thanked anyone else for asking. Except for Colby. He didn't want the boy to have any undue confidence. However, Colby just stood in the doorway, staring at Marvin like a beaten dog watching his master eat a steak dinner. Feeling magnanimous, Marvin threw a scrap. "Have you heard anything about what's going on at the hospital?"

"Yeah. Some guy went crazy. Must be wearing some kind of Kevlar vest or something because the news is reporting that bullets are just bouncing off him."

Bullets bouncing off? Exactly what Derrick had said. Marvin wished that the young man's presentation included even a shred of credence. Instead, he had Derrick yelling random words in his ear. Hardly a way to convince an individual to cease his current activities and put his life in peril. But if Derrick were right . . . ?

"Colby, why don't you call it a night? Head home early."

So beaten down, Colby didn't even register it as a reward. He almost asked why, but some part of his humanity still screamed from within, reminding Colby that he shouldn't want to still be at work well past eight o'clock in the evening. "Um. Okay. Thank you, Mr. Carver."

Once Colby left, Marvin did the same. The night was clear, but traffic was backed up. Closing off so many streets around the hospital took its toll. Curiosity swirled into impatience, prompting Marvin to park his vehicle and walk. It was less than ten blocks away, after all.

Blending in with the crowd on Second Street, Marvin joined the chaos; he listened to rumors blazing through the crowd and news reporters asking the police tactless questions only to be answered with terse no comments. Getting his fill of information, he discerned it better to find the facts with his own eyes. And the best way to do that was to become more covert.

Being as inconspicuous as possible, he moved away from the commotion a few blocks and then walked toward the river via an alley. Police manned temporary blockades, allowing only personnel vehicles through. The buildings in the area were either apartments or offices, all three stories or taller. Local residents meandered about small parking lots or smaller courtyards, sharing cigarettes, theories, and conspiracies. They would occasionally shift topics of discussion, but the crackling voices of a nearby police walkie-talkie would pull them back into the imminent situation. Realizing the best action was inaction, Marvin found a comfortable area to stand about a block away from the hospital and Front Street. However, he didn't have to wait long.

While the locals seemed more fixated on only those they knew, Marvin exerted little effort to remain anonymous and focused on the police. He heard far more rippling static from the walkie-talkies than usual. Sliding along one of the buildings, he moved closer to one of the barricades on Front Street. The walkie-talkies and car radios erupted with voices and intermittent gunshots from the hospital.

"He's moving! He's moving! He's—" *Sssshhh.*

"There! There! Stop him!" *Sssshhh.*

"Get the babies outta here! Move!" *Sssshhh.*

"Fuck! Nothing's taking him down! Noth—" *Sssshhh.*

"Who the hell's that! Some guy in a mask is—" *Sssshhh.*

More voices interrupted, barking out orders and commands. Police scattered, all but abandoning the blockades. Marvin crept closer to Front Street to get a better view of the hospital. Officers from all over swarmed the hospital. More gunshots. Yelling. Screaming. Crashing. Then Marvin saw a large man launched backward into the air. Arms flapping and legs flailing, he flew in a low arc, plopping right in the center of the Susquehanna River. Although Marvin couldn't see around the building, he heard more commotion. He recognized Michael's handiwork, pushing the large, bulletproof man into the river.

Now the police ran in circles, not sure if they should pursue the lunatic thrown into the river or the oddly dressed character who did the throwing. Marvin saw a unique opportunity and took it. Sprinting as best as he could in dress shoes and a suit, he ran unnoticed across Front Street and down the bank to the river's edge. He so dreaded ruining a suit by jumping into the dank river, but he ran risk vs. reward projections through his head. If this man in the river was truly bulletproof, it would be worth the risk. And investing was all about risk. Marvin dove into the river.

Thanks to the absolute reign he held over his body, the swim was almost recreational, even while wearing his clothes and shoes. He regulated his heart-rate, controlled muscle exertion, and doled out the oxygen from his one and only breath where necessary. He formed a thin membrane over his eyes, allowing him to keep them open without the river's irritants infiltrating them.

Swimming in the general direction of the splash, Marvin adjusted his bio-chemistry accordingly. He shifted the design of his inner ears to hear unusual splashing or gargling, adjusted his rods and cones to see better, and shifted the nerve endings close to his skin to feel abnormal heat sources and vibrations in the water. Surprising even himself but saving self-congratulatory praise for later, Marvin found the man with ease.

Obtaining his target, Marvin swam to the shoreline opposite from where they came. While dragging the large man to shore, Marvin commanded the man's diaphragm to contract, forcing the water out of his lungs. The big man coughed and sputtered, but once his bearings returned, he lunged at Marvin, wrapping his meaty hands around the businessman's throat.

Stone froze, every nerve in his body rippled with electricity and exploded. He wanted to scream, but his whole body seized. He felt nothing but pure pain. He felt . . . he felt? After relinquishing his grip, Stone fell to his knees, panting. "How . . . how'd you do that?"

"Rule number one. Don't you ever fucking touch me," Marvin said, standing as tall as a liege over his bowing subject.

For the first time in days, reason crept into Stone's mind. "Okay. Okay. But . . . I can't feel anything. And you hurt me."

Without bothering to ask, Marvin grabbed Stone's wrist. "Hmm. Very interesting. Your skin cells have all but solidified as well as increased in number and density. No wonder you can't feel anything. You're but a breath away from being walking cement."

"Can . . . you fix me?"

Still holding onto Stone's wrist, he slapped the bald man's face with his other hand.

"Ow! What the fuck, man? You . . . hey! I felt that! You did it!"

"Now, don't get your hopes too high. I can fix you temporarily. Judging from the way your skin cells are reacting once I free them from my will, the fix will probably last an hour."

Stone's shoulders slumped. Dejection washed across his face. "An hour. And only *you* can fix it."

"Yes. But, as fortune would have it, I'm looking for a fellow with your skills to be in my employ."

"Work for you?"

"Yes. You'll have to be all but indentured to me, with saving your life and all, but there will be a salary and other perks."

Stone pulled his hand out of Marvin's grasp. He sighed and felt . . . *felt* . . . his tears run down his face. He worked so hard to escape from his brother's chains only to freely shackle himself to another master. "Yeah. Fine."

Marvin smiled. He received another roadmap. He hired an employee who would come in very handy. And he learned that this bulletproof man had sleep apnea a few years ago . . .

CHAPTER
51

Philadelphia, Pennsylvania

LaKeisha stared at herself in the mirror and smiled. She had been smiling ever since she woke up about an hour ago. She couldn't help it; last night was incredible. She got laid.

That wasn't the only reason why she smiled, though. She had sex two nights before, and three nights before that, a couple times the week before that. Each time was with a different guy, within minutes of meeting them. Well, usually they weren't formally introduced or anything, more like an instant connection. She'd see a guy, he'd see her, then came the kissing, pawing, gnawing, and slamming. And the guys were all cute, too! Not just cute but hot!

Looking in the mirror, she realized that she still got "it." She was still pretty. Time added a few lines, and her love of corn chips might have added something to her cheeks and chin, but she knew she was still pretty. She had mysterious dark eyes and a big bright smile, still with all her teeth, not yellowed since she didn't smoke or drink coffee. She looked at her frumpy body and wondered if she was so pretty that men started overlooking the extra pounds? Maybe it was the new "in" thing? She never looked at fashion magazines, so she had no idea about the latest trends. Maybe curves were back? Big curves! Maybe she was the new "it" girl?

Stepping back from the mirror, LaKeisha struck a cheesecake pose, one hand on her accentuated hip, the other holding her kinky hair up. She laughed as she imagined this image on the cover of a magazine. Her breasts sagged, but they were big, and one thing she knew in life was men loved big tits! If she turned the right way or wore the right jeans, she could camouflage her belly. And she liked the curve of her hips under the right circumstances. Whatever she had that drove men crazy, she prayed she'd never lose it. Some fucked her too rough, but she'd take the bad with the good.

She stepped out of the bathroom and crossed her kitchenette to the living room in two strides. Both her children lay on their stomachs, propping their heads up on their hands while watching television. LaKeisha looked at them and smiled. She was content. They were content.

Thoughts of taking the kids out today danced through her head. A walk around the block? A nice breakfast at Friendly's? She just wanted to do something special with them today. However, her train of thought was derailed by a light knock on her door.

Peeking through the peephole, she saw Camilla. LaKeisha jerked her head back and frowned as if the peephole tried to poke her eye. Camilla? LaKeisha hadn't seen or heard from Camilla since . . . the club where the bitch punched her in the face. LaKeisha wanted to get angry but really couldn't. Camilla had been her best friend since first grade. And she certainly wanted to know why Camilla punched her! "Whatchyu want?"

Camilla's shaky voice barely made it through the door. "Hey, sweetie. I . . . I jus' wanted to 'pologize for . . . you know . . . buncha stuff. I'm really sorry, sweetie. I miss you."

LaKeisha sighed and thought, *She lucky I got some last night!*

"S'okay," LaKeisha said, opening the door for her best friend. "But why you punch me?"

Camilla stepped into the apartment and froze, confused by LaKeisha's question. "I . . . I don't know. I really, really don't. I thought about it every day. *Every* day. An' I still don't know. I was jus' . . . jus' . . . mad."

"At me?"

"No, sweetie, not at you. Jus' *mad* at everything. I'm so, so sorry. I . . ."

LaKeisha smiled, waved her hand, and sucked her teeth. "S'nuthin'. It's all good."

Camilla's body slouched as the weight of the world slid off, and she exhaled in utter relief. "Oh, thank you, sweetie. I was so scared to call you an' I kept wantin' to visit earlier but got all nervous an' shit. I'm so . . ."

Camilla paused as she looked at LaKeisha's face, her smile. Camilla knew that smile. A broad smile crept across her face, ready to ask a question. She waited long enough to peer at the children, making sure they weren't paying attention to anything other than the television. Just in case, Camilla took a step closer to LaKeisha and whispered, "Girl? You get some last night?"

"You know it," was all it took to get both women to laugh as if their friendship suffered no hiatus.

"Who? Anyone I know?"

"I dunno. Some guy."

Still whispering, Camilla leaned in closer. "What? Oh, sweetie, give me the details."

LaKeisha peeked over to make sure her kids weren't listening. "Last night, a little after midnight, I ran to the 7-11 for some snacks. I'm walkin' across the parking lot to the front door, right? But then I see this hottie workin' the key to his car door. At first, I didn't think he got a good look, 'cause he looked up at me an' looked back down. He looked Puerto Rican, with nice brown skin and dark black hair and one of them thin mustaches I like. An' big arms like I like, too. But as I got closer, he musta seen somethin' he liked, 'cause all's it took was a smile an' next thing I know, we back of the store by the dumpster, pumpin' away."

LaKeisha replayed the events in her mind. Pants around his ankles, he pinned her to the wall for an hour and a half. His small dick felt good to her, no over-stretching her vagina, no smashing into her cervix. Like the other men during her unprecedented run of good booty fortunes, he didn't speak, just grunted like an animal while he humped away. She felt his semen splash inside her at least once, but she was certain he came twice more. But, like the other guys, he didn't stop to reload—he just kept pushing.

Even after a good night's sleep, LaKeisha was a bit sore between her legs, but it was worth it. As she gave Camilla more details, the soreness dissipated, replaced by a familiar warmth. Her nipples even hardened just thinking about it. She knew her flimsy shirt would do little to hide them. However, she didn't know how Camilla would react.

"That good, huh?" Camilla asked, staring at LaKeisha's nipples trying to burst free from her shirt.

"Umm, yeah?" Confused, LaKeisha took a step back. Licking her lips, Camilla took a bigger step forward.

"They look good," Camilla gave a throaty whisper as she reached out and squeezed LaKeisha's breasts. "Big."

"Hey!" was all LaKeisha could come up with, too shocked to comprehend her best friend's actions.

She pushed Camilla's hands away, but they snapped right to LaKeisha's breasts like magnets and pulled her close. A tiny stream of saliva flowed from the corner of Camilla's mouth. "I know you've thought about this."

LaKeisha had thought about trying things with another woman. But not like this and certainly not with Camilla, whom she had known most of her life. And by God, not with her children twenty feet away! *This can't be happening*, she thought as she tried to squirm from Camilla's firm grasp. *Grabby hands bitch pissin' me off!* No luck. Camilla pulled LaKeisha in for a kiss, her tongue so deep in her mouth LaKeisha had to fight herself from gagging. *This is crazy!* With one violent push, LaKeisha separated herself from her ravenous friend. "What the fuck?"

Camilla wiped her mouth with the back of her hand as her eyes glossed from lust to rage. "Me? You whore! You fuckin' tease! Spreadin' your legs for fuckin' strangers! An' not me? Fuck you! I hate you! Fuckin' kill you, bitch!"

Still seething, LaKeisha couldn't believe her ears. "You come to my house an' grab my tits an' talk shit to me in front of my children an' . . ."

LaKeisha looked over to her children to see if they still watched the television. And she wanted to cry. Her children, her babies, were rolling around on the ground, fighting. Not just toddler wrestling, but hitting and kicking and screaming at each other with anger no eight-year-old or six-year-old should ever know. She was so distracted she never saw Camilla's punch coming.

Right on her cheekbone. Windmilling her arms, LaKeisha fell back, landing hard on her backside. Camilla strode toward her with an animal's swagger. She curled her fingers like claws and bared her teeth. Standing over LaKeisha, Camilla growled hateful profanities as her saliva foamed at the corners of her mouth. The icy knife of pure terror plunged itself into LaKeisha's heart. She never thought her friend capable of this, and that frightened her to the bone. Then Camilla froze.

Her breathing shifted to short, panicked puffs, and Camilla's eyes widened bigger than plates. Shaking, she put her hands in front of her, shielding herself from LaKeisha. Tears streamed down her face as her lips quivered.

"Stay away! Stay away!" Camilla screamed as she ran out the door.

LaKeisha turned to her children to see them both standing, their arms wrapped around each other, shaking like they just saw the devil himself. Crawling to her knees, she whispered, "Babies?"

With tear-choked sobs, they both ran to her and hugged her tight, beyond the capability of their little muscles. "We're scared, Mommy! We're scared!"

LaKeisha held their trembling bodies tight and cried. Something was wrong with *her*. And she was scared, too . . .

CHAPTER
52

Camp Hill, Pennsylvania

What the hell did I just do? Michael asked himself, sitting in his Ford Explorer. He had been sitting outside his house for over half an hour, now well past ten o'clock. Sarah was in bed and Claire was probably glued to the television, watching the news. How was he going to explain this?

They had a spat earlier in the evening, forcing him to go to his on-campus office. That was over four hours ago! He had never been out that long after a fight before. He hated lying to Claire, especially since she was a lawyer—she made a career of breaking down liars and tearing the truth from them. But, good Lord, how could he tell her the truth? *Gee, honey, I got this crazy ability to "push" things with my brain, and I've been hanging out with other crazy people who can do crazy things, and we were the ones at the hospital fighting a bulletproof man and getting cops killed.* His stomach sank at that thought.

A dozen police officers. Every time Michael blinked, he saw their lives snuffed by the hands of a madman. But he helped save men, women, and babies. Plus, if he, Emma, and Derrick didn't get involved, maybe that psychopath would have killed the cops *and* everyone else, including the babies. But did he sign the cops' death warrants by getting involved? Maybe they could have handled it? That was a preposterous notion! Their bullets were as effective as confetti! His involvement helped some and hurt others. But which side of the line did his actions truly fall? "Dichotomy," he whispered. "Noun. Division into two mutually exclusive and contradictory groups or opinions."

Michael stepped out of the truck and ran his hands over his shirt. After the hospital incident, Michael jammed his mask and Under Armour shirt into a plastic bag and hid it under the spare tire. He wanted to throw them in the trash, but knowing his luck, the cops would find them, work their CSI magic, and peg Michael for being "The Masked Pervert" or "Fetish Man." Sometime this week, he'd have to find a way to burn them.

As soon as he opened the door, he heard Claire call out. "Michael?"

"Yeah?" His voice cracked, not knowing what to expect.

"Oh, God!" She sprinted from the living room to the foyer and threw her arms around her husband. "I'm sorry. I'm so sorry for arguing with you. I was being silly and immature and . . . and . . ."

"Whoa, whoa, whoa. It's okay." Michael learned early on that he could get more mileage out of not *officially* accepting her apology. It took a big man to accept an apology, but a man with wings and a halo acted like he didn't even need one in the first place. "What's all the fuss?"

"The hospital . . . did you hear about the hospital? Of course, you did; you were probably caught in all that traffic."

Traffic? Michael thought. *Perfect!* "Yeah, the traffic was a nightmare, and my cell phone was dead."

"I know it was stupid, but I couldn't help but think you were . . . I don't know . . . one of the dead people. There were twenty-eight deaths, Michael. Mostly police, but some bystanders, too. And I thought maybe . . ."

"Hey, it's okay. I'm fine. Seriously."

"Oh, God," Claire sighed. She hugged him again and ran her fingers through the back of his hair. "Your hair's wet."

Oh crap! Lawyer-mode! "Front Street was a parking lot. Lot of us got out of our cars and hung out, trying to figure out what was going on. Hot night."

Claire smiled, then grimaced, crinkling her nose. She stood on her toes and moved close to his face and sniffed. "You smell like . . . leather?"

"Cheap ball cap I had on. Crazy thing must have reacted to my expensive, exotic shampoo."

Claire sniffed again and then smelled her hands. "Yeah, probably. I told you not to use that crap."

"But . . ."

Claire paused, realizing how she sounded. Her eyes welled with tears again. And again, she hugged him. "I'm being a bitch again. I'm sorry. It's just a lot of stuff going on with me. At work."

A couple well placed lies, and he was free as can be. But, God, he *hated* lying to his wife! "Honey, it's okay. Let's just call it a night and go to bed."

"Sounds great to me."

Of course, it sounded great to her—she was the one who actually got a good night's sleep! In fact, even better than usual. After a few hours of constant worrying, the relief threw her into the deepest sleep Michael had seen in a year. He, on the other hand, only stared at the ceiling all night. He wasn't even sure if he blinked, let alone closed his eyes for any discernable length of time. Not to mention the throbbing in his leg and hip from falling on the cement hospital floor. No matter what position he tried, comfort eluded him. And then the alarm went off.

Michael walked through his morning like a zombie. He barely remembered to give his daughter a kiss and a hug before she ran off to the bus stop without her shoes. He couldn't even enjoy his coffee.

"Is something wrong?" Claire asked, extra perky and extra rested.

Yes. Yes! Crazy abilities. Pushing. Put myself in mortal danger. Saw people die. "No. Why?"

"You look like hell. Sure nothing's wrong?"

Just tell her. Just show her. She'll understand. "It's . . . I just got a call. One of my students was involved with the mess last night and is in the hospital."

"Really? I didn't hear the phone."

Oh, come on! Tell her already! She's your wife! It'll all work out. "Cell phone. When you were in the bathroom. Gonna go visit her."

I suck!

"Oh. I'm sorry to hear that. I hope she's okay."

Yeah, me too, Michael thought as he drove to the hospital. He knew Harrisburg Hospital would be a madhouse trying to get everything cleaned up from last night. The fire departments and police departments, as well as civic-minded volunteers, did a great job. There was no structural damage, mostly bullet holes and bloodstains, a few expensive pieces of equipment that insurance companies would have to pay for. The hospital was far from capacity, with most new patients still being diverted to other area hospitals. However, Emma was wounded in the hospital, and Michael couldn't imagine any corporate bureaucracy stupid enough not to keep her there. Luckily, his assumption was correct.

Michael felt like a criminal returning to the scene of a crime. Was anyone he walked past here last night? As much as he hated the mask, he thanked God he had one. But he still kept his head down and turned away from everyone else. He even walked with a slouch and a slight limp just in case some hardcore crime scene investigators watched him through the surveillance cameras trying to match his body type and movements to the guy in the leather mask from the previous night.

The floor Emma was on came out of last night's fiasco unscathed. If one were to judge the hospital on this floor alone, one would never know of the insanity that had taken place twelve hours before. If anything, the activity was lighter than usual, with staff helping on the ninth floor and lobby as well as most patients being diverted. Emma even had the room all to herself.

With a light tap on the door, Michael entered. "Hey. How is she?"

Derrick sat next to Emma's bed, his eyes so bloodshot it pained Michael to look at them. The young man scowled. "Okay. No thanks to you."

Groggy, Emma turned her head to Derrick and patted his hand, "Now, now, dear. He did what he had to. He saved us all."

Michael smiled and walked further into the room. "That almost sounded like you took my side for once, Emma."

Emma turned to Michael and regarded him with half-shut, sleepy eyes. "The painkillers. Makes me tolerate insufferable shits like you."

Michael frowned and then Derrick smiled. Emma giggled and turned back to Derrick. "I said 'shit.' Oop! I said it again."

"I'd like to have some of what she's having," Michael quipped.

"Yeah. Sure," Derrick replied.

Michael sighed. "Derrick, I just don't get you. You wanted this. You wanted to play dress-up and beat the bad guy. And we did. Did you think it was going to happen in a vacuum? Didn't you think people were going to get hurt?"

"Yes. I did actually. But I thought 'people' would stick around and help."

Michael rolled his eyes. "Derrick, there were a dozen cops. With guns. Pointing guns at *me*. I had to run."

"Whatever." Derrick turned his attention back to Emma. "Do you need anything?"

"Just you two to stop fighting," she slurred.

"Don't worry, Emma," Michael said. "I just stopped by to make sure you were okay. I'm going to go now."

"See you soon," Derrick replied, goading the professor.

"No, Derrick. There is no next time."

"Sure there will be." Derrick's voice seemed hallow and flat, reaching into Michael, talking to his soul. "Do you really think we're the only special ones. The three of us, Marvin, and that big guy? There are more, Michael. Good or bad or indifferent. We're like ambassadors for this. You want to keep it private? Well, others don't. It's up to us."

"No, Derrick. Again, there is no us." With that, Michael turned and walked out the door.

"You liked it, didn't you?" Derrick asked, his voice holding a maturity Michael thought him incapable of. "Playing the hero? Scoring the winning touchdown. Saving the day."

Michael shoved his hands in his pockets and scuttled down the hallway, frowning. Damn it. Derrick was right . . .

CHAPTER
53

Hershey, Pennsylvania

Marvin flipped through the pages of the latest issue of *Forbes*, impressed that a doctor's office waiting room kept current on their magazine selection. The waiting room of Central Pennsylvania Sleep Institute differed very little from any other doctor's office waiting room. Muted gray colored the walls, carpet, and furniture. The area was open and clean while one wall-mounted television showed news and another showed a soap opera. It always amused Marvin that the receptionist was tucked away behind a sliding Plexiglas window in every doctor's office.

It had been five years since Marvin last stepped foot in this office. Sleep apnea. Thelma had forced him to come here, saying she had concerns about his snoring, that it might be a symptom of something larger or potentially danger-ous. He always thought it just annoyed her. But she demanded, and he caved. After some tests, Doctor Zillin suggested a procedure that included breaking and rearranging the roof of his mouth. It was painful indeed, but he lost quite a few pounds, the aftereffects of having his jaw wired shut. Of course, as soon as he could open his mouth again, the weight came right back, and he returned to being a pudgy, middle-aged man. Marvin laughed at those memories as he continued to scan *Forbes*.

Just as impatience dictated that he must check his watch, a nurse entered the waiting room. "Mister Carver?"

With smiles and pleasant conversation, Marvin followed the nurse to an exam room. It might have been the same one as the last time he was here, but they all looked alike. While alone, he read every brochure and medical book he could find. Nothing helps roadmaps like other roadmaps. After the standard wait time of a tectonic plate movement, the doctor finally arrived.

"Marvin Carver?" Doctor Zillin asked upon seeing the fit and trim patient, with a healthy head of hair, remembering a pudgy, balding man in this office five years ago.

"Why yes, Doctor Zillin. I assume you've noticed I'm no longer quite the bumbling wretch when we first met."

Zillin extended his hand as well as a warm smile. "You simply must tell me your secret to living well, then."

Marvin smiled a shark's smile and took the guppy's hand. "The secret to living well? For you, that's quite simple. Tell me the truth and don't even think about trying to bullshit me."

Confusion swept across Zillin's face, wondering what his patient meant by such a cryptic response. Then he became downright perplexed as awkward sensations rippled from his crotch. Marvin felt the good doctor was due an explanation. "The awkward sensation you're feeling is your penis shrinking, although you didn't have much to begin with. I will be more than happy to restore it and even grant you a few more inches if you cooperate."

The fear of truth stabbed the doctor like an emasculating spear. "Cooperation? Cooperation with . . . ?"

"Simple. I ask you questions. You answer them. As you can probably surmise, I have become rather special. I've even met others who are just as special, and the one unifying factor is we have all had some form of sleeping disorder in our lives. So, Doctor Zillin, what exactly did you do to me five years ago?"

"I don't know what you—" The doctor stopped, unable to continue past the pain of his testicles contracting into his abdomen. His eyes slicked with tears as he inhaled through his nose.

"I was hoping to avoid this whole torture thing by starting with your manhood, but I guess you're just not as big a fan of your testicles as other men."

In between labored gulps of air, the doctor forced out, "But they'll kill me."

"I have a feeling 'they' will understand. And I assure you, there are worse ways to live than die."

Tingling and prickling danced up and down Zillin's arm. As he looked at his left hand, he watched a bubbling blister form in the middle of his palm while each fingertip exploded into a massive cauliflower shape like perverse pink popcorn. Closing his eyes, he couldn't contain his sobs any longer. "Okay. Okay. I'll show you."

Color returned to his hand, fullness and then some returned to his crotch, relief returned to his heart. Zillin wiggled the fingers of his left hand and then grabbed his crotch. Eyes still wet with tears, Zillin looked at Marvin.

"Yes, you'll now dazzle your wife and be the envy of the locker room. For now. I suggest you step with alacrity, or I'll take it all away," Marvin said, releasing Zillin's hand.

Zillin walked and Marvin followed. Down a hall, through a "restricted" door, around a bend, through another "restricted" door, down another hall, through a door offering a warning that an alarm would sound if opened. No alarm sounded.

Marvin followed the nervous man down an unassuming hallway leading to an equally unimpressive office. Zillin, voice quaking, said to the man behind the desk, "Sir? This gentleman, Marvin Carver, is here to see you. He is one of our . . . special . . . patients."

Matthew Matthews glanced up from his computer monitor, then did a double-take. "You used to be fat! And bald!"

Marvin frowned, not expecting that response from a man he had never met before. "I did the 'work' myself. Now, unless you'd like to see what else I'm capable of, I suggest you give me some answers."

"Hey, now. No need for threats here. I know what you can do," Matthews said. He offered a dismissive hand wave to Zillin, waiting for the doctor to leave before he continued. "I find it quite impressive that you figured out where to come for answers. So impressed that I'm going to tell you everything. In fact, I'm very curious to see what you do with the information. Just give me a second and I'll be right with you."

Cautious, Marvin took a seat while Matthews typed, "Move Marvin Carver to number three."

CHAPTER
54

Pittsburgh, Pennsylvania

The dance club was alive. It breathed laughter and voices. Its heart pulsed to the beat of the music. It blinked in strobe. Smoke machines belched fake fog, gently blanketing the writhing bodies on the dance floor. Lasers flickered with the music, creating geometric shapes along the walls, floor, and ceiling. The club was filled to capacity with happy, horny people. Candice was neither.

She started the night happy and horny, vamped up for a night on the town with her best friend, Mandy. Now, she watched her friend play kissy-face with Bob, whom they had just met. She didn't even know how it happened. One minute they sipped drinks at the bar, and the next minute two guys, Bob and Kevin, bought them drinks. And Mandy jumped all over Bob. Candice didn't think he was all that cute, but he sure seemed like a real smooth talker. But Mandy liked him and Candice felt it her duty to play the part of wing-woman tonight. Plus, she learned that Kevin fixed computers and owned his own house. Not a bad start, she thought, but he lacked conversation skills.

Mandy and Bob moved their public displays of affection to the dance floor, grinding against each other in lascivious ways. Candice looked at Kevin and smiled. He smiled back, awkward and crooked. They sat at a table for four in a darkened corner away from the dance floor. They could feel the vibrations of the thumping music without needing to scream over it. However, Kevin still barely talked loud enough for Candice to hear.

"So," she started. Conversing with Kevin had been difficult at best all night. His responses were too regimented and robotic for her tastes. But three beers later, she decided to try one more time. "You ever been to this club before?"

"No."

"Mandy and I usually start here. There are a few others we hit. Which ones do you like?"

"This is my first one."

"Oh? That's . . . nice." The discomfort level raised, and Candice turned to see her friend's lips embrace Bob's. "You good friends with Bob?"

"We work together."

"Yeah? He do the same thing you do? With computers?"

"Yes. We're both hardware technicians."

"Good job?"

"Yes."

Candice felt her ability to continue this wane and her attention diminish. Her alcohol-laced hormones guided her eyes from tasty stud to hot hunk. She glanced away long enough to watch Mandy lead Bob from the dance floor toward the nearest exit. "I see Bob and Mandy are hitting it off."

"Yes."

"I take it you don't dance?"

"I never tried."

Candice's inebriation exceeded her patience. She could take no more of this, and she fulfilled her duty as wing-woman as best she could for far too long. She and her friend shared a cab over, and she knew of another club two blocks away. The thought of how Kevin would make it home never crossed her mind. In one gulp, she finished her drink, then gathered her purse. *Never tried to dance before?* she asked herself. *Even guys who live with their mothers went dancing. Kinda creepy. Heh. Probably gonna kill me and hack me up in little pieces. I gotta get outta here.*

"Well, Kevin, it was nice meeting you," Candice said, standing. "But I have to get going now."

As quick as one flash of the dance floor's strobe light, she disappeared.

Kevin sat befuddled. It was obvious he had no choice but to leave as well, to follow her and take her back to his place to experiment on her. He didn't have high hopes for this meeting; after all, she was no prostitute, and this was his inaugural time trying to meet women in this type of setting. However, he was still perplexed at how poorly the experience went.

He answered all of her silly questions! Why was this not working? Very little separated humans from computers—humans *were* computers! Just made from different components. So why didn't they act like computers? Every human was equipped with even a basic sense of logic. After all, the logical process helped humans evolve past being rudimentary apes. Why did it stop now? Or did it simply escape a *woman's* comprehension? Nonsense. Kevin often observed Bob and many other men he worked with behaving in rather irrational fashions.

Especially when women were involved. Maybe women's lack of logic sapped men of their rational thought? Again, nonsense. Kevin had no irrefutable proof for any of his hypotheses. In fact, his actions reflected irrational behavior since his desire to understand women stemmed from wanting to be with Debra. However, his irrational motives surfaced because he wanted *to be* with her, not because he *was* with her. He . . . he . . . *he* was a variable he had yet to study.

All of his experiments revolved around understanding women. He collected data about women, their behavior, their feelings, and their reactions to a multitude of stimuli. He never questioned the validity or quality of the stimuli themselves. He tested their reaction to what *he* did as opposed to comparing and contrasting their reactions to what another man would do. Using only his reasoning and thought processes, he presented only a fixed amount of stimuli, only a handful of scenarios and reactions, all according to his sense of logic. Surely, other men would offer different responses to women's questions. Maybe he had to first study men before having the means to properly study women?

Kevin followed Candice outside to the sidewalk and past the parking lot. She ducked down an alleyway, a shortcut to the neighboring block and closest dance club. Wires wiggled like salivating snakes from his watch, and Kevin started down the alley after her. But stopped. Adding her to the study would yield no unique results. Turning, he left the alley. Candice, in blissful ignorance, escaped while Kevin walked back to the parking lot, where he found Bob and Mandy leaning against a car, kissing.

Mandy had suggested they leave the club and head back to her place. Never passing up what Bob often referred to as a gift from the Booty Godz, he accepted. The whole way out of the club, she was grabby and kissy, impatient for what Bob had to offer. He wanted to get to the sidewalk and hail a cab but couldn't resist the urges of the delectable Mandy. His tongue sought hers as they fell against the nearest car, locking themselves in a groping embrace.

An inexplicable chill ran up Bob's spine, forcing him to open his eyes. There stood Kevin, three feet away, spectating the kissing and fondling. Startled, Bob jerked back, breaking the torrid embrace. Mandy was about to express her dismay, but she bolted up when she saw Kevin leering at her. Out of instinct, she backed herself against Bob while covering her breasts with her arms.

"Kevin?" Bob asked with as much patience as he could muster. "What's up?"

The chubby hardware technician extended his arm and displayed his unique watch. A dozen wriggling wires bolted from the watch like multicolored lightning, striking both Mandy and Bob. Neither of them even had a chance to scream . . .

CHAPTER 55

Carlisle, Pennsylvania

Sunshine crept through the slats of Haley Mitchell's blinds, only half shut. The position of her bed kept the sun from touching her. However, the beams brightened the room. Haley awoke with a smile for the first time in over a month.

Finally accepting this room to be *her* room, she removed her CPAP mask, placed it on *her* nightstand, and jumped out of *her* bed. It had been a guestroom her aunt and uncle converted for her, and that had been how she felt—a guest. Not because of anything her aunt and uncle had done—well, Aunt Becky had been morbidly depressed this whole time—but because Haley refused to believe she'd be living here the rest of her life. She clung to her childish fantasies that it was all a dream; her parents would ride up to the house on a white horse and whisk her away, taking her back home. Today was something new. Today, this was *her* home. *Her* room.

The room wasn't pink like her other room had been, but since the walls started as light azure, Uncle Joe painted some clouds on them and the ceiling last week. At the time, she was still too deep in the well of self-pity to care, but today she liked them. *Her* clouds on *her* walls.

Haley missed her parents so much that a fire started in the pit of her stomach every time she thought of them. She could never let go, and she knew that. But she had to move on, move forward in life. She even had a therapist to help with that. Uncle Joe and Aunt Becky were her new parents now, and she'd just have to cope with that. They tried hard. Well, Uncle Joe more so than Aunt Becky, who still struggled in the quagmire of depression. But she was getting better. Aunt Becky had a therapist, too, who gave her pills.

Wearing her pink flannel pajamas, Haley slipped her feet into her pink, fuzzy slippers and went to the dining room for breakfast. But no one greeted her. A pang of fear pinched her heart as she felt her throat constrict. No smells of sizzling bacon or frying eggs. Not again! This *cannot* be happening again! "Uncle Joe? Aunt Becky?"

"Out here, sweetheart," Uncle Aunt Becky's lilting voice danced from the porch.

Relief swept through Haley's body. She made her way to the porch and witnessed something odd—Aunt Becky smiling for the first time in months. Haley couldn't control her face; it returned the smile, broad and toothy.

Aunt Becky sat on the floor, and Uncle Joe sat on one of the loveseats, and he smiled broad and toothy as well. Haley couldn't help but ask, "What's going on?"

"Well, why don't you come here and see for yourself, princess," Aunt Becky answered, waving her arm to beckon the ten-year-old girl.

Tentatively, Haley walked further into the room. She chided herself for being so nervous. These were her relatives. They would never do anything to harm her. But after what she had been through these past few months, she remained skeptical about surprises, no matter how nice they might be.

Haley still treaded lightly. She couldn't help it, almost tiptoeing, stretching the suspense longer. Putting one hand on the arm of the loveseat, she peeked around and saw—a puppy. An adorable, floppy-eared, golden-coated puppy with paws too big for its body. Haley's heart melted.

Squealing with excitement, Haley knelt next to Aunt Becky and held out her arms. Without hesitation, the puppy jumped into her arms and licked Haley's nose as if she were the one thing it had been missing all its life. Giggling, Haley tried to get a hold of the squirming young dog. The ten-year-old girl couldn't be any happier.

"Thank you! Thank you so much, Aunt Becky and Uncle Joe," Haley said as she turned to look at her uncle, wanting him to see her smile. He didn't see it, though. He was unconscious and slumped over on his loveseat.

Confused, Haley turned to her aunt for an explanation. But Aunt Becky was just as confused. Then her eyes widened and mouth opened and closed with no words, looking like a middle-aged fish. She collapsed. And Haley saw a dart sticking out from her aunt's neck.

Time slowed as her heartbeat sped up. She just lost her parents, and now something strange had happened to her aunt and uncle! Why was this happening to her? Panicked, she jumped to her feet as she heard the whistle of something buzzing past her. She looked out the sunroom window to see a man in a blue uniform with gray body armor and helmet, pointing a gun at her on the other side of the screen, now with three holes in it.

Haley screamed. Fear wouldn't let her do anything else. But she felt warm, the strange warmth she hoped she'd never feel again. It started at the top of her neck, at the back of her head, just like before. And like before, it spread through her whole body.

The uniformed man with the gun swore and tried to run but spasmed instead. His hands shook and his knees wobbled; his head flopped from shoulder to shoulder. He tried to scream, to call for help, to pray to God, to call out his wife's name one last time. All he managed was a dry, raspy gargle. In one anticlimactic instant, it all ended with a dull puff, as his body disintegrated, a pile of dust all that remained.

Panting harder than her puppy that now hid behind the loveseat, Haley saw more uniformed and armored men coming with more guns. They ran toward the house, pointing and yelling.

"She took out Parker!"

"Stupid idea! In broad fucking daylight!"

"Hurry! Hurry! Get her before she gets us!"

"Cops'll be here in three minutes. Easily!"

"Fucking Matthews! Fucked this all up!"

"This is why she's number one on the list!"

Haley ran back into the main part of the house as darts zinged past her. She ran into the dining room and toward her aunt's and uncle's room. Their room had the attic stairs. She heard "cops" and "three minutes." Maybe she could hide in the attic that long? If not, the small air vent seemed easy enough to kick out, and the one oak tree grew too close to the house, its branches perfect for climbing. But she also heard "Matthews." Detective Matthews? He seemed like a nice enough guy when she last saw him, and he certainly kept his promise to not tell her aunt about Rascal. Why would he . . . ?

She sprinted through the living room to get to the hall leading to her aunt's and uncle's room. Halfway through, the main door exploded off its hinges, dust and splintered wood flying through the air. Haley screamed and kept running as more men piled through the door.

"There! There! There!"

"Get her!"

"Shoot!"

"Hurry! *Hurry!*"

"Fuck!"

Haley lost her footing and fell against the hallway wall. The warmth flooded her body again. She turned to break the levy and release the deluge. The man closest to her disappeared into a puff of ash. But there were plenty of men behind him, all shooting.

Her arms and legs stung. And itched. Why were they here? Why did they want her? Did Aunt Becky and Uncle Joe know what happened to her parents? Had they found out it was her and told someone? But she had a new puppy, and it needed her! It was new and it wouldn't know what to do . . . or where . . . where to . . . go . . . Needed her . . . Aunt Becky . . . Uncle Joe . . .

As she lost consciousness, she hoped she didn't snore too hard since she was falling asleep without wearing her CPAP mask . . .

CHAPTER
56

Gallitzin, Pennsylvania

Adam heard the scratching. He knew Nora was nearby and commanded her wood-gnawing minions to facilitate a search and rescue for him. However, he felt her long before the scratching. Her presence rolled through his mind like a late evening fog. While hanging from the rafters in the barn, he scrolled through his memories like flipping through a scrapbook containing crystal-clear photographs. Now he could only think about the rafters, the way the wood creaked as he and Robert swayed.

Despite the omnipresent pain, Adam found himself wondering about his actions these past few months. Why did he need Nora? His new body possessed more than enough strength and speed to survive in the wilderness alone. And it wasn't like Nora was the most stellar company, especially after meeting Samson. Why did Adam feel the need to be with them? To protect her? Over the past few hours, the questions slipped from his mind, and now he found himself comforted that Nora was nearby.

Adam looked over at Robert and wondered how he fared. Actually, he wondered if the teen-turned-half-rabbit was still alive. Robert's thin, sallow chest wasn't moving as far as Adam could see. Adam heard no breathing either, just the drawn-out creaks of the rafters. And the scratching.

To Adam's surprise, Robert mumbled, "What the hell is that scratching?"

"Ressscue."

Incensed, Robert turned his head and scowled at Adam. "What?"

"Jussst . . . wait."

Robert rolled his eyes and went back to hanging his head. "It's annoying."

The scratching continued from behind them, a nonstop noise that neither captive could ignore. It was indeed annoying, like sandpaper grating from ear to ear. But it continued, louder, faster. Then it stopped, immediately replaced with tiny squeaks and little squeals. Robert's head snapped up and twisted as far as it would twist. He even tried to jerk his torso. "What's that squeaking? Is that mice? I hate mice! What's going on, Adam?"

Adam pulled his thick lizard lips back into a smile. Mice and chipmunks, groundhogs and squirrels, ran into the barn through the hole they created. A few creatures stood on their hind legs, ears turning from side to side, noses twitching, eyes peeking at every corner and crevice the barn had to offer. Adam knew that was Nora's reconnaissance. The rest of the animals scurried along the floor to Adam and Robert.

"Aah! What are they doing?" Robert yelled as they jumped from the ground to his legs. Dozens crawled up his thrashing body to the rafters, specifically where the hook holding the chains was embedded. "Get off! Get off!"

"Calm . . . down," Adam said, allowing dozens of creatures to use his body to make their way to the rafters. "They . . . are here . . . to help."

"What? You can't be . . ." Robert cut himself short as he looked up. Mice and squirrels and chipmunks attacked the wood around the hook with the fervor of rabid, starved animals. If he had peeked over at Adam, he would have seen the same thing.

Adam fell first. Thinking ahead, he landed on his good leg, but it mattered little since he hadn't used it for well over a day. He put his other foot down for balance, which only ignited a fire within his thigh. His tail twitched, attempting to aid his equilibrium, but that failed as well, and down he went on the hard dirt floor of the barn. A smile spread across his face—he was free.

Soon, Robert also fell. He crumbled to the floor upon release, having only one foot and not using it for almost a week. He sat up, no longer noticing the rodents scurrying around him, and looked at his hands, wiggling his fingers. Still unsure if he should believe what just happened, he let out a hoot and a holler. "WOO! I'm free!"

"No!" Adam snapped at his young cellmate, but the damage had been done.

Both boys heard the noises from outside, the guards rattling the chains as they unlocked the doors. "What's goin' on in there?"

Adam and Robert tried to stand, but their legs hurt too much to cooperate. Even using their arms and hands proved challenging. Out of instinct, they inched across the floor, away from the front doors.

"I'm sorry, Adam. I'm so, so sorry," Robert whimpered as he squirmed. Heavy streams of tears matted the fur under his eyes.

The chains clanked to the ground. The doors flung open. Three gun-wielding silhouettes blotted out the waning sunlight. The scowls on their faces became apparent as they entered the barn. Albert and his lifelong hunting buddies, Morton and Bart, each pointed their guns and walked over to their captives, caught mid-escape.

Training his gun on Robert, Albert asked, "How'd you get down, boy?"

Robert, trembling to the point of convulsion, curled into the fetal position, his misshapen hands over his head. "I'm sorry. Oh, God, I'm sorry!"

"Leave him . . . alone!" Adam shouted as loud as his raspy voice allowed.

Morton strolled over and pointed his gun at Adam's head. "So you feel like talkin', huh? How's 'bout *you* tell us how you two got down?"

"Uh, Albert?" Bart asked. "Look atchyer feet . . ."

Albert did as his friend suggested and saw mice. A dozen gray field mice scampered across his shoes. With a swing of his leg, he kicked most of them off. "Git!"

Before he could even put his foot back down, four dozen more appeared. Stunned, Albert watched as they all ascended his leg, prodigious belly, and chest, aiming for his open mouth. He tried to clamp his jaw shut, but it was too late. Without so much as a squeak, mice made their way in.

Albert dropped his gun and clawed at his face. Terror wiped his mind clean as instinct took over. He swept away handfuls of mice, hardly enough to stop the attack. Gagging and retching, he tried to close his mouth but couldn't. Already inside, the mice showed no sign of slowing. Albert felt their feet clawing and teeth biting, burning tunnels of pain shooting through his chest and gut. His friends rushed over to help, but their efforts proved futile. Pink foam frothed from his mouth, and his eyeballs rolled back into his head. Convulsing, he fell to the ground and curled as his muscles contracted. He gurgled bloody froth until the last twitch.

Angry and confused by watching his lifelong friend die in such a bizarre fashion, Morton did what he always did when angry and confused—he grabbed his gun and started yelling. "What the hell was that?"

Although the gun and the question were pointed at Adam, the reptilian teen sat in silence. His tongue flicked in and out of his mouth, tasting the musty barn air as it filled with fresh blood. And more friends.

A river of snakes rushed across the floor from the hole in the back wall, aiming for Morton. Still unsure of what was happening, Morton shot at the snakes, blasting a few to meaty chunks and ribbons. He pumped and shot again. A third time he pumped, but he couldn't pull the trigger. The snakes reached him, slithering like scaled lightning up his body. Hundreds of teeth pierced his arms, legs, neck, and face. Screaming and doing the dance of the damned, he dropped his gun and pulled at the reptiles. He managed to rip away a few but not enough to stop the fury. "Bart, git over here an' help me!"

Bart backed toward the exit, away from the devil's creatures.

"Come on, Bart, you fuckin' coward!" Morton shouted his last words. The ranks of the slithering army consisted mostly of black snakes and garden snakes, but enough rattlesnakes and copperheads found a way to inject their venom into Morton's flesh. Much like his recently deceased hunting buddy, Morton's muscles flexed beyond his control. He fell to the ground and vomited blood while coughing foaming mucus from his lungs. After his last twitch, the dozens of snakes made their way home to Adam.

Robert stared in disbelief, his skin crawling as more snakes slithered over and blanketed Adam. He looked at Albert, then Morton, and hated himself for feeling happy to see them like that. Their demise was savage and brutal, but it felt damn good to watch them die! Hearing the ominous pump of a shotgun, he turned toward Bart, still backing toward the door. Unable to pick a target, the gun muzzle bounced from Adam to Robert to Adam to random squirrels to Albert's dead body to Adam again. "Don't move! Don't nobody fuckin' move! I'm gettin' the sheriff. I'm gettin' the sheriff. I'm gettin' the sheriff."

Robert's eyes widened, not because Bart waved the shotgun around, but because of the bear standing on its hind legs behind the scared redneck. With a barn-shaking roar, the bear caused Bart to wet his pants. And that was the last thing Bart ever did in this life.

Quaking, Robert couldn't take his eyes off the bear mauling Bart in the corner of the barn, even when a naked Asian girl walked in, followed by a large cat-creature. As casual as an early evening summer stroll, Nora took the keys from Albert's belt and unshackled Robert. She smiled and stroked his furry face. "I'm Nora. You're free now."

Nora stood to free Adam while Robert stared at the stubby fingers of his fur-covered hands. "I'm free. I'm *finally* free! *Free!*"

Using every ounce of rage and hatred he could muster, Robert dragged himself to Albert's corpse and hit it. Then again. And again. Even though Albert no longer felt pain, Robert continued slamming his fists against the body. Harder and harder, laughing and crying with every punch as tears streamed down his face. "You hear that, fucker? I'm free! Free from your sick redneck fuck psycho hell!"

Nora crouched next to Robert and put a hand on his shoulder. "It's okay. It's over now. They can't hurt you anymore."

Robert turned to her, wrapped his arms around her, and buried his face into her chest. His body shook from the outpouring of emotion, and his shoulders shuddered with every heart-wrenching sob. He hurt so bad that he didn't even care she was naked.

Getting feeling back in his good leg and tolerating the pain in his bad, Adam, with dozens of snakes dangling from his body, stood and walked toward Nora. "We should . . . go."

"No," Nora said, petting the pitiful creature clutching her. "We have to do something, Adam. This . . . this is the future if we don't do something *now*, if we don't carve out our own future. Tonight, I'll gather an army. Tomorrow, this town will fall."

Even as she spoke, animals and birds of all sizes and species flowed into the barn, the first to be drafted. Samson slinked into the corner opposite the bear. And from the shadows, he watched Robert . . .

CHAPTER
57

Camp Hill, Pennsylvania

"You're home?" Michael asked Claire as she walked through the door.

She paused to regard her husband, sprawled out on the couch covered in newspaper pages like a derelict in an alleyway, wondering why he was home on a Friday himself. Realization sunk in as she forced herself to keep walking, not to look suspicious, as she heard her daughter's heavy footsteps thunder across the ceiling, followed by a raucous squeal. July Fourth weekend—no school. Hoping her husband would buy her alibi, she answered his question with, "July Fourth, silly."

"And you have off?"

"Why is that so hard to believe," she said with a smile, continuing the ruse.

"Well . . . you're a lawyer. First, you're trained in a military-style boot camp in mind games and lying. Second, you work twenty-five hours a day, eight days a week, holidays be damned."

"Oooh, you think you're so funny." As playful as a kitten, she ran into the living room, jumped on her husband, and dug her fingers into his ribs. They laughed as newspaper parts flew through the air and drifted down like ink-stained snowflakes. She loved him and loved how easily distracted he was. In less than four seconds, she made him forget about his line of questioning. If it were only that easy with opposing council! But she took the day off for a doctor's appointment, and she didn't want Michael to know. She even crept from the house before he or Sarah woke.

"That's my job. Being funny," Michael replied, mounting a counterattack tickle offensive.

"Your job is to bore young adults to tears with dusty old books by dusty old writers."

Michael mandated a cease-fire, pausing to register his wife's comment. He looked her square in the eye and replied, "I'd find that offensive if it weren't so damned true." And went right back to tickling her again.

Out of nowhere, a squealing mass of blonde hair bounded across the living room and jumped on Michael. "Tickle Daddy! Tickle Daddy!"

"Oh no! A Sarah-bomb! Aarg!"

Father and daughter tickled and played and laughed. Claire watched and smiled, laughing every time her daughter did, swept away in the contagious tidal wave of unbridled happiness and joy. That little girl's laughter was simply addictive. Unable to resist, Claire again jumped into the fray, sitting on her husband's legs to pin them down while aiding her daughter in the tickling.

"Okay!" Michael screamed in between fits of laughter. "I give! You two must stop, or I will pee on the couch."

Sarah jumped off her father. Without thought or reason, she extended her arms out from her sides and started spinning in circles. Getting faster and faster, she squealed, "Pee pee daddy! I have a pee pee daddy!"

Before Michael could retaliate, biology did it for him; Sarah became so dizzy that she flopped down on the floor, panting from all the recent excitement.

Satisfied that her husband forgot she was home when she shouldn't have been, Claire stood, releasing his legs, but not before a few more pokes to his ribs. He laughed and whispered a sexual reference under his breath to her. She winked back a reply, knowing he'd never find out that she took off work for a doctor's appointment today.

Claire strolled to the refrigerator and procured a premade, prepackaged smoothie shake. After a few gulps, she watched her daughter, back still on the floor, continue to spin in circles, using her head as a pivot point. Claire laughed. She hoped Michael noticed how much pent-up energy the little girl had and he'd change his mind about not letting her play sports.

Michael watched his daughter spin in circles, still lying on the floor. *God, she has so much energy*, he thought. *I hate to admit it, but Claire might be right about letting her play sports. I'd hate for her to feel like we're forcing her, like she has to. Like I had to at that age. But she seems like she could use something to do.*

He looked at Claire and saw exactly what he thought he'd see—her giving him the "I told you so" look. He sighed and arched his eyebrows, giving her the "yes, I know you told me so, and I know you're right" face.

"Hey, Sarah," Claire said after finishing her smoothie. "What would you like to do today?"

"*Shopping*!" she shouted as if her mother stood four states away.

"Shopping?" Claire pondered for a bit and realized that even though it wasn't the greatest exercise, it did involve walking, and it would get the girl out of the house. "Okay. For what?"

"Shoes!" she shouted as loud as possible again.

Michael sat up and looked at his wife in utter disbelief. Claire could only return the same look of shock. They watched each other as if they could read each other's minds, sharing the same memories of their daughter having to be reminded to *wear* shoes every day and going to school at least once a week without them. This same little girl who had no concept of the virtues of footwear now demanded to spend the afternoon shopping for shoes. Claire and Michael laughed.

Sitting up and having no idea why her parents had tears in their eyes, Sarah looked from one to the other and asked, "So, are we going?"

Claire and Michael laughed again.

"Yes, dear, we most certainly are," Claire answered, composing herself by sucking air in through her nose and exhaling slowly through her mouth. "Just as soon as you get ready."

"Yay!" Sarah jumped up and sprinted from the room. Her tiny feet thundered up the stairs and boomed across the ceiling to her room. Claire and Michael savored a longing look into each other's eyes, knowing this was one of "those moments" they would cherish and laugh at forever. They both mouthed the words, "I love you" as Hurricane Sarah rumbled back downstairs.

"Ready!" the little girl announced, jumping back into the living room with her arms extended, Olympic gymnast sticking-the-landing presentation style. She pulled her hair into a ponytail like her mother's and held a small sequined purse so pink Michael assumed it to be radioactive, sans shoes.

Claire smiled as she walked over and put her arm around her daughter's shoulders. "Let's leave Daddy here and go shoe shopping."

"Yay! Bye, Daddy!" Sarah hollered as she grabbed her mother's hand and pulled her toward the door.

Trying to keep up with a little girl bristling with energy, Claire barely got out, "Bye, honey! Love you!" before the door slammed shut behind her.

Laughing, Michael turned on the television to watch the news while he cleaned up the scattered newspaper. He didn't get very far with his cleaning project. Once his finger hit the "power" button, he immediately regretted his decision . . .

CHAPTER
58

Harrisburg, Pennsylvania

"It's done."

Marvin smiled from ear to ear upon hearing that. He replied into the phone's receiver, "Thank you, Mister Stone. Well done."

"You'll . . . uh . . . you'll be by in a couple hours, right? Hook me up?"

"Yes, Mister Stone. I may be a demanding boss, but you'll soon learn that I always reward my employees whenever they perform exceptionally."

"Glad to hear. Could you pick me up some beer and hookers while you're at it?"

"Nothing but the best, Mister Stone. I'll be by your apartment with refreshments and entertainment before midnight."

"Okay. Bye."

Marvin returned the phone to its cradle and reveled in the fact that he would be president of his investment firm within the week.

After rescuing Stone from the Susquehanna River, Marvin employed him and set him up with an apartment in one of the buildings his company owned. Upon discovering his new employee's proclivity toward unsavory activities, Marvin decided to use him to run equally unsavory errands. Once completed, Marvin would reward the brute with his magic touch, allowing the man named Stone to feel. Although Marvin doubted Stone's mental stability, he was sure that being denied the sensation of touch brought out the monster within the man. Insanity seemed the only logical recourse when presented with such a situation. However, due to Marvin's "therapy sessions," Stone can go almost an entire day before losing all sense of touch. And just like every addicted employee under Marvin's control, Stone's need for therapy outweighed everything else.

This latest errand Stone had run for Marvin involved the current president of the investment firm. As with most executives who live in ivory towers, the president was well into his AARP years with his waist exceeding the limits of his belt. A heart attack loomed in the man's future, and Marvin had plans to help it along. But no matter how much control Marvin held over his employees, he couldn't control the rumors that spread after the few, yet coincidental, untimely deaths the investment firm faced. No matter how natural a heart attack might have appeared, speculations would surely abound. Especially from Thelma, who knew of Marvin's ability but not of the extent he had been using it. Fate intervened by dropping Stone in Marvin's lap.

Every investor and shareholder lived with the constant fear of scandal or corruption infiltrating the companies in which they invested. And the investors and shareholders of Marvin's investment firm were no different. Thanks to Marvin knowing the president's schedule and that he was luxury cruising the Caribbean, he sent Stone over to his house to strategically plant a few kilos of cocaine. Thanks to Stone's prior occupation, the cocaine had been easy enough to procure. Marvin planned on making an anonymous phone call to the police in an hour but first wanted to savor the moment. And what a delicious moment it was!

When word of the president's illicit pastime would leak to the press, and in today's day and age, the inevitability was a constant, the investment firm's share price would tumble. Not only their price but the prices of the companies in which they had a controlling number of shares. Marvin estimated a twenty percent decrease in the parent, five to ten in the subsidiaries. And every company nestled under the venture capital arm would surely suffer the most. Marvin was prepared to exploit them all.

Due to his volcanic rise toward the top of the corporate ladder these past few months, he found himself in a position with quite a bit of disposable income; income he used to make a few investments himself. Two restaurants, a few rental properties, and a small, upstart office supply distribution company later, all employing workers with an unyielding dedication to succeed, he acquired a taste for wanting more. The price retraction after the media's upcoming feasting frenzy set Marvin up for just that—to get more!

After the news and subsequent termination of the president, the board of directors would have no other choice but to name Marvin as president. And while the firm's stock prices and many of its holdings plummeted, Marvin planned to mortgage his house as many times as possible and borrow even more money against the companies in his personal portfolio. Then the sky would no longer be the limit for him. Or his family.

"And why are you all smiles?" Thelma asked, entering his home office.

"You," Marvin replied, pulling her onto his lap. With warmth and love, he placed his hand on her protruding pregnant belly. "And my sons."

She kissed his forehead and then ran her fingers through his hair. "You're so sweet."

"You make me that way." He rolled his eyes up to watch her fingers as best he could.

Thelma noticed her husband watching her and stopped, then giggled. "Sorry. I can't help myself. It's been years since I could last do that. It just feels like . . . like a dream."

"Well, if it is, you're the best part, and I never want to wake up."

"That's only because you gave me *these*." Thelma laughed and pointed to her breasts, swelling with milk and testing the confines of the DD brassiere holding them back.

Marvin laughed as well. He again patted the triplets in utero. "*Those* are because you gave me *these*."

Her fingers found their way back to the soft black froth atop Marvin's head. "I believe you had something to do with them as well. So . . . was that one of your new friends on the phone?"

Marvin tried not to frown. After Thelma had met Michael and Claire, he told her about the time Michael, Derrick, and Emma visited his office. Since then, Thelma referred to them as his "new friends." Little did she know that Marvin hated Michael, found Derrick annoying, and thought of Emma as nothing more than a doddering old fool. He just didn't have the heart to tell her the truth; she liked the idea of him having friends, and she enjoyed the occasional dinner with Michael and Claire. "No. A new employee actually."

"But they've called before, though."

Not sure where her line of questioning might lead, Marvin gave a very guarded, "Yes."

"That was them last week at the hospital, wasn't it?"

Thelma knew that they had abilities like Marvin. Just last week he pranced around proud as a peacock, showering himself with self-congratulatory compliments because he shared secrets with his wife while Michael didn't. The only thing he didn't tell Thelma was the true extent to which he used his abilities. But semantics like that mattered little, and he deemed that information immaterial in the workings of their happy marriage. "I believe it was."

"Did they call you then? Ask for you to join them?"

"Yes and yes. But I declined. It was far too dangerous for a soon-to-be father with no formal training in handling extraordinary situations like that. I tried to convince them to avoid the situation and allow the proper authorities to handle it."

Thelma continued running her fingers through his hair, developing a methodical, almost hypnotic rhythm. "Excellent choice, dear."

More than a bit surprised by his help-those-in-need wife's statement, he let slip, "Really?"

"You are absolutely correct about putting yourself in danger. Plus, what if your little secret got out? Millions of people would beg you to cure them of whatever ails them. Millions more would demand you make their muscles bigger and waists smaller. Nonstop media coverage. And I'm sure the government would want a word with you. It would be utter madness. No, my dear, you made the proper choice."

Stunned by his wife's intuitive perspective, he took her free hand and kissed the back of it. Obviously she thought of entire scenarios about glimmers of ideas he hadn't even dreamed of. "I assure you, I promise to avoid any situation that jeopardizes our safety or secret."

"I'm glad. Be careful of your new friends, though. Michael . . . seems very persuasive."

Why would she think Michael to be persuasive? Well, he did wear an arrogant demeanor like a cloak. And again, she seemed ignorant that the initial request to join and further instigation came from Derrick. "So, why are you so concerned all of a sudden?"

In a motion so fluent it seemed rehearsed, she snatched the remote control from his desk and used it to bring the television to life with the current news. The town name, "Gallitzin," ran across the bottom of the screen while an attractive blonde holding a microphone talked to the audience. ". . . mixed stories from the residents who have escaped. Some say dozens of rabid animals are running wild, forcing the residents from their homes. Others claim there is a . . . girl . . . who is somehow controlling these animals to attack. A few even believe they've seen . . . lizard- and cat-like monsters. Whatever is happening in this sleepy little town, the local authorities have . . ."

Monsters? A girl who can control animals? If that were true, and Marvin had certainly lived through enough these past few months to entertain the ridiculous notion that the story might be true, the implications would be limitless. The entertainment value. Better yet, the scientific value! The *very profitable* scientific value! Marvin had to find out. And if this girl could control animals, he had to have her. Marvin realized he was about to lie to his wife . . .

CHAPTER
59

Camp Hill, Pennsylvania

Michael watched the television and became angry. Three months ago, if he had seen these images, he wouldn't have believed his eyes. He wouldn't have believed the news program. He would have laughed and thought those in charge of the news station nothing more than tie-wearing dupes. *This is nothing more than a stunt,* he would have thought. *A group of kids trying to get attention.* But not now. Not today. He knew there was no dishonesty in what he watched. It was real.

The camera work was a bit shoddy, certainly not a cameraman from a large news channel. The caption listed a town in western Pennsylvania, and the reporter was pretty enough. Behind her, Gallitzin resembled a ghost town with tourists waiting to inspect the attractions. Michael didn't focus on the reporter of moderate beauty or the fidgeting throng of onlookers glancing between the camera lens in front of them and the empty streets behind them. Two state police officers and orange sawhorses stood between the people and the town's main street. Michael saw the remnants of a head-on collision, crumpled cars and broken glass, as well the damage done to the storefronts lining the street. The shops no longer had windows, and the sidewalks rippled with dunes of broken glass. Doors struggled to hang on to one hinge while the occasional awning lay in the street. Then, the cameraman zoomed in as far as he could, bouncing between blurry and clear, trying to find the balance of getting a close shot and getting a clear shot, trying to maximize the shock value of the dead bodies.

Michael leaned forward in his chair and squinted, his right hand rubbing between his cheeks and chin, up and down, examining every inch of the television screen, looking for a clue. To most of the viewers, this was a mystery. To Michael as well, but he knew more answers than most. He stared at the street, riddled with carcasses, animal and human alike.

Michael counted three bloodied people on the ground, each with a large firearm by their side. Even small-town media had its fascination with gore, the panning camera lingering on the disemboweled guts or the neck missing its throat a little too long. The camera made its way to the dead animals, dozens of them. A few deer lay dead, as well as a mountain lion. Dogs and cats made up the majority of carcasses with an unsettling number of traditionally adorable woodland creatures. Raccoon, groundhog, fox, and squirrel parts were scattered and splattered across the town buildings. Every animal met its end by gunshot. Every one of them. Michael knew next to nothing about guns, but he knew enough that a rational person would not use a high-powered shotgun to stop a squirrel.

The camera pulled back to the young blonde with the microphone. "And now we're going to show you some home movie clips that happened to catch some of the action earlier today that can only be described as bizarre. We have to warn you, some of the images are graphic."

The young reporter on the edge of town clipped away, replaced by a brunette bombshell in green lingerie standing in a living room. She smiled while twirling a lock of her Aqua-Net hair and shifted her weight from one leg to the other, causing her natural D cups to jiggle and ripple. She tilted her head and, with a two-pack-a-day voice, asked the man holding the camera, "So, you like?"

The world knew it was a man because he replied, "Fu[beep] yeah! Mmm-mmm. You're so fu[beep]ing hot! I'm gonna—"

The living room door exploded off its hinges, cutting the amateur cameraman short. Although the images jumped and jerked, Michael had little trouble seeing the large black bear burst into the room. The woman's blood-curdling shrieks ended as the bear sunk its teeth into her face and disemboweled her with one swipe, intestines dangling from its claws.

The man with the camera ran. Dizzying images whipped back and forth across the screen like a carnival ride. Floor, wall, floor, shredded woman, floor, wall, floor, while the man screamed, "Fu[beep]! Sh[beep]! Fu[beep]!" The man ran through his kitchen and out the back door as half-second glimpses of his neighbors evacuating their own homes, being chased by crazed animals, filled the screen.

With headache-inducing abruptness, the screen shifted to the product of another camcorder. The television transported the viewer to a squalid kitchen, the camcorder operator focused on the forest right outside the window, but Michael could not help but let his eyes linger on the monstrous pile of food-encrusted dishes threatening to topple from the sink. He ignored the rubes yapping to each other with their unsophisticated western Pennsylvanian drawls and pulled his eyes to the focus of their conversation—a convoy of animals and birds, all shapes and sizes, predators and prey, marching in sync through the forest from right to left. A large blot of green flashed between trees. Then farther in the distance, a streak of orange. However, the image froze on the orange streak, and the news producers zoomed in on the frozen image. Blurred and grainy, the image almost looked like a human shape. Michael knew the image was real, despite the flashback to the late-seventies media frenzy of Big Foot sightings.

The reporter continued repeating that neither citizens nor authorities could explain what had happened today. But Michael knew. And whatever specifics he lacked, he knew the one person who would have them should be calling soon. In hopes of accelerating the process, Michael snatched his cell phone, ready to push the "accept" button when the inevitable call came. Planning for the conversation, Michael thought of ways to let Derrick down easy, ways to say "no" to driving out to Gallitzin to hunt down the source of why the animals went psycho or track down the mysterious orange creature. Orange creature?

Icy pins prickled their way down Michael's spine as he realized something. Against his better judgment, he understood that something strange had happened to him to give him his "pushing" abilities. The same strange thing also affected Emma and Derrick and Marvin. He never considered that there might be physical effects to whatever gave them their abilities. Sure, the large man that they encountered at the hospital obviously went through some form of metamorphosis. Would Michael go through the same kind of transformation? Turn his skin to steel? Or change him to a mythic orange Sasquatch? His stomach churned at the notion, unable to stop his imagination from painting him orange and green while adding seven more arms, a dozen new eyeballs, and a few twisted horns for good measure. Why the hell hadn't Derrick called yet?

No clock in his house could tick, but Michael heard each second click, echoing in the cavern of his now empty soul. He never even wanted to admit he had special abilities, but now he had to know more, had to know if one day he would awaken next to his wife as some Kafka-esque monstrosity. Able to take no more, he pushed "talk" on his phone and dialed Derrick's number.

"Yeah?" came from the other end.

"Derrick? It's Michael. Have you seen the news? Seen what's going on in Gallitzin?"

"Yeah."

"You think it's . . . you know . . . special? Like us?"

"Without a doubt. Heading out that way soon."

"Oh. Well, I called to let you know I won't be joining you. Last time was my last time, so don't . . ."

"S'okay. We didn't plan on calling you since you made it very clear that our last time together was your *last time*."

"Oh. So . . . you going alone?"

"No. I'm with Emma right now. Marvin's coming over to speed up her healing, and then the three of us—"

"*Three* of you?" Michael all but shrieked, jumping from his chair. "Marvin's *joining* you?"

"Yeah. Like I said, we're waiting for him at the hospital and—"

"Don't leave until I get there!"

After hanging up the phone, he found a sheet of paper and scrawled a quick note to his wife. "Students called, wanted to organize a last-minute field trip. I'll call soon to explain. Love bunches, Michael."

That was the *worst* lie *ever*! But he could hardly help it. Derrick's flights of fancy were one thing, but Marvin's involvement was a whole separate matter . . .

CHAPTER
60

Philadelphia, Pennsylvania

Matthew Matthews strolled past the cookie aisle in the grocery store and thought of simpler times, the ones as a child with his grandparents, enjoying the special moments of sharing a glass of milk and a dozen cookies with them. Good times before they died in a car crash a mere two months after they received custody of him when his parents were killed in a mugging. Matthews shook his head to snap from his little daydream and looked around the grocery store, a term he used loosely. It reminded him more of a convenience store, barely bigger, with shelving that only came up to his shoulders, presumably so the employees could monitor any shoplifting attempts since there were no security cameras. There were three checkout stations, two of them manned by teenagers, neither of them possessing the enthusiasm or attitude to care about shoplifting. Matthew noticed a stock clerk trudging around, taking empty boxes to the backroom and returning to the floor with full ones, as well as a frowning manager patrolling the aisles.

Impressed by the number of patrons, Matthews continued looking at the snack foods. Even if he and the two undercover agents weren't in the store, it would still have a healthy traffic volume. Trying not to be too conspicuous, Matthews glanced at his partners. They all wore bulky jackets to conceal their equipment and meandered around the store. Luckily, the manager was the only one who seemed to notice but too busy to care. Two more agents waited in a van in the parking lot. However, if their target didn't show up soon, Matthews and his agents might have to call it a day and think of a plan B.

Glancing at his watch, Matthews wondered why she hadn't shown up yet. She received her welfare check today, and then she'd go to the bank and end her trip here. For the past three weeks, his men watched her. This routine was the only one she followed to the minute each week. She had to be here soon.

Matthews thought of getting her at her apartment but didn't like the variables. It was on the fifth floor of her building, confined quarters, and limited escape routes. Plus, he observed she knew many of the neighbors, and if the extraction went awry, as did the one with Haley, he knew the neighbors would be more than happy to intervene. And odds were, her neighbors had better weapons than he and his agents did. He didn't want to pull her from her apartment, but that might be the new plan if she didn't show up soon.

Still no show. Matthews decided to call this mission a failure. He grabbed a handful of beef sticks, figuring he might as well make the trip worthwhile, and looked up to see an explosion of hair enter the store. LaKeisha had finally arrived.

He fought the instinct to duck and opted to turn, keeping his back to her. Making eye contact with one of the other agents, Matthews offered a slight nod. The agent moved to a more advantageous position.

Waiting until she grabbed a handbasket to start her weekly shopping trip, Matthews slid his hand into his coat pocket, gripping the injection gun. He didn't want a scene; the sedative loaded in the gun would make LaKeisha loopy but suggestible and still able to walk. The other agents had tranquilizer darts if things were to get out of control. Matthews hoped for a smooth extraction but knew how the real world was.

LaKeisha wandered down each aisle toward Matthew's location. He had to time this right, couldn't let her see him. She turned down the aisle next to his. Keeping his back to her, he spun from his aisle into hers. He saw her turn her back to him and decided to take a chance. At a brisk pace, he aimed right for her, his finger on the injection gun's trigger. He wanted to grab her by the arm, tag her, and escort her out with no one the wiser. No such luck.

LaKeisha looked right at him and smiled. "I thought I saw you when I came in."

The effect was instant. She wore a thin shirt and tight jeans. And no bra, which became very apparent to Matthews as he saw her large, hardened nipples press against her shirt as if trying to escape. His sudden erection hurt as he walked closer. He scolded himself for deciding on such a stupid idea! He and his team should have taken her at her apartment. No matter how hard he tried to fight, he couldn't help but stare at her tits and remember how good her soft body felt against his. With one final effort, he reached into his jacket and pulled out a small filtration mask.

After putting it on, he gulped the filtered air as if he were lost in a desert and just found an oasis of cool water. He wasn't sure if her powers of persuasion were mental or chemical or other. But the techs back at the lab found traces of pheromones on his clothing from the last time he met her. Pheromones strong enough to melt away his inhibitions. But the filtration mask worked. However, once LaKeisha saw it, she started to back away from him.

"What the fuck is *that*?" she asked.

The two other agents put their masks on, causing quite a stir with everyone else in the store. Taking a chance, Matthews lunged for her but missed as she pulled away. His hand slipped from his pocket, holding the injection gun. And she saw it.

Scared, she dropped her basket and ran. And since she was scared, anyone without a filtration mask became scared. Frightened. Panicked. Running around in a blind frenzy.

This could have gone better! Matthews thought as LaKeisha ran to the emergency side exit, away from him and the other agents. The only good news was the employees were too panicked to call the authorities, and the emergency exit was not hooked up to any alarms.

Matthews and the agents, with their tranq guns drawn, pursued. The exit led to a small alley where trash cans and other waste were kept. At one end came the other two agents from the parking lot. LaKeisha ran the other way.

"Go around! Cut her off!" Matthews ordered the agents from the parking lot.

LaKeisha knew where she was and knew enough not to want to be there. Knew this was where trouble lurked. But if that fucking white boy thought he could fuck her, disappear, then come back with some weird-ass mask and a few of his friends . . . well, that ain't how things were done around here. She turned a corner down another alley and found what she knew she'd find.

Eight men, skin ranging from shades of creamed coffee to the color of tar, loitered in the alleyway, rolling dice. They all wore baggy pants and designer tank tops or basketball jerseys. A couple wore no shirt at all. They all had frowns, even when smiling, and bodies forged from prison steel. And they all looked at LaKeisha, sweating and panting, like a pack of dogs would a wounded rabbit.

All of the men stopped their game and approached LaKeisha. She knew they were gang members, heavy into dealing drugs and other things if the price was right. They started talking tough, toying with her, taking advantage of a woman walking into their alley. They frightened LaKeisha at first. Then she thought of Matthews and what just happened at the grocery store, forcing her to put herself in this situation. And that made her mad.

Surprised, LaKeisha watched as the men turned on each other, taking their aggressions out. A couple stood chest to chest and barked. Others displayed their toughness through body language and endless strings of profanity. Until LaKeisha intervened. "Hey!"

Once she got their attention, she pointed to the other end of the alley where Matthews and four of his agents, all wearing filtration masks, stood. Just looking at Matthews made LaKeisha angrier. The gang members frothed and fumed, gnashing their teeth. In a blind rage, all eight ran toward the intruders. All eight were gunned down.

Paralyzed in shock, LaKeisha stared at the bodies. Were they dead? Why didn't they pull their own guns? Why'd they charge with their bare hands like crazy animals? She couldn't move as all five masked men moved closer, guns drawn. One pulled the trigger.

The tranquilizer dart stung like a yellow jacket bite. LaKeisha pulled it from her neck and looked at it. Then collapsed as her world went black.

Matthews moved fast enough to catch her before she hit the pavement. He ordered his agents to pull the van around and keep the prying eyes of passing pedestrians to a minimum. As he cradled the chubby black girl in his arms, Matthews smiled. Despite how poorly the actual capture went, he got her. He could now move forward with his plans. He could now move forward with his plans for Haley . . .

CHAPTER
61

Gallitzin, Pennsylvania

"This is stupid," Michael whined. Dried leaves and small twigs crunched and snapped with every tentative footstep. The stench of decay and mold intermingled with the smell of sweaty leather. The random bird chirps and tree creaks sounded strange to Michael, making him uneasy about exploring an alien environment. He hated forests and cities, and this expedition reaffirmed his belief that suburbia was the pinnacle of mankind.

"Why?" Derrick asked. His voice came through the Bluetooth in Michael's ear with crystal clarity. Michael hated it, the Bluetooth attached to his right ear, the tight leather mask jamming it seemingly into his brain. "Just because you didn't think of the plan?"

"Plan? You call this a plan? The four of us just meandering around the forest looking for God knows what?"

"Well, Professor," Marvin's voice piped into Michael's head. "Until you have an idea that's actually better than the ones you tear apart, we have little choice but to use my ideas."

Michael stewed with those words. Especially since Marvin was right. The whole drive there, in the back of Marvin's Hummer H2 with a private driver, the four of them squabbled about what to do. Any idea that Marvin, Derrick, or Emma had, Michael shot down. Someone had to be the voice of reason, and it was obvious to Michael that he was it. Not to mention that once again, Derrick's foresight to buy ski masks for this adventure failed to include Michael, who had to be relegated to wearing the leather biker's mask he so loathed. That irked Michael, as did traipsing through the savage world of Western Pennsylvania's forests. "I'm just saying that it feels like we're rushing in headfirst again. The last time we did that, Emma got hurt."

"And I'd gladly make that sacrifice again if it means saving people's lives," Emma said, her stern voice cutting from Michael's right ear all the way to his left.

Michael rolled his eyes while still tiptoeing among the tall trees as if any one of them could reach out and harm him. "That's not the point. We need to think of the danger involved. The authorities closed the roads into the town for a reason. And we don't even know if someone is even behind this. Maybe it's a few rabid animals? We didn't take enough time to think things through."

"Well, thank you for your concern, Michael," Emma replied. "But we need to find out what's going on here first before we assess the level of danger."

Michael paused to think of a witty comeback but noticed the forest stopped making unnerving noises. No chattering or clicking, chirping or creaking. The only noises he heard were his crunching footfalls. Even the wind seemed to have run away. "That's odd."

"What?" Derrick asked. "Did you find something?"

Slowing his pace, Michael looked around. "No. It's just everything went . . . quiet."

"That'd probably be because of me," a voice came from behind Michael.

Turning, Michael winced as Derrick shouted, "Who said that? Who's there?"

Samson stood before Michael, claws protracted and anxious teeth glistening with saliva. Unable to believe his eyes, Michael froze, terrified. His heart exploded, pouring ice into his throat. His eyes widened to the point of pain. Samson stepped forward; Michael watched the corded muscles ripple beneath the pelt of orange fur. Fear strangled Michael, allowing only the merest of whisper, "A . . . a . . . a cat . . . creature . . . thing."

Samson stopped and his face soured from Michael's comment. "Well, what kind of freak walks around the forest wearing some kinda fetish biker mask with zippers on it?"

"Freak?" Michael repeated, dignity pushing fear out of the way for prevalence. "Look who's talking?"

Samson smiled a Cheshire grin. "At least I ain't talkin' to myself."

"Talking to . . . ? It's a Bluetooth."

"Well, it don't matter what color your teeth are, I'm gonna have to kick 'em in." Then Samson pounced.

Surprised by the speed, Michael barely had time to prepare a push. By the time Michael felt the ball of warmth at the base of his skull, the half-man, half-cat was already in the air. Fur raised and hissing, the corded creature of fury arced downward with claws extended and jaws ready to rend flesh. Falling to the ground, Michael released the warmth, smacking Samson square in the chest.

Releasing an eerie yowl, Samson arced back into the air. A trail of loose fur floated to the ground as he twisted his body. With one final flip, he righted himself and dug his claws into a tree, stopping himself. After regaining his bearings, he climbed down the tree and charged toward Michael again.

Surprised that the creature continued its attack, Michael stood. This time, he was prepared. Doing his best to take a deep breath, ignoring the leather smell, he concentrated. Fire raged within him, burning for escape. And once the creature came within ten feet, Michael released it. Again, the mysterious and invisible energy slammed Samson's chest, and again a cloud of orange fur remained. Michael pushed Samson with such force a rooster tail of leaves and twigs plumed behind the cat-creature as he skidded across the forest floor. With a flurry of throaty growls, the claws of Samson's hands and feet scrabbled to cling to the dirt. Once again, he needed the aid of a tree to stop. And once again, after stopping, he charged Michael.

Unnerved by the creature's sheer determination, Michael focused and pushed again. This time, the cat-monster did not go quite as far and regrouped twice as fast. And charged again.

Each spitting hiss sent a chill down Michael's spine. He could see nothing but claws shredding leaves and spraying dirt as it ran toward him. He pushed again with less-than-optimal results. Knowing all too well how a mouse felt, Michael ran. The flight instinct took over. Legs churned and arms pumped. Desperate, Michael turned and pushed again, the effect diminishing. Of all the ways he envisioned himself dying, being torn to shreds by a cat monster in the middle of a forest certainly wasn't one of them.

As an overweight trucker, Samson never had natural grace. But as a mutated half-man, half-cat, grace was his new companion. The first time Michael telekinetically threw him through the air surprised Samson. He assumed that whatever happened to him and Adam and Nora had to have happened to other people, but he never suspected he'd be flung into the air by a guy in a biker mask who talked to himself. The second time Michael pushed him, he allowed his new, natural grace to take over, compensating with pure instinct. Each successive push was nothing more than a minor obstacle that Samson's body was prepared for.

Dodging Michael's mental attacks or compensating for the ones that connected, Samson continued his charge. He ran toward Michael, shifting from hind legs to all four limbs. He smelled the fear in Michael's sweat. He could almost taste the blood beating in Michael's heart, each *thud, thud* mimicking his own. Samson knew it wouldn't be much longer now that Michael tried to flee. Enjoying the nice little chase his prey offered, Samson smiled as he readied his muscles for one final pounce. But quickly changed his mind.

Michael turned one final time and opened his mouth to scream, or so Samson thought. Instead, his jaw snapped open, dropping to his chest as his lips retracted to expose rows of broken glass teeth, saliva dripping, tongue snaking and whipping to three feet long. The veins and tendons in his neck pulsated and grew, his skin staying taut around them. His clothes turned to rags, unable to contain the exploding muscle as he grew to fifteen feet tall.

Samson, fur puffing all around his body, stopped his attack and retreated. Hissing and spitting, the cat-creature scurried away, leaving a befuddled Michael in the dust. Standing there, wondering what he could have possibly done, Michael looked at his hands. Nothing unusual. He then touched his chest, shoulders, and face. Other than leather and zippers, he felt nothing out of the ordinary. It wasn't until he heard the crunching footsteps from behind that he realized what had happened. From behind a thick oak tree stepped Derrick.

"Derrick! You scared the crap out of me!"

"I scared you? So, the freaky large man cat thing had no effect?"

"You know what I mean."

Rolling his eyes, Derrick shook his head from the lack of gratitude. "Come on. We gotta find Emma."

"Why?"

"Haven't you been listening to your Bluetooth? She's facing something like you did. Some lizard thing."

"Listening? Sorry, I was a bit preoccupied."

Derrick shook his head and rolled his eyes again as they jogged toward Emma . . .

CHAPTER
62

Pittsburgh, Pennsylvania

Kevin Keller took a deep breath and exhaled slowly. Bob had taught him that the best way to display confidence was not to jump into a situation while nervous; that'd be like a batter taking the plate with two strikes already. A few deep breaths, clear the mind, try to anticipate, but stay away from too many detailed possibilities. Today was the day. After three months of practice and studying and preparing himself, Kevin was going to do it. He was finally going to ask Debra Verone for a date. And it had to be perfect.

Kevin's plan was risky with countless variables, and he was really going to put himself out there. But as Bob taught him, the more over the top the setup, the more difficult it would be for her to say no. Go grandiose without crossing the stalker line. Kevin was pretty sure his idea would work. He had spent all day yesterday running probability programs with his studies and experiments. The outcomes for this scenario had all been favorable.

As quietly as his girth would allow, he crept up behind Debra, working at her computer in her cubicle. She didn't notice him behind her. Hunched over her desk and cloaked in lethargy, she pecked away at her keyboard, barely noticing the changes she made to her spreadsheet. Last night she went on another date, an attractive man she met at a bar last weekend. As with most attractive men, she was finding out, he spent the entire dinner talking about himself, what he did for a living, his sports car, and the winning touchdown he made over two decades ago during the state championship in high school. Was this to be her fate? How her heart would feel for the rest of her life? Just as she thought of picking up brochures on becoming a nun or a lesbian, an instant message popped up at the bottom of her screen.

KevinKeller01: Good morning, Debra. How are you today? [Press ctrl-alt-F2 to reply.]

Sitting up in her chair, Debra couldn't help but smile. She had worked here for ten years and never knew the system had instant messaging capabilities. Pressing the proper key combination as instructed yielded a new window with Kevin's message repeated and a flashing cursor next to an ID she assumed was hers. She read the ID three times, grinning like a schoolgirl, and replied.

PrettyEyes00: I'm doing much better, now. I didn't know we had IM here?

KevinKeller01: We don't. I'm special.

PrettyEyes00: LOL!

Debra giggled, but Kevin couldn't understand the humor she found in his last statement. But as Bob taught him—just roll with it.

Leaning back in her chair, Debra nibbled on her index finger, waiting for a reply. She then remembered this was Kevin she dealt with. Even though he displayed a boldness never seen before . . . it was still Kevin. She decided to help him out.

PrettyEyes00: I really like the ID you came up with for me.

KevinKeller01: I just call em like I see em.

Debra giggled again, never imagining Kevin talking like this. This seemed more like . . . Bob. Was this Bob? A sadness washed through her. If this was Bob communicating with her, did he think he was helping? Or was he just mean? A pig like all the other men? She shook her head, trying to shake out the bad thoughts. As she tried to formulate a response to fish for information, another IM popped up.

KevinKeller01: Do you like blue suits?

What an unusual and abrupt question. *That* certainly seemed like something Kevin would say! Feeling better that this might be Kevin, and a bit guilty for doubting him, she answered.

PrettyEyes00: I most certainly do. I think they make a man look dashing.

KevinKeller01: Do you like snapdragons and lilies?

Not understanding the logic behind this line of questioning, Debra chuckled. Was he flirting with her? He *had* to be! He flat out said she had pretty eyes. But the suit question? And the flower question? She was intrigued and needed to find out what was going on.

PrettyEyes00: Absolutely. They're both beautiful flowers.

KevinKeller01: Hypothetically speaking, if I asked you out on a date, what might you say?

Placing her left hand over her mouth, she couldn't believe he had just asked her out. After all these years. She knew he had a crush on her but never fancied him to be her type. An unusual feeling passed through her—he just asked her out via the internet. But her mind, maybe her heart, brought up images of last night. The boring time mixed with all the dull conversation. Corporate cliches like "think outside the box" and "step outside your comfort zone" flowed through her mind.

PrettyEyes00: I believe I might have to accept.

KevinKeller01: Turn around.

Debra turned around and almost fell out of her chair. Kevin stood in front of her in a blue suit holding a bouquet of snapdragons and lilies. It was a smart suit, a deep blue that matched his eyes, business-like but wearable for social functions. Debra had to admit she liked the suit. And the flowers.

Bob taught Kevin to never go with industry standards like roses or carnations when buying a woman flowers, because it lacked creativity. Sure, a woman would usually like any bouquet a man gave her, but she'd always love a bouquet containing flowers that no other man thought of. And Kevin saw the benefits as he handed them to Debra—her eyes misted up. "Kevin, that's . . . this is . . . wow. These are beautiful."

"Thank you," he replied. Keep it simple. Short answers were the best for now.

Cradling the flowers, showing both admiration and respect for the man who gave them to her, she looked at him, his suit. Nodding her head, her smile beamed. "And your suit is very smart, Kevin. You do look quite dashing."

"Again, thank you." Kevin smiled and offered a slight bow.

Debra closed her eyes and inhaled the fragrance from the flowers. She opened her eyes and squinted at Kevin. Looking over her shoulder, she stared at her computer monitor, then looked back at Kevin. She asked, "How'd you do that? Send me IMs while standing right behind me?"

Kevin smiled, one of confidence, not like the uncomfortable ones Debra was used to seeing. "Just a simple program."

"A program? A pre-made conversation? How did you know what my responses were going to be?"

Still smiling, Kevin moved his hands behind his back and tugged his sleeve over his "watch," now modified for wireless connection to the mainframe. "Just psychology."

Debra offered a wry smile. She didn't thoroughly believe him, but flirting with him was surprisingly fun. Nothing too heavy, just light enough to be engaging. "It's now a definite."

"Definite?"

"To your hypothetical question. If you were to ask me out, I would definitely say yes."

"Well, then," Kevin said as he stepped forward. As Bob taught, Kevin needed to do something classy yet smarmy. Unexpected, but not creepy. Running through his options, Kevin chose to take Debra's left hand with his right and gently kiss the back of it. "It would be my honor to pick you up at eight tonight."

"My goodness, Kevin," Debra said, brushing the fingers of her right hand across the base of her neck. "It's like you went on the internet and downloaded the perfect guy."

Kevin simply smiled and kissed the back of her hand again . . .

CHAPTER
63

Gallitzin, Pennsylvania

Emma rolled her eyes. Michael could be so insufferable at times. Sure, traipsing around a forest wearing masks was ludicrous, but there was no denying something was wrong here in Gallitzin. Even though Derrick no longer "vibed," or maybe he controlled it better, he said he felt there was someone special, someone like them, here. And Emma felt it was her God-demanding duty to help.

Why didn't Michael understand that? In fact, why did Michael even come along in the first place? He didn't like his gifts, and he shirked responsibility for them at every chance he had. He hadn't even told *his wife* yet about his wonderful gift! If Emma's husband were still alive today, he'd put Michael in his place!

Emma chuckled to herself, thinking of the disgusted look on Michael's face when Marvin suggested that they split up and move toward town through the forest to avoid the authorities. She swore he turned green! Emma had spent her fair share of time in the forest throughout her life. Plenty of it around her hometown for her to play in as a child as well as take romantic hikes and picnics with her husband. She couldn't fathom how an individual, especially a man, could get so flustered about walking through the woods.

The voices from her Bluetooth pulled her attention back to the surrounding forest. And reminded her of the potential danger. The severity of the men's voices threw Emma back to last week when she had been shot. She had been *shot!* A small-town senior, a "little old lady," was shot while fighting, *physically engaging,* a muscled man near three hundred pounds. A chill slid down her spine, right to where the bullet had pierced her skin. Phantom pains tugged at the healed wound. The fears returned as she heard the leaves rustle behind her.

The warm tingling spread through her body. It was ready to react, with or without her consent. Muscles tensed, she turned, making zero noise, and saw what made the noise behind her. If not for her ski mask holding it in place, her jaw would have fallen to the ground.

Before Emma stood a seven-foot-tall lizard with emerald-hued scales, standing on hind legs with arms and hands like a man. Brown copperheads and rattlesnakes draped over him like strips of hissing clothing. Black snakes and garden snakes roiled and rolled across his body. Emma didn't remember seeing any Biblical signs but knew exactly who this was. "Satan!"

The snake-creature reeled back as if the very word burned. Images of his father, his eviscerated guts, flitted through his mind. His father thought the same thing of him and told him so with his dying breath. As if talking to the image of his father, he said, "Adam . . . my name . . . isss . . . Adam."

Emma fought the electricity coursing through her, the urge to attack. This snake-creature was . . . or had been . . . a person. And he was young—Emma could sense it in his voice, the look in his eyes. "Adam. Are you doing this to the town, Adam? Are you making the animals attack the people?"

"Adam?" Marvin asked in Emma's ear. "Who's Adam?"

"No . . . Nora isss . . ."

Both Adam and Emma were poised to strike. Knees bent, hands in front of themselves, ready to block or attack.

"Nora? Her name is Nora. Can you take me to see Nora?"

"No."

"Adam, what she's doing is wrong. She's hurting innocent people."

"No."

"She has to stop this, Adam. She has to make amends and atone for her deeds. She needs to turn herself in to authorities."

"*No!*" And Adam lunged.

Feeling like pure electricity, Emma spun on her heel and dodged his attack. As if Adam moved in slow motion, Emma struck the back of his neck. Given the size difference, it did little more than knock him off balance.

Looking more lizard than man, Adam clutched the ground with all four claws, spun around, and leaped again. Tongue flailing and jaws open, Adam flung his body at her with outstretched arms. Emma timed her jump perfectly, kicking the back of his head. Again, she didn't have the weight to do any damage, only knock him to the ground.

Adam scrabbled to his feet, dirt and leaves spraying through the air, and lunged again. His outstretched hands missed the dexterous woman, but he planned for this. As she flipped out of his way, a dozen snakes shot from Adam's body like coiled springs. Recognizing which snakes were venomous, Emma either plucked them from the air or twisted to avoid their fangs. Grabbing two behind their jaws, she used them like whips to smack the others away. By the time her feet touched the forest floor again, she held two dead copperheads while two black snakes were attached to her legs. Emma dropped the carcasses and removed the black snakes. Although the bites hurt, she knew there was no poison.

Adam stood shocked. Even though he had reptilian features, Emma could tell he was surprised and had no idea what to do next. She prepared for another attack. However, he collapsed.

Marvin stood behind the fallen Adam, hand still outstretched from touching him. Even though he wore a ski mask, black pants, and a windbreaker, Marvin exuded an air of regality. He lorded over the twitching monster like a twenty-first-century gladiator, flush with victory. Even his voice mimicked his grandiose pose. "There's no need to panic, Adam. I pinched a few choice nerves, paralyzing you."

Wide-eyed from fear and tongue draped out of his mouth onto the ground, Adam looked up at the man who defeated him. He tried to fight, to stand, to simply *move*, but couldn't muster more than faint twitches. How was this possible? How could a man do this to him with a mere touch? Adam blinked and nothing more.

Marvin continued, "I learned much about you, Adam, in that single touch. Amazing what biological secrets there are that we think no one will find. You're only sixteen. And you have been robbed of your . . . manhood. I can help you, Adam. I might not be able to fix you right now, but after some time, time to study you, I might be able to find a cure."

A cure? It had been only three months, but Adam could barely remember a time before being a mutated freak. The faces of his family had been fading from his memories, all except the twisted, anguished face of his dying father. He could go back! He could explain and hope they forgive him. He could . . . no! This was impossible!

Still poised to attack, Emma walked toward Marvin. Leery of his intent, she listened as he continued, "I can see by the gleam in your eye that you would very much like to return to your life as the typical American teenager. However, there are some things I need you to do for me first."

Anything! Anything! Just make it stop! Just take it all back! Adam wanted to cry, but all he could do was wiggle his leaf-encrusted tongue.

Marvin squatted down close to Adam with his hand hovering over his reptilian chest. "I'm going to release you from your paralysis. You are going to cease your hostilities and take us to meet Nora. I assure you, if you attack my associates or me, I will do far worse things to you than knock you down. Blink if you understand."

Adam blinked. And Marvin did as promised. One touch and Adam had his feeling back. Marvin kept his hand on Adam's scaly shoulder as he sat up. Adam flickered his forked tongue to remove the dead leaves. Marvin asked, "Feel better?"

"Yesss."

Both men stood. "Okay, Adam, lead the way."

Adam started walking toward the barn in which he had been held captive. A smile crossed his face as he dreamed of returning to human . . .

CHAPTER
64

Gallitzin, Pennsylvania

Derrick and Michael found the barn. Finally. Marvin tried giving them directions to the barn from where they were in the woods, but the only thing that accomplished was giving Derrick a headache. Michael accused Marvin of giving bad directions and complained that all the trees looked alike. Marvin accused Michael of not being deft enough to follow simple directions. Nora sent a raccoon to find them and led them to the barn to expedite the process. Of course, Michael complained about how stupid he felt for following a raccoon.

Once they arrived at the barn, more animals greeted them. Four dogs stood by the barn, growling and exposing their teeth, foamy saliva spraying as they barked. Howling cats prowling along the roof arched their backs and puffed their tails. Squirrels and chipmunks skittered around, spitting and clicking their angry intentions. Michael hated animals, and this was why. The uneasiness intensified when they walked into the barn itself.

A black bear lumbered around, snorting its discontent at the new guests. A mountain lion prowled the perimeter, never taking its eyes off Michael. A ten-point buck snorted and shuffled its front hooves, wanting to charge. Owls and hawks and crows watched everything below them from the rafters. The warmth built at the back of Michael's neck, readying him to push, especially when he saw the creatures.

Standing with his arms crossed and back against the wall was the orange cat-creature Michael fought and Derrick scared away. In the middle of the barn was a seven-foot-tall lizard standing on its hind legs. While fighting the cat-thing, Michael thought he had heard Emma mention some sort of snake thing. This must have been it. Sitting against the other wall was a rabbit in the shape of a human, except missing a foot. But what really caught Michael's eye was the naked Asian girl with the onyx eyes.

"Nora?" Derrick asked. He jogged closer as he pulled off his mask. The animals bristled and ruffled but held their positions.

Michael couldn't help but say, "Derrick! Your mask!"

The girl frowned. "Who are you?"

Michael didn't notice that Marvin and Emma weren't wearing masks until Marvin spoke. "Seriously, Michael. Do you see any cameras here?"

Derrick ignored everyone except Nora. "It's me. Derrick. We met at that church camp back when we were freshmen. In high school."

Nora offered a condescending sneer and turned her attention back to Marvin. "Now, about your offer . . ."

"Wait," Michael cut in. "What offer?"

Marvin sighed but held his salesman's smile. "I just offered Miss Leung a job, and we're going over the details."

"What? A job? Are you serious?"

"When it comes to money, there is no other way to be. I was about to go into detail about the benefits of following certain rules, such as how she would be able to help animals far more working for me than she would attacking a town no one's ever heard of."

"What about the . . . those . . . them?" Michael pointed at Adam, Samson, and Robert.

Marvin chuckled. "Well, it's definitely refreshing to see you act as Nora's agent, pro bono. They're people who have gone through changes, just like us. Different effects, mind you, but they're still people. They're free to do as they choose. If Nora decides to come with me, they're more than welcome to come along. I would be happy to have them in my employ, and I would make sure they have more-than-adequate living arrangements."

"Employ? You're going to hire them? Doing what?"

"Well, Michael, Miss Leung and I hadn't reached that point in our negotiations. She has yet to accept my offer."

"But . . ."

"Michael," Emma interrupted. He looked over to see Emma inching her way to Derrick for comfort. Her arms were crossed over her chest, and her eyes were wide, unable to hide her fear of the situation. "Marvin is trying to bring about a peaceful resolution to this situation. If there's anything he can do to help . . . we don't even know why Nora is doing this."

"Nora's doing this because this town is full of redneck fucks!" Robert shouted.

All but ignoring the outburst, Marvin turned to Nora. "What is it that you want?"

Nora looked at Robert, then at Adam and Samson. She inhaled and glanced at all the other animals. "I'm in . . . was in . . . college. Penn State. I love animals and wanted to help them, protect them."

"Perfect!" Marvin clapped his hands together. Nora frowned, wondering why he was so excited. He saw her distrust and continued. "I will set up a facility for you. A clinic slash laboratory. You communicate with animals, so let's use that to help everybody. Imagine how much more efficiently we could discover new drugs, new cures, for *both* people and animals if we could communicate with them."

Still frowning, Nora snapped, "But that still means testing, still *hurting* them."

"Not if I can fix them." Marvin walked over to Adam and looked at the bullet wounds in the young man's shoulder and thigh. Marvin grabbed Adam's scaly arm and closed his eyes for effect. It had been three days since he had been shot, and the wounds had closed yet still seeped and exposed raw meat. Before everyone's eyes, the muscles reconnected and green skin grew over the top. If Adam were to wash away the dried blood, he would not be able to see the wounds, not even a scar.

Robert's jaw dropped as he sat up. With his cumbersome fingers, he pointed to his missing foot. "My foot! My foot! Do my foot!"

Marvin thought of coming up with an excuse not to. He neither liked the kid's attitude nor wanted to display how much power he truly possessed. But he thought he needed to comply to make the best of the situation. Negotiations always went better for heroes than bastards. Within a couple minutes, and a few moments of discomfort for Robert, his foot returned.

Holding his foot with both hands, Robert sobbed and wiggled his toes. "Can . . . can you fix me? And Adam and Samson? Make us normal again?"

Not wanting to concede *too* much during negotiations, Marvin walked back toward Nora and said, "Unfortunately not. Yet. Whatever has changed you . . . changed all of us . . . I cannot manipulate. However, if Nora decides to come with us, and you decide to accompany her, I shall make it a goal of mine to find a way to alter your appearance."

"I'm in!" Robert replied. "Nora, please. He's gonna try to fix us. Please."

Stunned from what she had just witnessed, she whispered, "You healed them."

"Yes, I did," Marvin replied.

"And you can do that with animals?"

"Of course," Marvin lied. He had no idea if he could or not, and he didn't particularly care. He just wanted what Nora had, wanted her roadmap.

"What will this clinic slash laboratory work on?"

"Your discretion. But before we get too far ahead of ourselves, I think it would be more prudent to set you . . . and your friends up with a new home where you all will be safe." Typical of a businessman, he extended his hand for her to shake.

Nora looked at Adam, standing tall and stoic, then at Samson, impassive and disinterested, and then at Robert, his hands pressed together in pleading prayer. Her mind roiled with arguments for and against. How could she trust this man? She *just* met him. But he and these other people had abilities like hers. They understood. If he gave her even half as much as he promised, she could do such great things for animals, for the world! And he was right about nothing getting solved if all she did was harass small towns. Plus, she'd have her three friends to protect her. And there were animals to be found no matter where they'd go, even in a city.

"Okay. I'll do it," Nora said, shaking Marvin's hand. And he viewed another roadmap. It was beautiful in its simplicity. Nothing more than telepathy and an understanding of the animal brain, a way to translate. She could see through their eyes, hear through their ears, smell and touch and taste. And *control* them all.

Marvin held the handshake a little too long, and Nora pulled away. Smiling, he removed his windbreaker and held it out for her to don it. "I know you will be remiss, Nora, but if you're to rejoin the outside world, a certain order of decorum is expected."

Nora accepted as Robert said to himself, "He talks so cool."

"Very well," Marvin continued. "So far, the local authorities and the state game commission are involved, but they're still in a state of chaos trying to deal with the citizens. Slipping out from here to my Hummer will be easy. But in a couple days, they will have the area scoured with deputized hunters, scared and with itchy trigger fingers. I suggest you send all your animal friends far away from here for a while."

"He has a Hummer?" Robert asked. He then turned to Samson. "You hear that? He has a Hummer."

Samson responded by bearing his fangs and growling.

"Dick," Robert replied and walked closer to Adam. "You hear that, Adam? He has a Hummer."

Marvin took a step back to allow Nora space to do what she needed to do. Michael strolled close to him and whispered, "Checkbook heroics, huh? This is what it comes down to?"

"The checkbook is the keystone that holds everything together."

Not able to refute the answer, Michael sneered and walked over to Emma and Derrick. And Marvin smiled . . .

CHAPTER
65

Pittsburgh, Pennsylvania

Debra sat across the table from Kevin and stared at him in disbelief. She felt a dopey smirk slide across her face, unable to stop it. She was on a date with one of the I/T guys, probably the nerdiest—no, not "nerdy." Maybe awkward? Sheltered? And she was having a good time. Not the most incredible or spectacular date ever, like bungee jumping or hang gliding, but it was certainly nice enough. Plus, the exciting bungee-jumping, hang-gliding dates usually came with immature and emotionally detached mannequins. But not Kevin.

Sure, he was a bit quiet for her taste, as quiet as she imagined he'd be. But he listened well, maintaining eye contact with her as she spoke. To the best of her knowledge, he hadn't even tried to sneak a peek at her cleavage. And when he did talk, his words were succinct, nice. On more than one occasion, Debra found herself checking his ears for any kind of radio transmitter, just in case someone fed him lines to say. A few times, she swore his words were Bob's.

They had both finished dinner, ready to start dessert. Debra had heard good things about this restaurant's cheesecake but needed a bit of conversation to feel comfortable. So, as she did many times tonight, she initiated. "I never knew you liked the theater, Kevin."

Kevin didn't. The first half of their date had been to see a musical, and he only took her there because it was all part of the formula to win her affection. "Of course. Did you enjoy the show?"

"Absolutely," Debra purred, sliding a forkful of cheesecake past her glistening lips.

Kevin knew she would. After examining the past three years' worth of her credit card statements, he cross-referenced with the most recently visited websites. Other than a few stops at dating and singles sites, she spent most of her time reading reviews for plays and musicals at the local theaters.

"Wonderful. So did I," Kevin lied.

After a few more bites and a couple more moments of silence, Debra asked, "So, Kevin . . . why computers? Why did you choose computers for a career?"

A sheepish smirk besmirched his face as he slouched a bit, trying to hide his blushing. "You don't want to know. It's stupid."

Now Debra was intrigued. This seemed like the first real response tonight. Even though she enjoyed every aspect of the evening, it felt a bit rehearsed, practiced. It felt like a date from a movie or television show that he once saw, all his words scripted. But her question obviously made him lose his place in the script. That was what she wanted. "Sure I do, so let's have it."

"No. It's kind of . . ."

"Oh, come on." Debra drew out her words, knowing how to modulate her voice to get men to do her bidding.

Kevin lifted his head, still blushing. His eyes were wide and bright, his smile innocent, like a child getting ready to talk about his favorite candy. "It's . . . I've always—this is going to sound so stupid—but I've always . . . known them. It's like I . . . I've always been able to look at a broken computer and immediately know what's wrong with it. I could always just follow a circuit and see where the interference is. Other people see just . . . boards and chips and wires and gears. But I see . . . I see living things. I know this is . . . is weird . . . but I can . . . talk to them."

Debra couldn't take a single bite of dessert during his whole speech. She was mesmerized. At first, she thought he was right about it being weird. But she listened to him with the same attentiveness he had given her all night. And she saw something different. He wasn't just some guy overzealous about computers. He was more. He possessed an artist's passion, a musician's devotion. Debra admired that. And found it very attractive.

Kevin felt the silence. This wasn't part of the plan! Why did he tell her that? Why did she even ask in the first place? In ten seconds, he went from having Bob's confidence to being the awkward geek from I/T again. He lowered his eyes and slouched. "See. Told you you'd think it's weird."

Debra reached across the table and placed her hands on top of his left hand. "It isn't weird, Kevin. And don't let anyone make you think it is. What you have is a talent, and you love that talent. Not many people can say that. And that makes you special. Very, very special."

Kevin smiled and looked into her eyes. Her words sounded sincere. He didn't need any form of analytical processing or Bob's help to realize she spoke the truth. She squeezed his hand. "How about we pay and go back to your place?"

Squeezing his hand was a good sign, he learned from Bob. "Are you sure?"

Debra smiled, bright and inviting. Her eyes somehow twinkled in the dim lighting. "Absolutely."

Kevin paid and they left the restaurant, hand in hand. In the car, Kevin's mind reeled. This was going to happen. She was going to be his. After countless probability matrices and statistical models and real-world experiments, this was going to happen. Kevin hadn't realized the profoundness of his physiological reactions. Sure, he was nervous the first couple times with the hookers, but nothing like this. She was going to be his!

Debra watched Kevin's face as he drove. He had a boyish grin, almost ready to giggle. *The big dope knows he's gonna get laid*, she thought. *But how's he know that? Now, why would I ever think he's a virgin? This can't be his first time. I can't imagine him a player, but he must have been with a few women before. At band camp or computer camp! Oh, behave—he's such a gentleman. A little too quiet but very smooth. Would he do this on a first date? I know I have before, but . . . well, look how all those turned out! Maybe we should wait?*

By the time they arrived at his house, Debra had waded through a moral quagmire. Even when they entered his house, she didn't know how the evening would end. Kevin opened a bottle of wine and poured a glass for each of them as they sat in the dimly lit living room, soft jazz floating from the stereo speakers. She knew she had to decide before things went too far.

"Kevin," she started, shifting uncomfortably on the sofa. "I . . . I know I've been giving off some signals tonight, alluding to . . . you know."

Kevin blushed and smiled, signaling he understood.

"But this is our first date. I've . . . well, you know . . . on first dates before, and things never worked out. But I think you're special. And I was hoping we could . . . umm . . . wait?"

No! This was too much! So close to completion and the scenario failed! What happened? Kevin executed all actions flawlessly. He made a minor slip when she inquired about his affinity for computers, but he recovered with grace, bettering his position. And now *this*? Unacceptable! He invested too much, planned for too long, to have it fail now! He didn't want to, but he saw no other course—he had to execute the contingency failsafe.

"That . . . that's fine. I completely understand."

Kevin sipped his wine as Debra smiled and exhaled a monster sigh of relief. "Oh, Kevin. I'm so glad. I was worried about what you'd say, but you totally put me at ease."

They both drank. Kevin put his glass down and smiled. "I want to show you something in my basement."

"Basement?" Debra asked, squinting as if trying to figure a riddle.

He offered a reassuring smile. "Weird, I know. But it goes along with what we were talking about earlier tonight. About why I like computers."

"Sure! I'd love to."

With a tenderness she had never known, Kevin took Debra's hand and led her to the stairs. Halfway down, he turned on the light. Debra tried to scream, but no noise came out of her mouth . . .

CHAPTER
66

Cresson, Pennsylvania

The Cresson Diner was no different than any other diner in America. Small, with a few tables along the walls of chrome-encased windows and a counter with stools. It even had its regulars, who shared smiles and stories of their families while peeking once and again over their shoulders at the table full of motley strangers. None of the patrons could figure them out—a woman well into her sixties, a young man probably not old enough to drink yet, and two middle-aged men. And all four wore black. They huddled close to each other and talked only in whispers.

"I don't think this is a good idea," Derrick whispered, noticing the occasional glare from one of the locals.

"We'll be fine," Emma reassured. "We're not from around here, and I'm sure everyone's on edge from what's happening in Gallitzin."

"My feet hurt," Michael reminded everybody as he choked down a bite of his burger. Grease ran down his arm. "Ugh. This is horrible."

"Apparently, you seem to have forgotten this was your idea," Marvin reminded him.

As he wiped away the grease with a handful of tiny napkins, Michael replied, "You're just mad that I guilted you into staying."

Michael was right; Marvin found this place just as unpleasant as Michael did. However, after he handled the situation with Nora in the barn, he found he had little choice but to comply with Michael's wishes.

After Nora commanded every bird, reptile, and mammal to stay at least three miles away from Gallitzin for a month, she and her mutated friends followed Marvin and his associates back to his Hummer parked along a dirt utility access road. Nora, Adam, Robert, and Samson piled into the back. The tinted windows put everyone's mind at ease about them being discovered. But as Marvin started to get into the passenger side of the Hummer, Michael threw a fit, hypothesizing that Marvin would strand them. Marvin promised to send a car for him, Derrick, and Emma, but that wasn't good enough. Marvin conceded, giving explicit directions to his driver on where to take the passengers and what to do with them when they got there. All four hiked through the forest to the nearby town of Cresson and found the nearest diner. Marvin placed a call for another car to pick him up, and all that was left to do was have an early dinner and wait.

"With one touch, I could give you laryngitis," Marvin mumbled, more to himself.

"Or grow a foot back, or heal bullet wounds, or fix broken bones. All of which is a far cry from the 'stop the sniffles' song and dance you put on for us when we first met," Michael replied, picking through his French fries, extricating the ones he deemed too soggy.

"It's called practice, Professor. You know, repetitive actions to enhance said actions. At the risk of putting them on the spot, both Emma and Derrick confided in me that they have been doing so as well."

"Uh-huh. So, if you can heal bones with a touch, can you break them just as easily?"

Michael risked another bite of burger, his hunger taking priority over taste, and stared at Marvin with calm eyes. The businessman stared back, eyes red with anger. Both Emma and Derrick stared in silence, listening to the sloppy smacks of the professor's mastication, waiting for Marvin to answer. Forcing his true feelings down, Marvin replied with an even tone, "I assure you, the thought has never entered my mind."

With those words, Emma turned away. They stung, not like the slap of a lie, but enough to make Emma look away. She stared out the window and watched what happened mere hours ago, watching the hulking form of Adam slump to the ground. One touch from Marvin rendered Adam immobile. That didn't bother Emma until Michael reiterated Marvin's potential in accusatory terms. Now, she couldn't even look at Marvin, wondering if he was lying, what he was truly capable of, and what motivated him.

"Emma?" Derrick asked, noticing her despondency. "You okay?"

"I'm fine, Derrick. Just a little tired."

"Not surprising in the least since you wolfed down three burgers," Michael said, still struggling with one of his own.

"She needs the extra calories with her increased metabolism," Marvin said.

"Really? So how do you know this? Learn it all from a touch? Know all our little secrets about our abilities?"

Marvin rolled his eyes. "Only the secrets I divined from high school biology. Logic dictates that since her ability runs through her whole body, her metabolism must increase to maintain her new level of performance."

"Is that so?"

"Oh, please," Derrick whispered in disgust as he stood.

Michael and Marvin looked at each other, then at Emma. They both asked, "What's wrong with him?"

Emma scowled at each man. "You two. You do nothing but bicker, and you never see the bigger picture. Together we have done two great . . . amazing . . . feats. We stopped a homicidal maniac a week ago, and today, just hours ago, we saved an *entire town*, maybe more. But neither of you is happy about that. Neither of you can see the good in any of those actions. You two are so much alike . . ."

"I'm not like him."

"Alike? Impossible."

"He's not like me."

"He's insufferable."

"He's pompous."

"He's . . ."

Derrick all but leaped back into the booth, slapping a folded *Pittsburgh Post-Gazette* newspaper down on the table. "Look. Look at this."

Michael and Marvin managed a quick game of tug-of-war with it before wordlessly compromising on keeping it in the center of the table. Only Emma noticed that Derrick was sweating and shaking.

Again, locked in competition, Michael and Marvin sped through the article in question, racing to finish first. In the process, neither caught the gist of the article. Michael looked at the quaking Derrick and said, "A few hookers have been murdered in Pittsburgh. So?"

Emma sneered at Michael. "Compassion. Noun. A feeling of deep sympathy and sorrow for another who is stricken by misfortune."

Michael sneered back. "That's not what I meant. Surely the world will weep, cut deeply by the loss of upstanding citizens like prostitutes. I meant, what does this have to do with us?"

"Did you even *read* the article? Or even look at the picture?" Derrick asked, sweat beads forming along his brow.

Both Michael and Marvin looked back at the picture. A naked woman was lying on her stomach on a motel room bed with dozens of chromatic wires sprouting from all over her body. Again, Michael and Marvin looked at each other, perplexed. Michael spoke for both of them when he said, "Creepy? Yes. I still don't see how this pertains to us."

"Technomage," Derrick whispered, sweat streaks flowing along his jawline.

"What?" Michael asked. "I don't know what you just said, but it seems like you're implying this murderer is special, like us."

"Yes. And we have to go and stop him."

Michael smacked the table hard enough for the contents to jump and clank and turn a few heads from the other patrons. He rolled his eyes, then his whole head up to heaven, pulling his lips into his mouth and biting them. His frustration could be seen in his clenched fists.

"Wait, Derrick. Technomage? What exactly does that mean?" Marvin asked.

"He . . . the killer . . . can control machines."

"Machines? *All* machines?"

"Yes. Probably. I think so. Look at the wires. The article said that each hooker had computer chips and small circuit boards embedded in their bodies."

"Even robots, perhaps? Control robots?"

"Yes."

Through clenched teeth and veins bulging from his temples, Michael whispered. "Dear God, Derrick, tell me you're fucking kidding me. Tell me you don't want us to go."

Emma put her arm around Derrick and used a napkin to dab away some of his sweat. "Michael, look at him. He's vibing again. We have to go. We have to go to Pittsburgh, if for nothing else, to help Derrick."

Still whispering, Michael grated, "No. No. No. No. No."

"Michael . . ." Emma continued but was cut short by Marvin's cell phone.

"Yes," Marvin answered. "Wonderful."

After returning the phone to his pocket, Marvin took a long sip of what passed as coffee in these parts. He dabbed his lips with a napkin and looked at Emma and Derrick. Smiling, he said, "Our ride has just arrived. Let us make haste for our next destination—Pittsburgh."

Michael's face reddened, his eyes ready to pop from their sockets. "I can't go to Pittsburgh. I refuse. I'm not going."

Marvin dug in his pants for his wallet. "Well, then I believe you'll have to find your own way back home. Shall I call a cab?"

Staring at the man across from him, Michael imagined doing unspeakable acts of violence upon him. He slammed his hand on the table again and stood before losing his judgment and inhibition. With a bull's snort, he turned and stormed out of the diner.

Assisting Derrick, Emma followed. Marvin tossed two fifty-dollar bills on the table and started out himself. However, before he could reach the door, a hairy-knuckled, meaty hand grabbed his shoulder from behind. Turning his head only, Marvin saw a man wearing a trucker's cap and a blue mechanic's shirt sporting a name patch that read, "Joey."

"We don't like strangers 'round here," Joey said, tightening his grip. "'Specially loud ones who think they're better than us."

Marvin's eyes moved from Joey's hand to Joey's face. "Well, then, I guess it's a good thing we're leaving. Now, if you'll excuse me."

Joey didn't let go. Willingly. This day, Marvin started a Cresson urban legend, about the time a mechanic named Joey's arm fell off his body, simply fell to the ground . . .

CHAPTER
67

Monroeville, Pennsylvania

"Pittsburgh?" Thelma asked.

Even through the Bluetooth earpiece, her voice conveyed frustration. Marvin simply figured it was pregnancy-induced discomfort. The raging hormones and all. Plus, biologically speaking, she was in the seventh month of carrying triplets. Hardly an easy task, he imagined. "Yes. I received word of a potentially lucrative business deal, and I wanted to check it out. I should be back late tonight."

"Uh-huh," Thelma grunted. An empty silence followed.

Marvin rolled his eyes. "What's wrong?"

"Business meeting?"

"Yes, dear. Business meeting."

"Uh-huh."

Marvin sighed, mustering the patience needed to weather the hormonal storm. "Are you going to tell me what seems to be bothering you, or will we continue playing this game?"

"I saw the news, Marvin."

The coldness in her voice chilled Marvin's spine. He thought he knew what she was referring to but opted for a more tactful approach. "And?"

"Gallitzin, Marvin. Gallitzin. The local news said the situation seemed to be taken care of. I've checked the internet, and there are rumors about a girl controlling the animals and other strange creatures. These same animals attacked a whole town and now have disappeared. The problem has been mysteriously solved."

"Thelma . . ."

"You lied to me, Marvin. I asked you not to go there, asked you not to get yourself involved. And you told me you wouldn't. You told me you wouldn't go."

"I needed to."

"No. No. You didn't 'need' to. You wanted to. For the past three months, it's been whatever Marvin wants, Marvin gets. I wanted you to avoid that situation, to stay home, to be with me, to forget about business just for a minute. And you promised. You promised and you broke it and now you're doing God knows what in Pittsburgh."

"Thelma, I'm sorry, but this is important."

"I'm important, Marvin! Your unborn *babies* are important! You've made more money in the past three months than we've made together in our entire marriage. I can't even comprehend how much you'll make next year! Money's not important anymore, Marvin. We have enough money now. We don't have a family yet. Family is important."

"Thelma, stop!"

"You promised!"

"I'm sorry, but this is a once-in-a-lifetime opportunity here."

"So is a family."

Marvin sighed, shooting his frustration through the airwaves. He ran his hand through his thick hair, his new favorite nervous tic when emotions ran high. "I'll explain everything when I get home. But if I don't do this deal today, soon, there's a good chance it won't be available again. Ever. This is huge. Huge."

Thelma went quiet, an icy quiet, her silence freezing the cellular signal. Her voice skated across the ice she created one final time. "I won't wait up."

A click, then silence.

If Marvin had been holding a traditional handset, he would have slammed it down. He was pretty sure that if he had a cell phone, he would have thrown it to the ground and stomped it out of existence. But his earpiece offered little substance, so he placed it in his pocket and chewed on his ire.

Sitting in the backseat of his second Hummer, Marvin watched Michael on the payphone along the outside wall of the convenience store. Michael forgot to bring his cell phone along and didn't trust using Marvin's Bluetooth. Michael paced in a small circle, tethered by the phone's metal cord. He had just told Claire where he was and prepared himself to get flayed.

"Where are you?" she asked, as if not hearing him correctly the first time.

I'm screwed.

"Pittsburgh. The students needed some extra credit and suggested an impromptu trip to the hometown of a couple famous writers."

Silence. Michael knew she wasn't buying it. She knew he was up to something. Then, still terse, she asked, "So, who are the writers?"

Not sure why, not sure how he even thought of it, probably because he peeked through the store window at the snack aisle, and just beside himself that he couldn't think of two legitimate writers off the top of his head, he blurted, "Stella Dora and Lorna Dunne."

What the fuck am I doing?!

"What? Those are cookies, Michael!"

"Who do you think they're named after? They're not made-up names, you know."

"Are you cheating on me?"

"*What?* No!" Michael almost laughed at the ridiculousness of the question. "Why would you even ask that?"

"Gee, Michael, I wonder why. One minute you're home with your family, and the next you're in 'Pittsburgh' with 'students.' What am I supposed to think?"

"Look, Claire, I know this sounds ludicrous. But you enjoy your job so much, and you have outside of work stuff with your friends like your reading groups, and . . . I don't know. I don't have that. My colleagues are so fake, and with all the school politics, I just dread seeing them off campus. You recently teased me about not liking my students, so I wanted to get to know my students better. I know this is impetuous and over the top, but it sounded . . . I don't know. I'm trying. I'm really trying with them."

Now I'm faking sincerity. Cad. Noun. A man whose behavior is unprincipled or dishonorable, especially toward women. Synonym: me!

Claire sighed. "Okay, Michael. I'm sorry. It's . . . you're right. You should really try harder with your students. This is . . . weird, but if it helps you help them, then I guess it's fine."

Holy shit! I did it!

"Just try to be home around midnight," Claire added, then chuckled. "Pittsburgh. You're crazy."

"Yeah. Crazy about you."

"You better be! Scaring me like this."

"I am. I love you."

They finished up their pleasantries and said their goodbyes.

Michael returned to the Hummer, glad that Derrick and Emma followed soon after so he didn't have to spend uncomfortable alone time with Marvin. However, once the vehicle started moving, Marvin made it uncomfortable anyway. "Nice chat with the wife?"

Ignore him and he'll shut up. Ignore him and he'll shut up. Michael stared out the window and offered a cursory, "Yep."

"So, what lie did you tell her?"

Michael answered with silence.

"Oh, come now, Michael. We all know you're lying to her about your abilities, lying through omission and all, so it only makes sense that you're lying to her about this trip."

Ignore him and he'll shut up, ignore him and he'll shut up . . .

"Silence? Oh, Michael, that is no way to be with your friends. We are your new friends now."

Brow furrowed, Michael turned. "I may be along for this stupid 'mission' of yours, but if you remember correctly, I was opposed. I don't even know why I came along to Gallitzin. Maybe out of guilt. Maybe curiosity or pity. But certainly not because of friendship."

Just as the words left his mouth, he saw the hurt expressions crawl across Emma's and Derrick's faces. He sighed and pinched the bridge of his nose, feeling stupid for engaging Marvin, especially when he knew the businessman was capable of trickery like this.

Michael went back to looking out the window, searching for the proper words—an apology, an explanation—while feeling three pairs of eyes watching him. Just as he thought he might have something, the Hummer slowed. "Why are we stopping?"

"Because I told the driver we're here," Derrick answered . . .

CHAPTER
68

Pittsburgh, Pennsylvania

"So, now what?" Michael asked, looking at the boxy two-story house. No lights were on inside or outside the house. Too much daylight was still present for the streetlights to come on, but Michael wouldn't be surprised if they were burned out.

"I don't think he's here," Derrick said.

Michael saw no garage and no car in the parking pad, so he assumed as much. He looked at everyone else in the car. Emma and Derrick stared out the windows with trepidation. But Marvin looked at the house with hunger in his eyes. Like a starving dog looking at a steak, Marvin said, "We're going in."

"What? You can't be serious," Michael argued.

"What we want is in there. So, we must go inside to find it."

"It? What *it*? You're talking about breaking and entering."

"Look, if this fellow is actually the one committing those murders, we need to be sure. Gather evidence and all that nonsense."

"If we wait . . ."

"If we wait, then there is a good chance we may have to confront him. If we go inside and find evidence, we call the authorities and leave them an anonymous tip."

Emma and Derrick looked from Michael to Marvin and back. Emma sided with Marvin. "Despite the fact that I hate the idea of breaking the law by trespassing, I think it's a good idea. If we see anything even remotely suspicious, we'll call the police. Right, Marvin?"

"Right," he lied, opening the door. He didn't look at the widow; he couldn't take his eyes off the house.

Michael, Emma, and Derrick exited the Hummer as well. Marvin opened the passenger door to tell the driver to circle the block every five to ten minutes.

"All right," Marvin started, still fixated on the house. "Do you all have your Bluetooths?"

"We shouldn't use them," Derrick said. "If this guy comes home and is truly a technomage, we'd be giving him a weapon with direct access to our brains."

Michael removed his Bluetooth and tossed it to Marvin. Marvin glared at Michael and put the earpieces in his pocket. "Very well. Michael and Emma should try the front of the house while Derrick and I look for a rear entrance."

Wanting to argue but knowing the futility behind such an attempt, Michael accompanied Emma to the front door while watching Marvin and Derrick sneak around to the back. As they reached the door, he asked, "Emma, why are you doing this?"

"I know this is hard for you to believe, but there are those of us out there who put others before themselves."

"Yeah, like Saint Marvin," Michael rolled his eyes as he knocked on the door.

"If the person who lives here is doing the things that the newspapers say he's doing, then I feel I have a moral obligation to—"

"No," Michael interrupted. "I don't mean just now. I mean the whole thing. The 'embracing your gifts from God' thing. Running around with Derrick and now Marvin, looking for what? Adventure? A thrill?"

Emma crossed her arms over her chest and turned her back to Michael. "I loved my husband."

"Yeah, I get that, but—"

"When he died, I thought I'd follow shortly after. See, young people always think and plan for the future when they get 'old,' like it's just a brief respite between middle age and the grave. And I thought like that as well when I was younger. But it's not. There are usually many, many tomorrows during that 'get old' time. Wives usually outlive their husbands. I knew that and accepted that, especially being married to a fireman. But I 'got old' and outlived my husband. Ten years' worth of tomorrows came, far more than I expected or thought about or truly planned for."

"Emma, I—"

"And I love my town, Michael. I know you probably think it's old and backward. But I grew up there and love the people. That town and those people became my life after my husband passed. They were there for me. The church

was there for me. And I accepted that. But then this . . . these abilities came
and . . . woosh! It was an injection of youth, a shot of life I . . . I never knew
existed."

Michael put his hand on her shoulder. "I'm sorry. This whole situation has
me uneasy, and I just didn't take the time to think about what it meant to other
people. I really didn't know it meant that much to you."

Emma patted his hand as she would a child. She turned to the house and
nodded at the door. "Well, since no one answered, shall we commence with the
illegal entry?"

Michael chuckled. "Yes, let's."

They walked back to the door and looked at it. Then at the nearby windows. "So," Michael chided. "You know anything about burglary?"

"Heavens, no, Michael," Emma replied.

Michael wondered what to do. Would slipping a credit card through really
pop the lock? Maybe they should try the windows first? Emma might have to
scale a wall to the second floor. Did she have the ability to do that? If so, how
far could she climb? Empire State Building, maybe? How many people would
pay to see that? The Amazing building climbing lady. And . . .

Click.

Michael snapped free from his mental intermission to see that Emma had
turned the doorknob. And the door opened.

"It's open?" Michael whispered.

"Appears so," Emma whispered back.

As Michael and Emma walked into the living room, Marvin and Derrick
entered the kitchen through the back door. Confused, Michael mouthed the
word "unlocked?" to Derrick. Derrick nodded.

The four slowly converged in the dining room, between the living room
and the kitchen, looking around for evidence of a homicidal maniac. Instead,
they found the typical abode of a bachelor. The kitchen was clean but far from
immaculate, marked with dirty dishes in the sink and an empty pizza box
stuffed in the trash. The living room was similar. Devoid of all forms of decoration, the furniture was newer but sparse. The entertainment center, complete
with an Xbox 360 and PlayStation 3, monopolized one wall while speakers
stood against the other walls. The four home invaders looked at each other and
shrugged their shoulders. Until they heard a moan from beneath their feet.

The hair along Michael's neck prickled as he fought the sudden urge to
release his bladder. Wide-eyed, he looked at everyone else, clearly shocked, and
asked in a whisper, "Basement?"

They all looked around until Derrick pointed to a door at the end of the hallway. Tiptoeing, they made their way to the door. Michael suppressed his desire to make a *Scooby-Doo* joke.

Marvin opened the door and started down the creaky wooden stairs. He could see a cement floor but not much else from his angle. But everyone saw the dull blue light of computer monitors.

"What's that smell?" Emma asked. Derrick smelled WD-40 and other machine part oils. Michael smelled stale sex. Marvin smelled blood.

Once at the bottom, Marvin pulled the chain of an uncovered overhead bulb, the base attached to one of the bare rafters. After the light washed through the room, he froze.

"What is it?" Michael whispered. Concern and fear swirled their way through him when Marvin didn't answer. He just stood there. Staring.

Michael charged the remainder of the stairs and stopped next to Marvin. And froze.

"What?" Derrick asked.

Michael answered without turning his head or even blinking. "Derrick. Just stop and take Emma back upstairs. Take her back upstairs and call the police."

"But . . ."

"Just do it, Derrick!"

Before anyone could say another word, Emma pushed her way past Derrick. Derrick saw no other option but to follow. They both froze when they reached the bottom of the stairs . . .

CHAPTER
69

Pittsburgh, Pennsylvania

Michael thought he had seen everything since he met Derrick. He watched a senior citizen move with the speed and accuracy of a martial arts master. He witnessed a man heal wounds with a simple touch. He saw animals that walked and talked like humans. But never did he imagine anything like this.

Against the back wall in front of the bottom of the stairs sat the torso of a man. Not even a complete torso. Michael stared at the chest, shoulders, neck, and head of the man, whose head lolled back, and unblinking eyes stared at the ceiling. Wires and cables and tubes from seemingly everywhere fed into the man. A nearby accordion-style cylinder extended and compressed, offering a slight hiss with every cycle. Liquids of all hues flowed through clear lines, into and out of him, some the color of blood. Michael's stomach lurched looking at this abomination, but his veins turned to ice as the computer monitor next to the man repeatedly produced the statement: "My name is Bob. Kill me."

Unable to stop himself, Michael kept looking around. There were worse sights. More torsos hung from the ceiling, against the basement walls, women missing their arms and legs, replaced by similar wires, tubes, and hoses. All of them had their bottom jaws removed, and in their place, hundreds of multicolored wires as if they vomited rainbow spaghetti. A round webcam substituted an eyeball in each of them. They all had rectangular computer chips in random places throughout their bodies that looked like hungry black leeches in the flickering shadows.

Another wall held the right half of a blonde, split with precision from vulva to skull. Michael couldn't help but imagine her caught in a spider web made from computer components and wires. Two monitors flanked either side of her, scrolling readouts from the variety of measurement instruments attached to her.

Marvin finally moved, walking to a bed in the far corner. The plain white sheets were stained, and a stale stench emanated from them. On the bed was a naked woman with short blonde hair in her late thirties, Marvin guessed. She was beautiful and had an athletic build. Marvin assumed her dead—her eyes were closed, and a leather strap tethered her hands to the bedframe. As with every body in the basement, wires and tubes fed into her, mostly from the ankles where her feet had been removed. On a nightstand next to the bed was a monitor, its screen alive with constant readouts.

Emma gasped and cried, then buried her face in Derrick's shoulder. Not knowing what to say, as if anything he could say would make the situation better, Derrick kept his mouth shut and put his arm around the frightened widow.

Michael crept further into the basement. Trying to avoid the atrocities hanging from the walls, he looked for a phone. So focused, he couldn't even bring himself to look at any of the computer monitors. If he had, he would have noticed the one message displayed on the screen attached to Bob changed to, "He's coming! He's coming!" Instead, Michael skimmed the desks, hoping against hope to find a phone. He noticed Marvin by the bed and walked over next to him.

"What the hell is this psycho doing?" Michael whispered.

"It appears he was experimenting on them," Marvin whispered back. He reached down and brushed some stray hairs from the woman's face. His eyebrows furrowed and his head cocked. He placed his fingers on the woman's cheek. Surprised, he turned to Michael and said, "She's still alive!"

As if on cue, her eyes flipped open and she grabbed Michael's arm. The cold claws of fear scraped from the base of his neck down to his bladder. Panic pinched his lungs, his breaths now quick puffs of air. He wanted to scream, wanted to pull his arm away, but froze. Time screeched to a halt as she looked at him and said, "My name is Debra. Please. Please help . . . he's here! Oh, God, he's here!"

With her warning, all of the partial bodies along the wall snapped to life. They jerked and flopped like freshly caught fish. Their bodies slapped against the wall as wires and tubes whipped around.

Michael yanked free from Debra's grasp and stumbled, falling onto a twitching body along the wall. Her pelvis thrust against his chest as his hands slipped to where the wires and tubes infiltrated her skin. He looked into her eyes, wide and frenzied from a mixture of horror and pain. Michael pulled away and puked on the floor.

The monitor beside Bob repeatedly displayed the message, "He's here! He's here!"

Emma and Derrick heard something from the top of the stairs. There stood an overweight man in his mid-thirties. They both noticed wires squirming like worms from his unusually large wristwatch. The wires sprouted and sank into the wall. And all of Kevin's hell broke loose.

The monitors flicked on and off, creating a strobe effect. With every third flash, red light bathed the room for half a second. Michael didn't know what had happened. He couldn't see, couldn't focus. The world appeared and disappeared faster than he could think or react. He stood, or thought he stood, his legs wobbled, and he wasn't quite sure which way was up. He reached out for support but stopped himself; he didn't want to touch anything, especially the flopping torsos.

Michael wanted to build a "push" charge but couldn't concentrate with the commotion. Run. That was all he wanted to do. Run. Far away. Run home. Run and hide and forget this place. Forget Emma and Derrick and, most of all, Marvin. He wanted to run. And to retch again.

His stomach roiled and boiled, swishing back and forth like a balsa wood boat on the waves of an angry ocean. His eyes widened, trying desperately to compensate for the flashing lights, trying anything so he could see. In brief glimpses, he saw wires whip and snatch Derrick, pulling him and pinning him to the wall. Was he still alive? Was he now a twitching torso hooked to machines? Emma flipped and spun and twirled. Things attacked her, but what, he couldn't make out. Something from the walls snaked in the air toward him. What? Wires? That was impossible! But they snapped forward, the tips of seven wires piercing his shoulder and upper arm.

"Gah!" Excruciating pain ripped through the entire left side of his body. Michael wanted to die just to make it stop—the pain, the fear, the insanity—all to stop! He staggered and stumbled. He wanted to cry for help, but the fire in his chest forced him to hold his breath, afraid that inhaling would only fan the flames. Dizzy. The lights, the agony.

"Stop!" Marvin yelled. "Or I'll kill her!" His hand rested on Debra's shoulder. With a thought, he raked the nerves in her shoulder and neck, bristling them with pain. She screamed and Kevin felt it through the complex web-work of sensors. Kevin didn't know how the intruder did it, but he knew that the threat was real. The strobing stopped. The lights came on. The wires ripped themselves from Michael's arm, and he cried out and almost fell over. But Derrick, very much alive, remained prisoner against the wall.

"Who are you and what are you doing here?" Kevin asked.

"We're special like you. We came to find you, talk to you about what you can do. You have some impressive abilities," Marvin answered.

"Talk to him?" Michael rasped, rubbing his arm, a combination of burn and itch. "Look at what this sicko did! He's a murderer!"

Marvin directed an angry glance at Michael. "We don't know anything, Professor. We don't even know his name."

"Kevin," he said as he descended the stairs. With every step, Emma moved farther away. "My name is Kevin."

"Very good. That's a wonderful start. So, Kevin, what are you doing here? What are you looking for?"

"Love," Kevin whispered, sending a longing glance to Debra.

"Love!" Marvin repeated, overjoyed. "What a magnificently noble quest! I'm on a quest myself. You see, I'm a businessman, Kevin. One with quite a few resources to help you on your journey. And you have some abilities I believe can help me with mine."

"You *can't* be serious!" Michael shouted, tears and snot streaming down his face as he walked closer to Marvin. "He's a monster! A freak! You need to knock him out and call the police!"

"Let's not be too hasty, Professor!" Marvin replied. "It would be a pity to have such skills wasted, discarded behind prison walls."

"No!" Michael yelled again. "Not this time, Marvin! We didn't come all the way over here and almost get killed so you could make a job offer to a murderer! You need to knock him out!"

"Michael . . ."

"Knock him out, Marvin! Knock. Him. Out."

"You mean like this?" Marvin asked as he touched Michael's hand. In half a breath, Michael's world went black . . .

CHAPTER
70

Camp Hill, Pennsylvania

Compunction. Noun. A strong uneasiness driven by guilt; a deep sense of regret. And Michael felt it through his whole body. He was tired, in pain, and alone, with no one else to truly blame except himself.

He sprawled on the loveseat in his living room, his back against one armrest while his feet touched the other, and stared out the large bay window. It was a beautiful summer day, but he saw none of that. He stared at the window like a movie screen, watching the terrible events of the past twelve hours.

It started with a phone call to Derrick. Why the hell did he make that call? Oh, that was right—insane jealousy caused by an insane ego. His deep sense of mistrust for businessmen, anyone with more money in their bank account, anyone more pompous, probably anyone smarter than himself, for that matter. He didn't trust Marvin. And when Michael had found out that the slimy businessman would be accompanying Emma and Derrick on a little adventure, Michael couldn't bear to be left out. So he invited—or rather forced—himself along. And it was no consolation that Michael was *right* not to trust Marvin.

They had met two special people during the trip, special with abilities like Michael. Two dangerous and severely unbalanced people. Both people had done horrible things, murdered innocents. Maybe hookers and a town full of rednecks were far from innocent, but they certainly didn't deserve what fate had doled out for them! These two people should be in jail or getting dissected in some lab. But Marvin showed his true colors as all betrayers eventually do. He hired them. He *gave jobs* to those two *monsters*! And left Michael, Emma, and Derrick stranded.

Pittsburgh's public transportation got the defeated and shell-shocked trio to a train station, the train station got them to Harrisburg, and a taxi got them back to the hospital where they had rendezvoused to start the adventure. Michael stewed as he drove home, nursing his arm where wires had pierced his skin during the attack from the freak who controlled machines, the "technomage," as Derrick called him. The only time Michael spoke was to ask flippant questions.

"What happened after Marvin knocked me out?"

They talked. Marvin offered Kevin anything he wanted.

"Why didn't you two stop them?"

Because Derrick had been pinned to a wall, held hostage, his life threatened if Emma made a move.

"Why didn't they kill us?"

Because Marvin said he took pity on lesser creatures.

Once they arrived back at the Harrisburg Hospital parking lot, Michael kept picking and picking, taking his frustrations out on a college kid and an old woman. Why was this happening? What was Marvin doing? Did Marvin know what happened to change them? Did he know the cause of these abilities? What did Emma know? What did Derrick know? What happened? *Why* was this fucking happening? Michael wanted to review how each of them met. Then Derrick dropped a bomb, one that obliterated Michael's soul. Derrick was why the people driving the cars at the mall crashed.

Michael replayed that day at the mall in his head, the day he saved an innocent bystander and himself by "pushing" two cars out of the way. Derrick confessed that he made the drivers see something other than reality, taking away their ability to sense impending danger. He also made the man with the headphones not see the cars, not hear the people screaming at him. Michael exploded; a flurry of caustic words flew from his mouth. Even after he reduced Derrick to tears, he continued to spit venom. "You're a murderer! You're a sick, twisted monster! You're no better than Kevin! Exactly the same as Kevin—killing people for your sick satisfaction. Experimenting on them for your own needs, like Marvin. You're Marvin and Kevin all rolled into one."

Michael only stopped once Emma intervened. And with that, he stormed off to his Ford Explorer, threatening to call the police if either of them attempted to contact him again. That was what Michael saw in his living room bay window as he sat on the loveseat. That ugly scene, over and over. Until his daughter interrupted his despair.

"Hi, Daddy! What's wrong?" she asked with a smile, still too young to discern the proper responses to other people's nonverbal cues.

"Well, Daddy did something stupid, and Mommy is really mad at him." Michael smiled when he looked into his daughter's doe-brown eyes. He stroked her straight blonde hair that fell across her shoulders, unable to picture a better personification of innocence as she stood in a light blue summer dress. She looked very much like Alice in Wonderland, but he couldn't help but feel that he was the one who tumbled down the rabbit hole.

"It's okay. You're always doing stuff to make her mad, but she still loves you. She has to. Wanna see the shoes I bought yesterday?"

Sarah spoke with a speed normally reserved for hyper cartoon characters. Michael heard the inflection of a question and said, "I'd love to," long before he understood the question or the ramifications of his answer. He lacked the foresight to guess that she'd be wearing them at this moment, and she jumped onto his lap. In her brand new, oversized hiking boots.

As the beige stompers dug their way up and down both of his thighs, Michael endured. He wanted to get mad but simply couldn't. Too fatigued and too appreciative of what he had with her—unconditional love. At least for a couple of more years, before she turned into a judgmental, unforgiving woman like her mother.

Michael sighed as he put his arm around Sarah. Squirming to get closer, which was simply not possible, she tried with vigor anyway, still digging her boots into his thighs. Finally getting comfortable, she stopped, rested her head on her father's chest, and stared out the window with him. Michael squeezed tighter and felt guilty for thinking of Claire as judgmental and unforgiving.

Last night, he returned home from his adventure a little before one o'clock. Claire wasn't happy. And she told him so in no uncertain terms. The long, sharp-tipped words she usually reserved for the courtroom stabbed Michael like spears. He stuck with the lame excuse of going to Pittsburgh on a field trip with some students. She knew the excuse was lame and a lie. She pushed on and again accused him of cheating. He tried to laugh it off, but as any good lawyer would have done, she accumulated and reviewed a list of late meetings, being where he shouldn't have been, and not being where he should be. He presented exhibits "A" and "B"—he smelled neither of alcohol nor perfume while his clothing was free from lipstick stains or tears, and his neck, cheeks, and lips had no suck marks associated with the passionate tryst for which he was being accused. Not good enough. So, he turned the tables and attacked.

It was an out-of-body experience, watching himself perform on a stage of desperation, watching himself in a nightmare he created. Never did he expect himself of such guile, never did he expect the words to come from his mouth— he accused *her* of cheating on *him*. He said the words without believing them at first, like a boxer wrapping his arms around his opponent so he could buy enough time for the referee to intervene. But the more he brought up his list of late meetings, being where she shouldn't have been, and not being where she should be, he wasn't so sure he didn't believe. Especially since she had no answers to "Why has the book appreciation group never met at our house?" and "If you meet twice a week, why aren't there more books lying around the house?" and "*Why* do you need to meet twice a week?" A lawyer with no answers, only guilty eyes.

The silence turned his bones to ice and his blood to slush. Watching the tears stream from her eyes made his sting. He hated seeing her cry. Hated *making* her cry even more.

The argument was over. He lost. They both did. Claire turned and stepped into their bedroom, shutting the door whisper silent, only the turning lock made a noise. Michael retreated to the couch for a night of fitful, comfortless sleep.

"Daddy?" Sarah asked, her voice muffled from burying her face in her father's chest.

"Yes, dear?"

"I'm bored."

"I know, sweetheart." Michael kissed the top of her head, pushing away thoughts of what to say to Claire, how to make things right between them, plans and strategies. "Let's—"

As if on cue, his cell phone rang. Michael knew he shouldn't answer it, but he did.

"Michael?" Emma asked on the other end of the phone, obviously crying.

Doing his best to turn away from his daughter, he conveyed his anger through a gruff whisper. "Emma, I'm hanging up and calling the cops. I told you . . ."

"It's Derrick. I think he went to kill Marvin."

Michael told Emma to meet him at his office. Hating himself every step of the way, he kissed his daughter and told her he had to go to work . . .

CHAPTER
71

Harrisburg, Pennsylvania

Marvin leaned back in the plush leather chair in his home office. He had a similar one in his downtown office—the president's office—but this one always felt better. The one at the downtown office was the king's throne, a general's battle chair, one in which he had to make decision after decision. This one, the one in his quiet home office, was his respite, his comfort after a long day of being king. There was a difference between eating food for nutritional purposes and savoring the tastes and flavors of a well-prepared meal.

It was late morning, and he could smell the warm aroma of his espresso wafting from the mug resting on his cherrywood desk. Before becoming rich and powerful, espresso was too expensive to drink on a daily basis, becoming a reward. But now, he enjoyed it every morning to begin his day.

He didn't need sleep either, able to keep the mechanisms of his body running with precision by mere thought. However, when he was paunchy, bald, and weak—he now referred to those days as the "Dark Ages"—he relished the thought of slumber, his only time to escape the cold, harsh world. Finding the world now neither cold nor harsh but his for the taking, he still slept at night because he enjoyed it, still felt a familiar sense of solace in it. But now, he was awake and excited. He readied himself to explore Kevin's and Nora's roadmaps.

After returning from Pittsburgh the previous night, he spent hours with his new employees. Kevin offered no problems; Marvin just set him up in an apartment in one of his buildings, a nice two-bedroom overlooking the river. Nora and her crew of mutated men proved to be a bit more difficult, logistically speaking.

With Colby's help, they made some space for them in the basement of the downtown office building. Since the young man, no longer the handsome, confident buck he first met, now so misshapen he looked like a slightly melted Mr. Potato Head, was one of the few people in Marvin's company who knew the full extent of Marvin's dealings. Some late-night emails were sent and restricted signs printed, warning away any nosy employees. Old couches were substituted as beds, and plenty of blankets were found. Colby even brought a dozen bags of fast food to help sate some appetites.

Marvin gave each of his guests fresh legal pads to write down anything and everything he could provide for them to assist in their transition. Adam and Robert had needed only one line each, writing the same request, "To be human again." Samson had listed every carnal desire that popped into his feral mind and used the rest of the pad to draw pictures instead. If the pictures weren't of him and Nora copulating in extravagant positions, they were of him with two Noras or even three. Impressed with Samson's artistic skill, even if he didn't have the cumbersome claws to negotiate, Colby took quite a fancy to a page with five very Nora-looking women demonstrating their affinity for one another. Naked. Colby tore that sheet from the pad and saved it for himself.

Nora was the only one who seized the opportunity and listed the kinds of equipment she would like for her laboratory and the conditions she would like for the animals. Satisfied that his new guests had the minimum requirements, if not content, Marvin decided to return home by two o'clock in the morning. Thelma was fast asleep. He made sure of that as he crawled into bed.

Now, Marvin took a sip of espresso, the warm liquid cascading through his whole body. He placed the mug on his desk and leaned back into the accepting softness of his chair. Closing his eyes, he decided to keep himself waiting no longer. It was time to view the new roadmaps. But his wife interrupted.

Thelma flung the door to his home office open with such force Marvin was surprised the hinges could still hold onto it. The dramatic entrance was more befitting for a snarling, fire-breathing dragon than a waddling pregnant woman with a distended belly. Little did Marvin realize there was nary a difference.

"We need to talk!" Thelma screamed.

Marvin smiled, chalking up all anger to her hormonal imbalance, something he lacked the proper knowledge to fix due to what constituted "normal" hormone levels. He usually used his abilities to manage her aches and pains. "Good morning, dear. I'm well, thank you for asking. And how are you this lovely day?"

"You lied to me!"

Marvin's fake smile faded, losing the mood to have fun with this argument. "Look, we went over this on the phone—"

"No. *You* went over it on the phone. You dismissed me like some petulant child."

"Well, when you act like one—"

"Don't you *dare* turn this around on me and try to make this my fault!"

Slouching in his chair, Marvin pinched the bridge of his nose, not to alleviate any sort of pain but to avoid looking at her. Like he did when he was fat and bald. "Thelma, you're being unreasonable."

"No. I'm not. Expecting my husband to keep a promise is not unreasonable!"

This was how she argued. How she always argued. They never argued much, but when they did, it was a battle. She always chose the field, picking some silly nonsense to get angry about and then picked and picked and picked. When she was spindly and allergic to everything, she felt so weak that the only way she could feel strong was to take it out on the one person weaker—her husband. Still not looking up, Marvin growled, "Things have changed."

"Yeah?" she continued her attack. "Things like honor? Decency? Trust?"

Something stirred within Marvin. Something deep and dark, but he had always controlled it, kept it deep and dark. But that was when he was weak. He snapped his head from his hand and stabbed her eyes with his. "No, but those notions and ideals are as malleable as clay. They cannot be in the forefront all the time."

"No, you're right, Marvin. When there's money to be made or power to be played, those ideals go right out the window."

Marvin stood. He always dreamed of standing up to Thelma when she got in one of her moods. For the most part, she was a doting wife. But when she got like this, she was intolerable. Inhuman. "And why is that so wrong? If I need to bend morality for a minute to get what we deserve, then *so be it*! Let's not forget that *I* got us this nice house. *I* gave you that pretty face and those big tits. *I* got *you* pregnant!"

"Not the first time!"

The whole world changed with those words. The air turned to poison and water to acid. Thelma clasped both of her hands over her mouth as tears and snot exploded from her face. Marvin took a step closer as his feelings crashed into each other like a bad freeway accident; anger rear-ended pity, guilt side-swiped concern, happiness was overturned and burning. "What?"

"Marvin," Thelma blubbered. "I'm sorry. I'm so sorry."

"What happened?" Marvin demanded.

Thelma could only quiver, her hands still over her mouth. "I'm sorry. I'm sorry."

Knowing he needed to accelerate the process, Marvin swooped in close to Thelma and grabbed her right wrist. He made her nerves squirm closer to the surface of her skin. The pain twisted its way up Thelma's arm; she stopped crying and gave a phlegm-filled burst of a scream.

"What happened?" Marvin asked one last time.

"Seventeen . . . seventeen years ago. It was seventeen years ago."

Marvin knew the timeframe, the two or so years their marriage had real problems. They had been out of college a few years, and they had been disappointed with Marvin's career. Working part-time doing busy work at an insurance company, she insisted he dust off his resume and find a new job. He refused, feeling his three years with the investment firm made a great foundation. The only time he ever won an argument, and it turned out that he was wrong. Their marriage hit a stage where the dreams started to fade, and the monotonous reality set in. No one married a prince or princess, just two regular people. And Thelma wanted one last taste of a fantasy world before she gave in.

Marvin's grip lessened as he moved her nerve endings back to their starting position, but he still held her wrist. He sighed. It happened seventeen years ago, back when he almost ruined the marriage. How could he blame her?

"And I got pregnant. I got pregnant and . . . and didn't know what to do. I love you, love you so much, Marvin. I had to . . . had to . . . get rid of it. But it had lasting effects, made it impossible for me to have another baby. Until now. Until you did it." Her words, garbled and saturated with tears, rasped from her mouth. Marvin did not hear everything, but he understood what she said.

"Who?" he asked, wanting just one more piece of information, just one sliver of a reason to trust her again, before he would pull her tight against him and tell her everything would be fine.

Too distressed, too weary from crying and harboring a seventeen-year-old secret in the pit of her heart, Thelma blurted out the truth before she could think of the ramifications of her words. "Michael Roseman."

Marvin clenched his hand. Thelma's wrist hurt, not because of an elaborate torture tactic of moving nerves but because he squeezed so hard. She watched in horror as blood vessels streaked her husband's eyes. His lips curled to reveal his teeth. She felt his anger slap her face. He stared, simply stared at her for an eternity.

Michael Roseman. That was inexcusable. Anyone else, any other friend or acquaintance. Even his brother. *Anyone* else he would have forgiven. Marvin understood—Michael would have been in his late teens and did what any horny teen would have done, succumbing to the wiles of an older woman, gaining a

"Mrs. Robinson" story to parlay over a round of drinks. He understood, but he could never forgive. He could not let this go without punishment.

Marvin's eyes darted over Thelma, a visual pat-down, as he searched for the proper punishment. He started with her face, but if he returned her former looks or made her uglier, it would also punish him. And too suspicious; people already gossiped about her getting plastic surgery. The same went for her breasts as well. A daily nerve twisting? Although he felt like doing that, she would find a way to leave him. No, he needed her to stay, unconditionally. Then he looked at her protruding belly.

"Marvin, no. Please, please, no. Anything but them," Thelma begged, her tears returning, knowing what he thought of doing.

Marvin looked her in her eyes, and his grimace of pain twisted into a maniacal smile as he said, "Abort."

Thelma screamed, guttural and inhuman, as she miscarried three fetuses, seven months old. Pain consumed her body, ripping through her so hard that she couldn't even pass out. She fell to the floor, writhing on her back. There was no end to the searing pain. Or the screaming.

Marvin felt a little sad about the loss of the babies—he wanted a family as well. He shrugged his shoulders to himself and relished the thought that he could make more. Satisfied that she learned her lesson, he waited for a pause in the screaming to say, "I'm going to the office. Call me if you need anything. But, here, first . . ."

Marvin picked up the phone, dialed 9-1-1, and tossed it to her . . .

CHAPTER
72

Hershey, Pennsylvania

White. White room. Bright white. So bright her eyes stung, and she could hear it. The white thumped and beeped. White was all she could see. Feel. Hear.

LaKeisha turned her head, and other objects came into view. They blurred when she moved her head again, rippling into focus only after she stopped moving.

Machines. Her heart. Her breath. The bright whiteness didn't make the noises—she and the machines did. Her heart thumped hard in her chest, her ears, the base of her throat, with a rhythm so slow that she forgot about it until it beat again. A beep from a nearby machine kept pace, one shrill pulse for every thrum that rattled her body. Her exhales had the raspiness of knuckles scraping against brick. Her inhales were silent, long, and slow, but her exhales were hard and quick.

LaKeisha was lying in a bed, she finally realized. With the white room and machines and hard bed, she thought she had to be in a hospital. *Hospital? Was there an accident? And . . . my babies?!*

A bolt of energy rippled through her, chasing the icy knife of fear down her spine. Jerking her whole body, she tried to get up but couldn't. Padded restraints bound her wrists and ankles. Resting her head back onto the mushy pillow, she knew she should have been mad or afraid, but she simply couldn't muster those emotions as she watched the world slowly come back into focus once she stopped moving her head. A sliver of pride sliced through her, proud of her sudden maternal instinct. *I think I'm drugged.*

LaKeisha was no stranger to marijuana but only if she scored it for free, at a party or friend's place. She enjoyed it but not enough to spend the money on it. However, she tried some pills once and didn't like them. The marijuana made her feel loopy and giggly and a bit free, because she wanted it to, because she allowed it to make her high. The pills looped her as well. More than looped, spun her, dizzied her in such an aggressive way that she imagined them as hands clamping down on her shoulders, shaking her like a half-filled paint can. That was how she felt now, shaken against her will.

Unsettled, she squirmed again to prove that the restraints were real. They were, much to her disappointment. Looking down, she noticed she wore a white hospital gown, stark against her dark coffee skin. However, the combination of medication and too intense light showed too many skin blemishes she had never noticed before. A dark freckle on her right forearm, a tiny gray scar on her left foot, the skin of her knuckles folded in funny ways whenever she extended her fingers.

"Hello?" The word struggled to free itself from her mouth, so she tried again, disheartened to hear only a whisper come from her mouth. "Hello?"

Turning her head again, she saw movement in her peripheral, the rippling part of her vision. By the time her world came back into focus, the movement was gone.

She tried to summon what she knew she should be feeling, frustrated that she couldn't. She should be scared. She wanted to be angry. But she just couldn't remember how to feel that way, like trying to think of a word or name she couldn't remember, just on the tip of her tongue.

Moving her hands and feet again, she noticed some give in the restraints. Not a lot, but it seemed to be enough to allow her to sit up. All the moving, the swirling of everything she saw, started to make her nauseous, so she closed her eyes as she pushed herself back with her feet and propped herself up with her elbows. When she opened her eyes, she wondered what kinds of drugs she was receiving.

A little past the foot of her bed, women sat in chairs, wearing the same style hospital gown she wore. All three slowly flowed from side to side while displaying silly smiles.

"Who are you?" she asked them, not sure if she even spoke. The fact that the women didn't answer, didn't even notice her with their stupefied stares, made her question if she was even awake.

To further convince her this all might be a psychedelic dream, two bug-eyed dog faces appeared over LaKeisha. She jerked her head back into the pillow and tried to raise her arms to shield her face. She blinked repeatedly, hard enough to make her nose hurt, bringing the world into focus. Not bug's eyes, but goggles;

not dog snouts, but air canisters. Like a fading ripple, two men wearing gas masks came into focus. The one man looked familiar.

"It's okay, LaKeisha," he said. "It's okay. Just relax."

LaKeisha recognized him—that cop she fucked; the guy who kidnapped her from the grocery store. Did he bring her here? He would have had to! Why? Again, she tried to move her arm, to pimp slap the sonuvabitch, but again the restraints kept her arm in check. She tried to gnash her teeth, then tried to cry, but something stopped her, made her feel numb and loopy again. "My babies . . . ?"

"They're fine," Matthews told her. "They're with your mother. Grieving."

"Wha . . . ?"

"Shh. Don't try to talk. Or think. We told them you were dead."

"What?" She felt his words punch her in the throat. But as soon as the shock hit her, it was gone.

"Don't worry. We told them you died trying to save some children from a burning building. Gave them a big fat check on behalf of the city of Philadelphia. Set up an educational trust fund for your kids. See if we can get them out of that ghetto when they get older."

Even if she didn't have some sort of drugs being pumped into her . . . drugs, had to be some kind of fucking drugs making her all fucked up . . . she wouldn't have known what to feel. They told her babies and her mama she was dead! But now they have some money. Her babies had a good chance, a *real* chance, for a future. Maybe all she had to do was lie there and take it, whatever the hell *it* was, and she could be a better mother here than there with them. Maybe she was better for them if she was dead. Was she dead? Big white place? Bright lights? Maybe she was in heaven, and these were the most fucked up looking angels ever, but angels nonetheless, helping her family. "Why?"

"Well, LaKeisha, you're a special girl. Have you noticed lately that the hot guys have been feeling the same way about you?"

A sheepish grin slipped across her face, just like her youngest whenever she caught him sneaking a snack that he knew he wasn't allowed to have. "Yeah."

"And also notice people get crazy mad whenever you get mad? Scared when you get scared?"

The smile slipped away. LaKeisha did notice it or maybe never noticed until now. "Yeah."

"All those instances were because of your pheromones."

"Who moans?"

Matthews laughed. "Pheromones. All animals have them. Primal, subtle scents our bodies give off to reflect our basest moods. Yours just happen to be very, very strong. Strong enough to affect the moods of the people around you. Which is why we're wearing these masks."

Impressed with herself for following the conversation so far, she pointed to the foot of her bed, to the three swaying and smiling women. "Like them?"

"Yep. Your pheromones are affecting them. We're experimenting, seeing if we can modulate your moods."

"To help people?"

"To help us, at least. See, there are other people out there as special as you, LaKeisha. We have one here, in another room not far away. She's a ten-year-old girl who can desiccate anything with a thought. That means she can turn anything to dust. She's an untapped weapon. We need to control her, control her abilities. But we hate to keep her sedated, not sure of the effects the medication will have on her. However, we have no problem sedating you and using you to keep her calm. Your pheromones are a much more natural sedative."

LaKeisha understood and fought hard against the drugs, fought hard to hold onto her sadness. A tear escaped from her eye. The women at the foot of the bed stopped smiling, and tears flowed from their eyes. Matthews watched this and sighed. To the other man in the mask, he said, "Knock her out and we'll readjust the levels."

As blackness framed her peripheral, as the tunnel vision irised in and pulled her into darkness, again she thought she had to be dead. But she wasn't in heaven . . .

CHAPTER
73

Harrisburg, Pennsylvania

"This is ridiculous," Michael said. His hands slid across the top of his desk as if he were smoothing the linen sheets of a freshly made bed. Emma sat across the desk from him, but he didn't make eye contact. He hadn't since she entered his campus office. "Ludicrous and insane."

Emma sniffed, fighting the urge to cry again. Her eyes, glassy and red, showed that was what she did all the way over to Michael's office. Feeling that sarcasm was the only language in which Michael communicated, she replied. "Are you going to give definitions of each word first, or are we going to figure out what to do next?"

Michael finally looked at her as he sank into his comfortable leather chair. "Oh, ha ha. Here's what we should do—you climb the tallest mountain with two stone tablets and pray to the first burning bush you see. That will solve all of our problems. In fact, let's join hands, sing 'Kumbaya,' and pray that Derrick comes to his senses and that, someday, my wife will forgive me."

Emma slumped forward in her chair, her shoulders no longer able to bear the weight of Michael's hostility.

Sighing and rolling his eyes, Michael ceased his verbal attack. "What happened?"

Emma told him, as if recalling the sounds of curdled screams and crunching metal of a car crash.

She and Derrick met at a café to review the events of the day before. Derrick was still upset about how things had ended, still licking his wounds from Michael's harsh comments. The young man took the professor's words to heart, thinking himself a freak. Those words might have been the very reason for his following line of reasoning.

Unable to sleep that night, Derrick stared at the ceiling, trying to think of how things happened, how they received their abilities. He came to a terrifying conclusion and shared it with Emma. There was one unifying factor he could think of—himself.

Emma had told him that his reasoning was flawed and inconclusive, down-right impossible. But he wouldn't listen. Derrick took a class that Michael taught. Derrick knew Nora from a summer camp. Derrick had a disease and spread it to everyone else. Nora spread it to the half-animal creatures. Michael gave it to Thelma, who gave it to Marvin. Derrick had started it. He then thought he needed to finish it.

"You told him about me and Thelma?" Michael asked.

"It was a while back, when I was mad at you."

"Great. But his theory is ridiculous. I met Thelma almost two decades be-fore I met him. And what about the hundreds of other unaffected people he undoubtedly met in his lifetime. And that doesn't explain you or that Kevin freak in Pittsburgh."

"I know," Emma agreed. "I tried to explain that to him, but he wouldn't hear of it. He was so upset."

"Excellent. We all know he's so stable to begin with, and now that he's upset—"

"Don't forget, Michael, *you* were the one who upset him."

"Sure. Blame me. Whatever happened to 'Thou shall not lie' and 'Thou shall not *kill*?' He killed people, Emma. *Murdered* them."

"He didn't know how to use his abilities. He wasn't controlling his abilities; they were controlling him."

"And that makes it okay?"

"No, but now he is trying to atone, trying to find ways to make things right. He looked to *you* for help but couldn't find it. So, he's now off to Marvin's office to . . . do God only knows what. Fight him? Stop him? I don't know."

"Yep. Blame me again, Emma."

In a huff, Emma crossed her arms over her chest, looked at the ceiling, and threw herself back in her chair. "This is why I can't sleep either. This is why I've been using my mask again."

Michael pinched the bridge of his nose, trying to fend off a headache. But Emma's phrase "my mask" bounced around his mind like a bullet shot in a steel room.

My mask. My mask. My mask.

Hand still in front of his face, Michael peeked through his fingers to watch Emma cross her right leg over her left, her right foot tapping the air from frustration. "Did . . . you say, 'mask?'"

Dismissing his question, she answered with a curt, "My CPAP mask."

Michael froze as countless ice cubes slid down his spine. Nausea and realization wrestled with each other in his stomach. It all came together, dominos falling, one into another. He had apnea. During one of Derrick's marathon monologues, he mentioned he had apnea. Through casual dinner conversation, Thelma mentioned that Marvin had apnea. And now Emma, too.

Michael didn't need to replay the revealing conversations with Marvin or Derrick to recall that all three shared the same doctor in Hershey. He didn't even need to ask Emma about the details of her affliction. He just knew.

Weighing the pros and cons of telling Emma, Michael wrestled with himself. For the first time since Derrick butted into his life with this "special abilities" nonsense, Michael was finally curious about his abilities. He had never been one to enjoy puzzles or riddles, but this was too huge and fell right into his lap. He had to move forward with this. But without Emma's help.

"Emma. I'll get Derrick."

The widow looked back at the professor, confused by his tone. It lacked sarcasm or conceit. "What?"

"It's okay. You need some rest, so why don't you go back to wherever you're staying in the area, and I'll take care of this. It's only a couple of miles away, and he's probably trying to work up enough guts to go through with it. Plenty of time for me to pick him up and drop him off to you."

"Are you serious?"

"Yes." And he was. He felt that redemption was all fine and dandy but for the right reasons. He determined it would not sit well with him if he allowed the young man to throw his life away because he came to a wrong conclusion by following flawed logic. No, he would stop Derrick. Then he would finally find out how and why this was happening to him, to all of them . . .

CHAPTER
74

Harrisburg, Pennsylvania

Derrick stood before the Gunn & Dunn Investments building. Craning his neck, he looked up at the monolith, then back down at the smoked glass doors. This was it. The lone, brave knight, ready to storm the impenetrable castle and battle the evil wizard. And save the day. However, he never fathomed how terrifying being brave would be. He wanted to be the steel-nerved hero who rushed forth, guided by confidence and faith of overcoming adversity. But his hands shook. His stomach felt worked over by a taffy pulling machine. Ice water pooled in every pore of his body. But this had to be done. He had to end this. Like the knight donning his helm, Derrick pulled his hood over his head and entered.

The lobby bustled with people. Not a frenetic bustling like an anti-industrial, post-World War Two film, but plenty of people interacting. Derrick thought about using his abilities to make himself invisible but decided against it. If he did, he'd have to sneak all over the building to look for Marvin. He wanted a more direct approach. Plus, he was pretty sure the security cameras, and the armed security staff watching the cameras, would be able to see him sneaking around. And the further he walked into the lobby, the more convinced he became that no one saw him anyway.

The receptionist was the picture of perfection—perfect eyes, perfect smile, perfect teeth, perfect skin. Derrick couldn't help but wonder how much of her was God-given and how much was Marvin-given. "I need to speak with Marvin Carver, please," he said, trying to hide the shakiness in his voice.

"I'm sorry, Mr . . . ?"

"Derrick. My name is Derrick Sharper. And he's expecting me. This is an emergency."

Never losing her smile, she typed away at her computer and answered, "I have you in the database but no appointments for the day."

"He's expecting me." He wanted to sound suave and smooth but instead looked desperate and panicked.

"Sir, I . . ."

"Do you *really* want to take that chance?" He wasn't sure if he chose the right words, but they did the trick. She picked up the phone and called around, looking for Marvin. She smiled the whole time. Derrick noticed that her eyes shifted from emotion to emotion, but she kept smiling. Did Marvin do that? Did he have the power to manipulate the human body to that degree? Force a person to smile all day long? Every day? What else could he do? The possibilities multiplied exponentially in Derrick's mind, strengthening his resolve. Marvin *had* to be stopped.

After a few minutes of cat-and-mouse with the phone, the receptionist turned to Derrick and confessed, "He's in the basement."

"Basement?"

"That's where we keep our information technology department. Go across the lobby and use that stairwell there." She pointed to his destination, his destiny. And he went.

The stairwell was empty, no noise except for Derrick's heavy footsteps and raspy breath. He felt exposed under the sterile lights. His slightest footsteps seemed to thunder. Once at the bottom, he pushed a door that opened to a hallway, as sterile and cold as the stairwell. Overhead fluorescent lights bleached the immaculate walls, cinder blocks painted in gloss white. Derrick cursed himself, mad that he didn't have the savvy to recognize a trap until now.

He turned and placed a hand on the stairwell door, ready to retreat, but decided against it. Setting a trap meant that Derrick was getting close. Close to Marvin. He just needed to remember he wasn't a hyper spaz anymore. Remember that he faced off against others with special abilities, abilities they received from a disease he had given them, and held his own. The door handle shook in his trembling hand, and he realized he no longer had a choice.

The whole building seemed to shake from impossibly heavy footfalls. Derrick backed away, wondering what sort of dragon the evil wizard conjured. The door flung open with such a force that the handle caused chunks of concrete to spray from the wall. Bursting through the door came two hulks in black suits, followed by Stone.

Wondering how Stone survived their last encounter, Derrick's eyes snapped to him first. The bald man was even larger than Derrick remembered, his eyes even crazier, his smile more maniacal. But the men in front of Stone quickly commanded Derrick's attention. They each stood almost a foot taller than Stone, looking like towers but impossibly wider. Derrick blinked rapidly, trying to focus and make sure what he saw was real and not some illusion someone forced him to see, two professional wrestlers escorting a Lilliputian.

The monstrous men took their time approaching Derrick. Stone followed, laughing and cracking obscene jokes about how the men would sodomize Derrick. The men laughed at each joke, removing their suit jackets and ties as they strode closer to their target. Derrick didn't know true fear until he saw that their shirts did nothing to hide what was underneath. The material strained against striated muscle, and their veins looked like wires wrapping around too taut rope. They cracked their knuckles. The one man flinched his head from side to side to crack his neck. Then Derrick had a plan.

Surprising the three men, Derrick ran toward them. Confused, they stopped and watched him slip between them and skid to a halt. Anger welled within them like discontent magma as they watched the skinny kid flip them off. Neither saw Stone anywhere, assuming he fled back through the stairwell door. Their rage impeded them from further following that path of logic, and they attacked Derrick.

Derrick watched the mountains of muscle crash down on Stone. He chuckled to himself when he saw Stone's confused look after the one man punched him in the face. Derrick remembered that Stone felt no pain but was still impressed that he was standing after that blow. Satisfied his illusion worked, he continued down the hallway, leaving the large men engaged in fisticuffs.

The hallway pattern was standard and simple, but not knowing where to go made Derrick feel trapped in a maze. He made the next left, then the next right, then left again, knowing at the very least that he maneuvered farther away from muscle-maddened men. The fire exit signs from the ceiling and minimalist door numbers did nothing to aid his quest. But that was all just part of the trap, he surmised. To get him confused, unfocused. Along the way, he tried the knobs of any door that didn't need a keycard to open, but they were all locked. Maybe that was part of the trap? To give him nothing so he'd get bored and leave. *No!* he thought. *I started this mess, and I have to finish it.* Then he made one last right.

Nora stood at the end of the hall, wearing a white lab coat, her hands in its pockets. "Turn around and leave, Derrick. If you don't, you're going to die."

Derrick hadn't seen her since they were both young adolescents. But even then, she was brusque and to the point. "Nora, it's a disease. Your abilities, my abilities, Marvin's, everyone's, all a disease I gave you."

Nora laughed. "I finally remember you now. Summer camp, years ago. You were the naïve kid I fooled around with. You believed every ghost story, every Sasquatch in the forest story, everything anyone told you. Derrick, it's not a disease. You're just an idiot. Now leave."

"Nora, please. You don't belong here. You—"

Nora sighed. "It's been half a decade, Derrick. Get over it."

Without so much as a twitch or flinch, she sent a command. Two doors opened, one on either side of her, and out walked her lackeys, Samson and Adam.

Derrick remembered them from the forest. He remembered scaring Samson, but he had to slide into his mind to find his fears. Inside, he found a sick and twisted man. Derrick relived all the perverted things Samson did to truck-stop hookers and the sadistic way he treated animals. Any time he found a mouse in his motel room, he'd put it in the microwave for fun. Samson had a younger sister, and Derrick knew—*felt*—the things he did to her.

Samson skulked forward just as Derrick reentered his mind. With a perverted blood lust to fuel the feral fire, Samson pounced. Wading through the disgusting pool of memories, Derrick reacted out of reflex, grabbing a handful of horrifying images and holding them up like a shield. Samson fell to the floor, shrieking. Derrick twisted the memories and tied them in a knot, switching Samson with all his victims all at once: Samson was now his younger sister, forced to choke on his manhood; Samson was now the mouse jumping around the inside of the microwave while his insides boiled to eruption; Samson was now the hooker whose nipples he melted and disfigured with a hissing iron. The cat-creature huddled into a shaking ball of fur on the floor, swatting at the air, convulsing and frothing from his mouth.

"Nora, please," Derrick tried one more time. "Please stop this."

"Oh, *shut up!*" Nora frowned, her onyx eyes looking inhuman. She clenched her fists, and hundreds of lab mice spilled out from an open door. A torrent of white, speckled with dots of red, flowed toward Derrick. And Adam led the charge.

Derrick sensed Adam was only a teenager and a good-hearted one at that. He certainly didn't want to cripple him the way he did Samson. Adam's tongue flicked in and out of his mouth, and Derrick realized any illusion he cast for Adam might be useless. Merely tricking Adam's eyes would do nothing against the reptilian's sense of hearing or smell. And Derrick wanted to find Marvin, not exchange blows with his lackeys.

Falling back on old tricks, Derrick made himself invisible to Nora and then made her think her ally was her enemy. The avalanche of snow-white mice crashed into Adam, sending him to the floor. Within two heartbeats, hundreds of mice engulfed Adam, white blanketing the green. Derrick backed away while watching the massacre—Adam crunched a dozen mice with every chomp of his jaws, squashed some with his feet and hands.

Proud of himself for escaping danger twice, Derrick continued his search. Another hallway, then another, trying to open every door available, to no avail. He tried to keep his adrenaline up, reminding himself that pernicious surprises could lurk behind every corner, but it didn't stop the feelings of doubt and frustration. He needed to find Marvin. But how? Where? He decided to ascend the next set of stairs he could find and try again. His stomach knotted, thinking about how he might have to up his meanness level with the receptionist to get the answers he wanted as he followed the exit signs to the nearest stairwell. He turned the last corner and saw that he wouldn't have to interrogate her.

He found Marvin.

"Normally, I would applaud such tenacity. Maybe even reward it. But you're keeping me from a very important meeting." Marvin wore an expression of disapproval while he stood relaxed, hands in his pockets, suit jacket on, and tie loosened.

Derrick had contemplated killing Marvin, bringing a gun or a knife. But he knew what Marvin could do, knew he'd heal himself before a bullet or blade could even wound him. No, he had to fry his brain, like he did with Samson. He had to drive him insane, force him into a bottled Hell, and cork it. And he had to do it *now*!

Marvin strolled toward Derrick, the heels of his shoes making rhythmic echoes. Then the walls turned into curtains of fire. Marvin paused, shocked by the sight, then smiled. "Very impressive, Derrick. It is indeed life-like. However, I know this is nothing more than a charlatan trick." And Marvin continued walking toward Derrick.

The walls disappeared, but the fire remained and swirled around the two men, a vortex of flame. From the blaze came barbed tentacles, whipping and snapping at Marvin. Despite what truths he knew, he couldn't stop himself from dodging and parrying. He then laughed, chiding himself for falling for such a simple gimmick. He continued walking toward Derrick.

The floor under Marvin's feet rippled, turned to mush, and gave way. Marvin fell into an abyss where a gnashing maw of teeth awaited him. Ashamed for yelping at such a sensation, Marvin stopped falling. And stood. "I am not falling down a pit with nasty teeth at the end, Derrick. I am still standing on a floor. A *real* floor in the basement of my building." With those words, he continued walking toward Derrick.

Scared, Derrick tried using his own fears in the illusionary theater. A thousand disembodied mouths opened from nowhere, yawning with yellow teeth and swollen tongues. In unison, they spewed blood, feces, or vomit, dumping on Marvin. No matter how real it seemed, it didn't stop Marvin from reaching Derrick.

"I know it isn't real, Derrick! I know it isn't real!" Marvin shouted as he placed his hands on the young man's face, his fingers pressing against his skull. Maggots with blisters and pus oozing cockroaches burst from the back of Marvin's hands. "I know it isn't real!"

Derrick cried. It was over and he couldn't stop Marvin. His skull changed from bone to cartilage, from cartilage to loose strips of skin tissue. Marvin's fingers burrowed into Derrick's brain as his hands reduced the young man's head to pulp.

As if flipping a light switch, the world returned to normal. Panting, Marvin looked at Derrick's dead body lying at his feet. Cranial goo dripped from his hands, splashing on the floor with nauseating squishes. This time the knight didn't triumph, and the evil wizard won . . .

CHAPTER
75

Harrisburg, Pennsylvania

Michael parked his car on the fourth floor of the garage and ran to the elevator. He pushed the down arrow seven times, which he loathed when others did. An imbecilic manifestation of stress by those too stupid to alter their lifestyle choices and remove the stressors. And now he was one of those people.

He tried to remove the stress, he rationalized. But it kept creeping back into his life, kept forcing him to lie to his wife. And now that he had found another piece of the puzzle, what would he do? Knowing that at least four of the people with these abilities all went to the same sleep apnea specialist in Hershey made him question his resolve. Did he want to investigate further? Or should he just give the information to Derrick and tell him to have a nice life as long as he and Emma stayed out of Michael's. Derrick! Michael pushed the down arrow button three more times.

The garage was next to the Gunn & Dunn building, making Michael's foot time brief. But it seemed an eternity as a multitude of scenarios of Derrick's fate sluiced through his mind. Michael noticed a slight gallop to his gait, surprising himself once again.

Fighting the urge to be ill as he entered the building, witnessing the worst humanity had to offer buzzing around him in suit jackets and power ties, Michael made his way through the ornate lobby to the fake receptionist. Her smile was fake, as were her too round boobs, her tan, her hair color, and her whole damn demeanor. He wanted to tell her to unshackle those chains that confined her and not allow herself to be used by the bloodsucking leeches wearing thousand-dollar suits that squirmed all around her. Instead, he smiled at her and said, "Hello. My name is Michael Roseman, and I have an appointment with Marvin Carver."

After a few cheerful keystrokes of the computer in front of her, she replied with a sing-song voice, "I'm sorry, Mr. Roseman, but I don't have you scheduled for an appointment today."

"Are you sure? Could you look again?" Michael knew very well how lame he sounded but wanted to buy some time to think of a different tactic.

The receptionist followed through with the request, her smile never faltering. "I'm sorry, sir. Still no luck."

"Look, I know he's here. Let's not play any more of these silly games. Why don't you just tell me where he is."

The receptionist's eyes changed, flashing bits of anger. But her smile raged on, never disappearing even as she spoke. "I'm sorry, sir. I simply can't do that. If you'd like to set up an appointment, I could—"

"That won't be necessary." A voice came from behind Michael.

Michael flinched twice, once from the voice surprising him, then again when he saw to whom it belonged. A young man—Michael only assumed he was young because of his youthful eyes—wearing a brown shirt and khakis. The young man's receding—forsooth, retreating in full gallop—hairline betrayed his age. His shirt strained against the flab rolling over all sides of his belt, one deep inhale away from becoming untucked from his pants. However, the man's legs were thin, twig-like, making him look like a noxious candied apple on a stick. The young man continued, "I'll escort Mr. Roseman."

"Okay, Colby. Thanks!" The receptionist said, turning her attention back to her computer monitor.

Colby? Michael thought. *This whale of a human being is Colby? The boy was never thin, but to balloon to such astronomical proportions since the last time I've seen him seems . . . seems . . . is he missing more teeth?*

Indeed he was. Four more had abandoned his mouth since their last meeting. Michael's heart strummed the cords of pity and shame, unable to stop staring into Colby's mouth as he talked.

Colby chatted as he led Michael to the elevator, but Michael didn't hear a word. Not only did it seem like empty rhetoric, but the professor couldn't help but wonder how his legs didn't snap from supporting so much upper body weight. Michael found the maximum occupancy of the elevator to be two thousand pounds but was still a bit nervous, even though he and Colby were the only two occupants. Too flustered and awestruck to ask, Michael had no clue of their final destination, just up.

Once they hit the last floor, the doors opened to an extravagant waiting room, complete with another smiling receptionist. With a cursory nod to the receptionist, Colby led Michael into Marvin's office.

Even though the office was expansive enough to hide a small army, Michael knew Marvin was not there. The professor meandered around, shaking his head or sucking his teeth with contempt at every over-the-top decoration. He swore the desk and contents cost more than the GNP of most African countries. After absorbing as much disgust as he could, he turned to Colby and said, "So, do you know when he'll—"

Michael couldn't finish his sentence, interrupted by the blubbery man sobbing. "Help. Please, help me, Mr. Roseman."

Michael couldn't help but glance over his shoulder to look for another Mr. Roseman in the room, for certainly, the overweight young man couldn't have been talking to him. However, the realization that he was the only other person in the room compelled Michael to ask, "Excuse me?"

"I know you're special, like Emma, like Derrick used to be. Like Marvin. Please. Please, you have to help me."

"How did you know . . . wait . . . did you say Derrick 'used to be?'"

Colby's jowls jiggled with every stunted sob. "Oh, God. You don't know. I . . . I thought that's why you were here. I thought you knew."

"Knew? Knew what, Colby?"

"He's dead. Marvin killed him."

"*What*? How . . . ? When . . . ?" Michael couldn't hold on to reality. Colby's words spiraled through his mind, whipping their way along his chest and causing a frenzy in his stomach.

As Colby talked, he used his hands, spinning them in small circles almost as if he needed them to balance his prodigious girth. His belly, arms, and chins flapped with every movement. "Derrick came in to stop Marvin and made his way through security. But Marvin, he . . . he crushed him. Crushed his skull with his hands."

"But . . . but . . ."

"You don't know what's happened, do you? How you and he and everyone got your special abilities, do you?"

"You . . . know? Marvin knows?"

"Nanobots."

Unable to grasp what he had just heard, Michael contorted his face as if someone had explained God as a mathematical equation. "What? You mean those . . . those tiny little robots?"

"Yes. In your brain. In his brain. In all your brains. He told me what they were doing and how they were doing it, but I didn't understand."

Michael felt like he was sliding down an ethereal slope into a bad dream. Reality and logic didn't matter here. His gaze slid from Colby to the floor to someplace far away in the recesses of his mind. Microscopic robots? In his brain? Random images of the past three months flipped through his mind like pictures falling out of a photo album. He braced himself against the desk to keep from collapsing. "Did . . . someone call the police?"

Tears overflowed from Colby's eyes, streaking his face and giving it a greasy quality. He chuckled, wheezing. "Haven't you seen the employees, Mr. Roseman? They're slaves! Marvin made them addicted to this place. *None* of them can stay away from here for more than eight hours."

"What about you, Colby?"

Colby's jaw went slack, dipping into his pool of gelatinous chins. "Me? Are you fucking *kidding*? *Look* at me!"

"Colby, I—"

Tears streamed, his face reddened. The redder his face became, the more the tears flowed. Snot and spit glistened his lips as he ranted. "I used to be hot! I could get any girl I wanted, just with a smile. I was top of my class and got an MBA. Then I come here, ready to become a manager. Then *Marvin* fucked that up for me! And then started doing things—things I couldn't explain. Started doing *this*!"

Michael stared in stunned silence, not knowing what to say or even how to react. Colby waved his arms around in front of himself to draw attention to his gargantuan belly. "I mean, look at me! He did this all because he was too inept to get a promotion, because I got the job he wanted. Then this! This is Hell! This is fucking Hell!"

Michael's heart raced, keeping pace with the speed at which Colby lamented. His hands flung faster, his rolls jiggling with every swing. Michael felt his eyes start to close, a primal reflex to keep the images from his mind. The young man was losing it, this Michael was sure of. But he had no idea how to stop him.

Colby blubbered even more, grabbing chunks of his waist with his meaty hands. "Look at this! All because of a fucking job! I've gone days without eating, hoping and praying I'd lose some weight, even one lousy fucking pound. But no! I get fatter and fatter!"

Finally, Michael was able to break free from the spell and turn his head, just as Colby started to unbuckle his pants. "And he took my dick! I can't even reach it anymore. I have to . . . I have to sit down to piss, because I can't fucking *reach it*. I don't even . . . I don't even know if I have one anymore. Look. *Look!*"

"Colby . . . please . . . I . . . don't do this . . ." Michael stammered as he formed a visor with his hand and turned away. Every time he thought of a phrase, he instantly thought of how negatively Colby would react. He tilted his body away from what was surely a horrifying sight but found no alternative to calming the young man, so he twisted his head back for a guarded peek. Michael wanted to cry himself.

Michael saw Colby with his pants around his ankles and pitied him. Not only did his flab completely cover his privates, but his hips as well. Guilt and pity stabbed Michael's heart, having to witness such a spectacle. Then fear seized his whole chest and crushed it as Marvin entered.

Dark clouds of anger formed over Marvin as he assessed the situation. Michael and Colby were paralyzed with fear. Reacting first, Marvin swept across the floor to Colby and grabbed the young man by his throat. "My first thought was you might be engaging in a bit of corporate espionage, but now that I see your pants warming your ankles, I cannot help but wonder what other dalliances you might be perpetrating."

Tears streaming down his face, Colby could only manage a garbled, "No . . . no . . ."

A pinprick of nobility poked its way into Michael's heart as he stood and said, "Let him go, Marvin."

"Why, Professor, I had no idea you swing that way. Sure, all the signs are there, but you certainly must do something about your taste."

Michael knew Marvin didn't believe his own words; he only tried to goad him into a distracting dialogue. "He didn't do anything wrong. He was distraught, broken down from the miserable way you treat him and the other employees."

An evil smile oozed across Marvin's face. He turned to Colby, still crying. "Oh, Colby, I thought you were so happy in your employ here?"

"Marvin, stop it," Michael said, hoping he believed his own bravado. "This is wrong. What you're doing is *wrong*."

Marvin's sinister smile disappeared, shifting his countenance to pure hatred as he looked at the professor. "Wrong? You dare trespass into my building after sending your delusional lackey to assassinate me?"

"I didn't send Derrick, Marvin. What he did was wrong as well."

"Hmm. You seem to be proclaiming you know the difference between right and wrong. Let's put your resolve to the test, shall we?"

Marvin turned his attention back to Colby and flaunted his abilities. Colby's body rumbled and rippled. Muscles flexed and twisted, setting themselves up for work. His chest heaved and shuttered, his belly roiled. With a moan of pain and an expulsion of air, Colby released a spray of feces and flatulence against his will. But the muscles in his body didn't stop; they flexed harder, in different rhythms. The muscles in his chest pushed, his abdominal muscles throbbed, then tightened. With the speed of a lightning strike, Colby's rectum prolapsed.

Shaking with pain and fear, Colby tried to fight free from Marvin's grip, but Marvin held too much command. Every muscle in Colby's torso released, only to snap again with whip-like intensity, forcing his small intestines to fall out of his body. The onslaught continued, ribs cracking from the strain as Colby's body rebelled against itself. Large intestines snaked their way free. Colby's stomach fell out, landing on the floor with a sloshing splat. Liver, gallbladder, and spleen spilled out between gobs of yellow fat, spider-webbed in crimson.

Marvin finally released his prisoner. His muscles no longer where they should be, his entrails out, Colby flopped to the floor. Lying next to his organs, staring at them, Colby opened and closed his mouth like a stunned and gutted fish. His body opted to seizure as his eyes rolled up into his head and foam frothed from the corners of his mouth.

Michael felt his body seize as well, unable to do anything other than stare. He couldn't breathe, couldn't blink. He wasn't even sure if his heart still beat. His stomach twisted into a knot as the smells made their way to his nose. Until Marvin broke the spell, "He is still alive, Professor. Are you going to do the 'right' thing?"

Michael didn't respond. He couldn't. His brain refused to believe what he saw. It wasn't real. It couldn't be. It defied the laws of nature, of physics, of every science Michael knew to exist!

"Euthanasia is the 'right' course of action, wouldn't you say, Michael?" Marvin continued. "His suffering is obvious. And I know for a fact he could live like this for hours. I believe the only 'right' choice you have is to put him out of his misery."

Michael begged his legs to move. One step. Then another. Inching his way closer to the twitching blob that used to be a man. Making his way ever closer, Michael stared at things he thought he'd never see outside of textbooks. His legs continued to work, walking him closer to the innocent man suffering on the floor. Then he walked past him.

Breaking into an all-out sprint, Michael ran from Marvin's office, abandoning Colby, abandoning every moral he thought he possessed. He had never been in a situation like this before, but he discovered what he'd do. He ran. He ran from responsibility. He ran from the truth. He ran from fear. And he ran from Marvin's hideous laughter . . .

CHAPTER
76

Harrisburg, Pennsylvania

Adam crouched in the corner of the room as he watched Nora. He wore a lab coat in a futile attempt to feel human again by wearing clothes, but he still felt the chill of the cold cinder-block wall against his back. His arms wrapped around his knees, pulling his thighs to his chest as his tail curled around his ankles.

As silent as death, he watched Nora fuss over Samson. He watched as she stroked the cat-creature's orange fur, asking him if he was comfortable. Samson made no reply, only stared into nothingness, unbeknownst to anyone else, reliving the many hells he had created. Nora sat on the bed Samson lay on, like a mother doting over her child in a hospital. Or one lover longing for the other.

Adam felt a sense of satisfaction looking at the helpless Samson, now a vegetable forced to wear diapers. Ridiculous, yet resplendent. Adam knew the thoughts running through his head weren't very Christian. He knew his parents would have disapproved, reciting scripture about turning the other cheek or being a good Samaritan. But he didn't care. After the three months he had lived through, even Job would have given up. And so did Adam. Was there a God? Maybe He was just another human with special abilities. Just another man who could make people see miracles, like that kid Derrick. Or maybe He could heal the sick, like Marvin. Or enslave, like Nora.

When Adam first met Nora, she was just what he needed—a friend in his greatest time of need. Confused and lost, Adam leaned on Nora, allowed her grace and beauty to wash away his anxieties. He almost looked forward to his new and unusual life. But she wanted more, what he couldn't give. Then Samson came along.

Adam wanted to leave the two of them alone in the forest. But where would he have gone? There was safety in numbers, no matter how uncomfortable one of them was with the other two. That was what he'd told himself. Or was it?

After he found Nora, they never parted, except when they discovered the hillbilly insect freak. Wanting to protect Nora, Adam had used himself to distract the creepy old man, drew the arsenal of insects away from her. Had he truly wanted to protect her? *Yes,* he thought. That was something he would have done no matter the circumstances. But when he was separated from Nora, something happened. His mind cleared, as if awakening from a dream. And he had felt used.

The refreshing feeling had disappeared once he found that Nora had safely escaped the homicidal insects. Then he felt clouded again, his judgment impaired. His thoughts jumbled, even treasonous. Until Derrick attacked. Nora had explained that the young man in the hooded sweatshirt messed with her mind, made her think Adam was indeed Derrick, so she commanded an army of lab mice to attack the wrong target. But something more happened at that moment, something that Adam forced himself to hold on to.

Now he sat in the corner of a basement room of the Gunn & Dunn building they used as temporary living quarters. Feeling alone, he watched Nora stroke Samson's fur one last time before kissing his cheek and tucking him in for the night. Nerves had been working Adam's fingers; they tapped and wiggled, inadvertently shredding his lab jacket.

After she finished with Samson, Nora walked out of the room. Adam followed as he had done so many times before.

Almost midnight, the basement was empty except for the four unusual guests. Nora had yet to finish setting up her laboratories, so she had no need for any other employees to be around. She strode to her room, and Adam followed. He rationalized that he wanted to find privacy as they walked past the closed door to Robert's room, who hadn't left since arriving. But he knew it was nerves. A seven-foot-tall monster shouldn't be afraid, he thought to himself. "It . . . wasss . . . you."

Confused, Nora turned to look at Adam. "What?"

"Why . . . I ssstayed."

Nora smiled and placed her hand on his face. He pulled away. Her brows furrowed, but her placating smile remained. "Adam. I'm not sure what you're getting at?"

"You . . . sssee me . . . asss . . . a pet."

She winced and reeled her head back with a touch of melodrama. "Pet? Of course I don't see you as a pet. You're not a pet."

"Then . . . why . . . have you . . . been . . . controlling me."

"Controlling you? Don't be silly, Adam. Look, it's been a long day—"

"I can . . . feel . . . you in . . . my head!"

Nora sighed as she dropped her gaze to her feet. She shifted her jaw from side to side, thinking of what to say. She looked back at Adam, her smile gone, replaced by a sympathetic look of pity. "You were lost when I found you. Confused. Distraught. Your father tried to shoot you because he thought you were the devil. You needed help. You needed me to calm you down. Relax you."

"Why . . . keep . . . doing it?"

"Why keep you with me? Adam, you can't live in this world on your own like the way you are. No one would understand how beautiful you are, except me. And you're so young and naïve . . ."

"You're . . . only . . . three . . . yearsss older!"

Nora sighed again and took a step forward. Adam took a step back. Her face snapped stern. "Adam, stop this. I'm doing what's right for you. So I made you do a couple things, but it was to keep you safe. Look where we are now! We're safe and we can live and grow now. Yes, there are concessions to be made. I mean, look at me—I'm wearing clothes." She finished her sentence with an empathetic smile, hoping to pass her satisfaction to him.

"I thought . . . you were . . . a friend."

"I *am* a friend. I've been your friend since the moment we met. Now, why don't you go back to your room and get some sleep."

Adam's legs moved, one foot in front of the other, forced and awkward motions, like a dancer forgetting his routine. "You . . . didn't asssk!"

"I didn't need to ask, Adam. I knew you needed a friend. And I knew I'd be the only one you'd ever have. Now, come on, let's go."

His legs still moved, walking him closer to his room, his claws clicking on the tiled floor with every pained step. "If you're . . . my friend . . . then ssstop!"

She did not, knowing what to expect. "Adam, I can't. For your sake."

Adam twisted his head to look back at her. Tears streamed from his eyes. His autonomy was slipping away; he could feel it go. The cloudiness crept its way back into his mind. This was his last chance to be free. He believed it in his heart. With one last garbled sob, he begged, "Pleassse."

Nora sighed one last time, and Adam stopped walking toward his room. She wanted to say something deep and prophetic to convince him to stay, to convince him that he needed her. But she couldn't think of anything. She weighed her options and decided she would be too busy with her work and nursing Samson to control Adam all the time. Plus, she still had Robert. She couldn't pull his strings like she could with Adam, but she was a woman and had other ways to control men.

Finally free, the smog lifted from his brain. He could think and see and smell clearly now! His first thought was to disembowel her. His second thought wondered if she wasn't right, that he needed her to control him. But he shook both thoughts from his head as he tore and removed the remaining shreds of his lab coat. He took one last look at Nora and wondered if he would have stayed if she simply had asked him. "Good . . . bye."

Before Nora could reply, Adam scampered away on all fours clinging to the walls and ceiling as he went. She wanted to warn him, tell him that she couldn't control Samson or Robert because they remained human, despite their outward appearances. However, Adam became more animal every day. She knew the reptile he resembled would take over.

Within seconds, Adam wound his way out of the building. Well past three in the morning, he slithered his way along the bare streets, searching. He tried to keep to the shadows, being seen only by a homeless drunk staggering toward the nearest missionary shelter and a lonely cabby driving home. Finding the nearest manhole cover, Adam popped it off with ease and disappeared into the underground darkness, content to become an urban legend . . .

CHAPTER
77

Harrisburg, Pennsylvania

Marvin dried his hands, the Egyptian cotton towel gliding over his skin. He placed the hand towel, with a higher thread count than most duvets, next to the sink of the executive lavatory. Placing his fingers within an inch of his nose, he inhaled. Nothing. He finally removed the stench of Derrick's brains.

Grumbling about the day's events, he stormed from the restroom to his office and flopped onto his plush leather chair. He heaved a sigh with which only a burdened king could sympathize. Running his hand through his thick hair, he tried to calm himself. He ran his hand through again to satisfy a guilty pleasure, still enthralled by his regal mane.

He sighed again, his malcontent thoughts exhuming the day's melodramas from his mind. First, his wife forced the proverbial rod he would have rather spared. But she needed to understand that sacrifices needed to be made to maintain the new lifestyle she so quickly became acclimated to. Then the Derrick episode. Messy. And finally, dealing with the ramifications of inverting Colby's life, which coincidentally, led to the inverting of Colby himself. Marvin chuckled.

But after having Stone and a couple other muscle-bound mindless minions dispose of the bodies, he was now alone, shrouded in peace and quiet. He could now take the time necessary to examine Kevin's roadmap. Sinking further into the luxury of his comfortable chair, Marvin closed his eyes. He flipped through his memory and recalled the roadmap, placing it in the forefront of his mind, savoring it like a perfectly prepared gourmet meal. Before he began, he opened one eye to check on his door, making sure no last-minute intrusions reared to interrupt such a perfect moment. None. Splendid.

Closing his eyes once more, he focused on the inner workings of his brain, visualizing the synaptic roadways snaking through his mind. Bio-electrical impulses zoomed across myriad nerves, leaping from gap to gap with effortless precision. Like a blind man touching the face of his lover, Marvin took his time exploring, understanding every fold of his cerebrum and every lobe it formed. He absorbed the magnificence of the cerebellum, the magic of the thalamus, and primitive beauty in the simplicity of the medulla oblongata. As if discovering an ancient city on an archaeological dig that answered every modern mystery, he understood how truly similar humans were to other animals. He understood how creatures like Adam, Samson, and Robert were possible.

Once he felt he had learned an adequate amount of information, he searched for the needle in the haystack. But he knew where to look—he always knew. Every time he tried to pattern his brain after Michael or Emma or Stone, he always encountered a roadblock, an enigmatic entity causing him failure. Now he knew what it was and how to use it.

Simply following the ebbs and flows of neural activity, he rode the waves to the epicenter, the roadblock, the nanobots. He imagined them as obelisk-like citadels, only accessible by the worthiest. With his new roadmap, his new knowledge, Marvin was now worthy. It was time to go in.

Marvin accessed the roadmap he had procured from Kevin. The obese computer technician could communicate with computers and other electronics, his mind could simply translate random zaps of neurons into ones and zeroes.

Marvin created his concerto, like a master pianist playing a dozen keyboards at once. He moved neural paths, twisted axons, reshaped dendrites. He shifted entire regions. Following the roadmap precisely, certain parts of his brain configured exactly to Kevin's. Marvin tried to control the nanobots. Nothing. Anger welled deep within his belly, but he staved it off, hoping to think through the problem. The nanobots were the robotic gatekeepers to everyone's abilities, but Kevin could control robots, so Marvin should be able to control the nanobots. But controlling robots was Kevin's ability, and he would not be able to do so without the aid of the nanobots.

Maybe Marvin should make Kevin reconfigure the nanobots? He nixed that idea, not wanting to share his secret or put another person in any position to wrest away his power. Instead, he continued examining Kevin's roadmap, hoping he had missed something, hoping all he had to do was rearrange a few more synapses. Then it dawned on him. For Kevin to command robots, he first needed to communicate with them.

Relaxing, Marvin renewed his focus. Instead of attacking the nanobots, he "listened" to them, felt the connections between them and his brain. He observed and utilized the similarities. Zeroes and ones flowed through the nanobots' processors, while positive and negative ions flowed through his brain. The nanobots were translating their language to his, so all he had to do was sync up. Listen. Learn. Then he felt it, virtually saw how the nanobots said, "run." He quickly learned "go to." Soon he learned how they processed "if" and "then." The process became easier with every logical concept he learned. Faster with each command. The information streamed through him like rivers of lightning. Until he tied it all together. He figured out how to unlock the gates.

Marvin's eyes snapped open as he accessed a different roadmap. He molded his brain to the precise shape it needed to be. Then he felt it. A warmth building within his neck, at the base of his skull. A pinprick of fire, at first, but it grew to a controlled inferno. He held out his hands and released the blaze, invisible flames scorching from his shoulders to his fingertips and beyond. With the force of an exploding grenade, waves of air rippled from his fingers to his desk, producing an equally dramatic result. His desk slid backward, then tipped over, all the contents plumed into the air or crashed against the nearest wall. He could now do what Michael could.

Marvin tried to catch the loose sheets of paper fluttering to the ground, hoping to mimic Emma's speed and accuracy. Instead, he seemed as slow and clumsy as ever. He concentrated, communicated with the gatekeepers, and finally followed Emma's roadmap. Half the papers had fallen to the floor now, but with laser-targeting precision, he plucked the remaining sheets from the air. He laughed, almost giddy, drunk with power.

Plucking a pair of scissors from his desk drawer, he held them over his open palm, wielding them like a knife. It seemed that he could utilize only one ability at a time. So be it. His neurons shifted and moved; chemical transmitters changed flow. He now had Stone's abilities and commanded the cells in his hand to mimic Stone's. He stabbed his palm. Then again. And again. No effect, not a single scratch or even the sensation of the cold steel bouncing off his skin. Nothing.

Laughing, Marvin fell back into his chair. He did it! He cracked the code. A tear escaped from his eye, traveling down his cheek. He did it. A wry smile twisted his lips as he realized that he had lassoed the horizon and reeled it in. The world became smaller, tiny enough to fit in the palm of his hand. With his new abilities, he could do anything. And he decided what he would do first thing tomorrow—revisit the Central Pennsylvania Sleep Institution and get more . . .

CHAPTER
78

Camp Hill, Pennsylvania

Michael sat at the dining room table. He forgot why he chose to sit in this chair rather than in the kitchen or living room. No one sat in this room. Not even for holidays. They never used the dining room, and it had a mystical quietness to it, as if noise chose not to use this room either. Maybe that was why he picked it, because it seemed devoid of life, just like his soul.

Resting his elbows on his knees, Michael wrung his hands together until his knuckles hurt, but he couldn't seem to stop himself. Maybe the self-inflicted pain was some form of retribution? Some form of penance for walking out on a dying man. But what could he have done? Seriously? Kill Colby? Even though it would have been euthanasia, it still didn't seem justifiable. It wouldn't have been like taking a doddering and decrepit pet that lived beyond its years to the vet for one last visit. This was a person! Colby was no pet! But Marvin sure thought so.

Hanging his head low, chin to chest, Michael still couldn't find an answer to what he should have done. He knew what he shouldn't have done, which was what he did do. He ran. Abandoned Colby. Just as he abandoned Derrick, leaving them both in the vile clutches of Marvin. *No!* Michael admonished himself. *I didn't kill Derrick! I didn't kill Colby! Marvin did!* But he still felt like he may as well have pulled the proverbial trigger.

Maybe he should have killed Marvin? Yeah! Right! Murder one of the richest men in Harrisburg. In cold blood. Sure, it would have been self-defense, even if just technically, but who would have believed Michael? No one. Especially with a disemboweled young man writhing on the floor. Tell the police that Marvin did it? That Marvin had special abilities to control the human body? And thinking of Marvin's powers, would Michael have been able to do it? Sure, he could have used his push abilities to slam Marvin into the wall a few times, but would that have been enough? Would he be able to split his skull like a melon before Marvin could heal himself?

Michael shook his head, trying to derail his train of thought. He shouldn't be thinking like that! He wasn't that kind of person. But what was the use of having these abilities if he didn't help people? Oh, God, that was Derrick and Emma talking. But Michael felt like he should have done something! Claire would know.

Michael stopped wringing his hands and rubbed them across his face, as if washing it sans soap and water. He would tell Claire. He had to. Even if he wanted to ignore his abilities, he still needed to fess up, inform her why he almost ruined their marriage.

The front door opened, and Michael heard the beautiful sounds of his daughter's laughter and voice, her usually infectious joy unable to penetrate his heart. He couldn't even bring himself to chuckle at her squeals as she thundered up the stairs to her room. Then his heart turned to ice as his wife walked into the dining room.

Claire paused as she crossed the threshold, frozen mid-stride, her keys dangling from her fingers over her open purse. Her brows furrowed as her head cocked to the side, her look asking Michael what he was doing here. Michael wasn't sure if she meant "here" to be "the never-used dining room" or "the house."

This is it, he told himself. *The monkey comes off my back, the weight off my chest, and whatever other metaphors I can think to mix. I'm telling her. I'm telling her right now.* "We need to talk."

"Let me guess—about your *students*."

Claire's words punched him in the chest. Just the word "student" made him think of Derrick. Without thought, his mouth just spoke. "Derrick died yesterday."

"Well . . . what? One of your students died?"

"His name's Derrick. He was only twenty-three," Michael replied, voice soulless, in a trance.

Claire took a step back and connected the dots, completing a puzzle that lacked all the pieces. "So, you really *did* go to Cresson? And Pittsburgh?"

"Yes," Michael answered, not quite hearing his wife's words.

"For Derrick."

Knowing the conversation didn't seem right, Michael snapped out of his stupor and lifted his head to look at his wife. "What?"

"You went to Cresson and Pittsburgh for Derrick. Because he was dying."

Don't do it, Michael told himself. *I can't be this low. I can't be this much of an asshole.*

"Yes. He had friends he wanted to visit before he went."

Apparently, I am this much *of an asshole!*

Claire's angry eyes softened. She placed her purse on the floor and stepped closer to her husband. "So, why didn't you tell me sooner?"

Tell her now! Tell her the truth now!

"I don't know. I think he wanted it to be personal? He didn't want many people to know. And you . . . you're so damn caring that not only would you have all but let him move in with us, you'd probably whip up fourteen different fundraisers for him. Derrick wouldn't have wanted that."

What the fuck is my problem! I suck, I suck, I suck, I suck! Emma's right—I'm going to Hell!

Cracking a faint smile, Claire stepped closer. "You really think I'd do all that?"

Forcing his mouth to curl upward, Michael replied. "Yes. With blimps and doves and fireworks and a Barbra Streisand concert."

Why can't I just tell her? Why? The most amazing woman in the world, and I can't tell her!

But Michael knew why. Deep in the recesses of his mind, in his brain, lurked tiny machines that became all too apparent once he noticed his wife might forgive him. What were they doing? Michael swore he felt them moving around inside, setting up tiny little homes and replicating, taking over. The more he thought about it, the more his head itched. Claire made a supreme gesture of forgiveness by closing the gap between them and sitting on his lap. Michael scratched his head.

Claire's expression reflected her thoughts of his odd behavior and asked, "Fleas?"

"Probably. I *was* in Pittsburgh after all."

Laughing, Claire leaned into him for a deep hug. "Jackass. I love you."

"I love you, too." Michael twisted his arm around her to scratch his head again. Nanobots. Robots. Injected? Implanted? During his sleep apnea surgery all those years ago? It had to be. The Central Pennsylvania Sleep Institute in Hershey. He remembered it well; it was an outpatient procedure, and they broke his jaw. Wired shut for six weeks after; he lost a good ten pounds. He needed to drop the weight but took exception to the discomfort. But his answers lie there. Tomorrow. Tomorrow he would go there and get—no, demand!—answers. Then he would tell Claire. *I can't tell her what I don't know.*

"Just promise me that when you find out something like that again, you'll tell me."

A smile crept across his face, now more confident that he made the right decision to withhold information until further, more conclusive research. "When I find things out, I promise I'll tell you."

Tomorrow . . .

CHAPTER
79

Hershey, Pennsylvania

Michael stood before the Central Pennsylvania Sleep Institute Building and scratched his head. The infernal itching refused to subside. His psyche could not relinquish its hold on the concept of microscopic machines rummaging through his brain. Convinced they caused the itching, he scratched his scalp with obsessive fervor and entered the building.

"Is Doctor Zillin still a part of this practice?" Michael asked the receptionist.

She offered a pleasant smile, tried to keep from watching Michael claw at his scalp, and replied, "Yes, he is. Do you have an appointment?"

Scratching a different part of his head, knowing the nanobots were wreaking havoc in there, Michael answered, "No. But I need to speak with him. Now."

The receptionist could no longer ignore the scratching, and her eyes glanced upward. She wanted to let this crazy man know that this was neither a dermatologist's office nor a psychiatrist's office but rather a sleep specialist institute. But it was close to the end of the day, and she felt no particular loyalty to Doctor Zillin. With a smile, she took the crazy man's name and called the doctor. The crazy man declined her invite to sit, opting to pace instead. And scratch his head.

Within minutes, a door opened to the waiting room, and a nervous man with a nervous smile appeared. "Michael Roseman? I'm Doctor Zillin."

Michael strode with vigor to the doctor. "I remember you. We need to talk."

Too angry to notice that the doctor didn't even ask why, Michael followed the doctor down a small hallway lined with doors, leading him through an entrance labeled "restricted access." Curious, Michael decided to save his tirade until after the doctor swiped his keycard and revealed another long hallway. Once the doors shut behind him, Michael spoke. "I was here three years ago for a sleep apnea surgery, and—"

"I know," Doctor Zillin replied, still nervous, but obviously not because of the irate English professor.

"You know? You were . . . are . . . a part of . . . of this?" Michael yelled, pointing to his head.

"Yes," the doctor offered, leading them through another set of doors and to a stairwell.

"That's it? Nothing else? No hint of why? Why you did it? Why me?" Michael was so mad, he never realized they descended the floors into the depths of the building.

With his back to Michael, he kept walking, unwavering in his silence. Like a diminutive juggernaut, the doctor kept moving forward through one final set of doors. Again, Michael followed him through, and this time, he was greeted by a dozen guns pointing at his head.

Michael froze mid-step. Normally, he would have had to struggle to keep his bladder from releasing, but after fighting with Stone, Samson, and Kevin, guns no longer seemed so ominous. However, he knew they were still lethal. He raised his hands and turned to look at the room.

White. The walls were white as well as the floor, the ceiling, and the lab coats of every person not holding a gun. And it went on forever—the expansive room seemed to have no horizon. Michael knew very little about science, but he knew enough to recognize this as a laboratory. A white computer on every white desk, machines on workstations and tables, and even a few dangled from the ceiling. Michael saw lasers flash, watched centrifuges spin, looked at the graphics and readouts of every beeping monitor. Printers spat out reams of paper coated in graphs and charts and endless oceans of data. Scientists had their arms in accordioned gloves, dissecting animals and organs inside transparent cubes while others manned the computers attached to them. Entire rooms made from transparent walls populated the area. Most were empty, but two had inhabitants: one, a medium-sized black woman, lying in a white hospital-style bed attached to vital sign monitors and an IV drip; asleep in the other room, on another hospital-style bed, was a young blonde girl that Michael estimated to be his daughter's age.

Michael looked from gunman to gunman, spread throughout the room. He estimated he could push three, maybe four at once, but the others would easily finish him off before he had a chance to run, duck, or push again. He spun around as he heard a voice from behind him say, "You can't do it."

Michael turned to see Matthew Matthews standing next to one of the gun-men. "Do what?"

"Don't play coy, Professor. It's quite unbefitting. We know all about your monodirectional telekinetic bursts. Even though your ability's special, it's not enough to take out all the guns. And that's why we have you so low on our list."

"List?"

Matthews smiled, relaxed and confident about the current situation, and stood with his hands in his pockets. "List of special people like you, Michael. We have you all ranked by how useful you are to us. Numbers one and two are in the Plexiglas rooms. You're number twenty-three in Pennsylvania."

"Twenty-three?" Michael snapped, almost insulted. A chill ran down his spine as he truly thought about the number. He only counted ten that he knew of, plus the two in the see-through rooms. How many were there?

"Your abilities are limited, Michael. Sure, they can be used as an offense, but your range is weak."

Michael dropped his eyes as he thought about Matthews' words. "Offense? Range? We're . . . weapons? You put fucking *robots* in our brains, *against our will*, to make *weapons*?!"

"I knew you were a professor for a reason. Let's just say we're a company that makes weapons. More specifically, biological."

"Biological? You mean you're trying to create weapons-grade diseases?"

Matthews let loose a sarcastic laugh, one laced with past pains. "Trying? Ha! Did! We've made plenty. We've made viruses that would rot out the guts of any animal they got into. We have bacteria that make a person drown in their own blood. We've created things Satan hasn't even dreamed of! But we did it all here. And therein lies the problem."

"Problem?"

"Yes. Right now, this lab is self-sufficient, enclosed, sterile, and set at an unalterable sixty-eight degrees. Every sub-lab and research area can be altered to create a hospitable environment, perfect for any culture we create and harvest. Unfortunately, the world outside this lab isn't like that. Every time we've created the perfect weapon, we would release it only to watch it die or mutate its way into nothingness. The deadliest disease to come from this lab? Gonorrhea! We certainly can't threaten millions and make billions from crotch rot!"

Michael scratched his head again, thinking about the nanobots. His emotions swirled from his throbbing head to his churning stomach. Men pointed guns at him. Countless freedoms had been, or were being, violated. He had been lying to his wife. Fear. Anger. Sorrow. All for money. He felt the familiar tingle form at the base of his skull. "So you decided to use innocent people as guinea pigs?!"

"Our division was almost axed until some egghead decided we were taking the wrong approach. We always had the technology to bioengineer microscopic life forms. Recalibrating them to engineer microscopic computers was a snap. A simple program to have them find the right spots in your brain to dig in, and we had ourselves a new potential weapon. Since this is the foremost medical facility devoted to sleep-related problems, we knew we'd get test subjects from all over the state."

Michael clenched his fists. Anger began to dominate fear and sorrow, pushing them away. "You sick son of a bitch!"

Laughing, Matthews put his hands in front of him, shielding himself from the professor's harsh words. "Whoa! It wasn't my idea. I just run this facility and collect a nice big paycheck. And you have a respectable ability. At least you didn't get turned into a mutant animal creature."

Michael turned to the two glass rooms, people in lab coats buzzing around them like bumblebee drones. "And them?"

"Ahh. The black girl has an incredible gift. Her pheromones have mind-altering effects. Quite impressive, too. The little blondie? Well, she's number one on the list. The most powerful person on the planet, that we know of. She can turn you to dust with the blink of an eye."

"I've heard enough!" With that, all eyes moved to the voice to see Marvin grabbing two of the gunmen by the backs of their necks. Their guns fell to the floor, as did their fingers. They both stared at their newly stubbed hands as their fingers still twitched on the floor like thick worms. "Michael, why don't you release the ladies, and then all of us can make our exit."

Michael didn't know how Marvin made such a surreptitious entrance, but he was certainly thankful for it. Then the thought of being thankful for Marvin made him nauseous . . .

CHAPTER
80

Hershey, Pennsylvania

Shooting. *Always shooting with these money-hungry secret operations bastards,* Michael thought as he ducked behind a nearby desk. *All probably Republican, too!*

He peeked around to see all the armed guards focused on Marvin. His stomach lurched as he watched the bullets bounce off Marvin as if he were made of . . . Stone. Frowning from the inconvenience of it all, Marvin strode forth, the walk of a pharaoh, a god-king among ants.

Thoughts swirled through Michael's mind, colliding with each other. How did Marvin do that? Was he always able to do that? Michael shook his head, needing to focus. He looked at the captives in the two clear cells. The scientists crouched behind desks and islands and workstations. Abhorring the thought of violence, Michael knew he had no choice.

Weaving his way from hiding place to hiding place, Michael made his way to one of the scientists and grabbed him by the collar. "Open the doors!"

Scared, the scientist trembled but did not respond. To prove his seriousness, Michael let loose his rage and pushed a handful of the scientist's colleagues, as well as the workstations they hid behind, in the fray. Arms flapped and legs kicked as half a dozen people flew through the air alongside small pieces of lab equipment. Michael turned back to the scientist he clutched.

Still, without words, the scientist handed Michael a keycard. Michael wasted no time using it, going into LaKeisha's cell first. After unhooking the IV, he tried to wake her, shaking her and tapping his fingers against her cheek. Frustrated, he grabbed the IV bag and tore it open, releasing the saline solution over her head. LaKeisha awoke with a jolt. "Wha . . . where . . . ?"

Like a slap in the face, Michael felt tired. Not so much tired but calm and relaxed, mellow to the point of not wanting to move. He remembered

Matthews mentioning that she affected people through pheromones. Digging deep, Michael fought the urge to curl up and take a nap while helping her from the bed. "Are you okay? Can you walk?"

Staggering her way to the door of the cell, she nodded. "Yeah. Jus' . . . jus' a little . . ."

Michael wanted to stay with her, escort her out of here, but knew that wouldn't be wise. He felt tired just from her being tired. What would happen if she came around and became frightened? Panicked? The last thing anyone needed was to panic. Michael thought of what they say about an emergency on a plane—put on your oxygen mask first, then help others.

Michael looked down a hallway lined with similar see-through cells and saw a door with an exit sign. "Okay. Okay. Can you see those doors there? Can you make it to them on your own?"

As if trying to shake off the blurring effects of alcohol, LaKeisha blinked hard and leaned against the wall as she stumbled forward. "Yeah. Yeah . . . I think I can."

"Okay. Good. Go through those doors and find a way out of here. And then run as fast as you can."

LaKeisha said something, but Michael turned his attention to Haley's room. Once inside, he ran to Haley's bed and unhooked her IV. He ran his fingers through the girl's blonde hair, and a tear welled in his eye as he thought about how much she looked like his daughter. Gently rocking her back and forth to wake her, he glanced up to see LaKeisha making her way toward the door. Away from her pheromones, he no longer felt tired as the adrenaline kicked into high gear. Sweat slicked his forehead as his heart bounced around his chest like a stray bullet. However, it almost stopped when he looked up to see how Marvin fared.

Marvin went on the offensive, his suit pockmarked and torn from bullet holes. Matthews screamed orders like a mad general while the gunmen changed positions, trying to flank Marvin. Marvin exploited the brief lull in the shooting by extending his arms toward three approaching gunmen. Michael froze as he watched them fly through the air. Marvin pushed them. He *pushed them*! How was that possible?

A chill slid down Michael's spine. *Marvin controls bodies—people's bodies. More like their biologics. If he could do that, could he steal special abilities? He must be able to. Bullets bounced off him like that psycho from the hospital. He pushed like I do.*

Upon realizing what Marvin could do, Michael looked back down at Haley and recalled Matthews' words: "She could turn you to dust with a blink of an eye." Michael redoubled his effort in waking Haley.

The girl awoke with a start but was too groggy to scream. "Wha . . . ?"

"Shh. It's okay, sweetheart. I'm here to get you out of this place."

"You are?" she asked, rubbing her still shut eyes.

"Yes. What's your name, honey?"

"Haley."

"Hello, Haley. I'm Michael. Can you walk, Haley?"

"I think so," she replied but only rolled onto her side.

Knowing he had no other choice, Michael picked her up, cradling her. She put her arms around his neck and opened her eyes. She saw and heard the commotion through the wall. "What's going on?"

Michael exited the room, not looking back. "Like I said, I'm here to rescue you."

"Oh, wow," her voice barely a whisper. "Who's the man in the tie?"

Thinking of only escape, Michael carried Haley down the same hallway he told LaKeisha to go, to the same door. "His name is Marvin. He's helping me."

The door led to a stairwell, which Michael was more than happy to take upward. However, they were greeted by more men with guns as they burst through the door.

Cursing his luck, Michael stopped. His arms were burning, tired from carrying Haley. She seemed more awake, so he put her down. She could stand on her own, and Michael kept her behind him, shielding her with his body.

Michael looked around and saw they were in a garage. Over a dozen plain white vans faced the outer walls on either side. Under each were hydraulic lifts. Workbenches full of tools lined all the walls. And Michael spied an exit. Still keeping himself between the gunmen and the little girl, he crept along, trying to make it to the exit, becoming more aware that the gunmen didn't want to harm the girl. There were four of them, and they each barked orders for him to stop or they'd shoot, but Michael kept moving, keeping his hands raised, telling them not to shoot. As he kept moving, they shifted their positions. He hoped to get them to bunch up so he could do one big push. Then they left the ground.

Stunned as their feet left the ground, all four gunmen stopped focusing on Michael. They each stretched their legs, trying to reconnect with the ground while windmilling their arms for balance. No matter what they tried, they continued floating higher into the air. All four went flying, slamming against one of the walls and falling to the floor with the clatter of falling tools.

Michael watched Marvin walk through the door using the same exit. Suit torn to shreds but not a single scratch on him, Marvin looked like a comic parody. "Now, Michael, you weren't planning on leaving without me, were you?"

With every step forward Marvin took, Michael took a step back, still keeping Haley behind him. He didn't know how Marvin stole abilities, but he assumed it to be through touch. "I saw you had things well under control."

Marvin laughed. "I most certainly did. And you performed quite admirably yourself, Professor. So, let me take it from here, why don't you?"

Michael knew where the exit was and kept creeping backward toward it. "I think it's more important that we get out of here and call the authorities."

"And the girl?"

"It's the best thing we can do for her. I'm sure the authorities will find her family."

"Actually, I beg to differ," Matthews joined in. He walked into the garage, followed by a dozen more armed guards. "The best thing for her is to stay here. As well as both of you. Now, if you two are done making a mess of things, we'd like to show you both where you'll be staying."

Marvin laughed. "I think not."

"To the contrary, Marvin," Matthews laughed back, stepping aside, allowing more guards into position. Eight more guards, four pairs, each pair carrying a loose net between them. "We know you can use only one ability at a time. You push the nets away, we shoot. You become bulletproof, we net you. So, let's do this the easy way, shall we?"

"No!" All eyes looked at the little girl with the big scream. She stood away from Michael, her fists clenched and her teeth clamped shut, anger in her eyes. She stared at Matthews and trembled. "You're a bad man!"

Realizing what was happening, Matthews turned to run. But didn't make it very far. His skin shriveled and his eyes bulged as he took one final gasp before exploding into a puff of dust.

"No!" Haley screamed again. She drove the heels of her hands into her ears and squeezed her eyes shut. Her body rocked back and forth as she stomped her feet. "No! No! No! No! No! No! No!"

The gunmen swiveled to target the little girl. Their guns crimped and bent like crumpled sheets of aluminum foil. Unarmed, they tried to run; half of them charged toward Haley; the other half tried to flee. All shriveled and turned to dust.

Michael turned toward Haley, backing away from her. She threw a fit, her young mind unable to comprehend what had happened to her. Or maybe she comprehended *too* much? He wanted to hug her and tell her everything would be fine but was too afraid to touch her. Then he saw Marvin approaching her with his hand extended.

The surrounding vans jittered, and the tools rattled, fell off the walls, and danced across the workbenches. The whole room quaked with the rage of a confused little girl. Images of Marvin possessing this type of power danced through Michael's head. Marvin was a megalomaniac. And Michael *could not* allow him to touch Haley. A warm tingle formed at the base of his skull.

Michael caught Marvin by surprise, pushing him off his feet and slamming him against the wall. Marvin's body hit a workbench and rolled onto the floor. His face, bloodied from a gash on his forehead, changed from confused to irate as he stood. By the time he made it to his feet, the gash disappeared. Michael felt the warm tingle return as he said, "Stay away from her, Marvin."

"Now, Michael," Marvin said as he used Michael's abilities against him, pushing Michael against a nearby van. "I thought we established that you were no hero."

Before Michael could react, he saw half a dozen screwdrivers flying toward him. They embedded themselves in the van, each less than an inch from his head. Marvin had used Emma's abilities as a warning that Michael could not allow himself to heed.

As he stood, he heard the metal in the vans and trucks creak and groan. The light fixtures swung wildly as the bulbs burst in pops of sparkling light. The tools on the floor clanged against the concrete. Haley still screamed and cried, having a meltdown. Michael cried out for her but doubted she could hear anything in whatever world she'd escaped to. "Haley!"

And Marvin continued his way toward her.

Michael pushed Marvin again. Just as before, Marvin slammed into the wall and workbench. He jumped to his feet with alacrity and stormed toward Michael. Marvin waved his arm, and Michael found himself suspended in mid-air. He flailed about but to no avail. Michael could feel the anger in Marvin's eyes as he approached. Panic gripped Michael as he thought about what Marvin would do to him. Colby's demise replayed itself in his head over and over, the images refusing to leave no matter how hard he tried to push them aside. Marvin strode forward until the van next to him imploded.

Shocked and a bit frightened, Marvin stopped, leaving himself vulnerable for Michael to kick him in the head. The distraction was enough as Michael fell to the ground. Getting to his feet, Michael focused and pushed Marvin again just as another van imploded. And turned to dust.

"Haley!" Michael yelled. But the little girl still screamed, still cried, still lost in confusion and rage. Another van crumpled and disappeared into a ball of ash. "Haley!"

Michael didn't know what to do. He wanted to run. Every fiber of his being told him to run. His legs were poised and ready to run. But he couldn't leave Haley. She was someone's daughter, a daughter just like Sarah. And he would never let Marvin have her.

Michael pushed through the pain, pushed past his fear. He tried to ignore the vans and trucks exploding into swirling clouds of dust. He readied the warm tingle at the base of his neck even though the walls cracked and windows shattered. Michael pushed Marvin again. The walls broke apart, patches turning to powder. Michael pushed Marvin again. The ceiling crumbled and fell. Instinctively, Michael crouched and protected his head with his arms. Surprise and relief rippled through him as he felt the cascade of dust. And then Marvin pushed him.

Michael slid across the ground, then rolled to a tumbling stop. He jumped to his feet, pausing at the awesome sight of the gray-swirling hurricane of dust that used to be a garage full of vehicles. Through the clear patches, he saw parts of the Central Pennsylvania Sleep Institute building eroding away to a similar fate. He also saw Marvin running toward Haley.

The whipping dust lashed at Michael's face and skin. He squinted while holding his hand out to protect his eyes. But he ran *toward* his fear, *toward* the danger. Just as Marvin came within feet of Haley, Michael pushed him away.

Coming within feet of Haley himself, Michael cupped his hands and mustered a bellow. "*Haley!*"

The little girl stopped screaming and opened her eyes. The dust stopped swirling and fell to the ground with an audible thud. Marvin walked toward Michael and Haley through the remaining nebula. Half of the building was gone, disintegrated. Haley looked around, looking up at the building's half-eaten carcass. The tears continued streaming from her eyes as she shook her head, mumbling, "No. No. No. No."

"Haley," Michael said, his eyes bouncing from her to Marvin. "Here. Come with me, honey. I'll get you some help."

Haley's blonde hair was sallow from the matting dust, her face ash white with caked clumps of gray along her cheeks, turning to paste from her tears. Her eyes were bloodshot, filled with horrifying visions no human should ever have to witness. She glanced at Marvin running toward her and then looked back at Michael. Remiss, Haley dropped her eyes to her hands, gazing at them as if they were responsible for picking apart a building piece by piece. She looked back at Michael and said, "There is no help."

Haley turned herself to dust and blew away on the wind like a gossamer dandelion.

"No!" Michael screamed.

Marvin stopped next to him, staring at the spot where Haley once was and yelled, "Fuck!"

Michael doubled over, resting his forearms on his knees to avoid collapsing. Replaying images of the past fifteen minutes, wondering why? And how? And what he could have done differently. All questions ceased once he realized Marvin stood next to him.

Standing straight and looking Marvin in the eye, Michael was done. Even though his newfound bravery was for naught, he gave up. He was done, not sure he could continue in a world where Marvin Carver flourished and Haley did not. But he was determined to meet his final demise like a man, on his feet with no begging. He looked death in the face.

Marvin laughed. "You look ridiculous, Professor, covered in white powder like an unsuspecting victim of a freak baking accident involving flour. Of course, I can't imagine I look much better."

Stunned, Michael couldn't stop himself from saying, "What? That's it?"

"Certainly you didn't take our little skirmish personally, did you? That was merely negotiations of a business transaction."

Marvin's words devastated Michael more than any punch. He contemplated the crassness as he turned back to the spot where Haley had stood mere seconds ago.

"Well," Marvin continued, tugging on his suit jacket as if it were still whole and new and clean. "It seems the parking lot is untouched. I suggest we depart before the authorities arrive. I would hate trying to explain this."

"Wait," Michael said, looking back at Marvin. "Telekinesis. How?"

"Simple," Marvin replied, patting Michael on the cheek. "I touched someone who is telekinetic."

In silence, Michael smacked away Marvin's hand. He turned and walked away . . .

CHAPTER
81

Camp Hill, Pennsylvania

Michael ran. But his legs moved as if he were a leaden statue, stiff and unyielding. His pursuer chased him with a howling screech that would drive most men mad. The distance between them closed, Michael unable to run any faster, his feet lifting higher and higher, but each new stride was no farther than the last. The hunter ran closer, reaching for Michael, and all he could do was laugh.

"Tag! You're it!" Sarah squealed between high-pitched cackles.

"Ugh!" Michael replied, placing both hands over his heart. He spun himself in a circle and fell to his knees. His head hung limply, then he fell to the ground, landing on his side. "I can't believe you got me!"

"That's 'cause you run like a dork, Daddy!"

"How *dare* you chide my running style!" Michael roared with mock ferocity. He snatched his daughter by her waist, whipped her through the air, and placed her gently on the ground. He rippled his fingers across her ribs, inducing spit-spraying laughter. Benevolence prevailed after a minute of tacit torture, and Michael stopped.

After Sarah caught her breath, she asked, "Are you and Mommy better now?"

"You bet we are, sweetheart."

"What happened?"

"Well, Daddy got caught up in some things that simply weren't important. At the time, I thought they were, but through some introspection..." He paused, remembering his audience was only seven years old. "After thinking about it a lot, I said, 'Duh, I'm being stupid,' because there's nothing more important to me than you and Mommy."

"Yay!" Sarah giggled with a smile that conquered her entire face.

"Yay!" Michael replied. "So, now what do you want to do, Creepy?"

"Pee!"

With that, Sarah jumped up and ran back into the house, the grass tickling her bare toes as she ran.

Michael laughed and looked at his bare toes. And laughed again as he stood. Mere months ago, going barefoot in the grass would have been too adventurous, but after seeing what he saw, almost dying on more than one occasion and almost destroying his own family, he realized that "adventure" was nothing more than perspective.

He walked over to the picnic table in his backyard and sat with his back toward his house, facing a small patch of forest, looking very out of place in the rest of the suburban development. Sipping from a can of soda, he thought of the Central Pennsylvania Sleep Institute building incident from three days ago. The day after it happened, he told Emma everything. She had a right to know, he decided. He then made it clear in no uncertain terms that he never wanted to see her again, no matter the emergency. She expressed her concerns about Marvin and the potential danger he could be. Michael expressed that it wasn't his problem. Their parting lacked fanfare.

Placing the empty can back on the picnic table, he wondered again if he should tell Claire. But why bother? There would be no more adventures, no more risking his life, and no more using his abilities. However, Marvin's last words tickled his brain, "I touched someone who is telekinetic."

It made sense to Michael that he was telekinetic. If he could push things, he should most certainly be able to pull them and lift them too. He stared at the soda can and allowed the tingling warmth to pool at the base of his skull. He glanced over his shoulder to make sure no one watched. Brow furrowed, he focused, concentrating on lifting the can. Nothing. The can didn't move, and neither did the warmth at the back of his neck. He tried again, wanting to pull the can toward him, imagining the tingling warmth was invisible fingers reaching for the can. Reaching . . . reaching . . . reaching . . . nothing! Frustrated, he threw the tingling warmth from his body, sending the can spinning end over end into the patch of trees.

Standing to retrieve the can, Michael wondered how Marvin could tap into the telekinesis but he couldn't. It was his own damn telekinesis to begin with, and he couldn't figure out how to use it!

Michael replayed the Central Pennsylvania Sleep Institute building incident over and over in his head, trying to remember if Marvin did something, a gesture, a look, to trigger the telekinesis. But he kept thinking back to Matthews' words as he told Michael he was number twenty-three on the Pennsylvania list. A chill ran down his spine as he wondered how many more people's lives that facility ruined. Then he froze as a terrifying thought eviscerated his mind. Matthews said *Pennsylvania*. That meant there were more facilities out there, still operational, still creating human weapons.

Michael scratched his head, certain he felt the nanobots rummaging around inside . . .

EPILOGUE

Camp Hill, Pennsylvania

Click.

"... bizarre incidents that happened three days ago. Authorities are still digging through the rubble of the Central Pennsylvania Sleep Institute building, although what remains is more like ash, looking for some clues as to what happened here. They are still operating under the assumption that this was the result of some form of blast; however, they—"

Click.

"... secluded medical building. By the time local police and firefighters arrived, the damage was done. These mysterious circumstances behind the destruction of the Central Pennsylvania Sleep Institute building have confounded investigators and—"

Click.

"... confirming with friends and relatives, left an estimated thirty-four dead. There were over a hundred employees who got out, but one unusual survival story. A young African-American woman was found among the wreckage, seemingly unharmed. But as paramedics tried to approach her, she became frightened and fled the scene. To add to the enigma of the Central Pennsylvania Sleep Institute building, the paramedics themselves became too frightened to chase her. With me now is one of the paramedics who first arrived on the—"

Click.

Claire flipped from one channel to the next, each station's local news crew still covering the unexplained happenings in Hershey. Sitting on her bed, she didn't notice as her mind wandered through a thick fog. For the past three months, she would have sworn that her husband had been lying to her. About what, she had no idea. He wasn't cheating on her, this she was certain. Sure, he had been disappearing off and on, but there had been no other signs. Michael was a smart man, but she knew he couldn't hide an affair from a lawyer! Was he lying? And about what? About the trip with his students to Pittsburgh? Michael *did* go there. Claire knew this from the bus tickets he willingly produced. And his story of taking a dying student out to see friends and relatives was plausible. Not practical, but Claire had been alive long enough to know that sometimes the truth *is* stranger than fiction. Maybe he wasn't lying to her. Maybe it was just her guilt manifesting these thoughts. After all, *she* was lying to *him*.

Not necessarily lying, she rationalized. *Just withholding information until I know all the facts.*

But she didn't know all the facts. Even with all the research she did while lying to Michael about attending all the book appreciation meetings. She winced at that thought—she had lied to Michael. Attending one or two to uphold appearances, Claire had used the meetings as a smokescreen to spend time at her office on the internet or at the library. *Poor Michael probably thinks I'm cheating on him.*

Concerned, Claire stood from her bed and walked to their bedroom window. Peering through the thick curtains in silence, she watched Michael play in the yard with Sarah. A quirky game of tag ensued; Sarah would chase Michael as he ran with silly, exaggerated steps until she tagged him, then he chased her and tickled her once he caught her. Claire smiled with a heavy heart and stepped back into her bedroom.

Claire had to tell Michael. She knew she did. But when? How? She had wanted to wait until she had better control of what she could do. Now that she did, when should she tell him?

Thinking of control, Claire decided to do her exercises. Staring at her bed, she felt a warmth build at the base of her skull. She relaxed her mind and focused, allowing the warmth to rush from her, as if willing her soul to flow to the bed. And lift it. While maintaining control of the floating bed, she glanced at her dresser. Soon that hovered above the floor. Then her nightstand, then Michael's nightstand. The lamps, too. The clothes hamper and the small chair in the corner of the room. She spent months secretly researching the different theories of telekinesis, from its origins to whack-job charlatans who hid behind false claims of having this ability. She figured out how she obtained it, where it came from, and how to control it. But now what?

ABOUT THE AUTHORS

BRIAN KOSCIENSKI & CHRIS PISANO skulk the realms of south-central Pennsylvania. Brian developed a love of writing from countless hours of reading comic books and losing himself in the worlds and adventures found within their colorful pages. In tenth grade, Chris was discouraged by his English teacher from reading H.P. Lovecraft and, being a naturally disobedient youth, he has been a fan ever since. They have logged many hours writing novels, stories, articles, comic books, reviews, and the occasional ridiculous haiku. To find out where they may be skulking next, visit them at www.novelguys.com. If you happen to see them at one of the various conventions they participate in, feel free to stop by their table and say, "Hi." They're harmless!